INTO THE VOLCANO

Into the Volcano

A Mallory & Morse Novel of Espionage

FORREST DeVOE JR.

HarperCollins*Publishers*

HarperCollins books may be purchased for educational, business, or sales promotional use. For information, please write: Special Markets Department, HarperCollins Publishers Inc., 10 East 53rd Street, New York, NY 10022.

FIRST EDITION

Designed by Amy Hill

Printed on acid-free paper

Library of Congress Cataloging-in-Publication Data
DeVoe, Forrest.
   Into the volcano : a Mallory and Morse novel of espionage / Forrest DeVoe, Jr.—1st ed.
      p.   cm.
   ISBN 0-06-072376-9
   1. Americans—Foreign countries—Fiction.   2. Intelligence officers—Fiction.   3. Istanbul (Turkey)—Fiction.   4. Cold War—Fiction.   5. Oceania—Fiction.   I. Title.

PS3604.E887I57   2004
813'.6—dc22   2004042888

04 05 06 07 08 NMSG / RRD   10 9 8 7 6 5 4 3 2 1

When will they come?
On a day like iron.
When will they come?
Never, then now.
How will they come?
Slow, then quick.
How will he greet them?
Greet them with fire.

—traditional Konoese chant

BOOK I Istanbul

1   *On Seraglio Point*

There's nothing worse than a summer cold, and van Vliet had a real beauty. Brimming eyes, swampy sinuses, clogged ears, and a raw throat that tasted of pennies; he'd had the lot since the beginning of May. Strolling down the esplanade, he couldn't smell the harbor scents of diesel exhaust and rope, or the toasted new corn from the vendors' carts. He couldn't hear the rush of traffic on the Marmara Highway. The sun glittering on the harbor seemed to shine for the benefit of others, for the old freighters and new pleasure craft, for the tourists in their toucan-hued clothes, for the Greek sailors and Stambouline wharfmen, as agile and purposeful as cats. Beside him, the cypresses of Seraglio Point climbed away into the flat blue sky, and behind them, the spires of the Blue Mosque retreated through the bright wet air into a splendid Byzantine past. Istanbul was splendid, all right, all twenty-five centuries' worth of it, and had twice been the center of the civilized world, but at that moment it seemed to have no place for a sweaty, middle-aged Dutch spy who hadn't been able to taste his food for a month.

Just van Vliet was a big, sandy-haired man with a projecting, somewhat shapeless jaw. He moved with the sleepy gait of a trained fighter, and the Turks gave him a respectfully wide berth as he ambled along the waterfront. He paused by a kiosk near the docks and scanned the front page of the day's *International Herald Tribune,* which the owner always displayed behind a dusty sheet of glass. An Air France 707 had crashed on takeoff. De Gaulle extended his condolences. Another shooting along the Berlin Wall. Khruschev had charged the West with "provocation." The Pathet Lao had taken two more hostages. U Thant had called high-altitude A-bomb tests "the manifestation of a dangerous psychosis." Scott Carpenter's Mercury capsule had overshot its target by two hundred fifty miles. So far 1962 hadn't been much of a year for anyone, except maybe the New York Yankees, who seemed to be on their way to back-to-back championships.

Van Vliet walked over to the balustrade, leaned his elbows on the railing, and stared out at the Asian Side.

He tried to be happy for the Yankees.

Eight years ago van Vliet had been a midlevel desk officer in the Binnenlandse Veiligheidsdienst, the Dutch Internal Security Service. Neither his colleagues nor his wife had expected much of him. Then his wife had left, and he'd seen how right she was to try again for something better. He'd said good-bye himself: to marriage, to women, and to Groningen. He'd let Gray recruit him for the Consultancy—until then, he'd never been quite sure that the Consultancy actually existed—and undergone six months' retraining in the pine barrens of New Jersey. The Jersey woods had been thick with pitch pines and red chokeberries. Van Vliet had been happy there. He'd loved the drills, unarmed and armed, and the hazards course, and the nightly seminars on tradecraft. He'd loved the orderliness and rigor of his days. For a while, he thought he'd actually managed to change his luck. But back in the field, once again he'd been—what did the Americans say?

A day late and a dollar short.

Three years ago Gray had asked him to head the Consultancy's Istanbul station. Van Vliet had known what the posting meant. Istanbul had become a political backwater, a place to tuck away men who weren't quite up to the mark. Van Vliet lacked, and knew he lacked, the inner strictness no good agent was without. He was prey to the weary twilit state in which the world seems too much trouble, to the drifting depression that is as deadly to the field operative as a rain of bullets.

The mouth of the Bosphorus lay before him like a sheet of oiled tin. To his right was the Sea of Marmara, an endless expanse of glaring gray water. It was dotted from the esplanade to the horizon with ships of every size, like a Renaissance exercise in one-point perspective, and grew bluer as it moved away from the city. To his left was the Golden Horn, and across it was Beyoglu, the foreigners' quarter where van Vliet had his office and flat. Beyoglu was a jumble of red-roofed buildings topped by the conical mass of the Galata Tower. At the base of the tower, one could just see the edge of a massive concrete hulk. Club Europa. It brought his mind back to his job. According to the papers, when completed Club Europa would be Turkey's biggest discotheque, with a revolving tempered-glass dance floor, a twenty-meter indoor fountain, and a rooftop heliport for VIP guests.

A nightclub with a heliport.

Van Vliet swallowed, hearing a series of clicks at the hinges of his jaw. After this many years in the business, he hoped he knew a front operation when he saw one. Club Europa was dirty, had to be. But he'd run it back every way he knew—financing, politicos, construction, even the architects—and hadn't come up with so much as a well-formed suspicion to take to Gray. He pulled out a sodden handkerchief and blew his nose, setting off a hellish squealing in one ear. He thought, for some reason, of his ex-wife's hands. They'd had an abrupt, startled way of moving—Helene herself always had a startled look. She'd been scanty and pale, and even if she'd been a man, he wouldn't have found her very attractive. But he'd loved her, and for a while, she'd loved him, too. When he'd had a cold, she'd made him hot tomato soup.

He sighed, boosted himself off the balustrade, and turned toward home.

The heat was stifling as he crossed the asphalt apron of the Eminönu docks and turned onto the Galata Bridge. A new tan Cadillac nearly grazed him with its tailfins. From habit, he made a mental note of the license. Ahead of him, the Europa was invisible now behind the illuminated Ülker sign. In twenty minutes he'd be back at his office. The Asker brothers would be back from lunch, industriously doing what little there was to do. The thought cheered him. Van Vliet had recruited and trained the Askers himself. They were young and gave a useful impression of naïveté, but they had strong nerves and alert, retentive minds, and he knew they were becoming good operatives.

What he ought to do, he realized, was turn them loose on the Europa. They had a deft touch with officialdom. They'd get farther than a foreigner like him. Why hadn't he briefed them before? He saw with distaste that he'd been embarrassed by the vagueness of his suspicions. He hadn't wanted to sound like an old lady in front of his agents. And there was another thing: he knew men on long, unpleasant assignments sometimes began to avoid comfort as though it were weakness. It would have comforted him to confide in the brothers. He remembered Gray saying, "This is a nasty job we do. It's a grave mistake to deny oneself little comforts." Like everything Gray said about the art and business of spying, it was true.

Van Vliet's spirits began to lift. He decided to stop off at his flat and have a shower. A cool shower and clean clothes, and then back to work.

Little comforts.

He lived in a high-rise on Jurnal Sokagi, conveniently close to his office. Though expensive, it was ugly, like most new buildings in Turkey, and made of concrete little better than sand. Istanbul's building inspectors were among the best-bribed in the world. *Heaven help us all,* he thought, *when the next earthquake hits.* He rode the elevator up to the twelfth floor, undid three heavy locks, and slipped silently inside his flat. After sixteen years of covert work, it was easier for him to be stealthy than to be noisy. In the bathroom, he deposited his sodden clothes in the laundry hamper and grinned at his hairy pink self in the mirror. He slid back the pebbled glass doors and stepped into the shower stall.

Van Vliet sighed as the cool water swept over his face and chest. He felt his mind clearing of self-pity and regret, felt his vigor returning. It had been a happy thought, this midday shower. He'd have to do it more often. He pictured himself in his air-conditioned office, in clean, dry clothes, briefing the Askers on Club Europa. You never had to tell the boys anything twice. He *had* been a goddamned old woman. What was that other thing Gray had said? "Don't ever fall in love with secrets, Just. It's a deadly habit to get into." Alone as he was, he nodded. Then he noticed himself nodding and grinned again. Soaping his face, he began to organize the case in his head. As he did so, the water slackened and then cut off. This had happened twice in the past week, and he waited, soapy eyes closed, for it to come back on.

If van Vliet hadn't had a summer cold, if his ears hadn't been stopped up, he might have heard three faint clicks then, from behind the bathroom tiles. He was Consultancy-trained, and if he'd heard those three clicks—even if he hadn't known what they were— he might have been able to throw himself clear in time. Even if he'd had to throw himself straight through the plate glass of the shower doors.

But there were three faint clicks. And he didn't hear them.

And then the showerhead let out a torrent of pale-yellow flame.

2 *Far Too Thin*

A lean, gray-haired, gray-eyed man walked up Madison Avenue in the morning sun and turned into a shop whose window read DAISY WRIGHT • NEW YORK LONDON MILAN. Inside, the store was empty except for two slender women by the cash register. One was very young and the other was very young-looking. Neither gave any sign of recognition as he selected a pair of dark linen slacks and carried them to the dressing rooms. He stepped into the third cubicle from the left, closed the door, and hung the slacks on a hook. He turned and stood facing the mirror, hands hanging relaxed at his sides.

He was five foot eleven and boyishly slender, though his shoulders were unusually wide, so that he seemed larger head-on than in profile. His face was narrow and deeply creased. His gray eyes were narrow and wolfish. His hair had been gray since his early twenties. He was thirty-four years old. He was quietly dressed in a dark jacket and slacks, worn looser than the current fashion. Since his survival sometimes depended on his ability to move quickly, he did not approve of tight clothes. The mirror slid silently away and he was gazing into the lens of a ceiling-mounted video camera. He ducked under the camera and proceeded down a short hallway, and the mirror slid back into place behind him.

The hallway was painted a janitorial pale green, and narrow enough that he had to turn slightly to keep his shoulders from brushing the walls. At the end was a forged-steel door with no knob or visible lock. A small microphone was mounted on the wall beside it. He said, "Please." Two stories below him, an oscilloscope plotted his voiceprint and transmitted it upstairs to a Univac 1206, which recognized it and tripped a relay, and the steel door before him slid open with a faint hydraulic hiss. Behind it was a cramped, window-less room painted the same pale green and containing several unoc-cupied olive steel desks. Each bore half a dozen phones and two tape recorders. He said "Please" again and passed through another steel door into a long, chilly gallery containing the Univac, with its rows of chattering printers and its three scurrying attendants, who ignored him, and then into another room containing a workbench, empty but for a miniature electric drill, and a man at a computer console. Beside the console was another door. In the opposite wall were two others. " 'Lo, Phil," said the gray-haired man, nodding to the man at the console.

"Hello, Mallory," Phil said, not looking up. "Briefing?"

"Hope so," Mallory said. He spoke softly, with a faint Texas drawl.

"What's it been, a month?"

"It's been too long," Mallory said.

Behind Mallory, the door hissed open again, and the older of the two women from the shop stepped inside, smiled at him, and spoke to the man at the console. "It's ten o'clock, Phil," she said. "Where's my signal?"

"I guess it's late, Daisy," Phil said.

Daisy came over to Mallory and straightened his tie. It hadn't needed straightening. She smoothed her hands down his lapels and said, "Where'd you get the jacket?"

"Hello, Daisy. I don't know. Some store."

"It makes you look a bit like a priest. That the idea?"

"I guess."

She examined the label, didn't recognize it, and let the jacket flop closed. "How come you know so much about clothes, Jack?"

"Considering I'm oilfield trash?" he drawled.

"That's it."

"I don't know anything about clothes, Daisy."

"That's what I mean. How do you know so much about clothes, when you don't know anything about clothes? Did you really like those slacks?"

"They looked all right."

"I'm glad. You can have a pair, if you like."

"Thanks."

"You never come around anymore."

"You wouldn't like me these days, Daisy. I'm too drunk."

"Well, you're getting a briefing, aren't you? Come by when you get back from the job."

"I'd like that," Mallory said truthfully, but without eagerness. The door at Phil's elbow slid open, and from within Gray said, "Good morning, Daisy. Come in, Jack. Sorry to have kept you waiting."

Mallory said, "So long, Daisy," and sidled into the room. It was almost completely filled with a conference table that seemed to have been scavenged from a much nicer office. Gray sat at the far end.

Mallory sat down diagonally across from him, and the two men regarded each other.

"You look bad, Jack," Gray said.

Gray was a small, fattish man with a large head thinly covered with dull silver curls. He wore spectacles, frayed corduroys, and an old sweater-vest. His cane stood in the corner, within easy reach. It was a source of chagrin to his agents that none of them could discover who he was. There was some evidence he'd once been in the Queen's Third Amphibious Commando. There was also a story that had gone around after the Korean War, impossible to verify, of a British POW who'd been tortured by the Chinese for some absurd length of time—two years, three years without a letup—first to obtain intelligence and later to refine their techniques upon an unprecedentedly resistant specimen. He'd eventually killed his captors, the story went, and walked the four hundred (or six hundred, or fifteen hundred) miles to Seoul. In every version of the story, the soldier was short and homely. About the next few years no one had any ideas, but it was a matter of record that early in 1954, a small, badly scarred man calling himself Stanley Markham had joined Madrid's Calderón heroin ring as a low-level enforcer. He spoke fluent Spanish with a heavy English accent and impressed everyone who met him with his savagery and shrewdness, and over the next twenty months rose through the ranks to become Rafael Calderón's number-two man. It was also a fact that on November 14, 1955, the entire senior leadership of the Calderón apparatus was slaughtered in a single afternoon, that three of its five warehouses were burned to the ground, and that a description of its principal distributors, drops, cutouts, and routes arrived at Interpol Brussels, postmarked two days previous. The ring's bank accounts, amounting to some three hundred seventy million Swiss francs, had been emptied out to the last centime. Markham's body was never found. Six months later, Gray appeared in New York and opened the Consultancy, working with an undisclosed and apparently limitless source of capital.

Gray's thick shoulders were lopsided and his left cheek was traversed by a deep, shining scar that seemed to have swallowed up his left ear. Nothing was left but a ragged nub, over which he hooked the earpiece of his glasses. His small plump hands lay primly on the table. The fingernails were dirty. The thumbnails were missing.

"You don't look well at all," he told Mallory.

Neither man thought the remark was funny.

"I'm aware," Gray continued, "that you deal poorly with inactivity, and I expect you to mistreat yourself somewhat between assignments. But the firm's invested quite a bit in you, Jack, one way or the other, and I also expect you to maintain yourself in reasonably good form. Your color is bad and you're far too thin. What do you weigh?"

"I dunno, Gray."

"You don't own a scale?"

"No."

"Buy one. You can expense it. From now on, you are to consider it part of your operational duties to weigh at least 160 pounds. I'd much prefer 170."

"I'll pick up a scale on the way home."

There was a silence.

"How well did you know Just van Vliet?" Gray said.

After a moment, Mallory said, " 'Did,' huh?"

"I'm afraid so."

"When?"

"Three hours ago."

Mallory paused again. "Well, we were partnered up on Tulsa, and I ran backup for him on that Darmstadt thing. You know all that. We had a few drinks in the in-between times. I guess we talked some."

Gray waited.

"I guess I didn't see why he was in this business. But he knew a lot. He was awful bright. His marriage, I guess you know all about that. Somewhere along the line he decided he liked the fellas better than the girls, but I don't think he did too well with them, either. He was a thinker. Maybe too much of one. I wouldn't have put him in the field, or even on a desk. I'd have had him training. I think he'd have been a good instructor."

"He was offered a posting in the Barrens. He preferred to remain operational."

"Yeah, well, I dunno. I guess he was one of the sadder guys I've met. It wasn't just the fairy stuff, it was how he was made. I suppose I didn't know him that well." Mallory shrugged. "I liked him," he said helplessly.

Gray leaned back. "One expects one's people to be killed from time to time," he said, seeming to address the ceiling. "But an elimination like this, so, ah, public. Provocative. One of our senior men. It's bad for business. Shakes up the clients, makes it harder for us to recruit. Unless, of course, it's promptly dealt with. The firm must respond, immediately and visibly, to van Vliet's death. I want you in charge of the matter."

"I'd like that," Mallory said. Then he said, "How'd it happen?"

Gray slid a manila folder across the table. It contained four letter-sized flimsies, typed single-spaced, and two glossy eight-by-ten wire photos. Mallory read the flimsies as he'd been trained to do, neither quickly nor slowly. When he finished, he could have recited much of their text from memory and paraphrased the rest. He examined the photos in turn. He slipped them back under the flimsies, neatened up the edges, and closed the folder. He slid it back across the table to Gray. His face was expressionless.

"Seems like a pretty fancy way to kill a man," he said. "Kind of showy, too."

"And highly technical," Gray said. "A classic Anton Rauth liquidation."

"You think it's Rauth."

"Quite possibly."

"We know yet who rigged the shower?"

"An independent named Lassiter."

"I know him. Jerry Lassiter. Claims he can booby-trap anything."

Gray nodded. "Nasty little fellow, but quite good. We've used him ourselves, of course."

"Seems like a place to start."

"Lassiter was killed about an hour ago behind a Tünel coffee shop. One 7.65 bullet through the forehead. Again, very much in the Rauth manner."

"If all this is such a perfect example of Rauth's style . . ."

"Exactly. It may not be him at all. What do you know about Rauth?"

"What everybody does. Some Czech rich kid, used to be an athlete. Fencer, right?"

"Yes. Czech, but a naturalized French citizen, and a former captain of the French saber team. He was widely favored to take the gold from Aladar Gerevich in the 1952 Olympics."

"Yeah, and he never showed up. I remember, there was some kind of kerfuffle. And now he runs guns."

"The Rauths were a very old Prague shipping family," Gray said, examining the ceiling again. "Originally of Austrian descent. Quite well-connected, so they managed to sell up and clear out to Paris in '48, just before the Soviet, er, Normalization. Anton's the eldest son. Exceptionally gifted in a number of respects, but his character's always been iffy, and he used to fool about with drugs. A few months before he was due to arrive in Helsinki, he tried injecting cocaine intravenously and gave himself a middle-sized stroke. Air bubble. Never properly learnt to use a hypodermic. It permanently lamed his right arm and, of course, put an end to his athletic career. Since that time, his sanity has been in question."

"Doesn't sound like he had much good sense to begin with."

"Perhaps not, but he's managed fairly well without it. In the past eight years, Rauth has become the world's single largest extralegal dealer in armaments, as well as a very considerable private provider of covert services. Built an organization quite like ours, in fact. Though he generally works for the Soviets and Chinese. Publicly, he is the director of KRW—Kamper Rauth Worldwide—a successful and, Analysis tells me, entirely legitimate reinsurance firm incorporated in the Seychelles. Headquarters in Paris."

"Where's Kamper these days?"

"No one quite likes to ask."

"I'm not following this," Mallory said. "If I'm Rauth, and Just's getting onto one of my jobs, I'd want him killed quick and quiet. This shower deal must have taken a couple months to set up. Why put on a big production number and get everybody buzzing around like flies on jam?"

"Perhaps Rauth wants the flies buzzing. Perhaps someone else wants flies buzzing round Rauth. I should mention that you have, in fact, dealt with Rauth before. Do you recall that kidnapping business two years back, the Danish consul's daughter?"

"I recall the daughter."

"Yes, I suppose you would. Well, Rauth was behind that, and hoped to realize a nice little sum from it. And he ran that laundry in Caracas. All contract work, of course."

"You never told me that."

"You had no reason to know. Another rather suggestive point. For a while, Istanbul was Rauth's covert-services HQ. The Turks kicked him out a year ago last spring. Favor to State. So Rauth bought a small island called He' Konau, about nine hundred kilometers east-southeast of Australia, and built a new base. His residence of record is in Paris, but he lives on He' Konau. Quite out of reach of international law."

"Uh huh?"

"Last fall, acting through intermediaries, KRW purchased Pedersen-Howe, a leading manufacturer of mining equipment. They paid somewhat above the market price. Of course, the company may have been undervalued. And recently, through a subsidiary called Origin Systems, KRW bestowed a large study grant upon an obscure crystallographer with the euphonious name of Herman Treat."

"What's he do?"

"Dr. Treat studies the effects of ultra–low frequency sound upon nonferrous igneous rock."

"That a real big-money field?"

"Not to my knowledge."

"What do you make of all this?"

"Nothing, yet. Too spotty. One last thing. Nemerov was seen last month in Istanbul."

"That's a good man," Mallory said glumly. "And he carries a 7.65. Used to, anyway."

"Yes."

"I guess Rauth can afford to hire fancy help like Nemerov if he wants. But using a guy like Nemerov, that'd tend to attract people's attention, too."

"Yes."

"This whole deal seems kind of like a trap," Mallory said.

"My dear fellow, of course it's a trap."

"What were you thinking of doing about it?"

"Well, I rather thought I'd throw you into it."

"I suppose that makes sense."

"Thank you. You are to go to Istanbul, investigate van Vliet's death, submit to any credible attempt at capture, discover from the inside the persons and rationale behind his liquidation, and escape."

"What if I'm not captured?"

"I fancy you will be."

"What if I don't escape?"

"We shall miss you."

"This isn't a one-man job."

"I'm glad you agree." There was a row of metal studs at Gray's elbow. He pressed one, and the door behind him slid open. The room beyond was empty but for a row of metal lockers, and had been painted a dingy cream, though not recently. A young woman was seated on a folding chair by the back wall, reading a paperback novel. Her name was Laura Morse, and she'd been seconded from the CIA for long enough that the Consultancy considered her part of staff.

She looked up and tucked the book into her purse.

"I've put Jack on the job, Laura," Gray called. "I trust you two don't mind partnering again?"

"I know how to follow orders," she replied in a cool, somewhat monotonous voice.

Laura Morse was thin but not frail, wheat-blonde, and rather aseptically beautiful. She had an air of disapproving of her own good looks. Ronnie Fellowes of the London station called her La Remorse.

Mallory grinned at her as she took a seat at the table.

On balance, he was glad they'd be working together. La Remorse wasn't much fun to know, but she was a first-rate operative and, as she'd said, easy to direct. She had the useful trick of growing more deliberate as a situation worsened. And, of course, there were her fighting skills. Before joining the Agency, she'd been one of the top competitive martial artists in the world, and was apparently still some sort of legend in karate circles.

"I don't mind," Mallory said.

"Good," Gray said. "You'll be the Cavanaughs again. They're getting a bit threadbare and we might as well finish them off."

"About time," Mallory said. "I'm sick of reading *Modern Alfalfa*." John Cavanaugh was a well-to-do grain broker, and Lena Cavanaugh was his bored and discontented wife. They lived in Darien, Connecticut, and had a son named Whit. Mallory knew a great deal about the Cavanaughs, and had they actually existed, would cheerfully have garroted John, drowned Whit like a kitten, and kicked Lena twice around the block. He said, "What do the local cops think we're doing in Istanbul?"

"You are selling next year's Thai rice. Your brokerage deals with Advance Global, and you knew Just in a business way. You're shocked at the death of a colleague. You can't resist poking around a bit. You consider yourself full of what is called American know-how and are persistent by nature. You are, in fact, something of a fool. Hence, no one the constabulary need worry about. Laura, you've come for the shopping and to keep your husband away from houris."

"How about the local spooks?" Mallory said.

"INSTA are expecting you, and believe you both to be CIA. Technically, this will be true. Langley are extending us certain, ah, facilities. INSTA will be eager to cooperate. You're to put them off. They're quite good and, unlike the local police, quite unbribable, and they'd keep you far too secure."

"Shallow cover?"

"Yes. We expect you to be blown. However, neither of you are to do anything to make Jack's capture easier. The people who arranged Just's death are quite competent enough to penetrate you in spite of all normal precautions. They're not to know we've seen a trap. It's barely possible they simply want to kill you there for some reason, so if it comes to that, don't let them. Jack, would you reach me down that bag from the shelf behind you?"

Mallory took down a pink Daisy Wright shopping bag and began unpacking it without being asked. He took out a pair of black wingtip shoes, not especially new-looking, and a pair of men's sandals. He looked up inquiringly. "Homing devices?"

"In the instep, not the heel. They'll quite likely discover them anyway, but we may as well try."

"I hope they go with your outfits," Laura said.

"They look all right," Mallory said. "Oxblood would've been better."

"Would you give Laura the little makeup business, please?" Mallory took a compact from the bag and tossed it to Laura. "It's all right, Laura, you can open it. Now slide back the—that's it." The shallow compartmented tray filled with blush and eyeshadow swung up to reveal a tiny screen, which flickered and then displayed a blinking amber dot, dead center. "You'll track the signal on that. Only receives when the inner compartment's open. Battery should be good for ten hours' use."

Mallory took out a small, chrome-plated gun with a pearl grip. Grinning again, he slid it across to Laura, along with a box of ammunition. She did not touch it. "Goodness, Laura, what a face," Gray said. "I'm afraid Lena Cavanaugh would never carry your Colt, so we've given you this. It's all right. Under that silly chrome, this is quite a nice Sauer-Suhl .32. Otto's given it a good testing on the range and I think you'll find it serviceable. Jack, you'll be all right with the Browning." From the accordion folder at his side, Gray produced two long, yellow envelopes. "Documents outdid themselves this morning. You might give Davis a word of thanks next time you see her. Visas, gun permits, a letter from Whit at summer camp, a prescription for Lena's tranquilizers, a phone bill with stub. Past due. Something to bicker about. Currency, traveler's checks. And here are your briefing packets—burn them before you depart, please—and first-class tickets on BEA. You'll fly out tomorrow morning. The Asker brothers were serving as van Vliet's 2IC's. I have no reason to believe they're less than trustworthy, and if you agree when you meet them, I suggest you consult with them intensively. I'll run you myself, Jack, and you'll run Laura and the rest of the team until you're captured. Once that happens, Laura, you'll take lead and run Jack, to the extent he can still be run. A bit unorthodox, this switching about, but, I think, reasonable under the circumstances."

Laura said, "Who decides when we switch?"

"You do," Mallory told her. "I'll be busy."

"Yes," Gray said. "Oh, by the way, you're to find and kill Just's assassins, of course, as gaudily and unpleasantly as possible. We've got to discourage that sort of thing. Well, I think that's everything. Laura, can you spare me ten minutes on that Kuwaiti affair?"

Mallory turned to Laura. "Do we need to talk now?"

She shook her head. She'd already been briefed. It was one of Gray's peculiarities that he liked to brief his agents separately. He briefed leads last. Mallory dropped the shoes and papers in the bag and stood. He told her, "Since we're running shallow, I'll meet you at the ticket counter forty minutes before the flight. Okay?"

"Fine. See you there," she said.

"And do remember, Jack. 160 pounds," Gray said. "In fact, you might go out the back way and get a bowl of pea soup at the restaurant. It's quite excellent."

"All right."

"It's not a suggestion, Jack."

"I know," Mallory said.

He sidled around the table, feeling faintly ridiculous, as he always did when he had to carry a shopping bag, and left the room by the door through which Laura had come.

Gray had laid out the Consultancy's offices himself and was probably the only one who never got lost in them. Mallory climbed a steel staircase along the back wall of a metal shop, squeezed between parked trucks in one of the motor pool garages, hit a dead end in a file room, and finally emerged through a door marked EMPLOYEES ONLY that let out next to the men's room in the Silver Crest Diner on Lexington Avenue. He carried his shopping bag to a table and dutifully ordered a Swiss cheeseburger deluxe, a chocolate milkshake instead of a beer, and a large bowl of split pea soup.

Gray was right. It was excellent.

3   *Don't Tell*

Something's happened, Mallory thought.

He was still half a block from his apartment. He carried two shopping bags: the Daisy Wright bag and another containing a new bathroom scale. Both were in his left hand. He was too well trained to carry anything in his gun hand unless he had to. He was not alarmed, not yet. A veteran agent's instincts are honed to unusual sensitivity, and are often set off by nothing, like radar picking up morning mist. He was alone on the sunlit street. If he was being watched from one of the hundreds of windows in the high-rises around him, there was no way to know. The windows of his own apartment seemed empty. The shades were open, as he'd left them. He recognized most of the parked cars, and they all seemed empty. Mallory had not broken stride, and now he walked through the front door of his building and handed the shopping bags to the doorman. "Hello, Benny," he said. "Tuck these away for me, would you? Any news?"

"All quiet, Mr. Mallory," the doorman said.

The lobby was tiled in beige and white marble, with a broad mirrored band running around the walls. Mallory could see half a dozen Mallories and Bennies confronting each other. He could see the doorman from behind. The back of the man's head was trimmed close, and bulged over his collar.

It looked dishonest somehow.

Mallory nodded to Benny and walked toward the elevator with both hands free.

In the elevator, the feeling began to fade, and then it came back strong as the doors opened. As he stepped from the elevator, he fetched out his keys left-handed. It was quiet. The air seemed slightly too warm. There was a scent in it, a fruity scent he couldn't identify. Halfway down the hall he knew for certain, though he couldn't have said how, that there was someone in his apartment. His gait did not seem to alter, but his footsteps became quite silent, and as he approached his door he took the Browning from its holster. It was a small, flat, snub-nosed automatic, and he brought it out and carried it so casually that a careless observer might not have noticed what it was. The heat was greater as he opened the locks of his door; he felt it against his knuckles. As the door swung open, the warmth and sweetish smell blossomed out at him, and he rushed forward to meet it, sprinting smoothly and quickly to the center of his living room, crouching to present a smaller target, gun drawn. A woman was standing near the door to his kitchenette. She froze, then slowly raised her hands.

She was small even for a Japanese woman and strikingly lovely, with long eyes and a delicate triangular face. Her legs were slim and slightly bowed. Her body was almost childlike except for the central delta of tangled black hair. She wore nothing but a pair of polka-dotted oven mitts. She stood there holding them above her head.

Mallory did not lower the gun. "I ought to," he said. "I really ought to."

"I make you *peach*-pie," she said meekly. "You don't like *peach*-pie?"

Holstering the gun, he walked slowly toward her. "It's Benny I ought to shoot. I ought to skin him and nail up his hide. I've told him not to play around about visitors. Even you."

She shook her head vigorously. "No. You must not be angry at Benny. Because I *force* him. I tell him I must be a surprise to you, and I make *big*-eye." She widened her long eyes to demonstrate. For a moment they shone, enormous, each one bigger than her tiny mouth. "I make big-eye. So Benny," she concluded, "don't have a choice."

"You're a dangerous woman, Itsy," he said, and kissed her. He pulled off her mitts and dropped them on the carpet.

"You are still angry?" Atsuko said, setting her hands on his chest.

"Yes."

"You don't like naked Japanese girl? I am naked here *all day*," she said, stirring slowly against him. "All day . . . all naked in your kitchen . . . little naked woman making you pie."

Mallory stepped around her and went into the kitchen. It simmered with the odor of peach preserves. The counter was dusted with flour. On the floor in front of the stove lay a rose-patterned kimono and a pair of minute cotton panties, where she'd dropped them when she'd heard his key in the door.

"Naked all day, huh?" he said.

He heard her cackling wildly, and then a pair of small arms wrapped around him from behind and she bit into his shoulder. He reached over and turned off the oven.

Mallory lay stretched out in bed, feeling the sweat dry on his face and belly. At the foot of the bed, Atsuko sat with her back to him, clipping her toenails with great concentration and a series of tiny clinking sounds. He was slowly tracing her backbone with his big toe. His clothes and blankets were scattered across the rug, looking indecent in the tidy little apartment. The Consultancy maintained apartments like this for him in New York, London, and Hong Kong. Logistics had furnished all three of them in the same anonymous good taste, and Mallory didn't know what they cost. He kept a set of clothes and a gun in each apartment, and, aside from this, owned little. Owning little suited him. It was one of the few things he'd liked about the Army. Each time Atsuko clipped another toenail, she added the sliver of nail to a neat row on the bed. She was humming a little tune. Mallory stroked her back with his foot and thought, *There isn't so much that's good about life, but there's this. And this is enough.*

Atsuko Shimura was a Japan Airlines stewardess who'd spent her New York layovers with Mallory for the past four years. She was the closest thing he'd ever had to a steady girl, and he'd given her a set of keys to his apartment. She usually showed up without warning. If he was out of town, she'd spend her layover there alone, quietly reading and watching TV, and leave a brief, misspelled note on his pillow. Atsuko had a degree in European history from Keio University, and would have liked to be a historian. "But a woman can't do academic in Japan," she'd told him. Now Mallory nudged her buttock with his toe and said, "What are you reading these days, Itsy?"

"Bobbin Session," she said with satisfaction. After a moment, Mallory decided she'd said *Bourbon Succession.* "About all the palace business, all the mess with the House of Orleans. I like Isabella. Nobody like her, but I do, because she is very—" Atsuko turned to show him a fierce face, with wrinkled nose and bared teeth. She clawed the air with one hand and laughed.

"Ever do any reading on Istanbul?" he said.

She did not stop smiling all at once.

Turning away again, she clipped the last toenail and added it to the rest, then counted to make sure she hadn't mislaid any. She scooped them up, rose, and dropped them in the wastebasket. Then she bent and ran a hand over her toes to see that there were no rough edges to inconvenience him. She climbed back into bed next to Mallory and cuddled against his side. By then she was no longer smiling. She touched a scar below his breastbone and traced it as it wandered along his ribs.

"That's a bad place," she said.

She lay a tiny hand between his legs, as if trying to protect him. He felt himself stirring beneath her palm.

"Uh huh?" he said.

"Istanbul is very old," she said, not looking at him. "Very big trading city for maybe five thousand year. It's right where Europe touch Asia, right between the Black Sea and the Sea of Marmara, and it's got the Golden Horn, best natural port in the world. So everybody's always fighting to get this place. Maybe 300 AD, like that, Emperor Constantine takes it over and calls it Constantinople. Makes it the new capital of Rome. He goes riding around on his horse, saying, *Here is the boundary. I know, 'cause last night an angel show me.* It's the first big Christian city, because Roman is getting Christian now. But that don't mean it gets peaceful. There's a big revolt in 400 and Justinian kill thirty thousand people in the Hippodrome. Thirty thousand. All in one day, and then a couple of Crusade come through. For a thousand year, it's like that."

Atsuko sat up cross-legged and brushed her hair out of her face. She took his sex in her hands and examined it. Then she kissed it softly and tried to lay it back where it had been. It didn't want to go. She looked off into the corner of the room, massaging it absently.

"Always fighting," she said. "Always blood."

She swung a leg over and lay herself across him like a blanket, trying to cover him up.

"Maybe 1400, 1450," she said, her cheek against his ribs, "the Ottoman take over and call it Istanbul. *City of Islam.* So now Istanbul is the big center of the Islamic world, the capital of Ottoman Empire. Just like it used to be the center of the Christian world and the Roman. And now, for a little time, everything is better. Everybody is welcome in this city now, all different kinds of Muslim, all the Jew that got chased out of Spain, a lot of Christian. Everybody come here to trade and study at the university. *Big* university. They invent Arabic number there. Got a lot of laboratory, observatory, so they can look at the star and see which way is Mecca when they pray."

He could feel himself, hard against her soft belly, pressing into her as she breathed. She wriggled a little, trying to get comfortable.

"It don't last," she said, and kissed his ribs.

"No?"

"No," she murmured. She'd begun to move against him, subtly, and her voice took on a faraway tone. "Goes rotten again," she said. "The sultan build a cage in the Harem and lock up all the prince there, so they can't be sultan instead of him. He starts to rob all the economy to build fancy mosque. Empty out the Treasury, melt down the lead roof to make coin. Pretty soon the Ottoman Empire start to come apart. The Janissary revolt and destroy the city. Everybody coming around, take away a piece of the empire. The Greek take a piece, the Serb take a piece, the Russian, and then the French take Istanbul. The last sultan die thirty year ago, in exile. Istanbul used to be capital of the world. Now it isn't even capital of Turkey."

"Itsy? Are you crying?"

"You are a stupid man, Jack," she said.

"Well, we knew that," he said. "Go on. Tell me about the place."

"Shut up," she said. She rose up, took him in her hands, and sank down on him with a little cry.

"Aww," he said, closing his eyes.

She bared her teeth as she worked to fit him inside of her, then fell forward and pressed her face to his chest so that he couldn't kiss her. He combed his fingers through her long hair and spread them across her shivering back. The face pressed against him grew slippery with tears, and her hips jerked and ground against his, but she made no sound at all except for a steady gasping. Soon she let out a long, quavering wail and was still.

Mallory wrapped his arms around her and went on moving, carefully, until he'd joined her.

He lay beneath her slight weight, thinking nothing.

Then he turned her wet, miserable face up to his and kissed it. She wasn't weeping now.

"It's a bad place," she told him. "Why do you care? Why do you got to know? Very big drug place, very corrupt, treacherous. But also very loyal. You kill a Turk, you better quick kill all his friend. A Turk is fierce, like an old Janissary. The bravest soldier in world. The bravest soldier, and the worst general, and all their history is defeat. All their history is just stupid men getting send off and die."

They were silent.

"You going to Istanbul?" she asked.

"First thing in the morning," he said gently.

"Oh."

"Yeah."

"Gonna sell them grain?"

"Lots of grain."

She got up off the bed, wiping her face with her palms.

"Don't tell me what you do," she said, and went off to finish the pie.

4 *The Lights of Beyoglu*

The rooftop bar of the Hotel Marmara has the finest view in Istanbul. Piotr Nemerov sipped his Haig & Haig and admired it. There was the tumble of moonlit roofs and neon signs, the Golden Horn jeweled with gliding ships, the illumined domes and spires of Sultanahmet, and beyond it, the dreamlike scatter of lights on the Asian Side. Nemerov was getting quite fond of Istanbul. They poured it down like Russians here, and because they had the very sensible idea that you shouldn't guzzle on an empty stomach, they set out platters of *mezes,* nice little bits of this and that. He was particularly fond of the *koç yumurtasi,* what they called ram's eggs. Balls, of course. He had a glass of good scotch in his hand, good food on the table, and his old GRU friend Sasha Kurski at his side. *Piotr,* he thought humbly, *it's a good life. You're a lucky son of a bitch.* Despite the great number of people he'd killed, Nemerov was a cheerful man who often stopped to count his blessings.

He turned now toward a movement he'd glimpsed at the corner

of his eye and saw a waiter walking across the room to them, bearing a phone on a tray.

The waiter bowed slightly and handed Nemerov the receiver of the phone. "For the sir," he said in English. The phone itself he set on the table, and then he retreated out of earshot to watch the cord trailing across the floor and see that none of the other guests tripped on it.

He was a good waiter, and remained carefully correct, but he didn't care for the big man at the window table, or for his two associates. In a convivial city that welcomed foreigners, they had managed to make their foreignness forbidding, even insulting. It was something in the set of their bodies and their hard, clean-shaven faces. The big man and his friend were obvious Russians. Though it was two centuries since the Ottomans had lost Crimea to the Czar, no Turk had forgotten the matter. About the third, younger man it was hard to say, but he seemed a nasty bit of business. Some kind of Slav. The waiter conceded that there were good Slavs, very good Slavs, but he didn't believe this was one of them.

"*Da,*" Nemerov murmured into the mouthpiece, then listened briefly. "*Do svidanya,*" he said and hung up. He held out the tray to the waiter, who took it with another bow and retraced his steps. When the waiter was out of earshot, Nemerov turned to Kurski. "Well, they'll be here in the morning. BEA 1140 from London. Traveling as the Cavanaughs again. They must think we're stupid."

"They'll find out how wrong they are," the young man said. He spoke Russian well, but with a thick Yugoslav accent. His name was Renko Tesic and he was a Serb who'd shaved his moustache to look more like the two Russians.

"I'll tell you when you can talk, kid," Nemerov said, not looking at him. "In a few years."

Renko was silent. A dull flush moved up over his pale, spade-shaped face, which was still lightly speckled with acne.

"Why are you so sure they know we're here?" Kurski said.

Nemerov smiled. "I don't know if they know you're here. But me? Sure. I've been here five months, Sashka. Gray's getting an old man, and the time will come when I can fool him for five months about where I am. But not now, and not soon."

"So you're blown," Kurski said. "And the operation?"

"I'm only blown to Gray, Sashka. And that's good. That helps bring Mallory here. The operation's still tight. If it wasn't, life wouldn't be so peaceful now." He popped another ram's egg in his mouth and chewed.

"The things you eat," Kurski said, shaking his head.

"As long as I'm eating theirs, instead of them eating mine," Nemerov said, chewing.

Nemerov and Kurski had been cadets in Moscow together, served in the GRU together, graduated to the Subdirectorate for Specialized Policies together and, at Nemerov's urging, left it together. Since going freelance they'd seen less of each other, but they'd been close friends for nearly twenty years. Kurski was bony, with a severe, thick-cheekboned face and close-set, watchful eyes. His thinning dark hair was swept back tightly against his skull. He was an assassin with a single area of specialization: the elimination of highly secured targets. Nemerov, on the other hand, had always been a jack-of-all-trades. A handsome, square-jawed man with tousled, russet hair, Nemerov was nearly two meters tall and thickly muscled. His belly was a low-slung basket of muscle, like a jungle cat's, and catlike, his hands were blunt but graceful. He sprawled easily in his chair, taking up plenty of space, his big leg almost touching Kurski's, while the smaller man sat upright, hands folded in his narrow lap. Both seemed quite at ease. In contrast, the young Slav, slouching in imitation of Nemerov, looked as awkward as a fourteen-year-old at a dance.

It was funny, Nemerov thought, how well Turkey had turned out. He'd grown up sixty kilometers from the Turkish border—like Stalin and Beria, Nemerov was from Georgia—and he still hadn't known a damn thing about the place before he'd come here. And he'd thought it might be dreary, with all those Muslim niggers, but it was fine. The *kharcho* and *kebabi* were almost as good as at home, even if they were a little underspiced. He'd found a couple of blondes in a house on Yeni Kafa Sokagi, good sturdy girls who spoke some Georgian and weren't fussy about what a fellow did, and they weren't underspiced at all. Nemerov had had his name written on them in henna, on their bellies and their rumps, so that either way he could look down and read it when he was on the job. Too bad if the other customers didn't like it. Of course, he reflected, he'd had it done in Georgian script, and the Turks probably just thought it was curlicues. So the woman part was all right, and they were making good progress at the site: three weeks ahead of schedule, and gaining. And he was working with Sasha again, and what could be better than that? The only thing that troubled him a little was the instructions he'd been given about Mallory.

Nemerov had met Mallory professionally, and for this job had been thoroughly briefed on him, and he considered that he and Mallory were much alike. They'd both been born poor in ugly little cities: Mallory in Corpus Christi, on the Gulf of Mexico, and Nemerov in Gori, on the banks of the Kura. Mallory's father had worked the oilfields and abandoned his family early; Nemerov's had worked the docks and died young. Mallory had been a white boy among Mexicans, and spoke their language like his own. Nemerov had been a Russian boy among Georgians, and did the same. Mallory had run the mile and won a track scholarship to the University of Texas at Dallas, then dropped out after two years, just as Nemerov would have done if he'd gone to university. Nemerov had been a champion javelin thrower, and practiced while the fifteen-hundred-meter men ran circles in the next field.

Like any man with something between his legs, Mallory had joined the Army. Like any man of spirit, he'd hated it. He'd been recruited by the CIA and later gone private, just as Nemerov had done with the GRU. They were both good-looking fellows, both ladies' men, and both had sense enough to avoid getting tied down. They were both good at their jobs. What was the difference between them? That they grew up under different flags? That one liked big blondes, like a normal man, while the other, according to the dossier, liked them little and dark? What was that, between two men who were men? They should be going out together and telling stories. They should be swapping lies all night. Mallory spoke a little Russian, apparently, and Nemerov loved speaking English. They should be out in the Flower Market tomorrow night, stuffing their faces and telling lies and getting each other good and stinking, and then he'd take Mallory back to Yeni Kafa and let him have a turn with the blondes.

Instead, he was supposed to deliver Mallory to He' Konau, alive and, Rauth had said, "undamaged." Undamaged, if you please! So Rauth could—what? What disgusting and unwholesome business did the little fellow have planned that required the victim to arrive *undamaged*—as if he were one of Rauth's little brides—halfway around the world? Nemerov had thrown the javelin, but his first love had been running, which he was too large and heavy to do well. What he objected to most was being asked to help inflict a disgraceful death upon a man who'd consistently run the mile in under 4:03.

"All this fancy stuff," Nemerov said broodingly.

Kurski said nothing.

"He deserves a clean death. He's a professional, isn't he?"

Kurski did not have to ask who *he* was. "We are not in the business of giving men what they deserve," he remarked.

"Look," Nemerov said, "something like the Dutchman, it's different, all right? You learn something doing it. You think, yes, it can be done this way, too. Once in a while, under certain circumstances. But every damn time? The money's good with Rauth, but the man's daft. Everything's got to be fancy. He can't even have a woman in the ordinary way, did you know that? And oh my, the things he does to them instead. And if anyone says a word? Listen, did I ever tell you what happened to Lowry?"

"Yes," Kurski said.

"We'd taken the big boat out for a couple of nights," Nemerov said, undeterred. "Sasha, you should see the boat. Like an ocean liner. But inside, like a spaceship, everything white, everything metal and glass, except the floors are teak, and always spotless, you know, polished. It's like trying to walk around on a skating rink. Impresses people, though, if you see what I mean. It's classy. What was I saying? Right, Rauth had to entertain some nigger business-man, Iranian, I think, and so out came the boat. And he had one of his little brides along. God knows where he finds them, but they're all the same: skinny, snooty-looking, perfect, like a movie star. Like out of a magazine. And Lowry had the cabin next to Rauth's. You see? So it's the last night, and the Iranian's gone to bed, very happy, the deal's on, the trip's a big success, and we're all relaxing on the stern deck and talking English and getting drunk, except for Rauth. He never drinks. And Lowry's pig-drunk, and he says, *Ah, Mr. Rauth, it's been very quiet in your cabin at night, you must be tired!* Because, you know, he doesn't like to do it right away. He likes to keep them around a few days, the brides, sort of *admiring* them, before—" Nemerov gestured delicately with one big hand, as if snapping some small thing in two. "So there's Lowry, all cross-eyed and red in the face, saying, *Oh ho, Mr. Rauth, I guess you must be tired!* And Rauth *leaps* to his feet, shaking, *shaking*, I swear to you! and for a moment I think he's going to bite someone. And he starts shrieking, *Put him in the Well! Put him in the Well!*" Nemerov screwed up his face and used a high, fluting voice quite unlike Anton Rauth's. Then he laughed and shook his head. "I told you about the Well?"

"Yes," Kurski said.

"So we go straight home and I have to put poor Lowry in the Well. For one little joke when the man was drunk. And then, of course, I have to hop around like a fool and find a new metallurgist right away, and meanwhile I can't even talk it over with Rauth to see what's needed, because he won't hear Lowry's name mentioned now. There is no Lowry. There's never been a Lowry. You see?"

"Yes," Kurski said. "I see."

"That's why I brought you along," Nemerov said earnestly. "I know this isn't your usual sort of job, Sashka. But I needed a sane man along, someone I could trust."

"You should have quit after Lowry," Kurski said. "The way to live long is to work for sensible men."

"Sashka," Nemerov said, his eyes crinkling with concern, "you're not sorry you came?"

Kurski leaned forward abruptly and took Nemerov's face in his hands. From the narrow, austere-looking man, the gesture was shockingly intimate. He gave Nemerov's head a shake. "Petrushka, my dear one," he said, looking into the big man's eyes, "next to you is always a good place to be. Because you're too dumb to die. You embarrass Death. It doesn't want to be seen with you."

Kurski settled back and refolded his hands in his lap. The two Russians gazed at each other peacefully.

"Why not take them at the airport?" Renko said.

Still gazing at Kurski, Nemerov whipped out a hand and cuffed Renko across the mouth.

The young Slav's head snapped back and his eyes went dead again. He gave no other sign that he'd been struck. Renko was long-legged and athletic-looking, and wore tight corduroy slacks, a burgundy leather jacket, and a butter-yellow silk shirt. His hair curled past the back of his collar. _Kid,_ he thought. _He calls me kid and smacks me around like a woman._

"Where are they staying?" Kurski asked Nemerov.

"Don't know," the big man said, draining his scotch. "Didn't ask. Wait, they told me anyway. The Pera Palas."

"A big hotel's good," Kurski said. "Lots of coming and going. I can have someone in the Pera in eighteen hours. Man takes sick in his room—food poisoning, say—and out the back way on a stretcher, all very hush-hush, and the management wants it even quieter than you do. And no one keeps things quiet like a good hotel."

"The stretcher, the airport," Nemerov said. "Will everybody stop hopping around and let a man digest his food? Why are you all in such a rush? Why are you all in such a hurry to make mistakes? We don't need to run after Mallory. He'll run after me. After van Vliet, he'll *fly* into my arms," he said, lifting his big arms. "He'll climb into my lap, he'll crawl into my breast pocket. Sasha, you don't think he will?"

"Yes, I do. But all this noodling about of Rauth's is insecure. I'd rather it were over with quickly."

"Ah, so do I," Nemerov sighed. "If it was me, I'd kill them both here, right away. Nice and clean, like Lassiter. What good do they do alive? Well, maybe not the woman right away. You could have some fun with the woman."

"You haven't changed a bit since the Academy," Kurski said fondly. "Brains in your pants. Do you know what they called her, at that Chink school she went to, up in the mountains? The Ghost Princess. They thought she was the reincarnation of some old Chink demon. They didn't think anyone who fought like that could be human. She'd tear you into bits and make you eat the bits."

"I wasn't thinking of a fair fight," Nemerov said.

"What idea," Kurski said, "do you have in that foul little head of yours?"

"Yes," Nemerov said, "you could have some fun with the woman."

5   *The Peony Crescent*

t was 0300 local time, and they were starting the descent toward Atatürk International. It was the last half-hour in which they could be confident nothing much was going to happen.

Mallory was surprised how lousy he felt. He usually loved the first hours of a job. It was usually a clean, alert, pleasurably tense time, before the first mistakes had been made and the first shots fired. It was a time to sit quietly as the plane or truck or boat carried him to his destination, and gather his strength for the fight. It was a time to be glad that the slack, idle time was over, and that he was working again.

But now Mallory found himself doing the most useless thing in the world. He found himself wishing things had gone differently.

He and Atsuko were used to missing each other when one of them wound up, by chance, in the other's city. But when they saw each other, they always spent two, three, even four days together. Atsuko was the only woman he'd ever spent an entire weekend with,

or wanted to. And this was the first time a job had called him away
from her after just a few hours.

The two of them never did anything very exciting during their
time together. She'd curl up against him and read as he watched college basketball or football. They'd play chess. She'd fix him *ramen* or
katsudon in the evenings; he'd fix her an omelette or flapjacks in the
morning. She'd teach him Japanese; he'd help with her English. If
the weather was good, they'd sun themselves in Central Park or
stroll along the East River. He'd take her to a French restaurant. She
loved French restaurants, all French restaurants, and was always
childishly excited to get dressed up and be taken out, and proud to
be out with him, and would keep looking around to make sure everyone was paying proper attention. In the evenings and mornings
she'd tirelessly massage his lanky body, and he'd knead her legs and
feet—her feet were smaller than his hands—as she sighed and
hummed. Mallory's mother had waited tables in bars and diners,
and he knew what it was to earn your money standing. They'd spend
a lot of time in bed. There'd be the slightly unusual pleasure of
unbuttoning and unzipping to find a body that was not new, but
familiar and known, of reclaiming what you'd already made yours.
The sex was always good with Itsy—no better, frankly, than with a
number of other women, but always good—and afterward, he never
found himself wishing he was alone. And sometimes, when she tired
of speaking English, she'd speak to him in Japanese. She'd tell him,
as nearly as he could make out, about her job and her fellow stewardesses, about funny or kind or difficult passengers, about what
she was reading and the monographs she'd start writing and sometimes finish and never show anyone, about the men she sometimes
stayed with in various cities around the world, and about being, like
Mallory, thirty-four: about the sorrows and fears of an unmarried
woman entering the last years of her youth. Her voice would lose
the bright, girlish tones she used in English. It would grow quieter,
wittier, wearier. And Mallory listened as if listening to music, some-

times vaguely, sometimes closely, recognizing one word in twenty, but understanding her, he guessed, about as well as people ever did understand each other. He and Atsuko wouldn't have done anything exciting together that weekend, but they would have shared a few days of calm and quiet pleasure.

Instead, he'd spent the previous evening studying and then burning his briefing packet while Itsy forlornly watched *The Saint* on TV. The show starred some kid named Roger Moore, who looked less like a secret agent than anyone Mallory had ever seen.

And now here he was again with La Remorse. She was flipping through a tourist guidebook as if looking for things to disapprove of.

He had to admit that Laura was beautiful, in her icy fashion. She was twenty-eight years old and had little in the way of breasts or hips, but somehow wasn't at all boyish, perhaps because she did have more than her share of superbly made leg. Her face was oval. He thought it was shaped like a melon seed. Her eyes were slate-blue, smallish, and slightly close-set. Her nose was long and thin, with an upturned tip, her cheekbones were high, and her lips were thin but flawlessly shaped. Laura's face was delicate, in fact, and would not have lasted long in a fight with an equal, but there were only six people in the world capable of striking her in the face, and four of them were very old men who had never left the mountains of China. Though she wasn't his type, she was pretty enough that he'd made a perfunctory pass at her on their first job together. She'd politely but emphatically blown him out of the water. He guessed he was lucky she hadn't coldcocked him, something she could easily have done without mussing her wheat-blonde hair.

He wondered what she'd had to say good-bye to the previous day. Laura Morse's personal life was a bigger secret than Gray's, but she was widely supposed not to have any. It was hard to imagine what she did when she wasn't working. She obviously spent a lot of time practicing her karate, though she seemed more diligent about it than passionate. She didn't seem to be passionate about anything but cars. She'd mentioned once that she had a new 3.5-liter Jaguar and a '43 Lancia Gran Turismo. She maintained them herself. It was the most personal thing she'd ever told him. Laura was an unusually skillful driver and insisted on doing the driving when she and Mallory worked together. It was fine by him. He wondered how she could keep cars like that on a CIA salary. Her folks, probably. She was supposed to come from money. She talked like it, that Boston brahmin drone, not quite nasal and not quite guttural. It was very cool-sounding. When, as Lena Cavanaugh, she'd kissed him hello at the airport, her mouth had been cool and her thin lips lifeless. The Cavanaughs' marriage was supposed to be in trouble, and he figured anyone who'd seen that kiss would believe it. *Imagine,* he thought, *having to kiss a mouth like that for the rest of your life.*

Not looking up from her guidebook, Laura said, "They've got the left hand of John the Baptist at Topkapi Palace. In a brass box shaped like a hand."

"Uh huh?" he said.

Outside, a band of cobalt blue dawn gathered above the horizon. It was only ten in the evening, New York time, but after thirteen hours in the air and a two-hour layover at Heathrow, he and Laura were tired. They'd been booked onto one of the new 707s. Mallory didn't much care for jets. They got you there quicker, but he missed that little moment at the beginning when the propellers started to spin. The new jets didn't feature much legroom, either. Of course, the fact that he was getting irritated about it showed the poorness of his mental preparation. *Somebody ought to give me a good kicking,* he thought. Beside him, Laura gazed blankly out the porthole. As usual, she was neatly and badly dressed. She'd grown up a genteel tomboy, and the Consultancy had long ago given up on her clothes sense, and now Logistics simply issued her an appropriate wardrobe for each job. Laura had, Mallory knew, a closetful of Lena Cavanaugh clothes in her apartment, but she'd still managed to pair a pale-oatmeal jacket with Kelly-green slacks. She sensed his gaze and turned to him, and he made himself smile. "Just a couple more hours, hon," he said in a conversational tone. "Bed'll feel good, huh?"

She nodded, then murmured, "At customs, you think?"

Her voice was almost inaudible over the dull roar of flight.

Mallory had thought all this through hours ago. He shook his head. "Too many people," he murmured back, his voice even lower than hers. They'd gotten pretty good at reading each other's lips. "Too messy. There's a long corridor leads out to the taxi stand. That's the first place makes any sense. Or the cab, more likely. But I'd guess we're all right till tomorrow."

"Hope so," she said. "I'm beat." She opened her purse and began to freshen her lipstick.

"Hon," Mallory said in a normal tone. "Where'd you get that?"

She stopped. "It's called Deep Coral. I like it."

"It doesn't like you back. That's for brunettes, darlin'. Makes a gal like you look bleached out. What else you got?"

Laura opened her purse and held out two other lipsticks, which Logistics had presumably issued her. Mallory selected a pale old rose and handed it back. She wiped her mouth clean with a tissue and did it over again in old rose, then looked at him inquiringly. He nodded, and she dropped the lipstick back in her purse and looked out the window again.

They did not speak again until they landed.

Customs was better organized than Mallory had feared, but he saw that the inspectors were examining about one set of luggage in six—randomly, from what he could see—and progress was slow. When he and Laura reached the head of the line, a trimly uniformed young man motioned them aside to a long metal table. It was in plain view of the crowd, which was better than a closed room on the side. Though it was unlikely he and Laura would be grabbed here, it was not impossible, and a closed room would be the likely first step. "Aw, hell, buddy," Mallory said. "What've we done now?"

"Purely a precautionary formality, sir," the inspector said. "If you would please?" He cast an eye over their bags and tapped Mallory's suitcase. "This one, I think."

Mallory swore softly and sincerely. His suitcase held both his Browning and his electric razor. The razor was Consultancy issue, an ingenious bit of West German engineering with a number of useful functions, none of which happened to include shaving. But the inspector merely hefted it to gauge its weight and replaced it in Mallory's toilet kit without comment. He raised his eyebrows at the Browning. "You expect Turkey will be so dangerous, sir?"

"We don't like taking chances anywhere," Mallory said. "The wife's got her own, if you care. I guess you'll be wanting these."

He handed the international gun permits to the young man, who caressed the State Department seals with his thumb and returned them.

"By all means," he said courteously. "No chances."

He ran his hands lightly through Mallory's folded clothes, scarcely disarranging them, then paused. With a look of careful blankness, he withdrew a damp-looking, shapeless package done up in aluminum foil and plastic wrap. The armed deputy behind them stepped closer. "Sir?" said the inspector.

Mallory could feel Laura looking at him curiously.

"It's a piece of peach pie," he said, stone-faced.

"I am afraid it is quite impossible."

"Yeah, well," Mallory said, "I thought it might be."

The corridor leading out to the taxi stand was not just long, but dim and lined with unmarked steel doors. But the doors stayed shut, and the Cavanaughs reached the end without incident, and joined yet another line of waiting travelers.

When they reached the head of the line, they began to squabble, and John Cavanaugh brusquely waved the couple behind them into the waiting cab. Another cab passed before they were able to resolve their differences and settle glowering into the third.

They were silent on the ride into town. The moonlit Sea of Marmara stretched out to their right, but the Cavanaughs were for some reason more interested in the lane to their left, where a number of heavy trucks were traveling the highway beside them, headed for the markets of Istanbul. But none of the trucks slewed over and forced the cab off the road, and the Cavanaughs reached the Pera Palas unmolested.

As they passed under the hotel's fan-shaped glass awning, Mallory fractionally relaxed. He'd studied the hotel's floor plans. Both the lobby and the elevator were absurd places to make a play. Unless there was someone waiting in their room, they were probably okay for the night. It was a beautiful old hotel, if a bit overelaborate, and Mallory hoped he'd get a chance to enjoy it. He noted richly worked rugs on the broad floors, chandeliers dangling by dark chains from the high, coffered ceiling, and walls of tallow-colored marble banded with stripes of darker stone. The elevator was an open cage of wrought iron and wood, and it groaned as it rose through the well of a spiral staircase, the stone steps of which bore a runner of dark crimson carpeting that seemed to ripple around them.

Their room was on the top floor, the sixth, tucked under the mansard roof. A ramshackle old bellman led them down a long hallway, pulling their suitcases along on a trolley, and Mallory tensed slightly as he opened their door. But the room, unless someone was in the closet or bathroom, was empty. It was a large, spotless room, shabbily elegant. In the center stood a single, queen-sized bed. Mallory swung around and said, "Excuse me, fella. But we reserved twin beds."

"This is your room, sir," the old man said, confused. "You have reserved."

"Not this room, buddy," Mallory said. "One with two beds. Two," he said, holding up two fingers.

"But this is your room," the bellman said. He looked from Mallory to Laura, and in his eyes was plain puzzlement that any man would object to sharing a bed with such a woman as this. "I am most very sorry, sir. But this is the only. There is a full booking presently in the hotel. We cannot provide such another."

"It's all right, John," Laura said.

"Look," Mallory said.

"It's all *right,* John. It doesn't *matter,*" she said witheringly.

Mallory found himself flushing. Laura was always good at these little scenes, sometimes uncomfortably so. He nodded, and the bellman opened the heavy curtains to demonstrate the view, and then closed them again against the oncoming dawn. Mallory handed him a ten-lira note, and he bowed and withdrew.

When the door closed, Laura began to stroll around the room, looking behind the curtains, the framed pictures, and especially the mirrors. "It *looks* clean enough," she said peevishly, peering into a lampshade. "But who knows with these Arab places?"

"They're not Arabs here, hon," Mallory said. He'd taken his electric shaver from the suitcase and was gently prying off the faceplate. Underneath were three miniature dials of knurled steel and two shining metal nubs. He drew out each of the nubs in turn, revealing them to be the ends of two whisker-thin antennae.

"*Whatever* kind of wogs they are," Laura said, still in her Cavanaugh voice.

"You didn't have to come, hon," Mallory said. Working with the tips of his fingers, he adjusted the tiny knobs until the shaver let out a low, regular hum. Laura was working her way clockwise around the room; he began to circle the room counterclockwise.

Perhaps ninety seconds later, they'd made a circuit of the room, bathroom, and closet, and Mallory switched off the shaver and gingerly tucked away the antennae. "Clean," he said. He kept his voice low. The most sophisticated technology in the world couldn't scan for someone in the next room with a stethoscope against the wall.

Laura sank sighing onto the bed. "Such a gentleman," she said, also quietly. "Thanks for looking after my maidenly virtue, Jack, but

I don't mind about the bed. It's certainly big enough, and it would have looked funny if you'd kept insisting." Pulling off her shoes, she began kneading her toes. "Ungh. Next time I want a cover where you're the one who wears the high heels. You'd probably enjoy it. Was my lipstick really that bad?"

"It didn't flatter you much. But it didn't have to. I should've shut up about it."

"You *are* in a mood," Laura said. "I thought you were just being Cavanaugh. Is Gray making you miss a date or something?"

"It's all right."

"You're in a mood, all right. She must have been something extra. Oh, no, wait. Oh no. Your Japanese girl was in town, wasn't she. Mitsuko."

"Atsuko."

"And *she's* the one who made that peach pie. And you never got to eat it, because you had to go. Oh, Jack, I *am* sorry. That really stinks."

"It's all right," he said, touched. "That's the job."

"That just stinks. Well, don't fret. They'll probably send a plump little harem girl after you soon enough, and that'll at least be a distraction. Seems the likely thing, don't you think?"

They were unpacking as they spoke, swiftly and efficiently. In seven hours, at noon, they were to meet the Asker brothers, and their first operational responsibility was to get as much sleep as possible by then. It might be days before they slept properly again.

"It's possible," Mallory said. "You'd think they'd learn."

"I know," she said teasingly. "They always fall in love with you instead." She paused with a stack of blouses in her hands and said, "I'm sorry about van Vliet, Jack. I never got to say. I know that you, well, that you were sort of friends."

"Yeah, we were, a little. Thanks." He couldn't think of anything else to say except, "Need the bathroom?"

"No, you first."

"Thanks."

When he poked his head out the bathroom door, he found Laura dressed in a plain, rather girlish cotton nightgown. It covered her to the knee, but Mallory still thought: *Jesus, those legs. You never do get used to them.* He himself wore a pair of pajama bottoms. She tossed him his toilet kit and joined him by the sink, and they stood brushing their teeth side by side.

"What do you think about the job?" she said around her toothbrush.

"I think Gray's slipping. But I've thought that before, and I'm always wrong."

"He says you've already had some dealings with Rauth."

"Looks that way. Caracas, and that consul's daughter thing."

"Ah yes. You and the Danish consul's daughter." She bent and daintily spat. "I don't like the job, either. I don't like anything about it. Doesn't it strike you as funny that Gray talks about all this as some kind of trap for the firm, but then only talks about you getting captured, not me?"

"Yeah, it struck me. But the notion that this is all some way to get at me, that's screwy. Say it's Rauth. Say he wants me dead on account of the laundry or the consul or whatever it is. Doesn't sound too professional, but let's say. Why bring me to Turkey to do it? It's a lot easier to kill me in New York. And besides, he'd know Gray'd send somebody, but how could he know it'd be me?"

"Easy," Laura said. Her lips were flecked with greenish foam and her breath was minty. "He'd know Gray would send one of his best men. He'd know it would be someone who does wet work. He might guess it'd be someone from the home office. All right. There's only about nine really first-rate agents on the New York desk right now. Only four of them work wet. Akers is still in São Paulo, Paul is on the Deutsche Bank thing, and Lutz just got out of the hospital. And if I know all that, so might Rauth. So that leaves you."

"And you," Mallory pointed out. "You might not be contracted, but by now I'd guess everybody considers you one of us."

"Yes, but that's the thing. I wasn't supposed to be free now. I was supposed to be on my way to Kuwait City. But State just pulled the plug on us without warning. Big kill fee. It just came through in yesterday's pouch. That's what I wanted to tell you."

Mallory rinsed his mouth and splashed water over his face. He rubbed himself dry with one of the thick white towels, thinking.

"I *will* need the bathroom now," Laura said.

He nodded and went back out.

Climbing into bed, he thought about setting the Browning on the night table. He decided against it. It would be messy enough if somebody tried a grab while they were sleeping. More gunfire wouldn't help. He'd have to trust Laura to stay alive and fight her way free. If anyone could do it, she could. She shut the bathroom door and he put out the light. In a moment, he heard the water running. She always ran the water, from modesty. Mallory grinned into the dark and writhed luxuriously against the cool sheets. It was a good bed. He'd shaken off his lethargy and knew he was ready to work. A good partner made all the difference. He stretched slowly and thoroughly and began to compose himself for sleep. It was pleasant to lie in bed and listen to a pretty woman puttering around in the bathroom next door, getting ready to join you. Even—he smiled again—if it was only Laurie. He heard the water shut off, and then the door opened, and for an instant Laura was silhouetted in the doorway, and he saw the dim outline of her body as the light shone through her nightgown: a slim pale shadow with two sharp dark spots where the worn cotton clung to the points of her breasts. Then the light went out and she walked noiselessly around the bed. She stood beside it for a moment.

"*As gaudily and unpleasantly as possible,*" she said, mimicking Gray. "I don't like it. I don't mind killing the people who killed van Vliet, I don't mind that a bit. But this whole make-it-ugly thing. I'll do whatever's necessary, but if it has to be something awful, I want you to think it up."

"They'll get dead some way or other," he said comfortably. "Let's go to sleep."

"And what I hate even more," she said, still standing, "is this business of using you as bait. Like staking out a goat in a lion hunt. I hate it."

"It'll come out all right," he said. "We'll think of something."

"All right. I just wanted to say that."

"Listen, Laurie? I'm glad Gray picked you to run my backup. This'll go a lot better with you along."

After a moment, she said, "Thank you, Jack."

She got into bed then and, as he had, wriggled against the sheets and stretched.

"God, this feels good," she said.

"Good night," he said. "We'll get up at eleven, all right? That'll give us nearly six hours' sleep, and an hour to eat breakfast and get over there."

"All right," she said. She yawned enormously and did not bother to cover her mouth. He saw the light gleaming faintly on her back teeth. "Gray doesn't even have a client on this one, does he?" she said drowsily. "This is on his nickel."

"We get him his intel, he'll find a buyer. Trust him for that."

"None of this adds up. If Rauth has a job on in Istanbul, why kill van Vliet in a way that's sure to draw attention to it? If there's no job here, why kill van Vliet at all?"

Mallory chuckled. "That's pretty much what I told Gray yesterday. Hush up now and let's sleep."

"All right," she said. "Good night."

She turned away from him then and settled on her left hip, and Mallory knew she'd soon be out. She always slept on her left side. It amused him that he knew this. But after all, he'd slept with Laura— next to her, anyway—oftener than any other woman, even Itsy. As the Cavanaughs, and the Pressmans before that, they'd shared a number of hotel rooms and had once been houseguests in a forty-room Maltese villa. They'd had to make do with a single bed then, too, and had been eaten alive by bedbugs. They'd slept side by side on the floor of a cargo plane crossing the Bering Straits. They'd shared a tent in the Mississippi woods. They'd slept in adjacent sleeping bags in an Argentine snowfield and in adjacent bunks—he in the upper, she in the lower—on the Super Chief to Los Angeles. He'd saved her life on that one. Not that she'd never saved his. But he had saved hers, and he felt, sleepily, that this gave him the right to ogle those legs of hers once in a while. They were only eighteen inches away from his. The left one was stretched straight out and the right one was drawn up. He could feel Laura's warmth and smell her combed hair and the clean cotton of her nightgown, and the light odor of her weary young woman's body. He could see her outline in the dawn light seeping around the velvet curtains. She hadn't much hips, but lying on her side like that, her small right hip was thrown into relief. A woman's hip, after all. He felt, muzzily, that the two of them had suffered a long time from a stupid misunderstanding. He reached out under the blankets and gently set a hand on her hip. It felt natural there. Her hip fit deliciously into his palm, and he stroked his hand slowly down to her waist. Her body stirred at last and, slowly, she turned to him.

As she turned, Mallory's hand slid up and around her ribs and, as if destined, settled on her small breast. It was firm and warm under the worn cotton, and the hard nipple bored into his palm. And at the same time, as she turned to him, her eyes filled with a look of drowsy purpose, her own hand slid lightly up his chest and, caressingly, along his neck, until her forefinger settled on a spot just under his right ear, which she gently pressed.

Mallory began to tingle from his scalp to his thighs, as if he'd touched a high-voltage wire. His hand lay limp on her breast. He doubted he could move it. He held himself very still.

"That, Jack," she murmured, "is a meridian called the Peony Crescent. If I press a bit harder, you'll go out like a light and wake up in quite a lot of pain. If I press harder still, you won't wake up."

Laura took her hand away, and Mallory breathed again. She turned her back to him, fluffed up her pillow, and settled herself once more to sleep.

"Good night, dear," she said over her shoulder.

Mallory lay there rubbing his neck.

Then he smiled crookedly into the darkness.

"Good night, hon," he said and went to sleep.

6   *A Good Chap*

An experienced agent doesn't need an alarm clock, and Mallory always trusted his body to wake him at any hour he'd chosen, or before, if there was any need for it. At about ten-thirty that morning, he noticed in his sleep that Laura was getting out of bed. Shortly afterward, he knew something was happening in their room, and that it didn't require his attention. He continued to sleep. Just before eleven, he woke and blinked into his pillow. Behind him, he heard Laura breathing deeply, almost panting, the rhythm of her breaths syncopated, with deliberate stops and starts, and he heard her bare feet moving softly on the carpet. He rolled over and found her in the middle of the room, wearing nylon running shorts and a T-shirt, performing her morning *kata.* He'd seen it often enough, but it was still impressive. There were dreamy, balletic glidings back and forth, and long, crouching postures, low against the floor, that made his legs ache just to look at them, and then all at once she'd whip an arm or leg forward or back and momentarily freeze in place before flowing inevitably into the next stance. Laura was an adept at half a dozen different schools, but her favored style was an old and obscure one called Floating Hand. He could never remember the Mandarin for it. And her hands and feet did seem to float, like hawks drifting in the sky. At the end of the routine, she stood poised and motionless with one foot planted on the floor and the other pointing straight up into the air, so that her legs were like the hands of a clock at twelve-thirty.

"Jesus," he said.

Laura lowered her foot, picked a towel off the dresser, and wiped her dripping face. Her T-shirt was splotched with sweat, and her narrow chest moved deeply and regularly. "Morning," she said.

"Morning. How high can you kick, anyway?"

Without warning, her leg lashed heavenward again. It seemed to carry her effortlessly into the air. Laura touched the sole of her foot to the ceiling and dropped noiselessly back to the rug, still holding the towel.

"Jesus," he said. "Nine feet, easy. And you weren't even trying."

"You shouldn't encourage me to show off," she said, grinning and wiping her temples. "It's really counter to the spirit of Piao Shou."

"That's it," he said. "Piao Shou. I always forget the damn name."

"How's the neck?"

"Little sore."

"Good. Teach you some manners."

"You're a bear-trap, Laurie," he said, reaching for the bedside phone.

"So I've been told."

He said, "Hello, room service?"

The apartment house on Jurnal Sokagi was only three blocks away. Freshly showered and lightly breakfasted, Laura and Mallory entered the lobby at five minutes past twelve. The place was working hard to look luxurious and ultra-modern: The commissionaire sat behind a long granite desk set with a long row of TV screens showing grainy, flickering images of the elevators and halls. They hadn't done poor Just much good. At the end of the desk stood a policeman holding a battered MAT 49 submachine gun. Beside him was a short, curly-haired young man in a dark suit. Mallory recognized him from the briefing packet: Talaat Asker, one of van Vliet's adjutants. Mallory shook hands with him and said, "Sad thing. Damn sad thing. Mr. Asker, my wife Lena."

"I am charmed," Talaat said, holding her hand in both of his.

He spoke briefly in Turkish to the armed policeman and then escorted them to the elevator.

Upstairs, another armed policeman stood beside a door marked with yellow and black police stickers. Talaat exchanged nods with him, then paused with a hand on the knob. He glanced at Laura uncertainly. "Inside will be unpleasant," he said to Mallory.

"I'm sure," Laura said mildly. "But it's what we came to see."

It had been less than forty-eight hours since van Vliet's death, and before the door was fully open, they smelled a thick, acrid stench: melted insulation, scorched carpeting, and plasterboard still damp from the fireman's hose. Beneath all that, a faint, sickening odor of roasted meat. The floor was muddy and the ceiling was dark with roiling smoke stains. In the center of the room, a young man sat in a straight-backed dining chair. He rose as they came in.

It was clear that Osman and Talaat were brothers: they had the same thick, straight noses and dark, direct eyes. Like many young Turkish men, they were handsome, and like most Turkish men, they had imposing black moustaches. They were both in their early twenties. Talaat, though smaller, was clearly the elder; there was something unformed about Osman's gaze. "Hello," Osman said as he shook their hands. The word seemed uncomfortable in his mouth. "I'm awful sorry about van Vliet," Mallory said, and Osman ducked his head in reply.

"Osman doesn't speak," his brother remarked.

"My Englis', to listen it, give you a bad head," Osman said, smiling apologetically. He touched his head.

"But his German is perfect, and he doesn't speak. He doesn't speak in Turkish. He stands there and he looks at you," Talaat said indulgently. "But he listens very much, and we know everything of each other. So you can speak to either with confidence." He did not sound confident himself. His eyes, like his brother's, were red-rimmed. "You are comfortable where you are in your hotel? They treat you well? You have no difficulties to come here?"

Like the chat at a family funeral, Mallory thought.

"They're treating us fine, thanks."

"I'm glad."

"Crime scene fellas all through in here? The police do their stuff?"

"The police," Talaat said savagely. He controlled himself and said, "The police have done what little they are interested to do. What little they are capable. More important, our own site team has completed an assay. INSTA has contributed a good lab man. There is nothing now that may not be touched."

"Good," Mallory said. "Let's see where it happened."

The smoke stains on the ceiling grew darker as they neared the bathroom. They seemed to billow overhead like the shadows of vast black blooms, and the charred smell wafted thickly from the bathroom door, which had been smashed from its hinges by the firemen. Inside, the plastic toilet seat had melted into the blackened bowl. The mirror over the sink had shattered, as had the glass doors of the shower stall and half the tiles within. A single red toothbrush in its holder was weirdly untouched. Against the back wall of the shower, and running down into the tub, was a tarry, clotted stain the width of a large man and about nine feet long. The mixed stench was nearly unbearable, and the Askers glanced uneasily at Laura.

"We read the initial site report," Mallory said, looking around. "Who wrote it?"

"We did," Talaat said.

"That was good work."

"Thank you."

"We know Lassiter bought it, and how. Anything else come up since you filed?"

"We have identified that the flamethrower is German, an old FmW-41. These is very common from the war. One buys such an item cheaply, and it is quite reliable. To choose it means only that the planning is professional. We have located the merchant who sold the device. Neutral, a man we use ourselves." Talaat shrugged. "We see little benefit in acting against him. He would not know Lassiter's client. For all he knows, the client would be ourselves. Lassiter rented the apartment next door three weeks ago under the name Gregory Fogg. The bathroom in that flat is next to this one. It has been all, ah, removed inside so as to install the apparatus. Everything very perfectly done. Lassiter has put a tap into the cables of the video cameras in the elevator and hall, and installed his own monitor. So what the doorman saw, Lassiter saw, and he knew when Mr. van Vliet was in the apartment and could activate the apparatus when he hears someone using the shower."

"Kinda convenient that the place next door was empty just then," Mallory said.

"The previous occupants was paid one hundred thousand lira to leave before their lease is finish. The arrangement is a usual one when a rich foreigner wishes a particular place. The previous tenants have identify Lassiter by his photograph. They was quite positive, and quite willing to do so. There is no reason to suspect collusion."

"But you've run a check on them just the same?"

"Naturally. We find nothing of interest."

"Prints next door?"

"None. Only the previous tenants."

Someone had had to scrape van Vliet from the tub; it was flecked with tiny scraps and dark curds. The brothers could not seem to take their eyes from it.

"Let's talk out in the living room," Mallory said gently.

There was a small dining alcove next to the kitchenette, and both Osman and Talaat tried to pull out a chair for Laura at the same time. Mallory sat down and rested on his elbows, gazing around the little bachelor flat. Glass doors let out onto a tiny balcony and a fine view across the Horn toward the Bazaar Quarter. On the coffee table were neat stacks of English, Turkish, and Dutch newsmagazines. Over the two-seat sofa hung a framed Edward Weston photograph of a bell pepper, gleaming like a nude girl crouched in the moonlight. Or, Mallory supposed, a nude man. On the end table stood a framed snapshot of a pinched-looking woman with short, fair bangs. Just's ex-wife. He'd shown Mallory her photo in a hotel bar in Tulsa. Mallory recalled the crime scene photos he'd examined in New York. The blackened thing in the tub had loved this pale woman very much. For just a moment Mallory was swept by rage, but it wasn't useful, not just then, and he forced it away. His voice was soft when he said, "You liked van Vliet, didn't you?"

The brothers' expressions did not alter, but, as if on cue, their eyes filled with tears.

"He was a good chap," Talaat said.

"I thought so, too. Got any suspicions?"

"None."

"No?"

"No. We welcome your advice very much. We have only one suggestion, and this we ourselves are already executing. We intend to know why Nemerov is in Istanbul, and where he is at present."

"That's not a bad idea. How've things been at the office?"

"Very quiet until this."

"No big new jobs? New clients? New clients for Advance?"

"No."

"Notice any change in van Vliet recently?"

"Perhaps he was a little sadder. But he was a sad man."

"Did he have a sweetheart here?"

"No. In the evenings maybe he goes for a walk. He has a small drink in a *meyhane,* he sits at home with his radio. Always alone."

"What did he do for sex?"

"Oh," Talaat said slyly, "Mr. van Vliet was a man. I am sure he did not go without the ladies."

"C'mon now, Talaat. I knew Just."

The sly smile vanished. "All right," Talaat said. "There are places in Taksim where a man can go and have a young chap, and sometime Mr. van Vliet went there. He was a fine man, a *good* man," he said pleadingly. "It is only because he didn't find the right woman to understand him."

"I guess he didn't, at that. Know where he used to go? Did he have a regular guy he always asked for?"

"We can find this out," Talaat said without enthusiasm.

"What was he working on when he died?"

"Small matters. Only small matters."

"You've thought about this already."

"Very much. In the last month he talk to us about nothing significant."

"All right. Then we need to find what he was working on that he didn't talk about. Site team check the place for anything that might turn out to be Just's notes?"

"Of course. There was nothing. No search had been made before ours, and the locks on the door had not been tampered."

"Who keeps the files at the office?"

"I," Osman said.

"Let's go there and check over the recent stuff," Mallory said. "I want to see what Just might have filed himself, without telling you two. I think that's where we start. Laurie, what do you think?"

"It makes sense," she said. "But I still think, alive or dead, Lassiter's our one real lead. We've got a pretty good file on him back in

Langley. I'd like to put one of our own analysts on this and have them cable me a précis of his recent contacts."

"Sounds good. Can you fix that up?" Mallory asked the brothers.

Osman nodded. "Very immediately," he said in his deep, hesitant voice. By now his face was shiny with tears he didn't appear to notice. Though not large, Osman had a wrestler's poise and a wrestler's densely muscled torso. His eyes sat in their sockets like hot, black stones. Mallory felt a fleeting moment of sympathy for whoever van Vliet's killers turned out to be.

"Okay," Mallory said. "We got Lassiter, any suggestive business in the files, and Nemerov, in about that order. Anything else we should know right now?"

"Only about Istanbul," Talaat said. "If you are to operate here, you must understand that Turkey is not yet a place of laws. Nor of institutions. Nor is it so simple that you can merely bribe anyone and have what you wish, as foreigners imagine. Though certainly there is very much bribery. This is a society where all is—relations. All is personal. This one is my brother, you see, and that one once did an injury to my cousin, and these is not convenient but they have done good business with my sister's family, and those is from my grandfather's village and will help me, and those is Anatolians and impossible. You see? It is all according to whom one knows. And this is how things are accomplish. Only in this way."

"It's not so different where I'm from. I know we'll be leaning on you two pretty heavily for the Turkish end of things."

Talaat looked relieved. "This was what we hope. And, ah, one last matter. Of Miss Morse." He addressed her for the first time, his dark face reddening. "We are concern that you might be, ah, when you are on the street? Alone, specially? That you might be troubled."

"That men will stare and make remarks and so forth," she said. "Yes, I'd heard. Thanks, but I believe I'll be able to take care of myself."

"It is a very bad local habit," Talaat said. "And a woman such as you, excuse me, so tall and blonde, is a dream for a Turkish man."

"For any man," Mallory said firmly.

"The last of the Southern gentlemen," Laura said.

"Of course for any man," Talaat said hurriedly. "I only mean for the Turk specially."

"Well, I can believe that, too," Mallory said. "Look, Gray's briefed you two, right? You know what I'm here for?"

"Yes."

"When they grab me, this becomes Laurie's job. Will you two have any problem taking orders from a woman?"

"We are modern men," Talaat said stiffly. "European men. There will be no difficulty." Then he glanced uncertainly at Laura.

"Good," Mallory said.

He looked around the flat again. A barren, lonely place. A tidy little place for a weary man who knew his best wasn't good enough. A place where he could rest after doing it anyway. *Poor son of a bitch,* Mallory thought. It did not occur to him that van Vliet's apartment looked much like his own. "Well, we haven't got such a bad start," he said, almost to himself. "We're going to take care of this the way Just would've wanted."

"Take care?" Talaat cried. "Take *care?*" he said furiously.

He began to weep.

"Excuse me," he said, "but how does one take care when a man is dead? God takes care of Mr. van Vliet now. It was once our job to do this, and we failed."

"That's slop," Mallory said. "You did your jobs then, and you're going to do them now."

"Oh, he was a good chap," Talaat said, sobbing. "And we failed him. And now it is very bitter that he must be revenge by strangers. But you was his friend? You was his friend. You are not a stranger."

"We were friends," Mallory said.

"He was teaching us, Mr. Mallory. He was teaching us very much. He was a good, good chap. You must remember that we cared for him. You must revenge him very much."

7 *Club Europa*

dvance Global Shipping was a busy office, and actually did a fair amount of shipping. As they entered, though, Mallory could sense a stillness and forlornness that hung in the air like a black wreath. The receptionist was a sleek young Turkish woman in a cranberry dress. The dress was provocatively snug, but it was plain that she, too, had been crying. She passed a practiced eye over Mallory and Laura and then went momentarily still, as even well-trained people often do when pressing a concealed button.

The reception area had been done up in blonde-wood paneling and ecru carpeting. Dim hidden lighting spilled down the walls. The room was bare of decoration, save for the opulent little receptionist and a discreet AGS in small chromed letters on the wall above her head. A six-foot-tall aquarium was set into the wall to their left and took up much of its length. It contained a variety of brightly veiled fish, which began darting in circles as the entire tank slid smoothly and silently to one side, opening a narrow doorway to the Consultancy's Istanbul station.

"Neat," Mallory said as they slipped through. "What if somebody comes in while this gadget's still open?"

"Belma surveils all the public spaces of the building, as well as the sidewalk outside," Talaat said. "She doesn't open if there is any question. And the mechanism bolts the front door until this passage has shut."

Mallory nodded. The room within was small, dingy, and crammed with government-surplus desks and expensive phones. They could have been back in New York.

The file room was comparatively spacious, though, and even equipped with a barred skylight. In the center were a scarred wooden table and two swivel chairs. Battered steel cabinets stretched floor to ceiling on all four walls, each with a combination lock. "These is all the bureau's desk files from the beginning. February 1958. To examine every file is many weeks of work," Talaat said neutrally.

"I'm guessing we only want files that've opened in the last three months or so. You've got log sheets on these?"

"Yes, on the front of the first folder in each series. Every addition must be noted. Within is a circulation log that tells who has withdrawn the file and when, and the date of return."

"These typed or written out by hand?"

"By hand. Yes, I see. Mr. van Vliet would only seldom open a file himself. Perhaps in this entire room, I think, are three dozen such files or less. And of course both of us know his handwriting well."

"Show us. And show us an example of yours and Osman's."

Osman thought for a moment, then went to a cabinet in the corner and dialed in the combination. He knelt, flipped through the bottom two drawers, and returned with three folders, which he lay in a neat row on the table. "Mr. van Vliet," he said, pointing. "Talaat. Me."

Mallory and Laura examined them. Then she looked at him and nodded.

"This red dot here the designation for hot files?" Mallory asked Talaat.

"Yes. It is peel off when the file is no longer so active."

"Okay. We don't want any hot files. If Just had a suspicion he was keeping quiet for some reason, he wouldn't draw attention to it with a red dot. We want files logged completely in Just's handwriting, from mid-March or later, with no red dot, that neither of you recognize by title. All right? Osman unlocks all these cabinets. Laurie, you write out your signal for Langley, and Osman'll get it sent through. Meanwhile, the rest of us will get going. Talaat, you start on this end, and Osman'll start at that end when he gets back, and the two of you'll work toward the middle. Laurie and me will start in the middle and work outward. We drop all the possibles on the table. There ought not to be too many. Laurie and me'll wind up pulling files you two'd've recognized, but that can't be helped. This make sense to everybody, or have I got something cranksided?"

"Nothing is cranksided," Talaat said, pleased. "Let's begin."

It took over four hours, and Mallory's back was aching in the first ninety minutes, and soon his knees were numb from hunkering over the bottom drawers. At the two-hour mark, Belma came in with sandwiches and a copper tray bearing four tiny glasses of tea. She was a small woman with a neat, glossy head and a luxuriously curved nose. She eyed Mallory appraisingly on her way into the crowded little room and again on her way out. Laura shot Mallory a sardonic glance, as if to say: *plump little harem girls.* At twenty past six that evening they were all gazing blearily at some crumpled sandwich papers and five file folders labeled in Just's neat, squarish script. Osman touched two of the files with a finger, said, "These I know," and stacked them neatly in the corner. That left three. They were marked DRACHMA/TL/DM, CLUB E, and POULSEN.

DRACHMA/TL/DM contained newswire printouts and a few pages of handwritten notes about a ring of Greek currency speculators. "It is possible," Talaat said, and stopped.

"Recognize it?" Mallory said.

"I am not certain. But Mr. van Vliet did mention the matter."

Mallory picked up the file and dropped it on the stack in the corner.

CLUB E contained newspaper and magazine clippings about a nightclub called Club Europa, currently under construction not far from the Galata Tower, and several pages of densely written notes on the club's financial and political history. "Third-biggest nightclub in Europe, when it's done," Mallory said, flipping through the file. "Glass dance floor—wouldn't want to wear a short skirt there, I guess—fountains, light show, fancy restaurant, helipad on the roof. Pretty good spread. This make any sense to anybody?"

The brothers shook their heads.

He dropped the file back on the table.

POULSEN held nothing but a few pictures of a young Norwegian actress named Nina Poulsen. They'd been clipped from newspapers and magazines, and except for the captions, the accompanying text had been trimmed away. Mallory frowned. "There's no info here at all. Even if she's dirty somehow, what good are a bunch of press photos? What's so significant about her face?"

"She looks a bit like the woman in van Vliet's apartment," Laura said. "The portrait on the end table."

Mallory stared, and then smiled sadly.

"Yeah," he said. "You nailed it, Laurie. She's about a mile prettier, but she looks a whole lot like Helene. Just's ex-wife."

The four of them were silent.

Mallory closed the folder and laid it gently on the stack in the corner.

Then he laid a palm on the folder marked CLUB E. "This is where we start," he said. "We'll keep pushing on Nemerov and Lassiter. But this is our priority."

"Why?" Laura said.

"Just a feeling."

"That's good enough for me," she said. "Talaat, Osman? Can you get us a car?"

"Yeah," Mallory said. "Let's go have a look at Club Europa."

"It won't be nearly as much fun," Laura told him, "as watching you do filing."

"Don't stop," Mallory told Osman from the back seat of the Consultancy's gleaming 1948 Mercedes. "But we can stare at it as we go by. Anybody'd stare at a thing like that."

In the architect's renderings in the newspapers, the club had looked like a cross between an Ottoman palace and a modern airline terminal. It was a design of notable vulgarity and considerable skill. But at present it was only a cavernous hulk of rough-cast concrete that seemed to soak up the slanting evening light and turn it to dark ash and shadow. Through a titanic open archway, they saw other vast archways within, alternately dark and lit with harsh arc lights. A yellow tractor laboring beneath them seemed a toy. "Like a Piranesi prison," Laura murmured.

"A what?" Mallory said.

"Just art history chatter," Laura said. "Ignore it. An old Italian who drew imaginary dungeons the size of mountains. Jack, have you ever seen cement mixers that size? Don't they look funny to you?"

"I observe," Mallory said, "a large concrete building, half-finished. Before it stands a large concrete mixer. I therefore deduce that the concrete mixer was intended to transport large quantities of concrete."

"Holmes, this is uncanny," Laura said. "Talaat, can you get us up someplace where we can see the whole area?"

Talaat glanced at Mallory. But Mallory was gazing out the window, apparently lost in thought.

After a moment, Talaat said, "This should not be impossible."

They get it now, Mallory thought. And like van Vliet before him, he thought, *You never have to tell these boys anything twice.*

"Thanks," Laura said. She sank back frowning in her seat. "I counted two armed guards among the workers. And not as many workers in there as I'd have imagined."

"I wouldn't worry too much about how many guys, hon. I've worked a little construction. Half the time the site's half-deserted, for all kinds of reasons. And it is around quitting time. But I saw the guards, too. Talaat, how unusual is that around here?"

"Perhaps not so unusual, in a project that is so large, and has been much spoken about, and is about to be close for the night. There is not very much petty stealing here, of the kind that is so common in America. But there is some. Still, I would expect that one guard is sufficient."

Laura hardly seemed to listen. "I'm with you, Jack," she said, frowning at the back of Osman's head. "So help me, I'm with you. There's a smell off that thing. It's dirty."

Mallory said nothing. Laura had joined the CIA as an analyst before someone in Ops heard about her martial arts ability and had her retrained for the field. She hadn't been as good at analysis as she proved to be at fieldwork, but when she was thinking hard, it paid to stand back and let her think.

"Perhaps here," Talaat said quietly.

He had parked the car at the crest of the Yeni Carsi Caddesi, under the shadow of the Galata Tower, looking northwest. Beside them was a mural of a lovely, black-haired boy, gazing gravely back at them with tears on his cheeks, standing in a field of huge, stylized tulips. The four agents sat and stared out the windshield. "This is Tünel we are in," Talaat said. "We are looking northwest toward the newer buildings. Toward Sisli. What are you seeking?"

"What's that big one over there?" Laura said. "The big greenish glass one."

Talaat twisted around and looked at her. "You have been briefed on this?"

"No. What is it?"

"Publicly, that is the Banco Lavoro Tower. A new commercial office building, of which the Turkish Treasury has taken five floors." He hesitated. "Privately—very privately—it is build above a very sizable, ah, system of underground vaults. Containing Turkey's gold reserves. Perhaps two hundred and sixty million American dollars' worth of gold. That building, Miss Morse, is Turkey's Fort Knox."

"Your gold reserves are in Ankara," Mallory objected.

"Publicly, only publicly. Mr. Mallory and Miss Morse, what I have just told you is most exceptionally secret."

"So secret you haven't passed it along to New York. It wasn't in our briefing packets."

"I am a Turk, Mr. Mallory."

"A quarter-billion in gold nobody's supposed to know about," Laura said slowly. "And maybe five hundred yards away, somebody's building a helipad you could land three Hueys on at once."

"Uh huh," Mallory said.

"It doesn't make sense," she muttered. "For God's sake, is Rauth planning to attack the Turkish Treasury with combat choppers?"

"And even if he did," Mallory said, "wouldn't he stage them across the border in Georgia? That's only fifteen minutes away as the Huey flies. Dunno how you'd get that far into Turkish airspace without a shooting war, anyway."

"You've thought of all this," she said.

"Keep going."

"All right. First, there's the heliport," she said, touching a finger to the back of Osman's seat. "That's the part that stinks the loudest. Second," she said, and touched another finger to the seat, "the building's just so damn *big* inside, and so much of it's blank walls five stories tall, and hardly any internal walls; just big arches. And that makes sense, if they're planning big ballrooms, but anything could be going on in there, and most of it would be hidden from the street. Third, how often do you hear of someone building a big new building like that for a nightclub, from scratch? Instead of, I don't know, renovating an old theater or something?" She shook her head. "But what I keep thinking of—it sounds crazy. But I kept thinking, the construction site? The drawings of the club from the papers? The whole thing seems like a great big stage set. For an opera. Something by Wagner. And I keep thinking, somehow that's part of what it's for. It's meant as a stage set for something. I know this doesn't make sense yet. You've probably thought of all this any-way," she said peevishly and for a moment sounded precisely like Lena Cavanaugh.

"I didn't think of the stage set part," Mallory said. "You're right. I want you to keep thinking about that. That and the cement mixers."

"Are you teasing me?"

"No." He turned to the brothers. "We'll want a full drill-down on the Europa and another on the gold reserves. That's all on the local side, so you two'll handle it. Keep referring back to Just's notes on the Europa and see if your intel matches his. Talk to the people he's talked to and see who looks at you funny. You know the routine. Whoever it is knows damn well we're after them, so there's no point in being dainty. Right now, though, everybody's office is closing, and I believe we're all through for the night. We'll meet at Advance at eight tomorrow morning and figure out some way for Laurie and me to help you drill. You two haven't slept yet, have you? Since Just died. You couldn't have drafted that report and run the site assay and the rest of it and slept, too."

"We will sleep," Talaat said softly, "when Mr. van Vliet's killers sleep."

"Nope. You'll go straight home, get a good meal, and sleep now. That's an order. When they grab me, I don't intend to have my backup yawning and blinking."

"All right," Talaat said. "Yes. You are correct."

"You've been doing good work, both of you. We'll meet at eight and do some more. Mind dropping us back at the Pera on your way home?"

"If you don't mind," Osman said in his deep, surprising voice, "there is one more visit that we must make."

He'd plainly practiced the sentence in his head.

Talaat looked at him, then nodded. "Yes. Though perhaps you and Miss Morse won't like to come with us."

"Naw," Mallory said, puzzled. "We'll come along."

The brothers were silent on the short ride across Beyoglu. The old Mercedes picked its way through a labyrinth of broad avenues and gnarled little streets, passing through blocks that glistened with wealth and those that seemed constructed of scrap wood and soot. Ten minutes from the Galata Tower, the Mercedes swerved abruptly to the curb. A white-capped traffic policeman seemed about to object, but took a second look at the car and its occupants and nodded. They were in front of a decrepit-looking old mosque wedged in between a multistory car park and an old office building topped with a billboard advertising Tamek Tomato Purée. Mallory reflected that they'd passed two large and beautiful mosques along the way.

"If you wouldn't mind to wait a few minutes?" Talaat said hesitantly, peering around at them.

"Not at all," Laura said. She was already fetching a worn paperback from her purse.

"I'll come with you," Mallory said.

"Yes?" Talaat said.

"Sure," said Mallory.

The entrance to the mosque was crowded on one side with empty shoes and sandals, and Mallory and the brothers removed their shoes and socks and left them there. On the other side, a row of iron spigots had been let into the wall, with a stone block beneath each one and a chair in front of it. Mallory did as the brothers did and quickly washed his feet and face.

Then he followed them inside. The mosque seemed far bigger than it had from the outside, and the absence of chairs and the expanse of threadbare Turkish rug on the floor made the space seem larger still. In the corner was a little gilded niche that Mallory knew indicated the direction of Mecca. What was it called again? The *mihrab.* Beside it was the *minbar,* a ladder-steep flight of stairs leading up to a tiny pulpit with a peaked roof. It jutted up into the air like the gnomon of a sundial. Beside and above Mallory was a curtained balcony. It was between prayer times, and only a few worshippers were scattered across the vast rug. The brothers walked out among them, sank to their knees, and prostrated themselves in the direction of the gilt niche, moving calmly and purposefully as swimmers taking their places on the starting blocks. Mallory stayed near the door. He stood with his right wrist loosely clasped in his left hand, in the traditional posture of a lawyer waiting for judge and jury to be seated, and bowed his head and gazed at the red, gold, and cobalt curlicues unwinding beneath his feet.

Five minutes later, the brothers rose together and walked back to join him, and the three men left the mosque, pausing to drop a few bills in the collection box.

"You was praying?" Talaat said shyly, as they pulled on their shoes.

"I was thinking," Mallory said.

"It is all the same God, you know," Talaat said encouragingly. "There is only one."

"At most."

"Ah, you don't believe?"

"I don't know much about that stuff. I'm glad you were praying for the job, if that's what you were doing."

"We was praying for true sight, and for strength," Talaat said. "We was praying that God should be pleased. We was praying for justice."

"Sounds good," Mallory said. "Next time, pray for Laurie and me, too."

"We was praying for you both very much."

"Thanks."

"Miss Morse prays? There is a woman's section in the balcony. We can give her something for her head. My handkerchief is quite clean."

"I think she's all right the way she is. Ready to go?"

"Yes," Talaat said. "We are ready."

"You take some walnuts," Nemerov said, seeming to take walnuts from the air with his blunt fingers, "and you thread them on a string, and you've already cooked down some grape juice, so it's thick, and sugared it up. And you soak the walnuts in the juice, you see? and sort of mush them all tight together on the string. And when they dry out, they're like a stick, but chewy, like sausage. *Churchkhela.* It's so good."

"The things you put in your mouth," Kurski said, smiling faintly.

He did not particularly feel like smiling.

It took a great deal to disturb Sasha Kurski. He had once arranged a gas-line explosion that killed the entire family of a Central African prime minister, including three small children. Even Nemerov had been upset about that one, when he heard. Kurski had not. He'd executed the job properly and been paid for it promptly, and that was all there was to be said about the matter. There was really only one thing that upset Kurski, and that was stupidity. And just now, stupidity was all around him. He'd stupidly taken on a stupid job to please an old friend, and it seemed his old friend was getting stupidest of all.

"I want to talk to you," he told Nemerov.

"I want to talk to *you*," Nemerov said. "I've been thinking about Mallory."

They were in Nemerov's suite at the Marmara, and Nemerov was sitting at ease in his desk chair, resting one foot on the edge of an open drawer.

"Yes," Kurski said. "You want to make a pet of him. You want him to play with your whores."

"No, no, that was all whiskey-talk. I've been thinking *seriously.* Listen," Nemerov said, and leaned forward. "I'm quitting Rauth."

"Oh?"

"You always give me good advice, Sashka. I'm taking your advice. I'm quitting Rauth."

"Good," Kurski said.

"After the job's finished, of course."

"Naturally. What about Mallory?"

The desk chair creaked as Nemerov leaned back again. "Do you know how old I am, Sasha?"

"We're the same age," Kurski said patiently.

"I'm thirty-eight, Sasha. I'm not so young as I was."

"I'm getting old listening to you. Piotr, what about Mallory?"

"A man like that," Nemerov said. "The Consultancy's best man, wouldn't you say? Close to Gray. A man like that must know a few things worth knowing."

"Doubtless."

"A few things worth something on the open market."

"I understood you."

"I'm not so young as I was, and I'm leaving Rauth. And it won't be so hard to find more work, this year, or next year, or five years from now. But what about ten years? Twenty? I've got to start putting a bit away. I've got to start being more like you, you slick little devil, and putting a few dollars away for my old age."

"No," Kurski said.

"You haven't been putting a few dollars away?"

"You are not going to double on Rauth. You are not going to sell Mallory on the open market. I can stop you and I will."

"Sashka," Piotr said. "Do I seem so foolish to you?"

"Lately, yes."

"Did I say a word, one *word*, about doubling? Did I say I wouldn't give Rauth his Mallory without a scratch, just as I promised? But listen, who says we can't have a little chat with the fellow ourselves before we wrap him up and put on the bow? Did Rauth say we couldn't do that?"

"You objected earlier to making things fancy. That would be fancy."

"I can be very persuasive," Nemerov said dreamily, "and never leave a mark on them. Not on the outside. With you to help me, we can be twice as persuasive."

"You are complicating an already complicated job. Mallory is to be delivered intact. The woman is to be neutralized, preferably killed. That's plenty to do right there, especially on top of supervising the Projekt. And I've yet to hear a single idea for bringing all this about. Except, of course, letting them climb into your breast pocket."

"You know, the courier came by this morning," Nemerov said. "Brought a little something for me from a sort of a buddy of mine at the Hyde Park Zoo." Nemerov opened the top drawer of the desk and withdrew a bulky padded envelope. It had been neatly slit open at one end. He withdrew a lightweight alloy dart gun and set it on the desk, then laid a plastic-wrapped packet beside it. Flicking open the plastic sheeting, he withdrew a gleaming dart the size of a ballpoint pen and fitted it deftly into the gun. He waggled the dart to make sure it was firmly seated, then turned the little gun in his hand, admiring it. "Nice?"

"Very nice," Kurski said.

"Kid," Nemerov shouted. "Hey, Ugly. In here."

Renko appeared in the doorway. "Yes?" he said somberly.

Nemerov shot him in the stomach.

There was a short, brisk hiss of compressed CO_2, and then the dart was quivering in Renko's belly. Almost at once the young man had snatched it out and was staring at it. He tried to raise his head to look at Nemerov and wasn't quite able.

He slumped bonelessly to the floor.

"Not quite a second and a half," Nemerov said, looking at his watch. "I wish he'd left the dart in, so we could have had a proper test."

Kurski said nothing.

Nemerov set down the dart gun, got up with a grunt, and ambled across the room. He bent down and felt the pulse in the young man's throat. "Steady," he reported. "I asked for the dose you'd use on a 150-kilo animal. So on a 75-kilo man, it'd kick in twice as fast. You're supposed to get about an hour's immobility, maybe ninety minutes. They gave us six darts."

"Of which you have now wasted one."

"Tested, Sasha, not wasted. I want to see how they work on a human." Nemerov nudged Renko's leg with a toe, making it roll laxly back and forth. He bent again, scooped the tall young man up in his arms—for all the effort he expended, he might have been picking up a fallen necktie—and carried him across the room, where he dropped him, almost gently, on the sofa. He passed his hand over Renko's chest, picked up an arm and let it fall, patted his cheek. He said, "I wouldn't mind the little weasel so much if he'd just kept his damn moustache."

"You'll push him too far."

"No. He likes being messed about. His sort need it."

"Only up to a point. What are you doing now?"

Grinning, Nemerov was unbuckling Renko's belt. With a brusque jerk he pulled the Serb's pants down to his knees, then rolled him over on the couch and arranged him so that his narrow behind was sticking up in the air. "That'll give him something to think about when he wakes up," Nemerov said. "Remind him why he had to leave home."

Nemerov dropped heavily into the desk chair again. He traced the edge of the desk with a finger.

"A 75-kilo man," he said dreamily. "Or a 50-kilo woman."

Kurski sighed.

"But it all fits together so nicely," Nemerov said. "They'll come for me. They're traveling as a couple; why should they go mousing about on their own? One dart for him, one for her, three left over for in case. Then they come to, and he's all tied up in a chair, and she's roped up across from him, spread-eagle. Not a stitch on. You see? And we say, Now, Mr. Mallory, we've got a few questions for you, and while you're thinking them over we'll be passing the time here with your woman. Oh, he'll talk. He'll blubber and plead and sing like a choirboy. Because if he doesn't tell us this, we'll do a bit of that to her, and if he wants us to stop doing such-and-such, he'll have to tell us so-and-so, and no one says *she's* got to remain undamaged. Oh, he'll be racking his brains, trying to think up more things to tell us. We'll empty him right out."

"And then?"

Nemerov shrugged. "And then we'll do all those things to her anyway, and then kill her, if she's still alive, and bundle Mallory into the copter. And there you are."

"What happened to a clean death for professionals?"

"Oh, I meant Mallory. Anyway, that's all off now. You can't keep things clean and tidy with Rauth."

Kurski was silent.

"You don't approve?"

"You know how I feel about all this noodling around. No, I don't approve."

"But Rauth says we've got to noodle. So we're going to noodle. And if I'm going to noodle, I'm going to have a little fun with it, and at the end, she'll be just as dead, won't she? It'll take five, six hours for the copter to arrive. Plenty of time for all sorts of things. The idea doesn't appeal to you, Sasha? She's never killed any of your comrades?"

"Probably."

"Then you can take a turn. You can go first, if you like."

"No." He looked down at Renko. "Any lasting effects?"

Nemerov shrugged again. "We'll see in a couple of hours."

The young Slav could have been a corpse except for the slow rising and falling of his shoulder blades. His buttocks were pale in the light from the window. It was true that Renko required a touch of the boot, but this was absurd. Much more of this and the boy would need killing himself. Kurski had little moral sense, but he objected to killing stupidly: in anger, for glory, or for an abstract principle. Worst of all was killing to cover up one's own incompetence. The USSR had been full of that sort of killing. Kurski suspected he was soon going to see more of it.

And there was his old friend Nemerov, who'd once been so shrewd and so capable, smirking away, dreaming of walnut candy and rape.

It's bad, Kurski thought. *It's going badly now. It's going to mean a lot of killing.*

8   *"It's Starting"*

Mallory flipped the brothers a loose, two-fingered salute as the old Mercedes rounded the corner of Asmali Mescit Sokagi and disappeared. Behind him was the entrance to the Pera Palas. He regarded it sourly. He'd begun the day in Just's charred flat, then been cooped up in the airless file room, and then in the old company car. The prospect of returning to the hotel held little appeal. He was beginning to feel stale and unfocused, something he meant to avoid at all costs while waiting for the other side to make its move. "How about a walk along the Istiklal?" he asked Laura. "Stretch our legs a little. A drink and some dinner, and then maybe an early night."

"Sounds good," she said. "I'm starving. Those damn files. I'm going to be a lot nicer to secretaries from now on."

"Tired?"

Laura knew what he meant. *If they grab me while we're out tonight, are you ready?*

"Fresh as a daisy. Let 'em come. I'm sort of excited, actually. I do think we've got hold of something already, even if it doesn't make any sense yet."

"The stage-set thing?"

She nodded.

"Rauth seems like a pretty dramatic guy," Mallory said slowly. " 'Course, we still don't know it's Rauth. But say it is. What sort of drama could he be staging at the Europa?"

"That requires a great big concrete vault and a helipad. Right. I don't know. I *am* hungry, though."

"All right. Let's walk up the Istiklal and see what we can see."

The late dusk of summer was closing in. From loudspeakers set in minarets and towers all over the city, muezzins began to call the faithful to their eight o'clock prayers. Laura and Mallory were silent as they strolled up the bustling street that had once been called the Grand Rue de Pera and was now the center of Istanbul's nightlife. Around them were the gates of old consulates that, in the days of Istanbul's glory, had once been embassies; there were tony apartment buildings, chic restaurants, and a constellation of old churches, some ornately tiled and domed like mosques, some built of bare, sunworn stone. The thronged sidewalks would have made it easy to shake a shadow if they'd wanted to, but by the same token made it difficult to tell whether they had one to shake. The detection of shadows is a matter of both observation and instinct. In a large crowd, instinct must predominate. They were both paying close attention to theirs, but by the time they'd reached the fountain of Taksim Square, they knew only that if they were being followed, it was by a professional. The uncertainty oppressed them. Some agents are skilled at entrapment and comfortable with waiting; others, with more active, direct natures, find it painful to surrender the initiative to the enemy. Both Mallory and Laura were the latter sort, and just then it was easy for them to play the part of the joyless Cavanaughs. *We'll have to take care of our nerves on this trip,* Mallory thought. *Especially Laurie.*

He looked down at her and said, "Grumpy little bitch, aren't you?"

She repressed a smile, though only someone who knew Laura as well as he did would have noticed. "Lay off, John," she said tonelessly.

In the maze of alleys above Taksim Park they found a promising-looking *meyhane:* a plain, deep-red awning, a half-curtained front window and, each time the door opened, a wafting of music from a flute, a violin, and drums. The scent of barbecuing chicken and lamb was first savory, and then, when they remembered the afternoon at Just's flat, briefly repulsive. Their eyes met. "All right," Laura said. "We're not going to turn vegetarian, are we?"

"Not this Texan," Mallory said. "Well, what do you think?"

"Yes," she said dryly. "I saw the belly-dancers, too."

"All right," he said, grinning. "We'll keep looking."

"No, I want to see them."

He raised his eyebrows.

"I'm always interested in muscle control," she said. "Besides, this is a good place to talk."

The tavern was a large, low-ceilinged room, dotted irregularly with square columns. It was noisy—Laura was right about its being good to talk in—and held a sprinkling of tourists in a dense crowd of locals. The old horn lanterns on the wall had been fitted with electric bulbs. Along one side of the room was a bar with a long mirror and rows of liquor bottles lit from below, Western-style, but it was faced in carnation-patterned tiles and featured a complex old coffee machine of worn brass. There were both red vinyl barstools and old overstuffed armchairs. Against the back wall was a fringed alcove in which the little band played. It included an ancient, fedora-wearing man solemnly tapping a triangle. The main room was crowded with round tables, and in the middle was an open square of floor containing a long barbecue pit over which dozens of chickens and lamb chops turned on spits. In front of it, the firelight gleaming on her torso and hips, was a gyrating young woman.

Or not so young, Mallory thought, as they were led to their table. And maybe not so good-looking. It was hard to tell. But none of the patrons seemed to mind, and neither did Mallory. Her eyes were magnificent, her arms were firm and round, and just then she was dancing slowly in the center of the floor, twisting like cigarette smoke in a still room, the movement flowing without interruption from her broad hips to the ends of her small fingers, on which she wore finger-cymbals that had yet to make a sound. There was nothing hootchy-cootchy about the dance. It was sad and solemn. And then the tempo began to increase, and she opened her immense eyes and seemed to be calling someone to her, in her loneliness, with her flowing arms and slowly rippling belly, punctuating her entreaty with little clashes of the brass disks in her hands. Laura and Mallory were given a table next to the floor—good tables were one of the advantages of working with a woman who looked like Laurie—and Mallory found himself fleetingly annoyed when the waiter appeared to see what they wanted.

Otto Roller, the Consultancy's Director of Logistics, was a noted gourmand, and had scrawled some emphatic notes on food in the margins of their briefing packets. They took his advice and ordered two yogurt soups, two green salads, a dish of stuffed eggplants called *imam bayilidi*—literally, "swooning cleric"—a swordfish skewered with peppers and tomatoes, fruity white Cankaya wine, and a stack of *pide* bread. *Nothing fancy,* Otto had written, *but this should get you started.* The waiter left and Mallory returned his attention to the dancer. She was approaching the crisis, her eyes closed again and her body seeming to contain the frenzy of a pair of lovers. Her legs, in their slashed trousers, had disappeared into a swirling of spangled fabric; her torso was a bright blur, and her upraised arms seemed those of a drowning woman. Then there was a crash of drums, and she stood motionless, face upraised, stomach heaving now with nothing more poetical than the need to catch her breath; a short, pear-shaped woman of better than forty with a sweaty, meaty face. Mallory, joining the barrage of applause, didn't give a good goddamn. "I think I'm getting interested in muscle control myself," he told Laura.

"She's good," Laura said, clapping hard. "She's *awfully* good."

The dancer was doing a sort of victory lap now around the edge of the dance floor, wiggling amiably from table to table as a few enthusiasts threw flowers from their table settings or tossed folded wodges of currency onto the dance floor. There'd be some sort of dressing room in back, Mallory thought. He wondered if she spoke any English or German. Not that he needed a common language— he'd done without one often enough—but it made things easier. The dancer reached their table, turned around, and pretended to grind her generous rear end in Mallory's face. She shot Laura a look of exaggerated triumph and, head high, undulated to the next table amid general laughter. Even Laura was laughing. She's one of the favorites here, Mallory thought. They'd give her at least half an hour's rest between shows. Probably through that door at the rear of the bandstand. Yep, there she went.

But, he reminded himself, he was on a job.

Ah well, he thought, and put his schemes away.

"Anybody?" he asked Laura.

Laura had taken a seat facing the door. "Three possibles," she said through her smile. "All Turkish. Heavy middle-aged man, dark-brown suit and sandals, square chin, no tie. Came in right after us. Maybe too soon. Tall young woman in orange jersey. Looker. Came in last. Thin young man in paisley shirt, longish hair, center part."

"Got 'em," he said after an idle-looking glance around.

"Let you know if any more come in," Laura said.

The food arrived and they began to eat.

"What kind of stuff did this Wagner guy write?" Mallory asked, spooning at his soup. It was delicious, cool and rich, but still somehow invigorating, and he chased it down with a sip of the white wine. He tended to drink a great deal between jobs, and with little enjoyment. But when he was working, he had a drink or two a day and enjoyed it immensely.

" 'This Wagner guy,' " she said. "Jack, have you ever opened a book in your life?"

"Once. It was full of words."

"Well, he wrote operas."

"I know that much, hon. I spent three and a half years in Berlin."

"That's right. I keep forgetting you were in the Army. Lord, you must've hated it."

"There wasn't much to do. I kept trying to wangle a pass to Bad Nauheim."

"Bad Nauheim?"

"Where Elvis was stationed."

"Of course. The *King*."

"That's right, the King. Greatest singer ever born. Listen, what's Wagner's stuff like? What made you think of him back there?"

Laura swallowed a mouthful of salad. "Hm. Well, there's always a hero who's got to pass some big test before he can get what he wants. That's not mostly what I was thinking of, though. You've heard of *Das Rheingold*? There's this ugly fellow, a troll, who feels the world's treated him badly. And he wants to get hold of a sort of special gold at the bottom of the Rhine and make a ring that will give him power over the world. And then, you know, look out. I keep thinking of revenge."

"Rauth wouldn't mind a little revenge on Turkey. They kicked him out."

"And he wouldn't mind some on you, maybe, and he probably wouldn't mind some gold. But this is all still very half-baked. I'd rather not talk about it yet, if that's all right."

"Sure. What do you think of the brothers?"

"Don't you trust them?"

"I asked you what you thought."

"They seem like such children. What's Talaat, maybe two or three years younger than I am? But he seems like such a boy. And at the same time, they don't miss anything, do they? Everything's wrapped tight on that desk. And they may cry a lot, but somehow I don't think they scare much. I think we can go the limit with them."

"How about if there's a scrap?"

"Oh, you know, you can't tell much by looking. They seem fit enough. Osman's a real little brute, and he moves quite well. The question is whether he's got any control."

"I like them, too. Tell you one thing I don't like, though. It's a mistake for the four of us to go around in a flying wedge like that. Keeps me too safe. No pro's going to want to make a grab if you're right there next to me. They know what you can do."

"I suppose," Laura said reluctantly. "On the other hand, it's easier to get you back if I know just when you've been taken and where it happened. I don't want to read about it in the papers. I haven't got oodles of faith in those homing things."

"Me neither. Let's say when I'm not with you, I call in every two hours on the hour to Belma at Advance, and you call ten minutes past. I miss a call, she lets you know, and you can decide whether to scramble the team."

"I'd much rather have you trailed."

Mallory shook his head. "Not if we don't know who's doing it and if they're any good. They get themselves spotted, and Rauth or whoever figures out we expect a grab, then this turns into double and triple bluffs and everything gets sloppy. I won't go quietly, Laurie. I'll make sure somebody sees. You'll find them and take it from there. So when we leave Advance tomorrow, we split up, all right? You take the Europa, I'll concentrate on the Treasury."

"How about the other way? No offense, Jack, but I was an analyst, and I'd do better with the financial end of things than you. And you know a lot more about construction and so forth than I do. And a *great* deal more about bars."

"All right," he said. "Hon, you're wolfing your food."

"You bet. It's good, and I don't think I'll get to finish. Fight with me," she said.

"What?"

"Fight with me. Looker at the bar hasn't taken her eyes off you since she came in. I think she's it. I think we're on."

"Hon, they got these women here they call whiskey dollies. They try to get men to—"

"I know, but she's only been looking at you, and none of the single men. It's starting. We'll fight, I'll stalk out, and once she's picked you up, I'll trail you. Get the brothers in if I can. Well?"

He hesitated, then nodded fractionally.

"Good luck," she said silently.

Then she stood and flung her napkin down in a fury. "Is it too much," she asked in a ringing voice, "is it too goddamned much to ask that you look at your own wife once in a while?"

Mallory did not raise his voice or his eyes. "Sit down, hon."

"You think I haven't seen her, too? That fat whore at the bar? That's what you like, isn't it? Well if that's what you want, you can have her. *I* won't make any trouble."

"You're making trouble now," Mallory said. "Sit down and be still."

"I've sat still for too *god*damned much," she cried, near tears, and shoved her way past him toward the door.

The room had not gone silent—it was not the sort of room that ever went silent—but they had the undivided attention of everyone in their end of it. Mallory stared straight ahead, wondering once again where the most inexpressive woman he'd ever met had gotten her acting ability. Then he looked levelly at each of the tables around him in turn until his neighbors stopped smirking and dropped their eyes. He stared at the door through which Laura had disappeared. Finally, he looked at the young woman at the bar.

She was gazing unhappily at the floor. Her round, black-browed face was almost brutally beautiful, but something in her downcast eyes was fragile, and made her provocative clothes look like a costume. Even the weightily voluptuous body seemed a sort of costume, something she was wearing on a dare, or as a penance. Though a bit tall for his tastes, she was memorably shaped. If they'd wanted a woman to get his attention, they hadn't done badly at all. Mallory dropped a handful of bills on the table, rose deliberately, and walked over to meet her. She raised her eyes and watched him until he was standing before her.

"Do you speak English?" he said.

"Yes," she said. Her voice was contralto.

"Would you like to buy me a drink?"

She showed white teeth then, very briefly. "I have no money."

"How'd you get that?" he said. Beside her was a tumbler of milky *raki* over ice and a smaller glass of lemon juice.

"The bar mans know me. I work near here. In a place like this one."

"Work?"

"Yes. Like what you was seeing."

"Show me."

"Show?" she said.

"Yeah."

She hesitated a moment more, then stood gracefully and raising her arms, gyrated once, with agonizing slowness, in a circle, then dropped her hands and gave herself a shake that left every bit of her joggling. "Work," she concluded.

The tables around them broke into applause and Mallory joined it, politely and soundlessly. It was the sort of thing, he suddenly remembered, Atsuko sometimes did to show approval. She'd bring her small hands close together at her breastbone, fingertips pointing heavenward like a praying Madonna, and clap rapidly and soundlessly, beaming. He felt a sudden pang of homesickness.

"My name's John," he said, taking the seat beside her.

"I am Ajda."

"Well, Ajda, seems like somebody ought to buy somebody a drink. Why don't I buy you one?"

"No, you must not. Because then I will be drinked."

"Drunk." He caught the bartender's eye, and the man nodded and came over with a glass full of ice and a bottle of *raki*. He set the glass on the counter in front of Mallory, filled it, and then topped up the girl's glass. He poured until it was almost brimming over, then righted the bottle with a flourish and said something rapid to Ajda and grinned. She shooed him away.

"What was that about?" Mallory said.

"He say to drink now I must spill, and then my fingers be wet. And then, I must drink, ah, suck the *raki* from my finger. And he enjoy that. There is a joke in how he say, but it does not in English. He is a stinking dog," she said cheerfully. "All my friends is a stinking dog."

"You need better friends."

"No. These is the good friends for me."

"You need better friends. Folks you can bring home to your mom and dad," Mallory said, and at once wished he hadn't.

"I have no mom and dad," she said. "I am dancing girl. So my family—" She made a pushing-away gesture with both hands.

"Disowned you."

"Yes. Disown. It is common for this. So this is the place for me. I am here with the good friends for me, who know me, and I can come and drink without money." She regarded her glass. "I will be drunk now. You want to drunk me?

"I don't mind."

"I am sorry you fight your wife."

"Me too."

"You should not fight."

"I've heard that."

"You should not fight. You should love your wife."

"I'll tell her you said so."

"She is very beauty."

"Uh huh."

"You don't think she is beauty?"

From force of habit, Mallory was trying to spot her backup in the crowd. It could be anyone, of course. Or, likely, someone outside in the street. He'd find out soon enough. "Yeah, she's beauty. And you know what she did last night when I tried to touch her? She gave me a good jab, right . . . " He touched Ajda's neck. "Here."

"That hurt you?"

"Puts you right out of business."

"She is a cold woman?"

"She is," Mallory said with feeling.

Ajda caught her heavy hair back from her face, ducked her head, and lapped quickly from her glass, like a cat from a dish, so deftly that it did not spill. Then she was able to raise the glass and take a ladylike sip. She flashed a victorious grin at the bartender. He shrugged.

Come on, girl, Mallory thought. *You were hired to do a job. Let's get on with it.* "I'm getting a little tired of being stared at," he said.

"Oh? I am accustom."

"Let's go someplace else."

"Yes," she said. "I know a good place. It is small, but it is quiet, and I have *raki* there and good melon."

And here we go, Mallory thought.

The young foreign woman stormed out of the *meyhane,* stopped short, and stared wildly around her. She was wheat-blonde, almost too thin, and dressed badly in expensive clothes. She looked up and down the street as if she'd never seen a street before. She was blinking back furious tears. After a moment of indecision, she set off diagonally toward a sidewalk café on the corner which, as it happened, commanded a good view of the door she'd just left. The maître d' tried to guide her upstairs to the family salon, where an unescorted woman would create less of a spectacle, but she seemed so upset that he decided not to argue when she pointed out a table on the sidewalk, or to rebuke her when she ordered a glass of wine.

As he showed her to her seat, the maître d' wondered what sort of man would be fool enough to mistreat such a woman as this. It would be pleasant, he thought wistfully, to console her. Had he been a decade or two younger, he would have attempted it. He brought her wine himself and then retreated to his station and watched as she took a sip and tried to calm herself by stroking her palms down the cool sides of the glass. She had not taken her eyes from the door of the tavern she'd just left. In there, of course, was the man she'd just fought with. Her husband? She wore a ring, which clinked on her wineglass. In any case, a simpleton, who didn't understand his good fortune. She was almost certainly an American, poor thing. No one made more of a mess of love than the Americans, not even the French, and at least the French knew how to enjoy their messes. But Americans were like children. Each little disappointment was the end of the world. The maître d' liked children, and he liked Americans, and he liked this one, who in addition to her somewhat under-nourished charms had a look of common sense. He suspected she knew the object of her affections was not worth the pain she suffered. Yes, one could clearly see pride and passion contending in that narrow breast. The maître d' had had his job for many years and considered himself a shrewd judge of humanity, and if you'd told him that Laura Morse was a professional putting on a show, he would have politely disbelieved you. The young lady, he would have maintained, was plainly and miserably in love.

He could always tell.

Laura lifted her glass with an unsteady hand and took a sip of her wine. She looked again at the door of the *meyhane.* She was thinking of the first time she'd partnered with Jack Mallory. He'd made a pass at her then, too. He reacted to a pretty woman the way a Venus flytrap reacts to being poked with a pencil. But he'd taken her refusal well, almost insultingly well, and behaved extremely well during the rest of the job, which had been far more difficult and dangerous than expected. She'd heard extravagant claims about Mallory's toughness and skill. It seemed that he deserved his reputation. When Gray had asked her to partner with him again, she'd accepted readily. The second job had been as tricky as the first, and, in the end, as successful. And then they were regular partners. And then it was too late.

Like any place full of secrets, the Consultancy was full of gossip, and she knew what people said about her. Rich prig. Frigid little WASP. La Remorse. She often wished she was as cold-natured as they all thought, but she wasn't, God knew she wasn't. It's just that she was picky. Of course, being picky didn't mean you picked the right one.

She didn't, frankly, consider Jack much of a catch. She knew a lot of handsome men. She knew a lot of brave men; she was brave herself. Jack was intelligent, though not interestingly so, and quite loyal, after his fashion. He always kept his word, whatever the cost. That was unusual. Perhaps that's what had gotten her started. He took very good care of his partners. If one got hurt or killed in spite of everything, he could be terrifying. That morning in van Vliet's apartment, when he'd noticed Helene's picture, Laura had seen a split second of blinding, savage rage, stifled before the Askers could notice. The whites of Jack's eyes had momentarily seemed to grow paler. His face and lanky body had gone as still as a sword in its scabbard. She'd seen Jack that way before, and it generally meant someone was going to die. For a minute or two Laura let herself daydream. She imagined that she was the one who'd been killed. She imagined Jack had that look in his eyes because of her. She imagined him avenging her, grieving over her. She guessed it was all pretty funny. She was painfully, stupidly in love with a man she didn't even want. Jack was full of little vanities, and prone to sulks, and, outside his field—this Wagner guy!—ignorant as dirt. He called her *Laurie.* He was becoming a drunk. His heart was cool and shallow. It wouldn't be much fun to be Jack's woman. With the possible exception of Gray, he had less love to give than any man she'd ever met. But then, she thought wryly, it was often those with the least to give who were the most generous.

Last night had been very bad. He'd reached for her as he might have reached for an extra pillow, to make himself more comfortable, and she'd still come terrifyingly close to disgracing herself. She'd almost given her body to a man for whom it would have meant no more than a cold glass of beer on a hot day. She was still shaken by her near-surrender. It wasn't that Laura considered her body so precious. She knew men admired it, and was professionally aware of glances from other tables. One pimply young man in a burgundy leather jacket was practically drooling. But often, it scarcely felt like a body at all—at the moment, her heart seemed to be beating in empty air—and if she withheld it from Jack, it was not because she valued it highly, but because to surrender it would make her humiliation complete.

The door of the *meyhane* opened; she saw Mallory's lean arm holding it open. And the looker in the orange jersey strode out.

Now, that, she thought desolately, *is a body.*

Laura had chosen a table next to a column, and was prepared to ease back behind it, but they turned away from her and started up the street. There were a fair number of people out enjoying the faint evening breeze. In a crowd that thick, she'd only have to give them perhaps five yards' lead.

Enough moping, she thought. Do your job.

Do your job. They were the most comforting words she knew.

No one had followed them out. Either the girl was working without backup or her backup was on the street. Quite possibly in this café. They were halfway to the corner. It was time. She had to follow them without the girl noticing, but maintain cover from the point of view of anyone surveilling her who didn't already know who she was, had to shadow them properly while not seeming to know how to shadow someone. It was a nice little problem. Now, how would Lena Cavanaugh look as she got ready to catfoot after her no-good husband and his new popsy?

She'd look as if she thought she was cunning.

The maître d' had followed Laura's gaze. So that was the husband. And there, of all people, was Ajda the dancer. He disapproved of the gray-haired man's character, but could not fault his taste. He watched sorrowfully as the American girl rose and fumbled out some bills—far too many, he judged—and then set off after them, moving with exaggerated stealth, a touching look of craftiness on her poor face. She'd follow them, she'd make a scene, and what good would it do? Well, she was young. Perhaps one day she'd learn. One thing was certain in life: there was always another lesson to learn. Sighing, he strolled over to clear her table himself. He somehow felt he owed her this personal attention. And it wouldn't do to let those extra lira go to waste. He did not notice the young man in the burgundy leather jacket as he drifted out into the street and, aimlessly, disappeared into the crowd that had swallowed the American and her faithless husband.

They're all making such a fuss, Renko thought, *but it's really quite simple. I'll just kill them like Piotr wished he could. And then he'll see I'm not such a kid. I'll just kill them.*

9   *How a Man Breathe*

enko Tesic was twenty-two years old and no one had ever much liked him. These days, this was understandable. He was an errand boy for assassins and a would-be assassin himself, with an unseemly enthusiasm for the work. But he had once been a perfectly prepossessing child, quick-witted, handsome, and good at games, and no one had liked him much then, either. Even at five years old, there had been a disturbing chilliness to Renko's gaze. He was silent and furtive and repelled by affection, and often stole what someone might cheerfully have given him. Asked to share a bag of candy, he would wordlessly hand the bag over and walk away.

When he was sixteen years old, one of his schoolmates took a fancy to him. She didn't like him, either, but he was tall, athletic, and the best student in school, and she thought it would be romantic to have a boyfriend no one else liked. He was, she told herself, a rebel. She took him walking in the woods, where he tied her up with her own clothes, raped her, and told her he'd kill her if she told anyone.

She believed him. That night, though, she bled so profusely that her family took her to the doctor. The doctor had seen rapes before, and the next night, the girl's two brothers went to see Renko. Renko had taught himself a sort of homemade karate from fights he'd seen on TV. He was mildly surprised to find it effective. He knocked one brother cold, snapped the other's neck, and made his way to Leningrad. His Russian was good, and Leningrad seemed a likely city for an ambitious young man.

In Leningrad, he became a courier for a gang of black marketeers. To better his English, he spent his evenings reading Dickens at the local library. After two years of regular attendance at the library's long, musty reading-room, he was befriended by an unmarried thirty-six-year-old schoolteacher who thought she saw sadness in his eyes. Renko tried to learn from experience when he could, and this time, after he'd bound and raped her, he killed her with a single thrust from the serrated American K-bar he carried in his right boot, and took pains to ensure that her body was not discovered until the spring thaw. All this came out in his background check when he was finally recruited by Rauth's network, including the fact that he had taken both women from behind. When Renko had come to the previous day with his bare buttocks in the air, he'd understood Nemerov's joke precisely.

In response, Renko had stolen the dart gun and the remaining darts and disappeared.

Let them worry, he thought.

And now he was shadowing the Americans. It was time for someone else besides him to get hurt.

Renko found it natural to be attracted to women who made him angry, and Laura Morse absolutely enraged him. It was not just that she was beautiful, though he felt she was certainly beautiful enough to annoy anyone. It was that look on her face. Even when she was shamming heartbreak, she wore the look of someone just a little too good for this world. That's probably why she was so skinny. She was too good to do anything as crude and common as putting food into that little mouth and chewing it. It had been a pleasure to leer at her at the café, to disgust her. He was pleased with the way that had gone. He'd have to remember that gambit. She didn't walk right, either, he thought as he followed her meager backside through the crowds. She didn't walk like a woman. Where had he seen that walk before? Yes, his sensei, the old Korean who'd trained him in Tae Kwon Do at Rauth's camp in the Urals. He remembered now, the bitch was supposed to be some sort of martial artist herself.

If he got his hands on her, just him and her someplace for an hour or two? He'd change the way she walked.

There. The American and the whore had disappeared into a shabby, glazed-brick apartment house off Kurtoglu Sokagi. Now the blonde would find an alley or—yes. There she went. It was, Renko had to admit, the same vantage point he'd have chosen himself. Once she was out of his sight, he cut to the left and padded rapidly down the street, looking for a back way into the alley. Round behind this pharmacy, he thought. He hoped there wasn't anything like a chain-link fence, that made noise when you climbed it. A brick wall or nothing. Ah, good. No wall. The blonde had sunk back into the shadows. She'd done it right. No one who wasn't looking for her would have seen her.

Renko began to walk toward her, silently, as he'd been trained to do. He'd had the foresight to fit the silencer onto his Luger before he'd set out that night. He'd already doctored his shoulder holster with a knife so that it would accept the silencer's length, and practiced drawing it that way, so that he wouldn't have to worry about snags. Not a shot to the back of the head, he thought. No style there. No fun. He'd have her face him, so he could see that snotty look on her face disappear for good. *Turn around, bitch,* he'd say. His English still wasn't as good as he'd have liked, but that seemed to have the right tone. *Turn around, bitch.* Like that. No emotion. Not even any interest. You're not so special. You're just another job. He was close enough now to see the streetlight glinting off her cheekbone. He slipped his hand into his jacket and drew out the gun. Then there was a sort of hitch or skip, as when the film momentarily slips from the sprockets in an old movie house, and he was flying through the air with empty hands.

He hit the cobbles rolling and sprang to his feet, pain scalding his left shoulder. The blonde was dropping his gun into her purse. She snapped it shut and looked him over.

"Nice fall," she said. "You've had some training."

Renko was silent.

She seemed to be waiting for his next move. He had no intelligent next move to make. When you don't know what to do, do nothing. It seemed important to figure out what she'd just done, and he closed his eyes and concentrated. He seemed to see her, as his gun left its holster, gliding smoothly backward. She must have taken a long backward step with her left foot, not looking around at him, dropping her purse as she went, then pivoted on her right foot and—he could almost see it now—taken the gun from his rising hand as if he'd given it to her. Meanwhile, her trailing left foot was swinging upward until she'd planted it against his breastbone, her slim leg flexed. Then she'd straightened her leg. And though he knew he must outweigh her by at least 25 kilos, he'd left the ground. By the time he'd returned to earth, her purse was in her hands again and she was tucking his gun away.

His breastbone was sore, though not as bad as his shoulder. She'd positioned her foot precisely for a heart-blow. If he was alive just now, it was because she'd taken a bit of care not to kill him. He was meant to understand that.

He opened his eyes.

"Figured it out?" she asked.

He did not respond.

"You were pretty good at the café," she said in a low, monotonous voice just loud enough for him to hear. "You had me sold. But the problem with that sort of bluff is, it makes people remember your face later. And then when you were tailing me, you did way too much stopping and starting and slaloming from side to side. There's a rhythm, a sort of flow to every street, and you never want to disturb that. You'll learn. If you live long enough. I doubt you're after my purse, but if you are, you can't have it. If you're after anything else, I advise you to look in the mirror. You're much too ugly. Do me a favor, would you? and leave now. It'll make a lot of extra work for me if I have to kill you."

She was making a little speech, enjoying herself, with both hands clasped around her purse, and on the word *work* he launched himself at her sideways, employing a maneuver known as Scything the Reeds. She did not stop speaking. She did not so much as alter her tone of voice. When he came to, he was sitting against the wall of the alley. She seemed to have dragged him there, and now she was flipping through his wallet. "Renko Tesic," she said. "Hello, Renko. And an Amtorg ID. How does a Yugoslav get one of those? I'll keep this, if you don't mind." She tucked his ID card into her pocket and tossed his wallet at him. It landed between his legs. "You're not a mugger. Not with one of these. I'd ask whom you're working for, but somehow I suspect you're working for yourself. Improvising. If anyone had briefed you, you wouldn't have tried anything as silly as shooting me at close range. All right, I'll ask anyhow." His gun appeared in her hand again. It was aimed unwaveringly at his groin. "Who do you work for, Renko? What's this about?"

He was silent.

"You understand me all right," she said, and pulled the trigger.

The report was no louder than a sneeze. Renko managed to hold almost perfectly still. He'd seen her deflect her aim at the last minute. The bullet struck the cobbles under his left leg and ricocheted down the alley. A fragment of stone leapt up and gashed his thigh. He kept staring at her.

"Well, your nerve's good, whatever else," she said. "But I've still got several more bullets."

"You don't want so much noise," he said slowly. "If you shoot me and you don't kill me, if you shoot me there, I'll make a lot of noise. I won't help it then."

"Then perhaps I'd better just kill you."

"You don't want a corpse here. You're busy."

She smiled. "Very good, Renko. I am. If we were by the harbor, I'd put you in it. But as things stand?" She put the gun back in her purse. "All right. Get going."

Renko picked up the wallet and slipped it in his pocket, then got to his feet. He didn't look at his ruined slacks, or the bleeding gash on his thigh. He thought of the trench knife in his boot and decided to leave it there. He'd balanced the K-bar for throwing and knew he'd be quite accurate from the end of the alley, even in this light, but didn't like his odds against an armed target that moved as quickly as this one. He felt sure that at least there was no expression on his face. There generally wasn't. He turned and began limping back up the alley. "Renko," she said softly, and, hating himself, he stopped.

"I am busy," she said. "I don't want a corpse. But if I see you again? Ever, at any time? I *will* kill you. Is that clear?"

The young man began walking again. Laura watched him out of sight. She didn't know when she'd seen a nastier-looking boy. Not entirely a clown, either. What *was* he up to? Either things were more complicated than they'd thought, or the other side was far less disciplined than she'd have thought. She felt a little better now. Action did that for you. And, she had to admit, the chance to take out your ill temper on someone else. She pulled her compact from her purse, freshened her makeup, and consulted the screen under the concealed panel. Jack was in the apartment building, all right. Third floor front, all the way to the left. Yes, there. She'd missed the light going on, but there'd been no light in that corner window when Jack and the girl had first entered the building. And that had been, what, six or seven minutes ago? She glanced at her watch. Not quite six minutes. Long enough to hang up a jacket, pour a couple of drinks, settle into a chair or sofa. She dropped the compact back in her purse.

With two guns inside, her purse was quite heavy. For a moment, it seemed an impossible burden.

The light in the corner window went out again.

Fast work, she thought.

"You'd think I'd be used to it," she murmured hoarsely, looking up at the darkened window. "You'd think I'd be used to it by now."

Mallory guessed it was about half past two in the morning. He was face down on Ajda's bed, naked and breathing slowly and regularly. Now and then he let his breath roughen into a snore. He did not, as far as he knew, snore, but he'd listened to a fair number of women do it and thought he could manage a passable imitation. Ajda had been awake for a while, he knew, and was now gently stroking the small of his back. He couldn't see her face. Though a small fan was blowing across them, they were both filmed with sweat. He felt the weight of one breast on his back, and the humid curve of her belly against his ribs, and her darkly creamy thigh across his. A good position to pin him from, if her backup were there and ready take him down. Mallory was half-exhausted with, among other things, waiting, and with the weary knowledge that they might be counting on his weariness. Ajda kept tracing tiny circles on the small of his back. The touch of her fingers seemed sad.

Six hours earlier, she'd led him through a door of cracked and grimy safety glass, and then past an open elevator shaft and up a staircase smelling of dust and cats. When she'd opened her own front door, he'd taken in her apartment at a glance. A single, untidy room, decorated with snow scenes clipped from magazines and tacked to the wall in frames cut from colored paper. In the corner, a small bathtub covered with a sheet of plywood to make a table. On it, a few clean dishes and a hot plate, the braided cord dangling free. Next to this, a chipped porcelain sink and the sort of half-pint refrigerator found in hotel rooms. The refrigerator was new. A bead curtain closed off the closet; the toilet enclosure had a narrow folding door, which was open. He smelled old plumbing and heard small scattered noises from the flats around them: muffled voices, the creak of old flooring, a drawer sliding shut. Mallory had come through the door relaxed but ready to meet an assault. Now he saw there was no one here and that he'd have to hold himself in readiness a while longer. Ajda locked the door behind them but did not fasten the chain. She couldn't, since its socket had been recently pried from the door jamb. A nice touch.

The hell of it was, he liked her. Of course, she might not know what she'd been hired for. They could have told her anything. It was quite possible, he thought grimly, that this was an ambush in which both of them were meant to die. Whoever killed van Vliet wasn't fond of loose ends. Every now and then Mallory had a fit of loathing for his job, and one overtook him now. He grasped Ajda by the waist, yanked her close, and kissed her roughly and contemptuously. Her keys clattered on the floor and her eyes widened, but she didn't pull away. She couldn't, of course, if she wanted to earn her pay. *Nice girl,* he thought furiously and, hooking his fingers under her shoulder straps, he jerked her dress and brassiere to her waist, so that her brown-nippled breasts swung free and she had to take a step sideways to keep from falling. He dragged her back to him by the arms and she kissed him, trying to match his roughness, to catch up with him, while untangling her hands from the snarl of fabric at her hips. Brusquely he undid his belt. She lowered her eyes and sank to her knees. A single clasp held her heavy black hair in place, and he plucked it loose and threw it in the corner. Her hair fell forward against his legs, and he ran his fingers through it, looking fiercely around at the empty room and the broken chain on the door.

That had been around six hours ago. And now it was half past two in the morning. It was a long time to wait to be captured or killed.

Well, half past two was a good time to make a move.

As if she'd heard him, she stirred, then rolled gracefully off the narrow bed and padded off toward the cabinet near the sink. She was trying to be silent, but every noise was magnified in the tiny, air-less room. He heard a cabinet open and shut. And then the unmistakable sound of a knife sliding out of a drawer.

Mallory moved restlessly, as if he'd just noticed he was alone and was wondering what had happened, then rolled drowsily onto his back. He gazed at Ajda's side of the bed and blinked. She was approaching again, her pace unhurried. All right. He sat up and swung his feet to the floor, looking around as if disoriented, his hands resting lightly on the edge of the mattress. Ajda was just settling herself on the foot of the bed. She carried a small tray with a half a cantaloupe, two small glasses, and a long knife with a wooden handle. The knife was quite old, and with a bright, gently undulating edge from being sharpened on a whetstone. It was freshly sharpened. "I am hungry," she said, not looking at him. "Are you hungry?"

"Umph," he said, sitting up and rubbing his face again. "Hello, hon. What time's it?"

The little noises of a large apartment building had vanished by now. There wasn't the least wisp of sound from the open window. Except for the steady sighing of the fan, everything was silent.

Ajda rose again and fetched a bottle of *raki* from the cabinet across the room. Returning, she stooped and poured a bit of it into each of the glasses on the tray.

"Yes, you are good actor," she said, pouring, "but I know you are not sleep. I know how a man breathe when he only pretend sleep." She set the bottle down by her feet.

"You do, huh?"

"Yes."

"I dunno, hon. I think I was out. What time is it, anyway?"

"It will be three. Why are you here? In Istanbul?"

"Told you, hon. Selling rice."

"Yes, you told me. Selling rice is so dangerous? Like this?" she said, and touched a scar on his chest. She touched one at his waist. "Like this?"

"Old hunting accident. I got messed up pretty good."

"Oh, hunting."

"Yep. Hunting. You're a suspicious girl, Ajda."

"In America you hunt with knives? This is with a knife. And this is with a gun and very old, and this is with a gun, but quite soon ago. So many accidents, all to sell rice? No. I am not suspicion. You are suspicion."

"Ajda, what's on your mind?"

"Who do you think I am?" she cried. "What do you think I do here? Why do you come home with me if you think I am a bad woman, and treat me, and treat me—" She couldn't finish.

Mallory regarded her, thinking hard. If she'd been hired to hold him for a grab, it made no sense for her to talk this way. If this was a longer game, if she was supposed to make him fall for her—

No, that was slop. Mallory had screwed up often enough to know the smell of a screwup.

"I booted this one," he said aloud. "Aw, I really booted this one good."

"Who are you?" Ajda said. "You are a thief, or a spy, or a drug man, and you think I am in this business. And you think I am tricking you. And you don't know what you are doing here. And you are in danger."

"I shouldn't've come here," Mallory said slowly. "You didn't need this, and you didn't deserve it. I'm sorry, Ajda. I'm awful sorry. I guess I been stupid lately."

"Yes, you are stupid, and you are in danger. I don't know anything, but I know this. You and your wife are in danger."

"Me and my wife," Mallory said, rubbing his face.

"Yes, I know she is not a true wife to you, but she is unhappy. And she is in danger. You are both in danger, and you should go to her."

She still wasn't crying. He guessed she'd run out of tears somewhere along the way. How old was she, anyhow? Her shoulders and knees gleamed faintly in the dim light from the window, her knees childishly round. She was lonely and didn't have good sense. Neither did he, but he knew how to take care of himself. She didn't. That was the last thing she knew how to do. Mallory was not a particularly compassionate man, but he considered that there was a lot of pain in the world; he hated to add to it for no good reason, and he knew that he'd just done precisely that. He touched Ajda's cheek and then kissed it, carefully, and she leaned against him. He kissed her mouth as gently as he knew how.

"Yeah," he said. "I should go to her. But not just yet."

Almost an hour later, Mallory was trudging through the predawn streets when he heard a familiar, almost silent tread at his back. He slowed and let Laura fall into step beside him, and together they walked past the Taksim Square fountain, which had been turned off for the night.

"Well," she said, "at least we know the homing thingie works."

"Does it now," Mallory said tonelessly.

"Like a charm," she said. "Have a good time?"

"I don't think anyone had much of a time. I'm sorry I kept you up late."

"I'm the one who ought to be sorry, Jack. It was my dumb idea."

He shook his head. "I bought in. Our dumb idea."

"Anyway, I had Osman relieve me and got a few hours' sleep, so you didn't keep me up. But the thing wasn't a complete waste. Someone shadowed us from the *meyhane*. Here." She handed him Renko Tesic's ID.

"What a beauty," he said. "How's a Serb get an Amtorg card, anyway? We should have the brothers run this."

"It's being run now. I had them print it, too, while they were at it."

"Good going. What'd you do to him? What'd he try to do to you?"

"Kill me, actually, which is puzzling. Came creeping up with a gun while I was keeping obbo. I didn't want to leave you, and I didn't want us cluttered up, so I took this and the gun and sent him away."

"Sure they weren't just trying a grab?"

"Could've been, I suppose. But he didn't have the right look. He looked too pleased with himself. I mean, until I knocked him down. He looked like he thought he was getting away with something. I can't imagine what he thought he was playing at. All I can think is, he's a junior man with Rauth, exceeding orders a bit in hopes of impressing the boss. Showing them his initiative and so forth. But that doesn't feel quite right either. He's very green, but not stupid, and he's got *awfully* good nerves. A cold one," Laura said approvingly. "And he fell very nicely."

"Still sounds pretty amateurish for the people who killed Just. Can you see Rauth using a guy like him? Say, to assist someone like Nemerov?"

"Sort of a trainee? Yes, but I can't see him liking it."

"Well. I guess he could be from some other outfit completely, or on his own. But right now that's all a little coincidental for me. All right. I like your theory. He's with them, but hotdogging. Looks like we've engaged them. Good thing is, they've given us an excuse now to act a little careful, so we don't have to waste time pretending we don't know they want us. We can just go bang heads."

"Suits me."

Mallory yawned hugely. "Lordy. We're meeting the brothers in four and a half hours, and I'm bushed. And it's too damn soon to get into the Dexedrine. Missing a little sleep didn't used to bother me."

"Well, does this at least make it up to you, a little, for having to leave Atsuko? She really was something, that big girl. Assuming you only have time for one Turkish girl while we're here, I'd say you didn't do so badly."

Laura's voice was light, and she wore a look of cool amusement. "You're a cold one yourself, Laurie," Mallory said without love.

"Poor dear," she said, laughing, "haven't you slept at all? Really, Jack, you ought to take better care of yourself."

10   *Steam and Stars*

The eight o'clock meeting was brief and to the point. Talaat presented them with temporary credentials identifying them as correspondent agents of INSTA. Laura had been given the courtesy rank of captain and Mallory was, for the moment, a major. These might, Talaat said sleekly, be convenient for them. It was an understatement. The embossed, saffron-yellow cards would command the cooperation of any policeman in Istanbul and most of the security agents, and Talaat had a right to look pleased with himself. Mallory examined his own photograph blearily. It appeared to be copied from the one on John Cavanaugh's passport. He wondered how in hell the brothers had managed to produce these in the middle of the night.

"It is arranged," Talaat said, "that Osman and Miss Morse will breakfast with Professor Sinan Garaj. Dr. Garaj is an economist at INSTA, and attached to the Currency and Trade Affairs Section. In such a way, he helps to advise the Treasury on security."

"Why's he talking to a civilian like Osman?" Mallory said, rubbing his eyes.

"Osman was Garaj's student in the University. He is, ah—"

"A protégé," Laura said.

"Yes. He has been very protégé of Osman. Of course, Osman still lacks clearance, and though Miss Morse has been cleared . . ."

"I'm a foreigner. And a woman," Laura said.

Talaat inclined his head. "But if Osman appeals to Dr. Garaj as an old protégé and a Turk, and Miss Morse does so as the highly cleared agent of a close ally, something might be arranged."

"I don't want much," Laura said. "I just want to know how to rob your Treasury."

"I am certain you are capable of delicacy. And Dr. Garaj has, ah, a fondness for the ladies."

"Always seems to come down to that, doesn't it? Anything else? Jack? All right then. You'll call in every two hours on the hour?"

"Starting at ten," he said.

"Good. Well, Osman, let's go get some breakfast. I could do with a bit of coffee."

She rose, bestowed a nod upon Mallory and Talaat, and left the room, Osman trailing after her, black eyes alert. Both of the brothers were pretty damn perky, considering they couldn't have had much more sleep than he or Laura. "You got a briefing for me, don't you?" Mallory said.

Talaat nodded.

"You two must've been working all night. I thought I told you to get some rest."

"Forgive us, Mallory Bey," Talaat said. "We slept as much as we were able. Truly, we feel quite rested."

Too excited to sleep, Mallory thought. *They think we'll have Just's killers soon. They're scenting blood. Well, I guess I can't blame them such a hell of a lot.*

Talaat said, "But you, Mallory Bey, if you will excuse me, you don't seem so rested. Perhaps we can take a little stroll while we have our briefing? If you are weary, I know precisely the thing. It will, what is the American words? It will fix you up."

The Cagaloglu Hamami was on Seraglio Point in the old city, at Prof. Kazim Gürkan Cadessi 34. It was not the oldest of the traditional Turkish baths, Talaat explained, having only been built in 1741. But it was perhaps the finest. And there, they were accustomed to foreigners. He led Mallory through the men's entrance and insisted upon paying his entrance fee, explaining, "When the baths were new, Mahmut would take the admission money to buy books for his library at Haghia Sophia, and I would have been pleased to let you give money for the Sultan's books. But now, of course, there is no Sultan, and this is simply another tourist business. And I cannot allow that you be treated here as a tourist."

The narrow passageway opened out into a towering square entrance hall. At the back of the hall, an arched door led, Mallory assumed, to the baths themselves. The air around them held a mild hint of the heat of the central chamber. The room was dominated by a three-tiered marble fountain surrounded by benches on which a scattering of Turkish men, the young lean and compact, the older ones unconcernedly paunchy, sat reading newspapers or sipping tea, gleaming like seals, nude but for a length of frayed plaid cloth around their middles. The walls were lined with wooden cubicles which looked as though they might be changing rooms. Above these ran a wood-railed mezzanine, perhaps leading to more of the same. Above that, the hazy, warm reaches of the august domed roof, lit by golden stained-glass windows and pierced by a single slanting ray from the oculum at the peak of the dome. *Like some old foreign church,* Mallory thought, and found himself silently saying, to whom he wasn't sure: *I'm sorry about Ajda. I guess I'm an ugly guy when I get riled. I hope she didn't mind it all too much.*

He and Talaat took two cubicles side by side, stripped, and locked up their clothes in rickety-looking wooden cabinets before wrapping their hips in the plaid sheaths. Mallory was moderately pleased that he was able to wrap himself properly without help. "You know to wear the *pestemal!*" Talaat said. "You wear it very well. You have been to such a bath before?"

"I been to the old Russian baths on Tenth Street. Back in New York. They're pretty good for a hangover. They don't give you a cloth like this, though. Just shorts."

"But the baths in New York, they are not like this?" Talaat said confidently.

"No," Mallory said. "They look like somebody's basement. They're not like this."

They passed through the wooden door and along a dark, warm corridor set with slender columns and pointed arches, and then opened the final door into the fierce heat of the *hararet*. It was another lofty room, though smaller than the first, and covered by a smaller dome pierced with tiny, star-shaped windows through which points of daylight pricked the rising steam. All around the room were marble basins with chromed taps. Talaat led Mallory to one of them, seated him on a worn stone stoop, and began working shampoo into Mallory's hair and then roughly but deftly massaging his scalp.

"That feels pretty good," Mallory said, as Talaat kneaded his occiput. "But for what it's worth, I did have a shower this morning."

"And now you are bathing again. This is a custom here. It is most vital for a Muslim to be clean."

"Uh huh? And what if you're not a Muslim?"

"It is vital for any warrior to be clean. One may be required to return one's body to God at any moment."

"Shouldn't I be washing myself?"

"In the *hamam*, one may wash oneself, or a friend may do so, or an attendant—a *tellak*. Today I am your *tellak*. Please close your eyes and mouth."

He dumped a bucket of water over Mallory's head, ending the discussion.

In the center of the chamber was a low, hexagonal platform of white and butter-colored marble, with a flat top slick with water. Talaat had Mallory lie on this, face down, and began scrubbing his back and arms with a coarse, soapy mitt.

"This that I am using is called the *kese*," he explained. "It rubs off all the old dead skin, so that you are like a child again. And this that you are lying on is the *göbektasi*."

"What they call the Navel Stone?"

"Ah! You know these things."

"Just what was in the briefing packet."

"And now I will turn you," Talaat said and, taking hold of Mallory's hip and shoulder, deftly spun him in a circle on the slick stone so that he was facing the other way. He worked Mallory's legs over with the *kese*, then scoured the soles of his feet. "The foot specially must be clean, because it is not a very clean part. Ritually. For example, you must never put your foot upon a Muslim's chair. It is a great disrespect." He cleared his throat. "I regret that I was not there last night to advise you. Ajda is well known in Taksim. She is well liked. She is not political and I cannot accept that she could be hired for such a purpose, to trap you. She is too, ah, emotional."

"I guess you could call her that."

Talaat sluiced Mallory down again and began working his fists down Mallory's spine.

"Miss Morse was very, I would say, understanding of the matter," he said cautiously.

Mallory had long ago given up trying to convince people that he and Laura were not a couple. He said, "Uh huh."

"She is a remarkable woman. Do you think that you eventually will be marrying her?"

"I doubt it."

"It is a great error not to marry Miss Morse. You will not find such another, who has courage and understanding. And intelligence. My own wife is intelligent. I find it a great advantage. And I believe Miss

Morse to be beautiful, in her way. When she is married she will be plumper."

"Now there's a thought. Got anything on that Amtorg ID yet?"

Talaat sighed and gave up. "We have received preliminary information. Mr. Tesic is a very bad individual, and wishes to be worse. He has raped twice, and killed more often. Professionally he has done nothing of interest, but it is certain that Rauth is developing him."

"Sure he's working for Rauth now?"

"It seems highly unlikely that he has left Rauth's employ since his last confirmed job for the man in January."

"Yeah, I guess Rauth's employ isn't all that easy to leave. What's the kid supposed to be doing in Istanbul?"

Mallory could not see Talaat's face, but he could tell the man was smiling. "He seems to have frequent business with the Laleli Construction Corporation."

"Uh huh? Why's that so good?"

"Laleli is the principal contractor of the Club Europa," Talaat said peacefully.

"Aw, sweet. Aw, that's almost too sweet."

"Yes. If you would turn over now?"

Mallory rolled over on his back and found Talaat's dark intent eyes gazing into his. They didn't match the smiling face. There was no joy in them. Mallory closed his own eyes, and Talaat began scraping his thumbs down Mallory's temples and then vigorously kneading his shoulders. "It was not difficult to ascertain Laleli's involvement. It is a matter of record. And Mr. Tesic is said to be producing a series of Russian-language articles on the project for Amtorg. For the Soviet press."

"Yeah, that'd work. Got anything else on Laleli?"

"Only preliminarily. But there is one interesting respect. At least three of the employees is Russians. And one, who is a supervisor of the project, is a large, a very large powerful man who is often speaking Russian with a Georgian accent."

"Sorta like Nemerov."

"Very much like Nemerov."

"Yeah, this's too good. They're just about hanging a sign out. They want us to come and get them, all right."

Talaat was grinding his thumbs into the hard sinews of Mallory's forearms. Finally he said, "So Nemerov is the one?"

Mallory opened his eyes again. "Easy, Talaat."

"He is the one?" Talaat whispered.

"It seems pretty obvious," Mallory said slowly. "But that doesn't mean it's true. It might just mean somebody wants it to seem obvious. All we got right now is guesses."

"Still, you yourself believe—" Talaat's voice trembled, and he broke off. Then he murmured, "No, don't tell us. Please don't, if we may not kill him. We believe in you, Mallory Bey. You was his friend, you will do what is right. But, please, if we may not kill him— Please. Don't tell us."

Mallory felt more refreshed than he'd thought possible as he strolled down the sun-warmed cobbles of Seref Efendi Sokagi. His eyes were clear, his step was light, and his shoulders felt slightly and pleasantly bruised from Talaat's thumbs. It had been three days since he'd had a full night's rest, but he felt relaxed and alert and disinclined to take the Dexedrine in his shirt pocket. *If they grab me today,* he thought, *I'll get plenty of time to catch up on my sleep.* It was blazingly hot, and since he would have been conspicuous in a jacket, Mallory had left his gun at the hotel. He'd left Talaat behind, too. If the idea was to get captured, then the more time he spent on his own, the better. Besides, this morning it suited him to be ambling along alone and empty-handed. It was not quite ten o'clock, but he'd just called Belma at Advance, and between now and his noon call had no obligations except to make his way over to Laleli Construction and follow his instincts. Mallory seldom permitted himself to be optimistic—it was, he felt, as dangerous a waste of time as pessimism—but just then he was optimistic anyway, and enjoying it. Every job had its screwups, and he felt they'd gotten theirs out of the way and were ready to do some work. Laleli Construction was on Bukali Dede Sokagi, behind the octagonal sandstone bulk of the Tulip Mosque. It was almost a kilometer off, and he might have gotten there faster by tram, but he was making the trip on foot for a simple and quite unprofessional reason. The Grand Bazaar stood squarely between him and Laleli. He might never be in Istanbul again, and he wanted to have a look.

For five hundred years the Grand Bazaar of Istanbul had been the largest marketplace in the world. It was a teeming complex of sixty-four covered pedestrian streets, punctuated by domed chambers and riddled with craftsmen's alleys and *hans,* the secluded courtyards in which many of the bazaar's goods were still produced. Within this hive swarmed twenty-five thousand traders, clerks, and artisans manning over three thousand shops, a city within a city, with its own mosques, law offices, brothels, and dentists. The main passageway was the Kalpakçilar. It was three stories high and roofed with a system of vaults, arches, and cupolas, all intricately painted and pierced with ancient sash windows. Beneath this lay an eighth of a mile of jewelry stores: some as formal as Harry Winston, some no more than a blanket spread on the stone flags, all glittering with necklaces, earrings, navel-ornaments, wedding bands, tiaras, pillboxes, charm bracelets, cigarette lighters, and neatly stacked ingots bearing the stamp of the Prophet. Mallory guessed it beat Neiman Marcus all hollow.

You could easily spend a week in here, Mallory thought, and still not be sure you'd seen everything, but all he had in mind was a half-hour detour on the way to Laleli. He turned off the street of jewelers and immediately found himself in front of a stall full of inflatable toys, dominated by a bulging Superman. Beside this stood teetering stacks of cheap cookware and an old man forming glass animals over a small blue flame. Mallory saw cabinets filled with old leather-bound books beside other cabinets filled with old *Life* magazines and before them, glass cases filled with French perfumes. He saw an endless vista of hallways stacked high with rolled carpets and kilims. He saw stalls bursting with gorgeous tulips, cut or potted, and with wire baskets filled with tulip bulbs. He saw praying Madonnas in porcelain and plastic next to suspiciously fresh-looking antique Russian icons next to framed quotations from the Koran in gold leaf and cinnabar ink. He saw televisions and power tools and an immense, gleaming lawnmower that was being examined by a bearded Jew in a black caftan. The air was filled with an echoing din made up of shuffling footsteps, vehement haggling, and music from unseen radios, and with a bewildering mixture of smells, from cardamom to new rubber tires to baking pastries to simple human sweat. *Someday I ought to take a vacation,* Mallory thought. *Just go somewhere warm and easy and follow my nose, with nobody paying me and nobody chasing me. Hell, I wouldn't mind coming back here, someday when I'm off the clock. Wonder if I got time to pick up some little doodad for Itsy.* He paused by a copper fountain to consider the matter and understood, suddenly and certainly, that he was being followed.

No one observing Mallory would have noticed that he'd realized anything. His face, behind a pair of mirrored sunglasses, remained amiably vacant. He looked like a bored American looking for the nearest cheeseburger, but he was watchful now, and thinking hard. On the whole, Mallory decided, being followed was good news. Assuming it was news at all—last time they thought they'd been engaged by Rauth, it turned out to be nothing but a lonely bellydancer. But say this wasn't a false alarm. What was he dealing with? He began strolling toward the Beyazit Square exit. Mentally, he closed his eyes. Sometimes, if you relaxed for a minute, some picture of your shadow would come to you, gathering in your memory out of half-noticed details, like a photograph in a tray of developer. After a minute you might see that whoever it was carried, say, a neatly folded newspaper, or walked with a rolling gait, or was wearing a blue cable-knit sweater. Sometimes, if you were lucky, you even got a whole face. But all that came to Mallory just then was shiny black hair and maybe a striped shirt, and that described half the men in Istanbul.

He left through the Gate of the Spoon-Makers and entered Beyazit Square, the sun striking his face like a spray of hot sand. He gawked, as any tourist would, at the University Tower. He gazed benignly upon the young students chattering in the park. He did not appear to be looking behind him, but Mallory's peripheral vision was unusually acute, and by the time he'd reached the shade of the Literature Faculty Building he was fairly sure of two things. First, his shadow was a clean-shaven Turk, tallish and a bit plump, wearing sunglasses, an untucked button-down shirt with fine vertical stripes, and a pair of baggy khakis. Second, either he was incompetent—and Rauth didn't hire incompetents—or he was executing an open shadow, a shadow Mallory was meant to notice.

Mallory had three choices. He could lose the shadow. That might be difficult, since his opponent knew the city and he didn't. But it ought to be possible. Having shaken him, though, what then? An open shadow is frequently used as cover for a true shadow, so Mallory might just wind up where he'd started. Even if the shadow was working alone, he still couldn't see what he'd gain: Mallory was heading for Laleli. That was presumably what Rauth expected. Why try to cover up? Why not head over to Laleli Construction as planned and let the shadow, or the shadow's backup, make the first move? But Rauth had already engaged them last night, and the shadow wasn't doing much of a job of hiding. What would it gain Mallory to play dumb? That left the third possibility, which was to do what he usually did, given his druthers. The third possibility was to take the shadow out.

He didn't have enough information to make good decisions. But the quickest way to get information was to make some bad decisions. You always learned something, even if you didn't enjoy the lesson. It was time to goddamn do something.

Number three it was.

Mallory took a theatrically emphatic look at his watch, shook his head—look at the *time!*—and began walking rapidly down the Ordu Caddesi. It was a safe bet his shadow was scrambling to keep up. At thirty-four, Mallory could no longer run a four-minute mile, but he could walk pretty fast when he wanted to. As the massive limestone piers of the Tulip Mosque came into view, he cut to the right and began working his way through commercial Laleli, sidestepping street-corner kiosks selling coffee and newspapers, and weaving around displays of luggage, spices, enamelware, transistor radios, and child-sized Ali Baba costumes for the tourist trade.

Laleli Construction was at Bukali Dede Sokagi 87, a squat, functional brick building with a Greek restaurant on its ground floor. Mallory passed it without a glance and strode around the corner. He was hoping for an alley, and found something better: a loading dock, hidden by a dogleg from the street, in which stood a Vespa, a delivery van, and a shedlike wooden enclosure crammed with bags of the restaurant's garbage. Mallory liked the setup. It was a good spot to leave the fellow in the striped shirt. Not dead, of course, but maybe a little discouraged. He could hear Striped Shirt behind him, out of breath and frankly trotting to catch up. And then, from behind the wooden shed stepped a tall young man in—despite the heat—a burgundy leather jacket, holding a K-bar trench knife with a relaxed three-fingered grip.

An almost handsome face with a blank, ratlike gaze. One that Mallory recognized from a confiscated Amtorg ID.

Renko Tesic stepped forward, gliding flat-footed and making no needless movements. Laurie was right: he'd been trained. But so had Mallory. Mallory threw himself sideways against the parked van, spun, and looked back just in time to see Striped Shirt rush into the alley, clutching a wooden-handled knife with an undulating edge and letting out a hoarse, womanish scream of rage, not at Mallory, but at the Slav in the leather jacket. Mallory recognized the old kitchen knife, and then the dainty hand that grasped it, and then the beautiful, black-browed face. It was shining with sweat and distorted with fury. *Sweet hopping merciful Jesus Christ*, he thought. *It's Ajda.*

An instant before, he'd been pincered between two enemies, and all he'd wanted was to be facing them both with a wall at his back. Now he was confronting an enemy and a damn-fool ally, and all he wanted was to be in the middle again. He launched himself from the side of the van directly at the belly-dancer, sparing a glance for Renko as he did—the kid was hesitating between the two targets—reached over her knife arm, and grasped her shirt by the far collar. It began to tear as he swung her around and, regretfully but forcefully, slammed her against the side of the van. The knife clattered on the asphalt and Ajda slid half-senseless to her knees. She didn't try to get up. The situation was manageable again.

The Serb feinted at Mallory's belly and then struck directly at his throat. Both feint and thrust were fast and well-executed, but they came a half a second too late. Mallory got under Renko's knife arm and knocked it skyward, then smashed his left foot into the Slav's ribs.

To his surprise, the kid kept his grip on the knife and let his torso twist limply sideways, robbing Mallory's kick of most of its force. He followed with a reverse side kick of his own, making use of his own momentum to swing a heel at Mallory's breastbone. Mallory rolled inside Renko's kick, passing within inches of the slashing knife like a matador working close to the horns, and head-butted Renko's temple as he passed. Then he was behind Renko, snatching a lid from one of the trash cans and raising it as a shield.

Renko was plainly stunned, but even so, his technique was admirable. He fell back and circled counterclockwise to keep Mallory from establishing a proper defensive stance, meanwhile switching the knife to his left hand. Mallory did not bother trying to shift his improvised shield. Renko could always countershift his blade faster than Mallory could countershift an unwieldy circle of sheet metal. Instead, Mallory pressed forward, tempting Renko with an opening to the right of his shield, forcing him to choose quickly instead of waiting for his moment. The opening was calculated but quite genuine, and Renko, seeing the risk, still chose to take it. He drove in and under Mallory's shield, and Mallory, moving faster than anyone might reasonably expect, chopped down on the Serb's left wrist with the metal edge of the lid, smashing the nerve center behind the thumb.

Renko's knife joined Ajda's on the pavement. It was over.

Mallory dropped his shield, locked Renko's right wrist in a disabling grip, and pulled him close.

"The other night," he said, "you used this hand to point a gun at my partner."

He yanked the young man's arm straight and, with the heel of his hand, broke it at the elbow.

Renko let out a tiny thin noise and was silent again, clutching his ruined arm above the elbow. Staggering backward, he looked hopelessly around for a next move.

Jesus, Mallory thought, following. *Barely a peep. That's willpower. This kid's trouble.* "I don't know what you're up to, Renko," he said. "But you cause a lot of problems, and I don't have time for it. Don't let me see you again. All right? Or you're going to wish I was as nice as I'm being today."

He drove a fist into Renko's chin, and the young Serb crumpled to the ground.

Mallory paused and listened. He heard no raised voices or running feet. Aside from Ajda's scream, the entire encounter had been pretty quiet. The girl was crawling along the alley now on all fours, the halves of her torn shirt dragging along the pavement. Mallory caught up and helped her to her feet. "You all right?" he said.

She blinked at him, then smiled beatifically and cooed something in Turkish. Her shirt was ripped to the waist. Beneath, it looked as if she'd tried to bind her breasts flat with a cheap cotton scarf. It was soaked with sweat now and giving way under the strain. She'd chopped her hair off in a crude imitation of a man's haircut. There was a cut on the bridge of her nose where her sunglasses had shattered. "Are you all right?" he repeated.

"He didn't hurt you," she said, putting her hands on his chest and beaming at him.

"No. Are you all right?"

"I think someone hit me."

"That was me. Anything feel broken?"

"Someone hit me. It hurt. I'm fine now," she said. The scarf slid to the ground. A moment later, she put up a hand to hold it in place. She stood swaying and beaming, one hand between her glistening breasts. Then she caught sight of Renko's body and stopped smiling.

"Cover yourself up," he said. "He's not dead. Cover up, now."

The young Slav was breathing deeply and roughly. Mallory turned and opened the door of the garbage shed. Plenty of room. Grunting, he swung Renko up on one shoulder, pivoted, and let him drop soundlessly onto the bags of garbage inside. He looked around for the trench knife, didn't see it, and closed the door again. He turned back to Ajda.

She was slowly and clumsily trying to tie the torn ends of her shirt across her bosom, calypso-fashion, staring at the shed all the while.

Mallory took hold of her shirt and neatly knotted it together, then tried to tug the ragged edges over her cleavage. "Ought to travel with a damn safety-pin," he muttered. He surveyed her. The effect was startingly immodest. Could she pass as a streetwalker? Not in baggy men's trousers, with her hair chopped off. She looked crazy. She'd have to pass for a crazy woman. As long as it got her home without being arrested. Then he remembered: Rauth's people had seen them together. They knew where she lived. She couldn't go home. "Ajda," he said, trying to keep his voice gentle, "what the hell are you doing here? What the hell did you think you were up to, following me around like that?" He touched the nape of her neck. "You cut off all your hair," he said stupidly. "You're a dancer. How in hell are you going to make a living with no hair?"

"I wanted to be a man," she explained. "So you wouldn't see me when I followed. I wanted to help you."

"Help me?" Mallory said furiously. "*Help* me? Jesus Christ, I don't know whether they brought me here to snatch me or kill me or for what, and I'm trying to pick up a few clues, and meanwhile I got to keep you from getting yourself stabbed in fancy dress and you're trying to *help* me? Don't you know by now what kind of guy I am? What kind of business I do?"

"You are a terrible man. I know this. All the men I love are terrible. I don't care. I love you. I love you and you are in danger and you don't know what you are doing here. Do you? Do you know?"

"Not yet." He was leading her by the arm out of the alley. It wouldn't do to be around when Renko came to and started hollering.

"And you don't know Istanbul."

"No."

"You don't know *anything,* and you come here and let them try to kill you. For what? For money? I want to keep you safe. I want to help you. I will do anything."

"You can help me by getting right the hell out of here. You can help me by going someplace I don't have to worry about you. Ajda, any time you're near me from now on, you're in danger. Have you got that?"

"Where are we going?"

"We're not going anywhere. You're going to the tram."

"I don't want the tram."

"You'll take one," he said as he towed her along. "You'll take the next one wherever it's going, long as it doesn't go too near your place. You'll get off nowhere special and stay in crowds till you find a police station, and then you'll tell the cops you're being followed. Tell them you were attacked and he tore your shirt. Don't mention Laleli—leave this place right out of it. In fact, keep changing your story. Make a fuss, act crazy, gather a crowd. By the time they toss you out, you'll have made it so hot that anybody following you's left. I hope so, anyway. Stay away from your place for the next few days. Even to sleep. They know where you live, do you understand that? Hang around the *meyhane.* Get a wig or something and dance extra shifts. Try to always be with a bunch of people. Scrape up an old boyfriend. You've mucked it up good, honey, and all you can do now is stay right the hell away. These guys may not know who you are, but they'll kill you anyway, just in case. Hell, you're not even listening. Look. Just get out of town. *Right now.* You got a friend in the country?"

"Yes, but I—"

"Call her. Then head straight for the train station. Got money for a ticket?" He pressed a wad of lira into her palm. "Here."

"I don't want this," she said, looking at the money with horror. "You must let me help. I love you."

"You picked the wrong guy."

"Is she so wonderful? You love her so much?"

"No, honey, I don't love her either. I don't love anybody."

Ajda jerked as if he'd slapped her.

She stopped short, took hold of his shoulders, and gazed into his face. She seemed to be watching some catastrophe a long way off.

"Oh God," she said, her eyes filling with pity. "Oh God, it's true."

She began weeping then, and he had no further difficulty with her.

11   *The Sunken Palace*

Mallory saw Ajda onto a tram on the Ordu Caddesi. She took a seat without looking at him and stared straight ahead until the car started. He watched it out of sight, then turned and, without seeming to do so, swept the crowd again with his eyes. There was nothing to see, which might only mean that someone had made sure there'd be nothing to see. She'd have to take her chances now. He hoped to God she'd be all right. He began walking aimlessly back down Ordu, thinking that Laleli was out of the question today, not with one of their men still in a heap in the alley, and that he hadn't liked the pity in Ajda's eyes. He wondered how Laurie was getting on at the Treasury. It was about time for him to call in to Advance. He'd just decided to go back there and try to pick up an unmuddied trail when he saw Piotr Nemerov coming out of a sandwich shop not a dozen feet away from him, stooping slightly to get though the doorway, holding a white paper bag imprinted with lime and magenta daisies. The crowd around Mallory was thin, and his eyes flicked to the side, looking for cover, but in the next moment Nemerov turned his way and their eyes met.

There was no point in doing anything else, so Mallory kept walking, and Nemerov ambled up to meet him. Mallory stopped when Nemerov was perhaps four feet away. Nemerov took another two steps until he was, in the Arab fashion, standing with his amiable, open face no more than a foot from Mallory's. He meant, obviously, to overawe Mallory with his sheer size. He succeeded. *Lordy,* Mallory thought, *what a damn bear.* The Russian was clearly as surprised as he was, and it wasn't likely he'd make a move in such a crowd. Mallory felt fairly sure that neither of them had the initiative yet, and that if Nemerov was going to grab him, it wouldn't be here. Mallory was half impatient, half relieved. No one would be eager to be captured by a man like Nemerov, but on the other hand, it was time to get the show on the road. What now? Improvise. "Hello, comrade," he said in his crude Russian. "It is a long time I don't see you."

"Quite a long time," Nemerov said in English. "Mr. . . . Cavanaugh?"

"Cavanaugh'll do."

"It suits you."

"Thanks."

"I was sorry to hear about van Vliet. A colleague of yours, I think? My office had some dealings with him. We sent a wreath."

"Thanks. I don't believe I know your name."

"Oh, make a guess. I am sure your guess is good."

"You look like a Nemerov."

"I accept the compliment. We will say I am Nemerov. Are you seeing the sights, Mr. Cavanaugh?"

"I'm here to tidy up van Vliet's affairs."

"Do you think that they will need much tidying?"

"I expect to have things mopped up pretty quickly," Mallory said.

"Well, they sent a good man," Nemerov said easily. "I'm sure you will repay their confidence."

What a damn bear, Mallory thought again. Nemerov had six inches on him and over a hundred pounds. It was one thing to read that on a briefing sheet and another to stand chin to chin with it. In the Army, Nemerov had been a senior instructor in unarmed combat—another thing he and Mallory had in common—and now, though nearing forty, he was in superb physical shape, with every last bit of Mallory's speed and skill and twice the muscle to put behind it. He held the flowered bag from the sandwich shop almost daintily. There was a kind of wit to his movements, an air of relaxed amusement. *If we ever mixed it up,* Mallory thought, *he'd take me like Sherman took Atlanta.* Mallory wasn't used to feeling physically unequal to a challenge, and it made him itch, but his voice was as casual as Nemerov's when he replied, "Aw, this won't take a good man. I just need to find some sorry little critters van Vliet must've been dealing with, who it looks like don't know their jobs too well anyway."

Nemerov raised his eyebrows. "Indeed? And how can you tell this?"

" 'Cause of the way they balled everything up. They got cute."

" 'Cute,' " Nemerov said. "I am afraid you will have to explain."

"Kinda obvious, isn't it? That whole damn barbecue they set up. All that showing-off, where a bullet would've done the job. That's not how a professional does things. That's just some sick kid thinking he's scary. He must have a bunch of damn fools to help him, too, 'cause only a damn fool works for a joker like that. So now all I need to do is find the fools, and they shouldn't take too long to straighten out."

Nemerov nodded thoughtfully. "You explain it all very clearly, Mr. Cavanaugh. I quite see what you mean. Van Vliet's death, this barbecue, must have been very unpleasant for him. Very exceptionally unpleasant indeed. But of course, once you have found your fools, the matter should be resolved very quickly. Perhaps I can even assist you to resolve it?"

"Friend," Mallory said, looking Nemerov in the eye, "I wouldn't dream of resolving anything without you."

A movement over Nemerov's shoulder drew Mallory's attention, and he caught sight of Sasha Kurski walking rapidly down the Genctürk Caddesi from the direction of Laleli. Kurski's narrow face was grim. Mallory recognized him from his file photos: he was a freelance assassin, and a good one. Specialist, too. Killing people was all he did. Gray had been wrong: if Kurski was here, Anton Rauth must want Mallory dead.

And if Mallory let Kurski catch up to Nemerov, there were any number of plays the two of them could make on the open street, right there and then.

It was time for some kind of Plan B.

Looming over Mallory had been good psychology but poor tactics. It put Nemerov in striking range. Mallory drove the edge of his forearm up under the hinge of the big man's jaw and leapt over him as he fell. The brightly wrapped sandwich spiraled end over end through the air, scattering paper napkins out over the moving traffic. Nemerov was rolling to his feet almost before he'd struck the sidewalk. And Mallory was running.

From the corner of his eye, he'd seen a brief pause on the traffic, and Mallory began by diving straight across the street, leaving Nemerov and Kurksi to flounder out into the honking cars. Across the Genctürk Caddesi stood another mosque, and, beside it, a cemetery with a green-painted iron fence. Mallory took it in a bound. When you're being chased, it's not a bad idea to head straight for places most people would hesitate to go: a street full of swerving cars and trucks, or a graveyard. He'd advised Ajda to be crazy. It was time to be a little crazy himself. It might be his only hope against two first-rate operatives working on their home terrain. The cemeteries of Istanbul often serve as parks, and courting lovers wander decorously between the headstones, which are ornamented with stone or metal images of headgear indicating the deceased's rank in life: a fez, an officer's cap, a wind-worn turban. Women's graves bear a stone floret for each child they've borne. The young couples looked on in shock as Mallory took the grave markers like hurdles. The back of the cemetery was a blank stone wall eight feet high; he leapt, caught hold of one of the iron spikes lining the top, and flung himself over, feeling a spike tear at his trouser leg as he cleared the edge. He landed in a crouch on the pavement on the other side, almost flattening a porter bent double under a pallet piled six feet high with braided bread. The man gazed after him expressionlessly, puffing at his cigarette, as Mallory dashed toward the Ordu Caddesi. At the end of the next block, he glanced backward and saw that Nemerov and Kurski had cut through a side-passage and were ten yards behind him, Kurski moving in a disciplined sprint, elbows pumping precisely, and Nemerov bounding along like a jaguar, grinning open-mouthed.

This time there was no break to be seen in the river of traffic along the broad avenue. Mallory swerved to the left, picked up speed, and then scrambled up on the rear deck of a moving car. The sheet metal dimpled beneath his feet with a loud clunk. Muttering *Sorry,* he half-bounded and half-toppled onto the hood of the car in the next lane. The stunned driver hit the horn and brakes at once, and Mallory, jarred loose, leapt instead of falling and caught hold of the slats of an old flatbed truck in the central lane, clinging to its side with his left hand and two fingers of his right. His feet dragged along the asphalt for twenty yards before he was able to solidify his grip and hoist himself aboard. Around him, the air was filled with cries and honking. The truck held a cargo of bathroom tile; Mallory scrambled across it and swung out on the slats on the other side. It was just overtaking a crimson city tram. With a last leap, Mallory landed on the very edge of the tram's back step. Clutching frantically at the old brass rail, he hauled himself fully aboard. He heard a burst of cheers and applause, and turned to see a clutch of delighted schoolboys aboard the tram saluting him, their teacher regarding him with amazement, and a black-bearded conductor stalking down the aisle, dark eyes filled with fury.

Still panting, Mallory dug another clump of lira from his pocket and held it out. The other hand he raised placatingly. He managed a drunken grin. "I'm awfully sorry," he gasped in German. In Mallory's experience, a drunk German tourist was capable of damn near anything. "I'm really most extremely sorry. I had a sort of a bet on, you see. With my friends? A bet? Wager? Excuse me, do you speak German?"

"A bet?" the conductor said in German. "Your friends make bet with you?"

"Yes, that's it. They bet me fifty marks that I couldn't get on this tram."

The man stared at him. Then, slowly, a white smile parted his black beard. "A bet. Your friends bet you this."

"Yes. That's right," Mallory said, grinning and swaying.

The conductor pushed Mallory's wad of money away and clapped him on the shoulder. Chuckling, he said, "I think maybe your friends get a little tired of you."

"You know," Mallory said, "I think they have."

Mallory made his way along the tram and dropped into a seat. Working to get his breath under control, he surveyed the situation. The priority now was to get to Advance and put a signal through to Gray. He also needed to get Laurie and the brothers together and discuss the logistics of a full-scale strike on Laleli, if that was the way Gray wanted them to go. The Consultancy's nearest response team was quartered in Bonn. There might not be time to wait for them. Mallory wished he knew for sure that he'd read the situation right. He didn't like even considering the possibility that, confronted with Kurski, his nerve had just plain failed him. He glanced at his watch: a quarter past twelve. He'd missed his call to Advance. Laurie would probably be flicking open her little makeup kit to see where he was. Or anyway, where those damn homing gizmos in his shoes thought he was. Meanwhile, it was barely possible that Nemerov had caught the number of his tram and would be waiting for him somewhere down the line. Mallory would have to get off in a few stops, preferably in a crowd, before Nemerov managed to intercept him. Where did this tram line go? They were coming up on the Basilica Cistern, Mallory remembered. He could rely on a good, thick crowd there; it was one of the top tourist attractions in Istanbul. Some people called it the Sunken Palace.

The Sunken Palace was in Sultanahmet, catty-corner from the Haghia Sophia. A vast underground colonnade, it had served as a cistern for the palace in medieval times and still held a few feet of water. It was supposed to be one of the architectural wonders of the world, but what Mallory mostly liked about it right then was that it seemed like a good place to get lost.

When the tram reached the Sultanahmet stop, Mallory followed the crowd out the rear door. The Sunken Palace was somewhere under their feet. Its entrance was located in a little triangular park adorned with a single stone pilaster, and Mallory decided to join the line waiting to descend. Once he was underground, he'd see about finding a phone. If they had a gift shop down there, as he suspected, they'd probably have other amenities as well. The key thing was to get the hell off the street.

He heard a car draw up behind him and glanced around. It was a navy blue Soviet Zil.

Kurski and Nemerov were just emerging from the backseat.

Mallory pivoted and moved toward the entrance, rapidly but without obvious haste, pulling the INSTA credentials from his wallet as he went. *"Police!"* he snapped, not remembering the Turkish word for police. Then he did; it was *polis*. Pronounced police. Jesus. *"Polis!"* he said again. Holding the embossed card before him, he strode past the crowd and headed down the stairs to the cistern. The crowd was already getting out of his way. Mallory had the gift of looking official at will.

Once out of sight of the street, he began taking the stairs two at a time.

It was a desperate move and probably a bad one. Mallory didn't know if there was a back way out of the Sunken Palace. The last thing he wanted to do was let them chase him into a dead end, but he didn't seem to be doing too well at shaking Nemerov and Kurski on streets they knew better than he did, and there was a chance that they hadn't taken the time to visit a tourist joint like this one; in which case they'd all be on unfamiliar ground. If only this were New York or Dallas, there'd be a real policeman here to mind the crowd. But Istanbul, God damn its soul, was too peaceable for that. He was on his own.

He reached the bottom of the steps and quickly scanned the vista before him; an immense subterranean chamber stretching off into the dimness in all directions and lined with rows of yellowish stone columns, hundreds of them, clear water lapping at their bases. Off in the distance, a great stone Medusa-head lay half-submerged on its side. Between the columns ran a system of railed walkways. The walkways were well-populated, but there was nowhere a man could fade into the crowd. He dodged and wove between the tourists, aware of a disturbance at his back that must be Nemerov and Kurski bringing up the rear. He could hear recorded harpsichord music, like a department store at Christmas. There was something he was trying to remember. Something that had been closed . . . A third of the old cistern had been sealed off, sometime back in the nineteenth century. He sprinted right at a fork and saw a brick wall that didn't seem to fit the rest of the architecture. That must be the bricked-up section. Why the hell should he care?

There was a steel door in the wall, and a maintenance man in a dark green coverall was just closing it.

All right. That was why.

Mallory took a shortcut across a corner by vaulting both sets of railings at once. The maintenance man looked up startled at his approach. Mallory held out the INSTA card again and opened his mouth to speak, but the man, with no further urging, opened the door again and stared open-mouthed as Mallory charged by.

Mallory skidded to a halt just inside and quietly closed the door. He looked for a bolt, or something to wedge the door shut. Nothing; just the loss of a precious second and a half. The steel door cut off the harpsichord music. He was at the edge of a cavernous darkness pierced by the occasional caged work-lamp. He smelled dank, still water and heard the whispery stirrings of rats. The walkways here were built of rough planks, with a single crude wooden handrail. If he ran on them, the booming noise might well be audible outside. If he tried to hide in the water under the walkway, the ripples would be visible to anyone who came through the door. The walls near him were unclimbable. There was a ladder fixed to the far wall, perhaps two hundred feet off. It might as well have been two miles. He'd been loping, as quietly as he could, along the walkway, and now he spotted an iron staircase leading up to the surface, perhaps twenty yards further on. The top end couldn't be seen. If he could reach it . . .

There was a burst of harpsichord music and Kurski and Nemerov stormed through the door behind him.

After that, it was over very quickly. Mallory turned and launched himself at Nemerov, unfolding a flying crane kick at the big man's throat, but a kick, like a kiss, must be heartfelt to be convincing, and Mallory knew in his bones he was done for. He had attacked only because he preferred to go out fighting instead of running. His kick would have killed ninety-five out of a hundred trained fighters. Nemerov belonged to the other five percent. The Russian deflected it along one cannonlike arm, still grinning open-mouthed, as if he were having the time of his life, and drove into Mallory with both huge hands. The old wooden railing splintered against Mallory's back, and they were in the water.

The water was less than waist-deep, and the stone bottom was slimy. The impact of their slithering feet and knees sent clouds of black scum up around them. Mallory found himself momentarily free and struck at Nemerov's eyes; his arm was caught by Kurski's small, firm hand and twisted, and then he was face down in the chill black water, being pinioned by both men at once. He did not struggle to free himself. That was, he knew, impossible. Instead, he struggled to hold his breath. The Turkish police, he recalled irrelevantly, were famous for holding suspects' heads underwater to encourage confessions. The name of the technique escaped him. His diaphragm began to heave helplessly, as if his lungs were trying to lunge through his throat, and then an icy cold gathered in his skull as he began to lose consciousness. Just as the darkness closed in, Mallory remembered what they called it, that thing the Turkish cops did. The *submarino.*

He was dimly aware of someone taking off his shoes.

12   *Like an Iron Flower*

Over time, every agent develops his own way of dealing with torture. Laura Morse, for example, had been schooled in techniques for separating her body from her mind, and used them.
To defeat the remaining pain and fear she would talk constantly,
calmly, and pointlessly on a range of subjects, including the ones
about which she was being interrogated. She was particularly
skilled at submerging information in a torrent of disinformation,
and her captors were never sure which, if any, of the several dozen
versions of the truth she might present to them was real. Mallory
hadn't had her training, and his response was simpler. He spoke not
a word, not even to swear, and instead screamed incessantly at the
top of his lungs.

It was impossible to know what time it was, but he felt fairly sure
it must be evening. Under torture, time can elongate or contract, but
certainly Nemerov couldn't have been working on him for less than
six hours. Mallory was in a side chamber somewhere in the Club

Europa, a raw concrete box the size of a two-car garage. Through a gap in one wall, he could see a fragment of the structure's huge arches and catacomb-like tunnels, along which faint streaks of daylight had been steadily retreating all afternoon. Perhaps an hour ago, the banks of arc lights outside had been switched on with a series of audible clacks, but the room he was in remained dark except for a single standing lamp attached to an orange extension cord that snaked across the room and out the doorway. The lamp had a fringed golden shade and looked oddly domestic. They'd tied Mallory to an old wooden chair, roping his calves to the front legs, his forearms to the arms, his upper thighs to the seat, and his chest to the back; they'd used a dozen double knots and fifty feet of new nylon rope to do it, and his chances of slipping free were nil. They'd done something else, too, which puzzled him: they'd wrapped his arms and calves in towels before tying him down, so the ropes wouldn't gouge his skin. Finally, they'd gagged him, for which he was on the whole grateful. It made it harder to breathe, but it hurt a bit less to scream for hour upon hour if you were screaming into a gag. His throat was still raw enough by now that it sometimes hurt worse than anything else. Now and then he felt like a child waking up in a dark room with a sore throat and wanting to cry for its mother.

At irregular intervals, Nemerov would remove the gag and say, "Well?"

Mallory would sit motionless, eyes closed, breathing raggedly until, after a minute, or five minutes, or a couple of seconds—Nemerov never let him know how long the respite would be—the gag was replaced and the work began again.

Nemerov worked without tools or any sort of apparatus: no cattle-prods, no steel rods, no vises, pliers, tubs of water, blocks of ice, awls, or lengths of rubber tubing. He worked exclusively with the strength of his immense hands and an impressive knowledge of the frailties of the human body. He seemed to know the location of every nerve cluster in Mallory's face and body and exactly how hard each could be pressed without reducing Mallory to unconsciousness; he seemed to know the precise spot where each muscle joined each bone, and exactly how much stress each ligament would take without tearing; he knelt unself-consciously before Mallory and ground the bones of his feet together; he placed a vast hand on Mallory's belly and another on his back, slowly mashed the breath out of him, and would not let him take another. He caused Mallory ferocious pain or mild pain or intense discomfort, moving from one to another with an almost musical sense of timing so that Mallory could never get used to what he was feeling. He paused for unpredictable lengths of time and let Mallory guess what was coming next. He did not shine the light in Mallory's eyes but kept it turned aside, so that, for Mallory, pain came out of the dimness at any time. He kept Mallory's chair facing the doorway so that Mallory could always see the freedom denied to him. He effortlessly lifted Mallory in his chair and turned him this way and that, like a sculptor working on a figurine, like a florist arranging a vaseful of flowers. He did nothing at any time that might leave so much as a bruise on Mallory's skin, but the pain came in waves, in bursts, in dull pulses, in endless streams, in churning floods that submerged Mallory completely.

To take his mind off what Nemerov was doing to him, Mallory tried to figure out why he was doing it. Part of the *why* was obvious: Nemerov wanted intel on the firm. It was a classic fishing trip, with no specific end in view. Where was the Consultancy's New York HQ? Where and who was the station and station head for Berlin? For London? For Hong Kong? Where did Gray live and under what name, who was Analysis, who were the cutouts for the New York–London pouch? The New York–Paris pouch? What was their Bonn dispatcher's workname? Was Carlo Heffernan a Consultancy asset? How were they paid by the CIA? By MI6? What were the firm's preferred frequencies, or did it use land lines? What was its basic code protocol? What could Mallory tell him about pending jobs? Again and again, with the same patient good humor, Nemerov told him, "You're being rather childish, Jack. You won't be rescued, you know. Your shoes with the pathetic homing mechanisms are currently on the feet of one of our junior operatives—not the one you left in the trash, of course, but a sensible fellow—who is at this time leading your bitch on a wild goose chase up the Bosphorus. The helicopter will be here to fetch you just before dawn. Oh yes, I won't pretend to you that we'll keep this up forever. But a night can last a very long time. And by dawn I expect you will have told me a number of interesting and profitable things."

So Nemerov was doing a little side-job of his own, and didn't mind letting Mallory know. It made a sort of sense. If he'd been torturing Mallory on Rauth's orders, he'd have been given proper facilities, not an unused corner of a construction site where they had to keep the subject gagged so his cries wouldn't be heard in the street. Everything about this deal looked improvised, and it was clearly Nemerov's affair; the look of fixed disapproval on Kurski's face, the few times he showed it, was enough to convince Mallory of that.

What interested Mallory, to the extent he could still be interested in anything but his pain, was why Nemerov felt free to take initiatives like this, while scrupulously keeping Mallory's skin unmarked; why Renko felt free to take quite contrary initiatives of his own; whether this was part of some impossibly intricate ploy of Rauth's, or whether Nemerov had just gone to hell as a lead agent and taken the operation's discipline with it. If the operation had really gotten sloppy as all that, there ought to be a way for an intelligent man to take advantage of the fact.

It's a damn shame, Mallory thought between blasts of agony, *that Gray didn't send an intelligent man.*

To someone in intense pain, thirty seconds is an eternity, and a full night might as well be a lifetime. Mallory felt, or imagined, cool evening air moving through the open doorway; he heard recorded dance music in the street, which began in the middle of a tune and ended in the middle of the next; he heard a distant mother scolding her child in a language, full of broad vowels and quiet sibilants, which he could no longer recognize as Turkish; he heard a jetliner passing overhead and was confused enough to think it was the helicopter come to take him to Rauth, and nearly wept from relief until he realized his mistake. But he had long since forgotten the helicopter, or where he was, or Rauth—had long since forgotten that there was anyone in the world but himself and Piotr Nemerov—when Kurski appeared in the doorway and said in Russian, "Piotr, it's almost nine."

Nemerov's look of good-natured interest became a look of good-natured regret. He sighed and patted Mallory's dripping cheek.

"Never a moment to oneself," he said. "Well, I'll be right back."

He followed Kurski out through the lighted doorway.

Mallory had had hours to think about what he might do if he were left alone for a bit. He'd had time to ascertain that his ropes couldn't be slipped or broken. He'd had time to see that they were not only stronger than he was, but stronger than the rickety old chair to which they bound him. He'd had time to think about what that might mean. He'd even had time to make a plan, but that had been sometime in mid-afternoon, an eternity ago. By now he'd forgotten his plan completely.

His body, however, remembered.

He sat and took a few deep breaths, gathering his strength, only dimly aware of what he was doing. He listened as Nemerov's footsteps faded and the roar of a heavy diesel engine in the street grew louder and began to echo. Something big was easing its way into the concrete hulk of the Europa. Some piece of heavy machinery rumbling down into one of the huge chambers beneath him. It didn't mean anything to Mallory right now. It just meant Nemerov had gone away, and he could . . . He took one last breath and heaved himself forward in his ropes so that the chair rocked slightly forward. He let himself rock backward, then heaved forward again. Backward and forward, until the legs of the chair began to leave the

floor, and then he gave a last forward lunge and was crouching and
teetering on the balls of his bare feet, with all four legs of the chair
wobbling in the air behind him.

Everything now, he thought, *everything or nothing.*

He heaved himself upright with all his strength. There was a
crackling of old wood as the pegs joining the front legs began to
splinter and one of the back slats split. The noise was lost in the
grinding of the big engine downstairs. His nose began to bleed. Red-
black drops spattered on the dusty concrete floor. If he fell forward
now, he'd split his skull, but at this point he had no particular objec-
tion to splitting his skull, and he told himself: *Give it even more now.
Goddamn you. Goddamn you. Goddamn your rotten stupid worthless
redneck soul do it now, now,* NOW, and with a long, rending groan and
then a sharp pop, the seat tore free of the armrests and back and
Mallory was standing, gagged and slightly stooped, with pieces of
an old straight-backed chair roped to his arms, legs, and waist.

He untied his gag, clouting himself across the ear with a piece of
chair as he did so, and took his first free breath. With shaking fingers
he unknotted his ropes and let the shards of wood and the sweat-
soaked towels drop to the floor. The towels were embroidered with
the logo of the Hotel Marmara. *They say,* he thought soberly, *that
that's a really good hotel.* The knots binding his right forearm to the
right armrest were too tight, and he gave up on them and limped,
dizzy and stiff-legged, to the doorway, the broken armrest roped to his
forearm like a splint. There was something he needed to do, something . . . He wanted a drink of water. The doorway opened upon a
titanic chamber whose coffered ceiling was lost behind the glare of
the arc lights. Mallory stood blinking and rubbing his sore left wrist.
Before him stretched a vast expanse of floor. Off to his left, that floor
dropped off a sort of cliff into an even larger open space. That was
where that big machine was grinding. Where Nemerov had gone. Better not go there. In the middle of the floor was a long metal house
trailer up on cinder blocks. Contractor's office. Little windows glow-

ing. Good. Out of the way there. First aid kit. Drink of water . . . *Damn* but his nose was bleeding. Moving like a sleepwalker, Mallory wandered out across the brightly lit floor, opened the door of the trailer, and went in.

The smell was familiar: stale coffee on a hot plate, old cigarette smoke. It was like any other contractor's office. He saw a coffee-maker, a small refrigerator, a card table and a few chairs, a transistor radio. The radio was softly playing some classical number. There were a couple of telephones, a row of filing cabinets, a desk and a drawing board. On the drawing board was a pile of blueprints. Seated before them was Sasha Kurski, his narrow back to the door.

The sight brought Mallory to his senses again.

He stood motionless. He'd apparently opened the door silently. But after all, it had been years since he'd made any noise opening a door, whether there was any need for silence or not. He glanced around the room. A coffeepot with a good stout handle, half-full of hot coffee, seemed the likeliest weapon there. He glided toward it without haste, flat-flooted on the dirty carpet. Mallory was never sure whether the floor had creaked or whether Kurski had noticed a reflection in the rippling plastic windows, but the Russian turned unconcernedly toward the door, and then in the same movement was out of his chair and heading toward Mallory with his mouth grimly set and his small hard hands poised to strike.

Mallory feinted with a left elbow and, as Kurski batted it away, smashed his right forearm, with the splintered chair-arm roped to it, against Kurski's cheek.

It should have shattered Kurski's jaw and left him unconscious, but no man is selected for the Sub-Directorate for Specialized Poli-cies without extensive commando training, and the Russian had whipped his head to the side at the last instant and let the blow skid off his cheekbone. As he fell, he scissored Mallory's leg in both of his, and the two men landed with a thump on the floor. They began a groggy and undignified scrabble for freedom. Mallory found his feet first and lunged for the coffeepot again. Kurski shot up a foot and caught him in the ribs, and Mallory flew over the prone Russian's body and smashed into the filing cabinet beside the drawing board, catching a corner with his hands just in time to avoid being brained. He hauled himself up and turned to find Kurski limping toward him. On the file cabinet behind him stood a mug full of pencils, a circle template, and a steel compass. Mallory hadn't consciously noticed them, but when he reached behind him, his hand knew where to find the compass, and he swung it around and buried it in Sasha Kurski's left eye.

Kurski stopped still and gazed at Mallory from his one good eye. He looked thoughtful and a little preoccupied, as if he'd just recalled an undone chore. The knurled handle and circular steel spring of the compass protruded from his left eye socket.

A single line of blood appeared around the compass and ran down his cheek like a tear.

He slumped to the floor.

Mallory turned and leaned against the drawing board. He was coldly awake, weak and nauseated but alert. He could run now and stand a reasonable chance of surviving, but with no notion of why Nemerov and Kurski were in Istanbul. Or he could take thirty seconds to review the plans before him and have a slightly worse chance of surviving, but with the information he'd been sent here to collect.

It didn't strike him as a difficult decision.

The blueprints were marked PROJEKT ABD. The top page made no sense to him. It looked like instructions for assembling an earthworm from a kit. A long, low-slung vessel built of thick, ringlike segments tapering down to a kind of a snout. He glanced at the scale: twenty-two meters long—say seventy-five feet—and armored from nose to tail. The thing was meant to run on what looked like caterpillar treads—in fact, there were caterpillar treads along the sides and top, too. What sense did that make? A drop of his blood landed on the paper with a faint smack, and he smeared it away and turned the page. There were what looked like three big drill bits nestled together at the tip of the snout part, and then a ring of smaller bits just behind . . . He turned another page and stopped. Mallory had never really learned to read a blueprint, but he knew he was looking at a sectional plan of the neighborhood around the Europa, with a tunnel, indicated in dotted lines, running between the basement of the Europa and that of another, bigger building down the slope. They'd drawn a helicopter on the Europa's roof . . .

Another drop of blood landed on the paper.

"Lordy," he whispered.

Clumsily, he folded the plans once, twice, three times, unbuttoned his bloody shirt, and mashed them inside. Rebuttoning his shirt, he glanced out the trailer's windows—*Jesus, standing in front of a window like that all this time*—and saw no one. He stepped over Kurski's body and began limping for the door. In the doorway, he checked the sight lines around the trailer, satisfied himself that he was unobserved, and recrossed the vast, brightly lit floor, forcing himself to move without hurry. The noise from the pit, he belatedly noticed, was deafening: the grinding roar of big diesel engines trying to move a load almost too heavy for them. Beyond the edge of the floor, he saw the boom of a crane. He noticed a shadowed gallery running along one side of the pit and, making his way to the corner of the wall, eased his way into it. Then he was able to move fairly quickly to a vantage point halfway down the gallery. He dropped laboriously to his belly, crawled to the edge, and peered over.

He was on the third floor of the Europa. Down below, in the center of a great floodlit void, was one of the big cement mixers that had excited Laurie's suspicions. Its barrel, which should have contained liquid cement, had split lengthwise in four hinged sections, and these had swung wide, blossoming open like the petals of an enormous iron flower to reveal the truck's cargo: a massive pentagonal ring of black steel, twenty feet across and about six feet thick.

Fifty feet away stood the front half of the earthworm-gizmo Mallory had seen in the blueprints. The body was segmented; it was built of those pentagonal steel rings. The cement mixer had just delivered another of them, and now they were rigging cables to it, getting ready to hoist it over to the gizmo and hook it on. He could see where the caterpillar treads would fit; he could see where the drill bits would go. He seemed to hear Gray's voice: *Acting through intermediaries, they've purchased Pedersen-Howe, a leading manufacturer of mining equipment.*

The hulk of the Europa was nothing more than a big concrete shed meant to keep away prying eyes. Inside, Rauth was building a huge burrowing machine. When it was done, it would tunnel under the Banco Lavoro Tower and empty out the vaults there like an anteater licking out an ant's nest, and then Turkey's entire gold reserves would be hauled up to the roof of the Europa and flown out of the country from a helipad that could fit three Hueys at once.

A quarter-billion-dollar payday, all in untraceable yellow metal. Revenge on the government that had kicked him out. The financial collapse of a U.S. ally. A chance to make a few hundred million more by speculating against the Turkish lira before the crash. It was loony, as loony as rigging up a flamethrower to burn a man alive in his own shower. But like the flamethrower, it might work just fine.

And that's what Nemerov had gone off to supervise.

Then Mallory thought: *Where's Nemerov?*

In the trailer, Nemerov knelt beside Kurski's body and carefully removed the compass from the ruined eye. He closed Kurski's good eye with his thumb. Then, kneeling with his gigantic fists on his thighs, he silently wept.

"I brought you to a bad place, old friend," he said at last. "I brought you to a bad place. But don't worry. Please don't worry. The American will die."

13   *"Good-bye, Mr. Mallory"*

ever had a chance, Mallory thought.

He was already thinking of himself in the past tense.

He'd been trying to orient himself, to find a way down to the street. He'd crept along the gallery until it ended in a raw edge spiked with rebar. Beyond it, a black void. Backtracking, he had another peek down into the pit, where the massive iron pentagon was pivoting slowly in the air, suspended from the arm of the crane. No Nemerov. Sticking close to the wall, he retraced his steps. It wasn't so good, not knowing where Nemerov was. Nemerov was a guy you wanted to keep track of. He pictured Nemerov stepping out from behind a column and for a moment fought down panic. He crept to the beginning of the gallery and paused at the edge of that immense expanse of dully gleaming concrete, stained with oil and marked with tire tracks. He guessed it was eventually supposed to be a dance floor. To his right was the trailer, its windows glowing, looking small as a doll's house. Way off against the far wall was a small open cage of steel mesh between two vertical orange steel booms. An elevator. Mallory stifled a short sob of gratitude and began limping toward it, keeping to the shadows and glancing around him, looking for vantage points from which Nemerov might catch sight of him. Then he paused. The elevator, he realized, had to be off-limits for him. He'd worked enough construction to know how loud one of those things was. If Nemerov had been supervising this site, he'd recognize the clank and whine, even over the roar of heavy machinery. On a big site, you learned to read the noises. He'd hear the elevator start up, and then Mallory would be trapped in a cage on a string, with Nemerov waiting for him wherever the door opened. Mallory needed stairs, fire stairs for preference, off in a dark corner somewhere. But in a building like this, the stairs could go in either before the floors were cast or after. Depended on who had the work. And would they bother installing stairs at all, if they weren't ever planning to finish? Meanwhile, Mallory had been limping steadily along the edge of the floor, keeping to the shadows and peering into every dark corner. The grinding of the crane's engine made it hard to think. Inside his shirt, the crumpled blueprints scraped his chest. Maybe they even showed where the stairs were. If he found a quiet corner to look at them . . . In what light? Instinctively he glanced back at the lit trailer and saw a vast shadow loom up in the door.

They spotted each other at the same time. And then Nemerov was rushing toward him as if he were on rails, and Mallory thought, *I never had a chance.*

The elevator didn't look likely, but everything else looked impossible, and Mallory was already sprinting toward it, or as close to sprinting as he could manage, the splintered chair-arm gouging at his ribs with every stride. By the time he'd covered ten yards, he knew it wouldn't work. He was too beat up. Nemerov was gaining. Mallory swerved toward a jumbled heap of supplies: rolls of wire mesh, plastic buckets of joint compound, a pyramid of twenty-kilo paper sacks of fine cement. He scanned them for a hammer, a plaster knife, a pry bar.

"Goddamn it," he whispered through his teeth, "gimme *something.*"

He skidded to a halt on one knee and tore at one of the sacks with clawed fingers, then grabbed it by the end and, as Nemerov approached, rose and swung it with all his strength. He saw Nemerov grin, a feral grin in a face wet with—what, tears?—and prepare to swat the sack away. But it disintegrated in midair, and Nemerov's head and torso vanished in a caustic, whitish cloud. The big man bellowed as the lime ate at his eyes, and Mallory was running again, Nemerov blundering after him, coughing and swiping at his own face. He was still a dozen yards back when Mallory reached the elevator, smacked the Up switch, and wrenched the cage door shut. After a sickening pause, the elevator lurched upward, and Mallory thought, *Up? Why the hell did I do that?*

The vast floor seemed to be sinking away from him. Mallory looked down and watched Nemerov race futilely across it. Then he stared numbly as the Russian took three long strides, leapt impossibly high, and caught hold of the mesh side of the elevator with hooked fingers. Nemerov was still coughing through a white twisted mask of a face, his streaming eyes a few feet from Mallory's own.

I need to get out of here. Why the hell did I send this thing up? Mallory thought.

He was trying to break Nemerov's fingers with his feet.

It was another wrong move. Even as he let loose his first kick, he realized he should have used the heel of his hand instead. His foot was too slow. And drawing back to get kicking room had given Nemerov the extra half-second he'd needed to clamber halfway up the side of the cage. Mallory smashed Nemerov's thumb, but the big man didn't pause. Mallory kicked again and missed, kicked again— and Nemerov was out of reach. Then, agile as a bear, Nemerov scrambled onto the roof of the car just before it slipped through a square opening in the concrete above.

And then they were rising through a cavernous mechanical space. Mallory saw vast cradles of girders waiting to receive giant ventilators and air conditioners. The roof of the elevator was steel plate. He couldn't see Nemerov now. Above them, a square of starlight grew larger as the car neared the roof. In another twenty seconds they'd be on the helipad. And then Mallory knew why he'd hit the Up switch.

He was going to die. Nemerov was too fast and too strong. Mallory was too beat-up and weak. He couldn't fight him and he couldn't escape him. The only thing left was to try and die right. And the way to do that was get up on the roof and throw the plans off first. The evening breeze had started up. Mallory could feel it swirling through the steel mesh. They'd go sailing out over downtown, crumpled blueprints wet with blood. Whoever saw them would pay attention. Maybe somebody would call a cop. Maybe somehow Laurie would get to hear, or the Askers, or INSTA—it didn't really matter. Once its security was breached, no matter how, Projekt ABD was an easy target for anyone with a badge, and Rauth would have to abort. Whatever Rauth had wanted here, he wouldn't get. Mallory could do that. He could still do that much. He'd taken the plans from his shirt and was wadding them up so they'd be easier to throw. It wouldn't work if they didn't reach the edge of the helipad. The elevator was nearly to the top. He heard Nemerov's feet shuffling above him, getting ready to jump, and he slid back the steel mesh door and got ready himself.

The night sky had blossomed open above them, blue-black and infinitely deep. All Mallory needed was one last burst of speed. Weary as he was, weak as he was, he still ought to be faster than Nemerov, if all he needed was one last burst. Especially since Nemerov had to be careful about going over the side and Mallory didn't—it would work just as well if he and the plans went over together. He hoped those two things gave him enough of a tailwind so he could get this last little job done. Nemerov wouldn't jump until he saw Mallory out on the helipad. He couldn't risk jumping first and having Mallory hit the Down switch and leave him up there. So Mallory could start running right away, while Nemerov would have to jump down and then get his feet under him first. *It could work,* Mallory thought. They were almost on the helipad. *Not yet,* he thought, *not yet, not—Now.* The car had not quite reached the top when Mallory scrambled onto the deck of the helipad and started sprinting toward the edge. He heard a deep grunt from behind and above him as Nemerov left the car roof, and he swerved hard to the right, making straight for the illumined bulk of the Galata tower. It was the last thing he'd ever see, rising like a huge spear through the lights of Beyoglu, rising across the shimmering black band of the Bosphorus, and then—he swerved sharply again— rising across the shadows beyond the river, all the endless black lands of Asia.

Jesus, it's pretty, Mallory thought, and then Nemerov smashed him to the concrete.

For a moment Mallory had no idea where he was. He only knew that someone was tearing it from his grip. Tearing what? Something important. He remembered how to open his eyes and saw Nemerov standing above him, powdered corpse-white from head to knees, rolling the plans into a rough cylinder and stuffing them into the back pocket of his jeans. "No," Nemerov said, panting deeply and evenly. "We can't let you take such souvenirs just now. We're still making some good use of these."

Mallory closed his eyes again for a moment. There was nothing he could do now, not a damn thing. Just try and go out fighting.

He was lying on his back, almost between Nemerov's feet. He launched a kick up at the big man's groin.

It was slow and wobbly, and Nemerov didn't bother to block it. He turned and took it on his hip, then reached down, grabbed Mallory under the arms as if he were an infant in a crib, and yanked him into the air. He set Mallory roughly on his feet, took the front of his shirt in one fist, and jerked him close. The Russian's eyes were raw and red. His face was covered with whitish grit except were his tears scored two shining channels down his cheeks, silver where they caught the lights of downtown, black in the shadows. "Do you know," he asked Mallory, "what sort of man you've killed, you filth? You skinny American filth?"

On the second "filth," he let go of Mallory's shirt and slapped him across the face.

Mallory's head seemed to shatter inside. He felt fresh blood squirting from his nose. He couldn't feel his feet, but didn't realize he was flying until he hit the concrete with a jolt that sent shards of pain through every part of him. Nemerov pulled him to his feet again. Mallory punched him in the jaw, more or less. The big man didn't notice. "Do you know what he was worth, this man you've killed? Do you know what he was worth to me?"

Nemerov had had something spicy for dinner. Chicken, maybe. This time the blow landed, not on Mallory's face, but on his ribs. An open-handed, left-handed blow, a slap, but it still folded him up like a penknife. Mallory felt a couple of ribs give way, and then Nemerov slapped the side of his neck and he felt himself flying again.

"Do you know what a man is, you little filth?" Nemerov said, following. "Do you know?" His arms hung ready at his sides. The left thumb, the thumb Mallory had kicked, looked broken, but Nemerov didn't seem to mind. Both hands were open wide.

He's going to slap me to death, Mallory realized. *Just keep slapping me till I die. Jesus. This is going to take some time.*

Mallory rolled over and began to stagger to his feet, just to be doing something, just so he wouldn't be lying there waiting for Nemerov to pick him up and hurt him again, and when he was half-upright, Nemerov picked him up and threw him toward the edge of the helipad. He landed with a short wail of pain. *Hell,* Mallory thought. *Hell, at least don't whimper. At least don't die whimpering.* Nemerov jerked him to his feet again. From blind instinct, Mallory stood. It was stupid to stand, but he was concentrating on not wailing again.

"You don't know much," Nemerov said. "And soon you'll know even less."

The immense open hand with the crooked thumb swung through the air again. Mallory didn't know where the blow landed this time, but when he opened his eyes again, he saw he was no more than a yard from the edge of the helipad. His clothes were soaked with blood now, and stuck to him everywhere. It was very uncomfortable. He couldn't seem to move his head. He wondered if his neck was broken. No, he could still move one hand. He tried to figure out which hand he was moving, and Nemerov kicked him in the ribs, so that he skidded even closer to the edge. "This is what you wanted, to jump? You wanted to fly? Well, I don't mind. If that's what you want, I can oblige you." Another kick, almost gentle, and now Mallory was no more than a foot from the brink. *Anyway, no whimpering.* "I don't think I'll hit you anymore, or you might go to sleep. And I want you awake. I want you to be very wide awake, all the way down."

Only a little longer now, Mallory thought. *Come on.*

Nemerov began to laugh. "Undamaged," he said, for some reason, and laughed harder. "Undamaged, by God!"

He sighed. "Good-bye, Mr. Mallory," he said, and drew back his foot.

"Turn around, Piotr," said Laura Morse.

Nemerov spun, and with a slim pale hand Laura kept him spinning until he was facing away from her again and then shattered his fourth cervical vertebra with two stiffened knuckles. He flopped to the deck like a heap of old clothes. Four brown hands seized him, and he slid rapidly away. Mallory peered after him, thinking, *Broke his neck. Like Hayes. Hayes? Hayward?* In Berlin he'd known a supply sergeant named Hay-something. Hay-something had flipped his jeep on the Potsdammerplatz and wound up a C-4 spinal who couldn't even wiggle a pinky. Mallory had sat with him in the rain, waiting for the ambulance, and the man never lost consciousness once, the whole time, just kept chattering nervously away about how walking was overrated anyhow and this way he'd save money on shoes. The guy could see and feel—he just couldn't move. What were the brothers doing with Nemerov back there? *Paynter.* That was it. Bobby Paynter, from Duluth. He thought Laurie looked very interesting. Mallory thought she was the most interesting thing he'd ever seen. It was the way she was staring down at him—he supposed he looked pretty bad—and then he thought he saw a sort of spasm flicker across her face, as if her face was reflected in a still pond and somebody had tossed a rock into the pond, so that for a moment her face flew apart and she was unrecognizable, but he must have been mistaken, because almost at once it was just Laurie again, cool and inexpressive, and she knelt and covered him with her jacket. "Here," she said. "You're in shock, or you will be."

Her voice was the familiar drab monotone.

"Plans," he croaked.

"Yes . . . " she said, looking over her shoulder. "Yes. Don't worry. Osman's got them." She smoothed her jacket carefully over his bloody chest, then seated herself cross-legged beside him. "That goddamned homing thingie. We were halfway to the Black Sea before we saw we'd been had. But then we figured they might've brought you here. And once we got to the site, I'm afraid we were able to follow the trail of blood. Can you understand me?"

"Yeah."

"Can you walk?"

"Dunno. No."

"Are you going to pass out?"

"Soon."

"All right. I'll have the brothers carry you down to the car as soon as they're finished."

"Finished?"

"I had to promise them. They'll be done in a minute. You're all right now. Don't look. I'm not going to look."

Behind Laura, Talaat was speaking in halting Russian. "You see us now, Comrade Nemerov? You know who we are? We are—of *Gospodin* van Vliet. You understand? We was—his men."

"No . . . " Nemerov whispered raggedly. *"No . . ."*

"Are you unwell, Comrade Nemerov? Are you—cold? It is a bad thing to be cold, Comrade Nemerov. A bad thing. Come, we will warm you."

Mallory heard the scraping noise of a metal cap being unscrewed, and smelled gasoline.

"I had to promise them," Laura said.

He grinned mirthlessly and passed out.

14   *Mrs. Cavanaugh*

Being dead was worse than he'd have thought.

For one thing, they hadn't buried him properly. It seemed as if they'd stuck him in the mud at the bottom of a dirty stream. He could feel a cold gray flow down his face and body, never stopping, and beyond it a weak flickering light, from the world up there where people were still walking around, not knowing he was down here, not caring. What had he done that was so bad, what could anyone do that was so bad that they'd do a thing like that? That they'd put you down here and just leave you? Was it because Nemerov . . . Or maybe they hadn't buried him at all. Maybe this was hell, and hell wasn't fire in the middle of the earth, but just a dirty gray trickle across your face for eternity and, just out of reach, the sweet living world you couldn't quite get back into, a dirty stream spilling over you and through you, inside where it was all broken, and it was awful, everything was just awful, except for the hand.

The hand was good. He'd been holding on to it, for how long, years? How many years? And when he couldn't hold on anymore, it held on to him, and kept him from slipping all the way under. Somebody up there didn't want him to slip all the way under. Someone was pulling him back up where he could still see the living world. Sometimes the hand went away for a moment, and then he tried to shout, but then something cool and wet would brush his forehead, his face, his throat, so gently, so cool! and then the hand would come back and he could get a grip on it again. As long as he could hold on to the hand, he might be able to stand it. But it was pretty bad, this being under the dirty stream, it was like when he was four and had almost drowned, in a public pool, and he'd gotten away from his older sister and floated off into the deep end, and he remembered being on the bottom, looking up at the sparkling surface of the water, dazzling shapes like lenses or fish moving back and forth on the surface, and the shadows of people, and knowing everybody else was moving around in the light up there, so sweet! and that he'd never be up there with them again. He'd once almost drowned . . . There was something about that. *He had once almost drowned.* When he was four years old. He had once been four years old, in Corpus Christi, Texas. His name was John Patrick Mallory.

He opened his eyes.

He was looking at a ceiling light with a round plastic cover. It was brighter on the left side than on the right. The ceiling was of old acoustical tiles. Someone had painted them. You weren't supposed to do that. If you did that, they didn't absorb sound right anymore. To one side of the light was a metal curtain rod, with a curtain, a white nylon hospital curtain drawn halfway back, and then he managed to turn his head all the way—it hurt to do it—and saw Laura Morse, sitting in a chair by his bed, holding his hand.

"Hello," she said.

He let go of her hand.

She shook her stiff fingers, took a handkerchief from her pocket, and wiped them. There was a paperback novel face down on her knee.

She looked very tired.

He said, " . . . lon'."

"Jack?" she said.

He tried to clear his throat. She took a cup of water from the bedside table, a paper cup with a flexible plastic straw, and held it to his lips. He took a few sips—raising his head, even slightly, sent stabbing pains through his collarbone and left shoulder—and sank back again the pillow. He cleared his throat. "Than'. Thanks."

"Easy," she said.

"How long," he said.

"You've been out nearly three days." She set down the cup and glanced at her watch. "Just . . . a bit under seventy hours."

He closed his eyes. He was trickling with cold sweat, and his stomach felt caved in. There were tubes in both of his arms and electrodes taped to his temples. His right hand was in plaster, his right arm was in traction, and his torso was thickly taped from neck to belly. They'd catheterized him too, of course. Mallory was just as glad he hadn't been awake for that one. He opened his eyes again.

"Plans," he said.

"In New York. Analysis got them the day before yesterday," she said.

He flicked his eyes around the room. "It's all right," she said. "I swept the place myself. I can't swear there isn't someone across the hall with a parabolic mike, but I'd guess we ought to be all right if we keep our voices down. Can you understand me?"

He nodded slightly. That hurt, too. He found that he wished she'd take his hand again. That was pretty funny. A little embarrassing, but funny. He felt pretty damn bad, about as bad as he could recall feeling. But on the other hand, he was alive. That was all right. That was the sort of thing you could get used to.

"We've got site teams at the Europa and Laleli," Laura said. "INSTA's interrogating the key men at Laleli, with Osman in attendance. I suspect they won't be as genteel about it as we'd've been. I hope they go easy on the civilians. You're at the German Hospital in Taksim. We are the guests of the Turkish government. They've sent quite a lot of nice fruit and candy, which of course you can't eat, and about a truckload of tulips and mums. It got a bit crowded, so I've given it all to the nurses."

He cleared his throat again. "Who're we?"

"Officially, we're still the Cavanaughs, and you are the victim of a mugging, which is ridiculous because they don't have that sort of mugging here. But the story doesn't actually have to hold. INSTA's been swarming all over us, and it's a pretty open secret that we're actually here on, ah, CIA business." She smiled wintrily. "The staff's all atwitter. And INSTA is *very* grateful. I believe they wanted to have the Army give us some medals, but I explained the Agency guidelines on that."

"Uh huh. How bad'm I?"

"Better than we thought. Three ribs broken, six cracked, a broken collarbone, a broken hand—two places—a dislocated shoulder, and a fair amount of internal bleeding, which has mostly stopped. *Very* badly concussed. But it was shock that nearly killed you. The internist said he'd never seen a man pounded like that outside of an artillery barrage. It was as if you'd been knocked down by the blast of a big shell. I guess Nemerov must have been quite a fellow. Around two yesterday afternoon they thought they'd have to operate to relieve pressure on the brain, but you saved the Turkish government a few lira and pulled through without it. And now you're awake. They told me they'd let you travel as soon as you'd been lucid for twelve hours. I explained that we'd rather be treated by our own doctor at home."

Mallory nodded. Dr. Chaudhury ran the Consultancy's secure clinic outside of Lexington. If Mallory had to be in a hospital, that was the one he wanted to be in. He noticed his eyes had closed again, and opened them. Laura's wheat-blond hair was lank and stringy, and two purplish arcs of fatigue were scribed into the pale skin below her eyes. She wore the same clothes she'd worn on the roof of the Europa. The white blouse was wrinkled. "You been here the whole time?" he said.

"Gray told me to see to your safety personally," she said wearily. "He was concerned about the possibility of retaliation."

"Gray had you sitting here seventy damn hours? You look like hell."

"Thanks," she said. "And you look like the first rose of spring."

A neat dark head crowned with a crisp white cap poked itself into the room. "Speaking!" the nurse said with a Teutonic lilt. "Our Mr. Cafanaugh is speaking!"

"Um, yeah," Mallory said.

The rest of the nurse bustled into the room. She was a tall, black-haired woman of about fifty-five, with alarmingly bright green eyes. "Speaking!" she said again, to Laura.

"I was going to ring for you in a minute," Laura said guiltily.

"This woman," the nurse said to Mallory, pointing so he'd know what woman she meant, "do you know that she has been here three days and three nights, and doesn't leaf your side? Ah, this pulse is a little more regular, and now you put this beneath your tongue? Thank you. And look at this fine urine!" she said, holding up the graduated bottle at the foot of the bed. "No blood in it at all now, and such a nice quantity! You know, Mr. Cafanaugh, when you come in here you didn't haf such a nice renal function, and quite a bit of blood, and your temperature, oh, I'm afraid I still don't like it one bit. Three entire days! Do you know, there is a young doctor here, and he thinks he is quite handsome. And all the time he is out *tom-catting*. It is all he thinks of. And so last night I bring him here, and I say, Look, Doctor. That woman is taking care of her husband. She is caring for him, and doesn't leaf his side, not for three whole days, not for a minute! And every time somebody comes in, you might think we are coming to *kill* him, the way she looks at us! Like this, so fierce! And that is loff. That is true married loff, and that is what you will never know, Doctor, until you stop *tom*-catting. And do you know, he understood me. You are a lucky man, Mr. Cafanaugh."

"I know it," Mallory said.

"And now you must rest, so you can leaf us and go to America. I will send the neurologist to look at your head," she said, and bustled off.

"She really is awfully nice," Laura said after a pause. "In spite of everything. Well, you'd better get some rest like she says."

"I guess I will."

"Do you want some more water? All right. Sleep tight then. At least until the neurologist comes."

"Uh huh," Mallory said, trying to get comfortable in bed. "Ow. Ah. You know, Laurie, you're an awful liar."

"Am I?" she said.

"Yeah, you are. Gray didn't order this."

"Why not?"

"He wouldn't waste you on sentry duty. And how many times's he lectured us on the mistakes agents make when they're tired? If INSTA's so damn grateful, they'd offer—hell, I'll bet a month's pay they *did* offer—to secure one stinking room for us. And Gray'd trust them to do it. He told us they knew their jobs. I'll tell you what happened. Gray said to come on home and let INSTA baby-sit me. And you told him, no thanks, you were going to stick around and make sure I got out of Istanbul safe. And that's why you been sitting here three damn days."

"Couldn't tear myself away, eh? Are you really that wonderful?"

"No, you are," he said. "I'm a lucky man, Mrs. Cavanaugh."

Laura regarded Mallory fixedly. Then she picked up her paperback and began to read.

"We'll see how lucky you are," she said, not raising her eyes. "As soon as you're fit again, Gray's sending us to He' Konau."

BOOK II   He' Konau

1   *Complètement*

There's nothing worse than a summer cold, and Jack Mallory felt a real beauty coming on. Still, strolling along the esplanade, he guessed it couldn't make him feel much worse than he already did. His ribs and collarbone had knitted, his fingers were clumsy but serviceable, and his bruises had faded. The gruesome headaches had passed, and he'd weaned himself from the methadone they'd prescribed for them. Even the rash he always got from surgical tape—they must have pulled a couple hundred yards off of him—had cleared up. Gray had sent him here to Cannes to recuperate, and Mallory was now strong enough to run two miles along the beach each morning. Tomorrow, he'd try three. By the end of the week, he hoped to be up to four, which he guessed was equivalent to about six on solid land. It wasn't pain or injury that depressed him; Mallory had a high tolerance for pain, and was able to find it stimulating if he had to. What troubled him was weakness, lethargy, boredom, and the memory of two months of helplessness.

Srinivasan Chaudhury's secure clinic was a gleaming little four-bed hospital just outside of Lexington, Kentucky. It was reserved for Consultancy operatives, and this had been Mallory's longest stay there. Two damn months. Even getting gutshot in Cape Town hadn't laid him up for as long as that. He'd been the only patient in the clinic—Tom Lutz had checked out the previous week—and there'd been no one to talk to but Chaudhury and a sour-faced male nurse named Waite. Mallory didn't care for reading. TV worsened his headaches. He'd listened to music and looked out the bulletproof window at his own little bit of Kentucky: two sun-bleached trees and a triangle of patchy grass. At the end of the first week, he'd begun going out with Chaudhury for slow, halting walks in the woods. A young woman named Sutton, who was on rotation from the Atlanta response team, had trailed discreetly behind them, her pale-brown eyes scanning the birches, a Bren gun swinging easily at her side. Mallory's right arm was in a sling. He gripped an aluminum cane in his left hand. Now and then he'd stop and lean against the stocky Bengali surgeon's shoulder.

"You are quite a remarkable specimen, Jack," Chaudhury had observed in his finicking English. "It is surprising—almost unsettling, I might say—that you are so soon vertical again."

"How come," Mallory had said, working to catch his breath, "how come you don't sound pleased about it."

"Gray asked me when you would be ready for the field. I told him you should on no account be reactivated for six months. He said that perhaps he might allow you two. He'll kill you, you know."

"Well, something's got to."

"It would be a great pity. You know, you are under no obligation to accept this or any other assignment. I am familiar with the terms of your contract."

"If Gray thinks I'm ready, I guess I'll go. He hasn't killed me yet."

Mallory had never turned down one of Gray's assignments. The thought of it made him uneasy. One day, if he lived long enough, he'd be too old to be useful to Gray. He couldn't imagine what he'd do with himself then except drink. Better to do the work when you had it, and die on the job if you had to, than be some old soak in a bar somewhere, gassing away about how you used to be a spy.

He'd felt strong enough to start walking again, but Chaudhury had remained motionless, his mournful, copper-hued face turned up to Mallory's, his large, hooded eyes disapproving.

"I like you, Jack," Chaudhury said. "But I do wish I saw you less often."

And now here he was in Cannes. Cannes was a fussy little pink-and-white town full of rich old people and pineapple palms. Since arriving Mallory had been, he thought, extremely good. He'd bought a scale in town, divided 160 by 2.2, and begun working his way up to 73.5 kilos, dutifully forking down three large meals a day, plus a dessert with dinner, though he hated sweets. He swam slowly through the tepid blue ocean, feeling the strength seeping back into his limbs. He drowsed in the sand, scratching sleepily at his chest, where the hair was beginning to grow back, and was in bed each night by ten.

His sleep, though, was shallow and riven by nightmares. He dreamed that his flesh was soft as the flesh of a baked chicken, and that Nemerov was pulling chunks off with his fingers. He dreamed he and Talaat Asker were chewing their way through the earth like worms. More than once he dreamed he was back in the hospital in Taksim and woke scrabbling through the damp sheets for Laurie's hand. He found it uncomfortable to think about Laurie. She'd sat by his bed for three days. Three days and three nights, holding hands with and talking to and bathing the face of a man she didn't even like. That wasn't like saving your partner's life, which was part of the job. That was something extra. He felt Laurie had stuck him with a debt he couldn't pay. Taking care of him like that, that was the kind of thing someone who loved you ought to do.

The whole thing made Mallory itch.

He went into a beachside kiosk, bought a ballpoint pen and a postcard with a view of the beachfront, leaned against the rail, and wrote:

> *Dear Itsy, well we got our grain sold but it was a tougher sale than we thought and so they sent me here to rest up. Pretty good huh? They got some pretty good beaches here. Some of the girls go around here without tops but nobody seems to be staring so I try not to either. You'd love it here with all the French food but I'd just as soon be eating peach pie. Say hi to old Queen Isabella for me and I'll see you around. Jack*

He read it over and thought, *I sound like a damn moron.* One of the things he liked about the Consultancy is that they never made him write anything. In a neat, neutral hand he added Atsuko's address and slipped the postcard into the pocket of his slacks. When he got back to the hotel, he'd have them put on the right postage at the front desk. Atsuko lived in Tokyo's Asakusa district, in the middle of a little neighborhood full of shops that sold fake food made of wax, meant for the display windows of restaurants. It was spooky how real the stuff looked, except the fish was usually a little too shiny. The soups and so forth were perfect, though. Itsy's flat was a grim little box with two slotlike windows, and she shared it with two other stewardesses, neither of whom much liked him, but he wished he was there now, having her fuss over him and tell him he was stupid and lecture him on the Bourbon Secession, even though they had to go to a Shinjuku love hotel any time they wanted a little privacy. It had been two long, rotten months since he'd visited with Itsy. Or, come to think of it, any woman.

A couple of those topless girls strolled by, wearing just about nothing but suntan lotion. The sun had darkened their nipples to the color of blackstrap molasses. The girls smiled at him and then looked away, but their bosoms continued to stare expectantly.

Two months. No wonder he didn't feel right.

Well, that, at least, he could do something about.

The two friends were a few yards down the esplanade. He guessed they were in their mid-twenties. One was pretty and the other plain, and they were airily chatting as if they thought he might be watching them. They'd worked hard on their tans, and on getting up the nerve to go without their tops, and were hoping, he suspected, to pass for French. The pretty little one might even have done so, but even if he hadn't heard them talking, the plainer one—as it happened, the one who interested him—couldn't have been anything but English. Gently sloping shoulders, thick strong limbs, big chin, neat fair hair; there seemed to be one like her behind every shop counter and reception desk in London, asking if she could help you sir, looking milkily complaisant and emphatically female. In a bathing suit, a woman like that seemed undressed. In a pair of tiny bikini bottoms, she was indecent. Mallory looked fondly upon her soft retreating back. He wouldn't mind, he thought, a little indecency. He decided against trying to catch up to them. Too much like rushing to make a train. Instead, he ambled off in the opposite direction, entertaining himself with thoughts of young Millicent standing, just as she was, at her cash register, asking the customers if she could help them, sir, and resolved to see what the afternoon would bring.

Le Boulevard de la Croissette stretched out before him, lined with decorous palms—which, like all palm trees, looked fake to Mallory, fake and stuck in crooked—and those endless formal flower beds foaming with pink oleander and purple bougainvillea. There were always a few poor bastards in overalls weeding away in the sun. Just looking at the gardens made Mallory tired, or at that dead-white beach they were always raking and fussing with. The whole town struck him as fancified, a whole lot of not much. But one thing you had to say for Cannes: there were an awful lot of women in it who looked like they might not mind a little flutter.

Mallory was walking west toward the Vieux Port, where the old fishing boats fought for space with the new oil sheiks' yachts. His hotel, the Majestic, was just coming up on his right. The Majestic was supposed to have one of the finest bars in Cannes, and he thought he might do worse than break his two months' abstinence with a bourbon and strike up a conversation or two. But as he approached the entrance, he saw a small woman with russet hair emerge into the sunlight, turn right, and begin ambling up La Croisette ahead of him. Mallory recognized her. She'd checked into the Majestic a few days before. A composed-looking girl in cheery, ugly clothes, with none of the forlorn jauntiness of most solitary women on vacation. He'd seen her sunning herself by the pool and been favorably impressed: square shoulders, narrow waist, round hips, and short, strong legs. A pretty young peasant's body, surmounted by an alert, snub-nosed, heavily freckled face. Mallory adjusted his stride to match hers and settled in to see where she might be headed.

The little redhead had a particularly engaging walk, and following her was no hardship. She wound up in an open-air café overlooking the docks on the Quai St-Pierre. Mallory approved of her choice. The local fishermen were the only people he'd met here that he had any use for. Mallory gave her a chance to find a seat and take a menu, then entered the café and walked deliberately up to her table. She watched him approach. He did not appear to cause her undue alarm.

"Is this chair occupied?" he asked in French.

"There are many seats available, monsieur," she said.

"But I think none is as nice as this seat."

In English she replied, "It seems quite ordinary. But do try it and see."

"Thanks. Your English is pretty good," Mallory said, sitting down.

"I'm from Montreal. We often speak English there."

"No fooling? Montreal in Canada? Thought y'all spoke Canadian there. What's the idea, trying to talk like Americans?"

"We are Americans. Only civilized."

"Live and learn. Wonder if they got any bourbon here."

"An uncivilized drink."

"That's right, it's American. Aw, I guess I can live with Dewar's. My name's Jack Mallory, by the way."

"I am Valérie Mathis," she said, offering a small firm hand. The back of it was lightly freckled. There were a few freckles across her fine round knees, and a spray of them across her sturdy shoulders. Her khaki shorts were rumpled and her halter was a graceless but charming triangle of striped cloth, fastened loosely to her body by laces at her waist and neck. It was the kind of blouse designed solely to make men want to slip their hands inside it. Whatever you found in there, he was willing to bet, would be freckled. "In fact," she said, "I know you, Mr. Mallory. By sight. I have seen you in the lobby of my *hôtel.*"

"Worshipping me from afar, huh?"

"I make a practice to keep watch on uncivilized men."

"I've seen you by the pool. I make a practice to keep watch on girls in yellow bikinis."

"Now let me see. Shall we discuss the weather? No, it is the same weather as always. Shall we discuss our home towns? No. I am sure your home town is most distressing. I think it's time for you to tell me big lies about yourself. How important you are, and how much money you make, and how exciting it is. That, I think, is the next thing."

"You first."

"No, there is nothing impressive about me. I am a schoolteacher. Schoolteachers are not impressive."

"I don't believe you're a schoolteacher," Mallory said. "I think you're just making that up to impress me."

"You are correct. In truth, I am a movie star. A tall movie star. But I am here pretending to be a short schoolteacher so as not to be bothered by the press. And now it is your turn."

"Aw, I'm too tired to tell lies."

"Then tell the truth."

"The truth? All right. Why not?" Mallory leaned close to her and glanced from side to side. "I," he whispered hoarsely, "am a secret agent."

He leaned back and tried to look modest.

Valérie clapped her hands together. "But how very impressive."

"It's nothing."

"No, how very impressive and exciting. And what do"—she leaned close and whispered—"*secret agents* do?"

"Battle evildoers."

"What kind of evildoers?"

"All kinds."

"Why?"

"They're nefarious."

"Now I see. And what nefarious evildoers have you battled?"

"Well, I'm not all that sure I should tell you."

"Oh, please."

"Well. All right. My most recent assignment—or caper, as we sometimes call them—"

"I understand."

"Was some guys who wanted to steal all the gold in the Turkish Treasury."

"Is there much gold in the Turkish Treasury?"

"There's enough."

"And how did they propose to steal it?"

"Tunnel straight through from China and take it out from underneath. See, that way they wouldn't have to carry it out. They could just drop it down the hole. They had two guys standing in Peking with a big net."

"How very ingenious. And what did you do?"

"I foiled their schemes."

"Just what I should have advised you to do. And now you are in Cannes, enjoying a well-earned rest. Recovering, no doubt, from your wounds."

"That's right. This'll be my first drink in two months."

"I am making you drink?"

"I'm toasting your eyes."

"My eyes are quite ordinary."

"I'm toasting your freckles."

"My freckles are extraordinary, and you are quite right to toast them. But I don't think, after all, you are a secret agent."

"Why not?"

"Because I have seen secret agents in films, and the waiter never ignores them."

"We are getting ignored pretty good, aren't we? Let's go someplace else. Take a ride on the roller coaster. Get a chili dog. Some cotton candy. Go for a spin in the bump-'em cars."

"We cannot do any of those things. This is not Coney Island. You are uncivilized."

"Darlin'," Mallory said, "you have no idea."

Mallory opened his eyes and wondered if he'd been napping. Valérie's right buttock, he was glad to see, was still in his hand. He gave it a squeeze, and she hummed sleepily. It was not freckled at all, as he'd imagined, any more than her high, girlish breasts; everything she kept hidden from the sun was a tender, creamy white. He couldn't remember the last time he'd felt this good. He rolled to his side and tried to take stock of the situation from his vantage point in the middle of the rumpled bed. Room service, he thought. There were a number of things he still wanted to do to her fetching little body, and some that he wanted to do again, but first they needed food, and he had no intention of letting Mlle. Mathis out of his bed for the next day or so. Maybe around Thursday they might get dressed. He could rent a boat. Take her out for a picnic on Ste-Honorat. The phone rang, and Mallory let out a grunt of displeasure.

Valérie reached for it. "What are you doing?" Mallory said. "Let it ring."

"But I must answer," Valérie said. "It is for me."

She gazed at him, her eyes clear and candid.

Then, brushing back her sweaty hair, she picked up the phone. " 'Allo?" she said, and listened. "Oh, absolutely. But *complètement*. In all details, without the slightest doubt. No, not at all. It is a pleasure. Until that time, then. *Au revoir.* Here," she said, handing Mallory the phone. "He wants to speak with you."

She got out of bed, picked up her halter, and began tying herself into it.

After a moment, Mallory said, "Hello."

"Hello, Jack," Gray said. "Have a nice vacation? I don't mind saying I've been a bit worried about you. But Miss Mathis assures me you're now quite fit for active service. Very capable girl, Miss Mathis. New operative from our Montreal station. We expect great things of her."

Mallory watched as Valérie's white rear end disappeared forever into her shorts. She noticed him staring and grinned. He was remembering telling her that he was a secret agent.

Gray said, "Well, if you're quite finished over there, would it be convenient for you to pop round for a briefing in, oh, say, half an hour?"

2   *Dummies*

he Parc Georges Pinard occupies the center of a cobbled cul-de-sac off Cannes's Rue Borniol. It's nothing much: just a tiny quadrangle of grass, four benches, and the bronze figure of General Pinard, seated in a massive armchair and flanked by two bronze young women. One is lightly clad and represents Wisdom. The other is heavily armored and represents Valor. All three stare glumly out toward the street as if they've given up all hopes of hailing a cab. The sky was just beginning to dim toward dusk when Mallory approached the monument, wearing jeans and a worn blue work shirt, and carrying a small satchel that might have held tools. The monument stood on a stone base seven feet tall, with an iron access hatch set into the back. Mallory circled around the statue and stood before the hatch, letting the pinhole lens in Wisdom's chiton get a good look at him. Then he selected a key at random from the ring in his pocket and slipped it into the hatch's lock. Since he'd been recognized, the key fit. He pulled the hatch open and, stooping, slipped inside.

Once through the door, Mallory was able to stand upright. He let it clang shut behind him and waited. After a moment, an overhead light in a steel cage flicked on, illuminating the small stone chamber. Another video camera mounted on the stone wall before him turned with a soft droning of servomotors and examined him more thoroughly. In the corner stood a dull-red tank of a neurological agent called Bofors CNR-5. It was equipped, Mallory knew, with an electrically operated valve, which would open if the camera's operators decided they didn't like him after all. Above his head was a dark, irregular bronze void: General Pinard's legs, and the base of his chair. A silvery armored cable snaked up into it and disappeared. This led to yet another video camera, which surveilled the park and street from the General's right eye. Before Mallory stood the railing of a spiral staircase, which was blocked off with a wedge-shaped trapdoor of heavy, safety-patterned steel. Next to the door was a small, dusty, green lightbulb. When this lit, Mallory stooped and lifted the trapdoor with a grunt.

The stairs led down into a small concrete room containing a bank of video monitors, a computer that might have been the baby daughter of the New York mainframe, and a scarred wooden kitchen table. On the table lay a set of bloodstained blueprints. Behind the table sat Gray and Laura Morse. Laura looked crisp and cool, as if it were always autumn where she was, and Gray looked just as he always did. Mallory eyed the gleaming trench that bisected Gray's cheek and wondered again how someone who looked like Gray was able to travel around the world unobserved. "Hello, Gray," Mallory said, pulling back the remaining chair. "Hello, Laurie. Thanks for the letters. Sorry I didn't answer better."

"That's all right, Jack," she said. "I didn't expect you to write me back lefty."

"Hello, Jack," Gray said. "Thanks for coming in on such short notice. You're looking very well."

"162 pounds," Mallory said expressionlessly.

"Very nice," Gray said. "Well. First of all, I want to commend you, as I've already commended Laura, for a quite serviceable job in Istanbul. Nemerov's death was front-page news all over Europe. Apparently he'd hung onto his old GRU ID, and when the body cooled a bit, the brothers left it in his mouth. I doubt there's anyone in the business who failed to receive our point. The Asker boys do have a touch. Subject to probation, I've left Talaat in charge of the station. Really, I'm quite pleased." Gray did not sound pleased. He had never been known to manifest pleasure, displeasure, or any recognizably human emotion. "However," he continued, "it must be said that the job has yet to be completed. You broke up Rauth's Istanbul operation—thereby exceeding your instructions, by the way—but you failed to discover its purpose, or the rationale behind van Vliet's death."

"Did we?" Mallory said.

"Yes." Gray tapped a finger on the plans. "I doubt you had a chance to examine these properly. But I have, and so has Engineering, and so has Miss Morse. Laura?"

Laura lifted a slim hand and pinched shut her nose.

"Quite so. They're dummies."

After a moment, Mallory said, "How do we know?"

Gray leaned back and looked inquiringly at the ceiling. "At present, Jack, gold is $35.35 the troy ounce. Call it $35 even. That's $420 the pound and $840,000 the ton. And we are asked to believe that Rauth meant to steal two hundred and sixty millions' worth of the stuff, or approximately, erm . . . 309 tons. Now. You'll notice that the provisions for moving the gold up to the helipad are rather sketchy, compared with the level of detail you see here and here, where the plans concern the assembly of the digging device. The remaining plans at the site are equally sketchy. But let's say more detailed plans were to arrive by zero hour, and that they somehow made it possible for Rauth to move three hundred tons of gold along the tunnel and up to the roof of the Europa in, say, three hours. He would still have to fly it out. Now, stipulating a fleet of Soviet Mi-6 Hooks, which are currently the most capacious cargo helicopters in the world, and which have a maximum payload—"

"All right, Gray. I get it."

"—of 16 tons, that would be at least 19 trips. At a maximum air-speed of 300 kilometers—"

"They'd be sitting ducks for Turkish fighters, and where would they run, anyway? I get it, Gray."

"Well, there you are."

"Why fix up dummy plans?" Mallory said. "I might never have seen them. I wasn't supposed to."

"They weren't meant for you. They were meant for Nemerov and Kurski. Rauth's far too intelligent to trust freelancers with his true objectives."

"The gizmo's a dummy too? Rauth was up to something in Istanbul. Some part of this business must've been real."

"No, the, ah, gizmo's real enough. We still don't know quite what to make of it. There's a cockpit in the nose with room for a single operator. The hull's articulated like the shell of a lobster, which permits the device to tunnel round corners and so forth. It was designed to resist quite astonishing pressures. There are perhaps five foundries in the world capable of fabricating such a hull, so it wasn't difficult to find Rauth's subcontractor, but there's no law against forging a bit of steel for someone, and anyway, the foundries all seem as mystified as we are. Engineering says the completed device would weigh as much as a small battleship. Which is why, of course, it had to be transported to the site in pieces. The drill bits, treads, and power train were all to come later. Rauth's team had a schedule, and were apparently sticking to it."

"Lester's been all over this, as you can imagine," Laura said. "He was rather funny about it. He said, 'With enough power and the right cutting face, you could drive this thing straight through the earth.' And then he started muttering, 'Of course, you couldn't get enough power. Not in a hull that size. Even atomic subs don't pack it that tight.' And then he said, 'But if it *could* be done, I'd hire Rauth to do it.' And he gave out that laugh of his."

"Isn't this all kind of academic now?" Mallory said.

"No," Gray said. "Rauth is rebuilding the device."

"Sweet Jesus," Mallory said disgustedly.

"If you would, Laura?" Gray said.

Laura passed a folder across the table, and Mallory opened it to find a stack of eight-by-ten aerial photos marked out with a grid of hairline crosses. They showed a cargo ship approaching a small, roughly oval island. Close-ups showed a large shrouded pentagon in the ship's hold. A sailor was checking the canvas tarp. Mallory could see the part in the sailor's hair. He grinned. "U-2 output. I guess I don't have to ask who our new client is."

"You don't, and I wish you wouldn't," Gray said. "But you generally do."

"This is He' Konau, huh? Volcano, looks like."

"Extinct. At least, these last two hundred years."

"Looks like they roofed over the inside of the crater with a steel dome. Built sort of like a camera shutter, so you can open it if you want. Sweet. And it's flat enough so you can land a chopper on it when it's closed. Likes his helicopters, doesn't he? I don't see where that freighter's going to dock. Hell, what's it doing in this one? Looks like it's sailing right into the island."

"Try looking at it under the glass," Laura said.

Gray said, "He' Konau possesses several marine caves. Rauth has enlarged one of them to create a very sizable underground dock. His factory, we are obliged to conclude, is inside the crater."

"So Rauth still wants the gizmo for something," Mallory said slowly. "He wanted it for digging a hole in Istanbul, and now he wants it for digging a hole someplace else. It isn't for stealing gold, and I don't know what else you've got in Istanbul, or anywhere, that would be worth the expense of building a gadget like that and getting it to the site. Probably isn't for stealing anything. I guess you could tunnel under, I don't know, Topkapi Palace or somewhere, and leave a bomb there, even an A-bomb, if you had one and were hacked off enough at the Turks." He grimaced. "But that seems like a lot of fuss when you could just sneak one in in the back of a panel truck and do just as much damage."

"One additional bit of information, possibly related," Gray said. "Analysis tells me that over the past eighteen months, a fair number of what she calls low-threshold actors—mercenaries, independent enforcers, freelance assassins and executants, that sort of thing— have been quietly dropping out of sight. Better than two hundred men in all. Each of them the sort that Interpol generally takes pains to keep in view."

"And you think they're winding up on He' Konau."

"I don't know."

"What's the little bastard up to?"

"I don't know. I want you and Laura to go to He' Konau and find out."

"Okay by me."

"Good. The Konau Archipelago is perhaps 900 kilometers east-southeast of Australia. Pali Konau is its principal atoll, and a close neighbor of He' Konau. In eight days, a submarine will drop you and Laura a few hundred yards off Pali Konau. You will approach the island underwater at dusk, establish a clandestine base there, penetrate He' Konau, and discover the aims and current status of Projekt ABD."

"Anyone living on Pali Konau?"

"Perhaps eleven hundred Konoese. Subsistence fishers and farmers, though the tribe owns a few lucrative marine oil leases and is not at all badly off. Their political allegiances, if any, are unknown, but since the western arm of the atoll is both uninhabited and shielded from the islanders' direct view, you should be able to conceal yourselves there for as long as you deem necessary. If you can initiate contact and develop a working relationship with the Konoese, so much the better."

"Why not go straight to He' Konau?"

"How did it look to you?"

"Like a fortress. All right. We'll pick our moment and sweet-talk the Konoese. Or wait, what do they speak?"

"Grammatically, the local language is quite similar to the principal Maori dialects, except that it lacks a nominative case."

"I guess we'll smile and point."

"You'll have one important advantage. The Konoese consider He' Konau *tapu*—sacred, forbidden. They believe that Rauth is profaning holy ground belonging to a sort of sea-dragon deity. In fact, He' Konau is known locally as the Dragon's Throne. As you can see here, the northern rim of the crater largely collapsed during the last eruption, and the cone does look a bit like an immense chair."

"If you've had a few."

"I'd imagine your scuba skills are a bit rusty, so I've arranged for Cardoso to arrive Saturday—excuse me, Laura. Guillermo Cardoso, a Bolivian salvage diver who worked with Jack on Operation Distant Drums. Cardoso will put you both through your paces and get you ready for the landing. You'll complete your underwater training on Tuesday and fly out to Australia the next morning."

"Good. What do we do till Saturday?"

"Core prep and unarmed drill. Chaudhury's no end vexed with me for putting you back in play. He probably told you. He tells most people most things. And it's quite true you've been badly banged about, so that even if Miss Mathis is satisfied with your, ah, physical condition, it might be as well for us to get you warmed up again. A bit of hand-to-hand and so on. Laura's kindly offered to take charge of it herself."

"Couldn't ask for better," Mallory said.

"Logistics will kit you out for the run when you get to Perth, but

I did want to add one small item." Gray took a fountain pen from his vest pocket and handed it over.

Mallory turned it in his hands. It was heavy and luxuriously made, the barrel a glossy black with dull orange highlights.

"The shell is a Waterman Superba. The mechanism was devised by Otto and Lester. One twist of the barrel and you have a low-intensity laser, visible for at least fifteen nautical miles. Seven minutes' maximum duration. Two twists, and you have approximately forty seconds of an industrial-strength beam that can cut an inch of plate steel. This is a prototype, but if it does well in the field, we're making it standard issue. In theory, it's waterproof. Let me know if you find it useful."

"Thanks," Mallory said, tucking it in his shirt pocket.

"Two final points. First, I'd like to say that you gave me a bit of a surprise, Laura, when you failed to return from Istanbul as instructed."

"I told you what I meant to do, Gray," Laura said.

"And that surprised me," Gray said. "Your countersuggestion did no actual harm, and so I accepted it, but I hope you'll remember— and you, too, Jack—that unlike Istanbul, the He' Konau run is to adhere strictly to protocol. Your prime responsibility is to return with data. Until I've had a full report, neither of you is to accept any significant risk to yourselves to help the other out of a pickle. If Jack is captured, Laura, he's on his own. If you're both captured, you are each to look out solely for yourselves. Is that quite clear?"

"Yeah," Mallory said.

"I understand, Gray," Laura said.

"Good. Secondly, I hope that both of you will remember that you are being sent to observe, not to interfere. This is pure intelligence-gathering. I'd be best pleased if Rauth never knew anyone had been there at all. It's quite possible that, based on your intel, the firm may be asked to terminate Projekt ABD, but we have not yet been asked to do so, and that, in any case, is not a job for two lightly armed operatives. It would take a small army to move Rauth off of He' Konau, and, should the need arise, a small army is what we shall send."

"If you say so," Mallory said. "But seems to me, you get a clear shot at an enemy, you take it."

"Once again, Jack, this firm does not have enemies. We have clients and projects. Rauth is, at present, a project. We oppose his interests only to the extent that we are paid to do so."

"Balls, Gray. If we're just guns for hire, how come we never hire on with the Russians, or the Chinese?"

"Because it's bad business, working both sides of the street. One's never offered the really big jobs unless one's trusted."

"Then why not just work for the Russians? They're the big spenders these days."

"Yes, these days. My dear fellow, they won't last. And I wouldn't care to be one of their contractors when they go to bits in twenty years or so. They rely far too exclusively upon fear as a motivating element. In the long run, fear makes people dull and passive. Of course, you Yanks rely too much upon greed, but greed's a bit better. Livens one up. I imagine you're due for a comeuppance sometime in the next century, but I expect the current dispensation will see us both nicely into our graves. In any case, we have a number of more ideological staff who mightn't be willing to service Communist clients."

"You got that right, Gray."

"You're more than ordinarily petulant this evening, Jack. I hope you're not still upset about Miss Mathis?"

"Yeah, Gray. Matter of fact, I am."

"Pity."

"It's what you ought to expect." Mallory laid the folder of surveillance photos aside and leaned forward on his elbows. He hadn't realized it before, but Gray was right. He was furious. He could feel it in his gut and throat, and read it in Laura's disapproving slate-blue eyes. Mallory's voice was quiet as he said, "Listen, Gray. You send me off to get killed on a regular basis. And I don't mind that. That's all right, that's the job. But this is the first time you've ever mixed into my private life. I don't want you to do it again."

"I beg your pardon, Jack, but if it suits the purposes of this firm, I most certainly shall."

"I hope it doesn't."

"Are you threatening me, Jack?" Gray asked placidly.

"I hope the day never comes when I threaten you, Gray. But keep out of my private life. And, as you like to say, that isn't a suggestion."

"Dear me," Gray said. "Perhaps Nemerov didn't hit you hard enough after all. Well, off you go, and we'll see what Rauth can do."

3 The Prettiest Girl in San Diego

Gretchen Cargill was the prettiest girl in San Diego. Everyone said so. Even the Honors girls, who didn't like her because she wasn't some kind of little genius, and Barbara Downey and Meg Levitas, who tried to look down on her because she wasn't built like them, like some kind of little cow, even they had to admit she was pretty. She was thin, but that wasn't a crime as far as she knew. Clothes looked good on her. And her hair was dark blonde and really thick, and if she wore it down, which was a real pain but sometimes she did it, because of the way guys acted about it, it was utterly comical to see them, if she wore it completely loose it reached practically to her butt, and she wasn't a short little girl like Barb Downey, whose butt was practically right under her head anyway. She was tall, thank God. Because she really didn't know what she'd do if she was short. Find some short guy or something. But this way she could do anything she liked, and someday she wanted to get serious about her modeling, and maybe be a singer, too, but right now it was thrilling to be a rich man's girlfriend, lazing around on this exotic South Sea island with a bunch of servants or whatever you called them, the guys in the uniforms, who'd do anything she told them to. You had to admit that was thrilling, even if she didn't exactly know what it was all leading up to, but that was part of what made it so exotic, and after all, what was the rush? She was only nineteen years old.

The whole thing was like a story. It was like a story out of a book, even while it was happening to you. First of all, Europe. Europe was a place she'd always wanted to see, because not only was it exotic, it was cultural, but my God what she had to go through to get her parents to let her go by herself. Even though it was her own money which she'd earned herself by coming in first in the Lady Coventry Face of Tomorrow contest. Which they hadn't even wanted her to enter, so how much did they know? So that was good enough, a year's exclusive contract for Lady Coventry, starting in New York in the fall, and New York was great but she was sorry, it wasn't Europe. It just wasn't. And anyway, fall was like months off, and New York wasn't going anywhere. Luckily, her father didn't pay much attention these days to anything that wasn't Barry Goldwater, and let's face it, her mother was always happy just to get her out of the way, and if there was something you wanted bad enough you could always run from his house to her house and tell them what the other one was supposedly saying until you got one of them to agree just to tick the other off, and the moral of the story was, Paris! With all the *incredible* shops there! Too incredible, in fact, because she wound up running through all her prize money in about five seconds. So she was sitting in the refreshment bar in the Galeries Lafayette, which, not everybody knew this, but you could get an absolutely perfect avocado cheeseburger there, and trying to figure out what to do next, when she looks up and there's Mr. Roth.

Anton Roth. She guessed, with a name like Roth, he would have to be Jewish, even if he didn't look it. But she wasn't prejudiced, even if she did wish Meg Levitas would break a leg and have to be taken to the vet and put down. Because that was because Meg the Maggot was a creep and a maggot and would be even if she was Christian, and what did it matter if a guy was Jewish and just the least little bit short if he had perfect manners and was so gorgeous it practically hurt to look at him? And he couldn't have been nicer. He somehow, and she wasn't the type to blabbermouth her life secrets to all and sundry, but he somehow got her telling her story, and he couldn't have been more sympathetic. But sort of strict, too, because he told her that it was highly improper for a young lady like herself to be in Paris unescorted. But you didn't mind when he said it. He sort of made it sound like she was too important or something, but that he sort of quietly admired her for getting away with it. He said her difficulties were not so great that they could not be resolved after a little discussion, and would she care to have dinner with him that night? No, no, not a restaurant. He didn't care for restaurants. If it wouldn't bore her too much, he'd prefer to give her something simple in his flat. There would, of course, be a chaperone. Like she'd ever needed one of those, but he settled her bill and led her out of the store, and there was this amazing old Duesenberg at the curb painted this dark sort of metal color, like a gun. The chauffeur was one of those black-pajama-uniform guys who she'd eventually got used to having around. He was her first one, and he handed her into the car, and then another black-pajama guy quietly got in behind them, a big one, and she realized he'd been just quietly following her and Mr. Roth around the store the whole time.

"I hope you don't mind Erno," Mr. Roth said. "I'm afraid my business obliges me to employ bodyguards."

She'd said, "Yeah? What kind of business?"

"Reinsurance," he said.

Well, she was terribly sorry, but she wasn't going to ask him to tell her all about *that*.

Mr. Roth had a place a few blocks from the Crillon, an old building with a creaky brass elevator, but everything very clean, and he had the top floor. It wasn't huge, like she would have expected. But it was perfect. The furniture was mostly kind of spindly-looking antiques, and not too many of them, and there was all this empty shiny wood floor, and a few really old-looking paintings of fruit and saints, and just one or two very modernistic pieces of furniture that looked like sculpture, and tall old windows everywhere with little balconies outside and flowers on the balconies. It was wonderful. It was like being in some pavilion, and dinner was delicious, even if she didn't know what everything was called. It was so good she asked for seconds, and Mr. Roth looked startled for a moment and then threw his head back and laughed and said You Americans fully deserve to rule the world, and gave instructions to have her brought more food, because apparently it didn't occur to anybody that anybody might want seconds. There was a chaperone there, just like Mr. Roth had said, this little woman in black pajamas who was about a hundred and fifty years old. But you somehow got the idea that it wasn't a good idea to do anything she wouldn't like. She wasn't darling. She was kind of terrifying, to tell the truth, but everything else was perfect, and she told Mr. Roth that it must be so wonderful to live here, and he said Oh, he didn't live here. This was a sort of weekend place. Would she like to see where he lived?

So that was, let's see, just four days ago and now here she was, living like some kind of princess in this enormous private suite of rooms, what he called her *apartments,* in this huge house or whatever it was, hollowed out of this extinct volcano she wasn't even going to try to pronounce, way off in the South Seas, and waited on hand and foot by this sort of team of women in yellow pajamas, who didn't seem to have any aim in life except take care of her.

Beat that, Barbara Downey. You'll be fat in five years anyhow.

Not that everything was absolutely perfect, because it actually wasn't. For one thing, she wished she knew what they'd done with her clothes and stuff. Because when she woke up the first morning they were *gone*, all the great stuff she'd gotten in Paris, like, not even her comb left or a pair of panties, so that she had her choice, be naked or wear this actually kind of gorgeous linen robe she found neatly folded on the foot of her bed. But a girl still wanted her own stuff. And frankly, she was getting a little lonely. She wasn't actually supposed to leave her apartments without Anton around, and apparently this insurance stuff kept him really hopping, if it even *was* insurance, because this didn't look like any insurance office *she'd* ever seen. It was sort of like a huge modernistic museum and sort of like something you launched missiles out of, and she got the idea that the place went down way underground, like way, *way* down, and every now and then the whole island would sort of *hum* for a minute and make all the little bottles on her dressing table rattle, as if something big was going on down there. Also, it's not like she'd been asked on a million weekends by a million guys yet, but when they did, she sort of assumed they wanted a little, you know. Fun. And Anton hadn't even laid a hand on her. The one thing he did, it was almost funny, the first night on the island after another of those amazing dinners, he took her back to her apartments and asked her to strip. Just like that. Strip. But very politely somehow, like he was asking to see her stamp collection or something, because he'd heard such nice things about it. So that you'd have felt kind of silly for saying no, and when she'd gotten her things off, he just sat there in this robe he wore when he came to visit, exactly like hers, only brown, with his hands on his knees, perfectly calm and composed, and just *looked* at her everywhere. And then he stood up, and took her very gently by the shoulders, and kissed her, just once, and told her she was perfect. Now, she'd pretty much stopped minding what guys did to her in bed by the time she was fifteen or something, but one thing, she did like a guy to be a good kisser. Not prissy-lipped or all tongue or all gulpy, and Anton was absolutely the best kisser she'd ever met in her entire life. In fact, what with him kissing her so perfectly, and just once, and her being naked like that while he told her how perfect she was, well, frankly at that moment he could have had her do anything you want to name, anything you want to name at high noon in the front window of Saks, but all he actually did do was tell her that he knew she was going to make him very happy, but that they should get to know each other a little better first. And then after that it was a good thing he was so polite, or she would have gotten a little bit ticked. Because then he started giving her these *instructions.* She thought she kept herself pretty nice. But he wanted her to be plucking things and waxing things and sort of marinating things she'd never even heard of, and there were all these lotions and whatever that her attendants, the yellow-pajama ladies, were going to apply to her. That was a little creepy, having them do that, she wasn't even allowed to brush her own hair or wash her own face, but you got used to it. The attendants weren't much company, either. For some reason they never looked her in the eye. So that was it, one kiss and then a bunch of foreign ladies massaging her with lotions. Yee-haw. She almost wondered if Anton wasn't some kind of fairy, what with not touching her and all these beauty tips, but if he was a fairy, then exactly what was she doing there on his little island? Hmm? Because let's face it, she wasn't exactly the kind of person guys wanted around because of her sparkling *mind.*

But anyway, it was still all very exotic. And you certainly had to admit he was gorgeous, except for the funny hand from the stroke, which anyway wasn't his fault.

But she wished he wouldn't stare at her like that, the way he'd started looking at her the last couple days. She liked having guys look at her.

But not like that.

So, Rauth thought, *she's finally beginning to feel a bit of fear.* It was astonishing how long it had taken. It bespoke a truly impressive degree of self-absorption. She was perched gracefully on the corner of her bed—she did everything gracefully—paging through the fashion magazines he'd had flown in for her. They were last month's, but she'd still been pathetically happy to get them. She was trying not to look at him. Her body was taut as the string of a kite. It was odd, how fear made ugly women uglier and lovely women lovelier. She was certainly very beautiful. She reminded him, just a bit, of the small Annunciation by Henryk Ter Borch, the one in the Hermitage. The fair little mother-to-be, just realizing she's been summoned. By a rather sniffy-looking angel. Gretchen Cargill. What a preposterously ugly name. No worse than Ter Borch, he supposed. No worse, he thought with amusement, than Rauth. The fineness of her nose and jaw, the length and spareness of her limbs and throat, the dense pallor under that barbaric American suntan—she was the most perfect one he'd found in years. The most perfect, in fact, since the Danish consul's daughter. And the consul's daughter—his hands tightened fractionally on his chair arms—had been taken from him and defiled, defiled by that witless, boorish, drawling—

No.

He wouldn't let himself think of it.

Rauth was sitting back in his chair, not quite slouching, legs lightly crossed. He looked, he knew, entirely relaxed. He was not. Ever since he could remember, Anton Rauth had experienced life—consciousness, breath, the beat of his own heart—as a sort of pressure that grew inside him day by day until it was, at last, unendurable. As a small boy, he could relieve it by running and jumping. As a very young man, he could relieve it by travel; at eighteen, he'd packed a rucksack and set off across India and Tibet. The family had had him discreetly shadowed. Eluding his father's operatives had been Rauth's first taste of covert action. For a number of years he'd been able to relieve the pressure through sports, and there had always been women, a great many of them. But eventually women began to fail him, too, and eventually he—his hands almost tightened again—had begun to fail them.

And then he'd tried drugs.

He glanced at his right hand. It looked to him, as always, grotesque, like the claw of a fiddler crab. He knew, however, that to others the deformity seemed slight. A certain awkwardness in the way the thick fingers joined the knuckles. A hint of brutality in palm and wrist. Most likely an inattentive man could shake Rauth's hand and never notice it. After the stroke, he'd begun to reshape his hand with weights and heavy steel springs from an auto supply shop on the Rue La Bruyère, and now it was far stronger than before, though still too clumsy to hold a pen or, of course, a saber. A bit blunt, a bit clublike, like the hands of Praxiteles's boxer. Rauth had always admired the boxer. A fine, bearded fellow, resting between rounds, his fists wrapped in strips of linen, just turning his head to the left as if he'd heard his name called. As if he'd been summoned, like the little Madonna. Rauth had worked until his right hand was strong enough to crush a dog's skull, and then turned his attention to his left hand and trained himself to write and even fence with it. He'd turned his attention to business, and found a degree of distraction there, if not contentment. He'd turned his attention to women again, and at length had discovered the cause of his difficulties. He was no longer an ingenuous boy. He had grown, one might say, more exacting.

And now here was Miss Cargill. It was really quite odd how long it had taken her to grow afraid. Unless you wanted to rush and botch things, there was really nothing to be done with them until they began, of their own accord, to understand, and over the past few days Gretchen Cargill had stretched his patience to the limit. It had, he admitted, sharpened his anticipation. In the end, it would heighten his pleasure. She'd had not the faintest curiosity about what he was doing on He' Konau, hadn't even bothered to learn the island's name. Or his own. Her perfect self-absorption was another facet of her perfection. He'd grown fond of her. It amused him to be taken for granted, like a servant. It amused him to be mistaken for a

Jew named Roth, to be chattered at by the hour. Listening to Miss Cargill talk was like listening to birdsong. She didn't bore him.

And, of course, she never would.

Rauth got to his feet. He felt his pulse in his throat and legs, slow and thick as honey.

It was time.

Okay, Gretchen thought as she watched him cross the room to her. *Okay. He's finally in the mood.* It was what she'd been waiting for, she guessed. There wasn't any reason to be nervous about it. *Put down the magazine,* she thought, *put it down, now,* but she couldn't seem to let go of it. And then he took it gently from her and set it on the night table, and somehow that was very terrible. He kissed her. He kissed her just like he had before, and somehow it was terrible, and she couldn't get her mouth to work, and then he slipped the robe off her shoulders and she was naked. She wanted to say something. There was a time once when she should have said something. It was really important, but that was a long while ago, and he was holding her by the shoulders and looking at her again, and saying, very softly, *"Perfect."* And then he set her down on the bed, and he wasn't doing anything, nothing that a bunch of guys hadn't done before, but she didn't want him touching her, want that hand touching her, and he was on top of her, gathering her wrists above her head and holding them there, gently, with one hand, and lots of guys liked that, but—And he was caressing her face with that horrible other hand, and touching the thumb to her lips. He was putting it in her mouth. He was making her suck it.

And then he put the hand around her throat.

She could move again. She tried to fight, tried to throw him off of her, but he held her wrists so tightly now, he was so strong, even stronger than she'd thought, and still doing things, and then he was cramming himself in down there, *into* her and she couldn't *breathe,* she couldn't *breathe,* and she was looking around for help and saw that old August *Vogue* on the table. And then she knew. She'd never read the September *Vogue*. She'd never see her mom again, or New York, or her bed at home with the ruffled quilt that she'd had since she was little and had the spot on one corner from cough syrup. And her arms wouldn't push him off, and her face was cold, so cold she almost didn't mind not breathing, and she'd never be teased by Barb Downey again, or hear any good songs, or eat anything good, any chocolate, any marvelous cool soda down her throat, she could see it, her life sitting out there in front of her like a meal they wouldn't let her eat, like being sent to bed without supper, everyone was sitting down to eat and leaving her out, hungry, in the dark, turning away from her, and the last thing she saw, dim, wonderful, impossibly far away, was the avocado cheeseburger at the Galeries Lafayette.

Rauth watched carefully as she struggled against him. He watched as she stopped struggling. He watched as she forgot she was meant to be struggling. And as the light faded from Gretchen Cargill's eyes, he felt a greater light grow within himself. And at last, when the light in her was gone and her emptiness was complete, the light in him spread out until it filled the entire world.

And then it was over, and he was lying, very still, on a dead young girl.

His eyes were closed now. He was afraid to open them. He was afraid to move. But the tension, the crippling pressure was gone. He could breathe. He'd be all right for a while. He felt the familiar, endless sadness that always flowed in after the light. It was crucial not to give way to it. He couldn't afford a depression now. There was too much to do. He propped himself up on his elbows and, navigating by touch, closed her eyes. He slipped her tongue back behind her teeth and gently shut her mouth. He rose and wrapped himself in his robe. Now he could look. It wasn't as bad as he'd thought. It never was. The marks on the throat were still pale. The new prominence of the closed eyes gave her a saintly air, like a martyr in ecstasy. It was important—It was important to keep in motion. He picked up the bedside phone and said, "Housekeeping." His voice was calm. "Rauth here. Have the apartments cleaned and aired, please. No, not this time. I won't want to see it again. It can be taken to the Well. Yes, thanks. Good-bye."

He replaced the receiver in its cradle and thought, *Over so soon.* Tears prickled at his eyes. He was afraid to look away from her now. Everything else, the entire rest of the world, seemed so ugly, so horribly alien and ugly. He took a breath, calming himself. The slim legs lay languidly open. Perhaps there was still time to . . .

No. He had himself under control now. No, it was out of the question. They weren't quite nice anymore, once they'd begun to cool. And a thing is either beautiful or it is not.

4 *All the Wrong Things*

Even in a high-speed minisub, it's sixteen hours from Perth to the Konau Archipelago, sixteen hours with nothing at all to do. Following standard protocol, Laura and Mallory had worked through the night before embarking, taken 500 milligrams of Demerol apiece once on board, and conserved air by sleeping through as much of the trip as possible. They woke around one in the afternoon with six and a half more hours to go. A breakfast of cold field rations and water killed a little time. Using the hand-cranked chemical head in the corner killed some more: five minutes just to decipher the instructions, ten minutes to rig a tarp to give Laura a modicum of privacy. Then Laura lay on her bunk in the sub's nose and read a well-thumbed Ngaio Marsh mystery while Mallory lay in the bunk beside hers and mused about Ajda's brown belly and, grumpily, about Valérie's white behind. The sub's driver was a Brit named O'Donnell. He sat behind and above them with his head and shoulders in the conning tower, which was formed of heavy glass and shaped like the canopy of a jet. If they looked around, they could just see his knees and his thermos full of milky coffee. He'd spoken to them just once, to forbid needless talk, which wasted air.

As always when he was aboard a sub, Mallory had a ringing headache and a mucky tongue from the recirculated atmosphere. The ceaseless moan of the turbines was driving him nuts, and so was the fine vibration it sent through everything in the sub. He was bored. He needed the head again. He wanted a drink. But in spite of all this, he was in a fine mood, and eager to get to work.

Back in Cannes, Laura had taken charge of him the morning after the briefing. She'd rented an old boxing gym in town and brought him there at seven, and had him change into a T-shirt and sweat-pants, which she'd purchased for him in town. Then, for the next two and a half days, he'd done his best to kill or cripple her with his hands, and in return had been knocked, kicked, flipped, and thrown repeatedly to the scuffed blue mat. Laura spoke little. She instructed by example. Sometimes she had him repeat a move, slowly, so that she could correct it with her hands like a potter shaping clay. By ten-thirty the first morning, he'd been too exhausted to lift his fists shoulder-high, and she'd had him take a long, hot shower, given him fresh clothes, and fed him steamed vegetables brought in by messenger from a restaurant in town and green tea brewed on a hot plate in the office. On her instructions, he'd taken a half-hour nap. Then she'd brought him out to the mat and begun again. In the next three days, Mallory sweated through eight changes of clothes. He ate five identical meals of steamed vegetables. They worked each day until seven in the evening, after which Laurie stood with folded arms and directed a hulking masseur as he pummeled and smoothed the kinks from Mallory's body. Mallory was fast asleep each night by nine-thirty, and brightly awake by six each morning, and found himself passing through weariness and pique to a state of detached observation where the trajectories of his and Laura's hands, feet, shoulders, and hips were, above all else, *interesting*. Early in the afternoon of the second day, he noted that the wrist parry she was applying to his roundhouse kick was a trifle high. He seemed to see it slip from the proper orbit before her arm had quite started on its journey. It required no thought to follow his kick with a slanting reverse elbow strike to the chin, slicing up and under her raised forearm, and he was not surprised to see Laura's head snap back as she spiraled half-senseless to the floor. He'd followed her down to the mat, launching his body across hers as she instinctively tried to roll clear, pinning her with the weight of his chest and bringing the heel of his hand up against the base of her nose. It was a venerable and lethal blow called Lifting the Veil, and, had he followed through, it would have driven the bones of her nose up into her forebrain. He'd stopped with his wrist just grazing her lips. All in all, he'd been pretty proud of himself. But not half as proud, it seemed, as Laurie had been. It had taken her a moment to gather her wits. She'd blinked, and then she'd beamed at him. Her smile had been wide, wild, almost adoring. He hadn't known she had a smile like that in her. He'd rolled off of her, and they'd gotten to their feet, and then she'd bowed to him and held her head for a long moment below his.

And then she'd returned to the attack, and spent the rest of the afternoon beating him, as usual, like a gong.

After lunch on the third day she'd said, "That's enough. We don't want you worn out. Nor me either, frankly." The twenty-four hours before Cardoso arrived were for rest. They'd gone to a matinee in town, a badly dubbed print of *The Guns of Navarone*. It had been pretty funny watching Gregory Peck talk French. Then they'd taken a twilight stroll along the Croissette, eaten a dinner of mussels and frites in a café by the Quai, and turned in. She'd given him a good-night kiss on the cheek. It was the first time they'd ever socialized outside of work, and Mallory had to admit it had been, in its way, a nice date.

A nice date with Laurie.

Laura seemed to sense his grin and looked up from her book. "You're thinking about that elbow strike," she said, her eyes merry. "You're gloating."

In deference to O'Donnell's instructions, she'd mouthed the words. Their faces were barely a foot apart, and it was easy for Mallory to read her lips.

Mallory didn't feel like explaining. He nodded. "I know it was just luck," he said, also silently, "but there's still not many guys can say they knocked down Laura Morse."

"It was *not* luck," she said, turning to him on her bunk. "You waited for your opening and then moved in on it. You did it beautifully. I wish you'd train, Jack. I'm not saying you should let me teach you, necessarily, but you could be so good if you'd just study seriously. I've actually, well, mentioned you to my master. You know, he'd love to teach you. He'd be honored."

"Trying to pack me off to China, huh?"

"No, I mean my American master." She looked away for a moment, then said, "Actually, I never trained in China."

"No fooling," Mallory said, surprised. "Everybody thinks you spent two years in Ch'ang-pai."

"I did." She paused. "In fact, I've never told anybody this. I think Gray knows."

"Yeah?" Mallory said.

"The China thing. It, it actually didn't go quite the way I've been letting people think it happened. The way I've been telling it."

He waited.

"It was—Well," she said. "My sophomore year of college, my master told me he couldn't teach me anymore. I'd gone beyond him, he said. He said he was holding me back, and he wanted to know if I'd be willing to go to China for a while, because there were only about three masters alive who were at the right level for me, and he'd made inquiries through his own master and, in short, probably the greatest living practitioner of Piao Shou, Master Wei of Ch'ang-pai, was willing to take me on as a disciple. Well. I knew how hard he must have worked to arrange something like that. Especially for a woman, an American woman. It was just a great honor, really."

She looked younger somehow, Mallory thought.

"I knew there was nothing else I'd ever wanted so much," she said.

"But you didn't go?" he said.

"Oh, I went, all right."

She paused again.

"Go on," he said. "Tell me about it."

"Well. I was going to be sort of sponsored by IACMA, who run the international circuit I competed on, and they sent a young black belt named Liu to meet me at the airport in Peking, a very nice boy from a local dojo who spoke a little English. It took us a full day on the train to get up to Ch'ang-pai. They put me up for the night at the dojo, and then in the morning Liu showed up with a rented jeep, because even though Master Wei only lived about ninety miles outside of town, it was in the White Mountains, over dirt tracks and through forests, and would take us most of a day. They were pretty rough roads. The ride practically shook our teeth loose. But I didn't care. It was, the scenery was incredibly beautiful. I was . . . very excited. We got to Master Wei's house around dusk and I almost ran up to the front door. He was waiting for us there. He was quite old. He must have been tall as a young man, but now he was all shriveled, with a little paunch and a dirty white beard with about ten hairs in it, and wearing an old pair of polyester slacks and a windbreaker over a ratty blue T-shirt. We knelt before him, and Liu explained who I was, and the master nodded and motioned for me to get up. And when I hadn't quite gotten to my feet, he kicked me in the face."

"Yeah?" Mallory said. "Doesn't look like he connected."

"Well, of course he wasn't really kicking me, not his best kick, because if he'd really wanted to kick me, I'd have been dead. He was just seeing what I could do. And when I managed to deflect, then he really piled onto me. And I was so happy. Jack, I was so happy. I didn't care if he broke my bones. I knew he wouldn't be doing it if he hadn't been taking me seriously, and I think I fought as well as I've ever fought in my life. We must have fought for ten minutes without stopping. You understand, that's an incredibly long time. Each round in a bout usually lasts just a few seconds, but this old man was fighting all around me, from every direction, like a blind man feeling all around a plant, say, to get its shape. I was one of the best competitive martial artists in the world by then, but of course men at his level can't be bothered to enter competitions, and he was so far above me that it's almost as if he wasn't fighting. It's as if I was fighting myself. Finally he stopped. I was ready to faint, but he looked just the way he had when he answered the door. And then he bowed to me, and said something to Liu, and I saw the most awful look on Liu's face.

" 'What?' I said. I was panting. I could barely stand up. 'What did he say?'

"Liu looked horribly uncomfortable. He said, 'He say he give us dinner, and tonight we can stay here. But in the morning we must go. He cannot teach you.'

" 'Can't *teach* me?' I said.

" 'Yes. He cannot teach you. He say—he say you already know everything.'

"Well, I grabbed poor Liu then and shook him. It was the most horrible disrespect to the master, but I'd completely lost control. I said, 'That's not true! That's not true! Tell me what he really said!'

"And Liu finally said, 'He say he cannot teach you. Because you already learn too much. You already learn all the wrong things.'

"Well, somehow I was able to bow to the Master, and thank him, through Liu, and make some kind of excuse. But as soon as we were out of sight of the house, I began to cry. I cried all the way back to town, and then I shut myself up in the guest room in the dojo and wrapped my quilt around my head so they couldn't hear and cried all night. I don't know if I can explain it to you. I wasn't even twenty years old. Everyone I'd ever met thought I was wonderful. I was my parents' favorite, and my brothers' pet, and all the boys thought I was pretty, and all the teachers thought I was smart. And I was a big deal on the karate circuit, the youngest Twelfth Dan in history and so on. I was just a spoiled brat. And I knew it, and I'd thought this was my chance to get serious, to begin my real, adult life where I wasn't just everyone's little darling getting gold stars on her book report. And this old man, who knew more than anyone else about the one thing in life that mattered to me, this man had told me I wasn't good enough. That I wouldn't ever be good enough. That all I knew was empty technique, just a bunch of tricks and stunts. That there was no hope for me.

"When I came down in the morning no one knew what to say. I'd lost so much face, and I think the dojo felt that they'd lost face, too. Poor Liu was at his wits' end. I guess he had a bit of a crush on me. Anyway, all of a sudden he blurted out, 'Master Morse, will you teach a class for us?'

"He had no authority to say this, none at all. But everyone started saying, yes, yes, will you teach? So I said all right. And that's how I first started teaching. When the first students arrived that morning, they were pretty surprised. They'd all heard I was going to spend the next two years up in the mountains with Master Wei. But I just announced the first form, in my horrible accent, and we went to work. I taught them the way I taught you. When they did something wrong, I knocked them down, and when they did it right, I didn't. It's how I was taught myself. It's really the best way. And of course, I don't speak Mandarin—I just know the names of the moves. Anyway, the students liked the class, and I had nowhere else to go, and I just stayed on, teaching for my room and board. And it's a funny thing. I was completely stone-faced with these people, because I thought they all knew how I'd failed. But in fact they had a completely different idea. I found out they were saying that when I first met Master Wei, we'd started sparring right on his doorstep—they got that much right—and that we'd gone on for a day and a night without stopping, that we fought so fiercely the sun set early and the stars were afraid to come out, and that, in that one day and night, Master Wei taught me everything he knew. And that when we stopped, he bowed to me, and told me I must have been studying for centuries, for many lifetimes, and he gave me a sort of a nickname, a *nom de guerre*."

"The Ghost Princess," Mallory said.

"Yes. Gui Gong Zhu. A Sung Dynasty princess who became a devil to avenge her lover's death. There actually is such a story. And he said that he would always think of me as Gui Gong Zhu, because I fought so fiercely and was so thin and white. Liu must have dreamed up the whole thing. He was so desperate to rescue the situation. I'm sure he'll go to his grave never telling a soul the truth. He's married now, with a little boy, and he still writes me a long letter every year on my birthday. Anyway. I think everyone sort of knew what had happened, but that was a dreary story, that no one liked to think about, and this story was so much better, and so they all sort of decided to believe it instead. And to this day, the dojo, which was quite an old and well-respected dojo, is known as the School of the Ghost Princess. They put up a new sign. It's quite a compliment.

"So I was in China two years. But I wasn't studying. And when I came back, I let people think I'd done what I'd planned. Because I was still so ashamed. It broke my heart, Jack. It was really the end of my martial arts career. I went on competing for another year or so, just sort of by rote, and then I quit and let the Agency recruit me. And that's the truth about the whole Ghost Princess business. I think some people on the circuit know, and maybe Gray. But I've never told anyone. You probably think this is all sort of silly. That it's silly of me to care so much about it."

Mallory said nothing.

"Ninety to drop, kiddies," O'Donnell said from above. "Might want to start gettin' your kit on."

They'd been silently lip-reading for a long time. It jarred them to hear an audible voice.

"It doesn't take an hour and a half to put on a wet suit," Mallory said to the driver's feet.

"When space's this tight? And you got to go one at a time? Yeah, I reckon it does."

O'Donnell was right. Suiting up in the open air is one thing. Suiting up on hands and knees in a thirty-two-foot minisub is quite another. It should have been part of their training in Cannes, Mallory thought. Also, they found they'd brought a near-empty container of corn starch, which divers sprinkle into their wet suits to help them slip on more easily. By the time they were both suited up and ready for the airlock, it was seven minutes to drop, they were both slightly winded, and Mallory had given his head a good crack against the wheel of the airlock door. O'Donnell helped them lift their tanks onto each other's shoulders and adjust each other's harnesses. They double-checked their equipment against the clipboard in O'Donnell's hand and then clambered into the airlock. The sub was at the drop point now, and no more than five fathoms deep, but surfacing so close to Pali Konau was an unacceptable risk.

The airlock was designed to accommodate one large, heavily equipped man in a pressure suit. Mallory and Laura, wearing only scuba rigs, were able to squeeze into it together. Mallory sat on the nylon-webbed seat, and Laura seated herself sedately on his lap, sideways so that her tanks wouldn't hit him in the belly, and then rapped twice on the door. They heard O'Donnell opening the flood valve and starting the air pump. In a moment, seawater was foaming up around their feet. They rinsed their face-masks in it, spat inside to prevent fogging, and rinsed them again. As he settled his mask on his face, Mallory spoke.

"Matter of fact," he said, "I don't think that."

Laura had her mouthpiece in and was adjusting her regulator. She looked at him inquiringly.

"I don't think it's silly at all," Mallory said.

He slipped his own mouthpiece in and opened his regulator, and a few seconds later the water closed over their heads.

It was sunset, and wherever they looked, massed spears of rusty light slanted down from the surface to meet them. On the surface, all would be dimness and dazzle, but there was no need to use flashlights if you'd studied maps of the terrain. For a clandestine landing, sunset can be preferable to dusk.

Mallory closed the airlock door behind them, spun the locking wheel and yanked it tight, and then closed a small hatch over the wheel. He pushed himself back from the stubby little craft and stretched his cramped back and limbs, methodically assuming a series of deeply arched floating postures. On the other side of the minisub, Laura was doing the same. O'Donnell watched impassively through the thick glass of his conning tower. Behind the conning tower was a smooth hump on the sub's back, and Laura and Mallory swam over to this, one on each side. Taking stubby keys from their belts, they undid a series of locks along the seam where the humped canopy met the main body of the sub. Moving in unison, they swung back the cowling to reveal a broad, casketlike fiberglass container with rounded edges and two shielded propellers at its rear. It was a watertight undersea sled containing an amphibious assault kit for two: guns and ammunition, a shortwave radio, clothing, a week's rations, medical supplies, cameras and film, surveillance equipment, and three small but powerful limpet mines. Mallory took hold of a nylon strap along its side, braced his flippered feet against the hull, and looked at Laura. She nodded: she had hold of her own strap. He nodded twice and as he heaved backward, she lifted her end and the sled slid sideways down the curve of the minisub's hull and came gently to rest on the bottom, sending up soft puffs of sand.

Above him, Laura was closing the cowling and making it fast again. Mallory was clipping a thick elastic lanyard to the sled's nose and to a loop on the back of his diving belt. He flipped open a small hatch on the sled's nose and withdrew a handheld control unit on a long coil of electric cord, which he carefully uncoiled, swimming slowly backward so that the cord wouldn't foul itself. Laura had joined him. All he could see of her face was two noncommittal eyes, colorless behind the glass mask and sometimes obscured by a momentary silvery cloud. They were wearing SEAL-issue stealth regulators, which broke their exhalations into bubbles as fine as champagne fizz. Laura nodded twice, and Mallory flicked on the sled's power switch. Eight feet away, at the end of its cord, the sled seemed to curtsy and then rose with dignity into the water. Mallory eased in the throttle and the sled crept forward to meet them. He lifted a thumb to O'Donnell, and then sketched a salute. With no sign of recognition, O'Donnell began to circle the sub around toward starboard and its long journey home.

Mallory and Laura individually checked the compasses on their wrists, and then scanned the sea bottom around them, mentally fitting it to the charts they'd memorized in Perth. The charts had been dark-brown and white. The ocean around them, though, was full of swelling, pulsing color. The shore was to the east, and its water was still as blue as blue curaçao; behind them, to the west, the water was as rusty as cranberry juice and boiling with red shafts of sinking light. To their left was the rippling disk of a parasol fish—a species of jellyfish, ruddy at the circumference and parchment-colored at the center, trailing lazy, blackish-purple tresses bearing, their briefing packets had warned, a particularly lethal toxin. It was moving the opposite way. Off at the lip of an underwater valley a bottle-green Hecht's lamprey hovered just in sight, grinning idiotically at them with a mouth of needlelike teeth. The bite was very nasty, but the fish was timid and only attacked when cornered. The lamprey was, in fact, the snakelike fish on which the Konoese had modeled their dragon deity. It was sacred but not *tapu,* and in fact made good eating for anyone who knew how to catch and bone it. A school of tiny, sun-yellow heptas with trailing azure tails swerved before them in unison, then swarmed around them toward some appointment. Mallory touched Laura's arm and pointed out an arc of rose brain coral off to starboard, which forked southward and mounted up nearly to the surface. The reef had been on the maps. They were within yards of the drop point, and no more than a hundred yards from shore. O'Donnell had done his job superbly. Mallory gestured with his chin and he and Laura began swimming deliberately forward, the sled trailing obediently behind them on its leash.

The water was warm, and Mallory wondered if they'd needed the damn wet suits after all. It was pleasant to paddle smoothly along and to know that in a minute or so they'd set foot on Pali Konau and begin the job in earnest. But Mallory was getting a bad feeling, a feeling they'd been either too clever or not clever enough. It was hard to say whether there was any good reason for it. Infallible instincts, unfortunately, do not exist. Ten yards from shore, as arranged, Mallory settled the sled down in the sand and switched off its motor. You couldn't move fast with a thing like that. They'd retrieve it after their initial reconnaissance on land. The feeling was stronger now, and Mallory wondered what, if anything, was to be done about it. Nothing, he supposed, unless they wanted to turn tail and swim after O'Donnell's sub. If something had gone sour, there'd be a crisis soon enough, and a crisis usually brings new choices. But right now, they had the plan or they had nothing. They anchored the sled and swam up the beach until the water was no more than waist-deep. Then, gathering their feet under them, they stood.

The Konoese are skilled spearfishers, using both the traditional thrust-spear and, when they have it, the modern gas-powered spear-gun. They are also old hands with the short knife, the weighted staff, and the bow and arrow, though the native bow might seem comically stubby to an American or European eye. But in battle the islander's chief weapon is the *atto,* or throwing axe. This is a thick, gently curved stick about eighteen inches long, set at the head with two or three tusk-shaped blades of sharpened abalone. The *atto* is similar in principle to the Native American tomahawk, though bigger and more carefully balanced, and has a vane of trimmed feathers to stabilize the weapon in flight. A skilled Konoese can take a gull out of the air with one at thirty paces.

When Laura and Mallory rose from the water, they found themselves facing a young Konoese, *atto* poised to throw, standing no more than ten paces away. On his left deltoid were tattooed three horizontal black bands, signifying a member of the warrior class. He wore a short necklace of alternating black and red coral, signifying a soldier on active duty. He seemed neither surprised nor pleased to see them. His brown feet were planted solidly in the sand, but poised for quick movement. His free hand was extended in a gesture they both knew well.

Don't move.

5   *Silver Moon and Golden Sun*

He looked about twenty-five, with a smooth, brown paunch and broad, rounded shoulders. His trunk was wrapped with a yellow cloth like a penang, which left his legs free to move. A canvas web belt, perhaps U.S. Army surplus, held a short knife with a leaf-shaped blade. His feet were bare. His black eyes were watchful and unexcited. The arm holding the throwing axe was as motionless as a tree trunk.

"I can take him, Jack," Laura said almost inaudibly. She'd spat out her mouthpiece and, though it would not have been noticeable to a stranger, was tensed for action.

Mallory opened his jaws and let his regulator flop down on his chest. He took a breath of the mild, sweet air and studied the young man.

"No," he said. "I think it's all right."

"I won't have to hurt him, not badly. Jack, I don't like this."

"Simmer down. We're all right for now."

"Masculine intuition, eh?" she said.

The young soldier let out a short series of whistles, and the leaves on the slope above them stirred and disgorged a dozen more soldiers like him, *atta* swinging at their sides, moving quietly and without fuss to form a loose semicircle behind him. Two of the soldiers held stubby bows and wore quivers of arrows. It was all right with Mallory. He'd decided it was talking time, and a man with arms and numbers on his side, Mallory felt, is usually more relaxed and readier to talk. Raising his voice, he said, "Hello. Speak any English?"

The young soldier spoke briefly to his men in a clicking, liquid language that sounded like wine pouring from a jug. Some of the soldiers were nearly twice the leader's age, but none seemed to question his authority. Four detached themselves, two on each side, and, tucking their throwing axes into their belts, waded past Laura and Mallory into the surf.

"Sprech' sie Deutsch? ¿Español? Français?"

"Un peu," the soldier said tonelessly.

Hell. It would be French. Mallory made a slight movement with his spread hands, indicating his mask.

After a moment, the soldier said. *"Oui. Mais lentement."*

Slowly, Mallory raised his hands and lifted the mask from his eyes. At his side, Laura did the same. He settled the mask atop his head, carefully returned his hands to his sides, and let the young man look him over.

"We are on your land," Mallory said at last in French, his voice mild. "And we regret this. Truly. We will do what you wish. Unless you wish to harm us, and then we will do what we must. What do you wish of us?"

"I don't wish things," the soldier said. "The Queen wishes. I go with you to there."

"We thank you," Mallory said seriously, "for the honor."

The young soldier lifted an eyebrow. Aside from this, the dark face remained impassive.

"I am named Mallory," Mallory said. "This is Laura Morse. May we know your name?"

After a moment, the young soldier said, "K'talo."

Then he added, *"Ne parlez-vous pas."*

Mallory solemnly inclined his head.

At a nod from K'talo, the archers nocked short barbed arrows and leveled them at Mallory's and Laura's throats. *Easy, Laurie,* Mallory thought. *Easy.* But she remained motionless, her face a blank. K'talo tucked his *atto* into his belt and beckoned the two of them forward onto dry land. He indicated their flippers and again said, *"Lentement."* Mallory and Laura bent, each conscious of the spots on their bodies into which the arrows were poised to enter, undid their flippers, and carefully kicked them away. Beneath the flippers, their feet were sheathed in tough but porous sponge rubber boots, snug as socks and reinforced at the sole with fiberglass and fine wire mesh. The soldiers regarded them quizzically. Two more soldiers stepped forward and bound Laura's and Mallory's hands behind their backs with leather thongs, while the archers covered them from up the slope, bracketing them as precisely as West Point grads. Then, at a gesture from K'talo, they all began walking.

The procession wound its way up the shallow slope. From its crest Mallory looked out across the atoll's central lagoon to a cluster of thatched roofs surrounding a big Quonset hut. He guessed it was where they were headed. Glancing back, Mallory saw that a soldier had tucked their flippers under his arm and that the four soldiers who'd waded out into the surf had retrieved the sea sled and were carrying it on their shoulders like pallbearers, one at each corner. It looked to be better than a mile to the Quonset hut. The sled weighed 280 pounds fully loaded. Mallory wished the men carrying it all the best.

If their hands hadn't been tied, it would have been a nice walk. The lagoon was a cobalt disk, silvered with the fading light of the dense blue sky. An outrigger canoe skimmed across it like a current-borne blade of grass. It was too dark to see the rowers. It was almost too dark to see the canoe. Not quite dead ahead, a single gap broke the near-perfect circle of the atoll. Through it, they could see a stretch of open sea and, beyond it, the jagged dark mass of He' Konau. There were four miles of open sea between the atoll and the neighboring volcano, but the distance seemed no more than a stone's throw. The sand was pleasantly firm underfoot. Even through his foam foot-gear, he could feel that it was warm but cooling fast. A distant bird let out a ratcheting sound, and a nearer one replied with a long moan, like someone blowing across the neck of a bottle. The trees bordering the beach were vinelike, with broad, wing-shaped leaves. Mallory had no idea what they were called. His briefing packet hadn't mentioned them as being edible, poisonous, or medicinal. Both his head and his gut told him the immediate danger had passed. He saw that Laura was watchful but calm. This was a disci-plined group. Everything depended on the Queen. Either she'd like what they had to say or she wouldn't.

When they reached the gap in the atoll, Mallory had a surprise: a pedestrian bridge spanned the seventy feet of open water. The walkway was made of heavy planks dressed with deck paint; they were slung from four creosoted telephone poles by cables braided from nylon rope. It was a modern suspension bridge, light and graceful, with plenty of room underneath for seabound boats. They stepped off the far side to find the village fading from view, shad-owed in the darkening lee of the atoll's arm. What he'd taken for a Quonset hut, Mallory saw, was a freestanding open barrel-vault, roofed with corrugated metal and open at front and back. A covered arena of sorts. In the darkness within, two torches had been lit, like eyes glaring from a cave. They were the only light in the village. Mal-lory saw now that the villagers had come out to meet them. They stood before their huts in a single mass, silent and still. Like K'talo, most of them were round-headed and plumply muscular. Their features bore a vaguely Chinese cast. The men were all tattooed: either stripes on the left shoulder or dots and stars on the left breast. The women covered their bosoms with brightly-hued sashes. Men and women alike wore their black hair in long ponytails and wrapped their hips loosely in penangs. Each of them carried a short knife almost negligently in one hand.

The soldiers led them through the silent crowds and under the arched metal roof that seemed to serve as town hall. Toward the back, lit by two torches, stood a polished Ruhlmann desk. Behind it sat a thin, wrinkled old woman. She was the first thin person they'd seen in town. She wore a pillbox hat, Jackie Kennedy–style, and what Mallory recognized—though he would never have admitted it to Laura—as a twenty-year-old Chanel evening gown, frayed but spotlessly clean. Behind the old woman stood two gigantic, heavy-bellied young men holding long staves.

Twenty feet from the desk, K'talo signaled for Mallory and Morse to stop. He seemed mildly surprised when Mallory knelt down and touched his forehead to the sand—Laura following his lead—and then hunkered back on his heels and waited, looking humble but entirely composed.

K'talo approached the desk, bobbed his head, and spoke succinctly to the Queen. She raised her eyebrows and turned to Mallory with a look of exaggerated surprise. "My grandson informs me, monsieur, that you speak French," she said in that language.

"Badly, Queen," Mallory said. "Very badly."

"A pity. It is a dignified and melodious language, and deserves to be spoken well. I have always tried to do it proper honor. There is a tradition that the queens of the Konau are educated in Paris. My accent was very poor when I arrived there, many years ago, well before you were born, but I had good teachers and they were able to correct the worst of my deficiencies. Have you been to Paris, monsieur?"

"Yes, Queen."

"What was your business there?"

"One time to arrange a sale of some private papers, two times to arrange that certain, ah, businesses will be caused to close, and one time to kill a man."

"Indeed," the Queen said. "Are you an assassin, monsieur?"

"I am a spy."

Laura didn't make a sound, but Mallory knew she was sighing.

The Queen was unperturbed. "And have you come to spy on us, monsieur?"

"No, Queen. We come to spy on a Monsieur Rauth."

Laura's silent sigh became a silent groan. The Queen looked politely interested. "And upon whose behalf do you mean to spy on Monsieur Rauth?"

"I regret very much, Queen, that I cannot say this."

"No?"

"I gave my word that I would not."

"I see. But this presents a difficulty. Because in the absence of any proof to the contrary, it is simplest for me to believe that you are acting not against, but for Monsieur Anton Rauth. You are American, I believe? He employs a very considerable number of Americans. We have been obliged to . . . entertain them before. And after all, monsieur, you and your companion have come, not to He' Konau, but to our little island, and not openly, but in what I assume was meant to be secrecy. Though I'm afraid that you and the operator of your submarine forgot that water, even at sunset, is transparent. At least for those accustomed to the sea."

"We come in secrecy, Queen, because we require—" Mallory paused. He was running out of French.

"Your Majesty?" Laura said. "If I may be permitted to speak?"

"Certainly, child."

"We required a clandestine base, Your Majesty, shielded from Rauth's view. This is our only business on your island. Since we could not know how you might regard our presence, we hoped to establish ourselves quietly and await a favorable moment to effect an introduction. We greatly regret the trespass."

"You speak quite passably, child," the Queen said, gazing off into the shadowed metal vault. "It would be pleasant to believe you also speak truthfully. What is your name?"

"Laura Morse, Your Majesty."

"And yours, monsieur?"

"Jack Mallory."

The Queen was silent. Her scrawny throat was wrapped in a choker of baroque pink and white pearls. Certainly uncultured and probably worth a fortune, crudely set as they were. Her dark, yellowish skin was freckled with age. Her white hair was drawn back into a neat chignon. Her eyes were immense and thoughtful. Her nose and mouth were broad and unlovely. She was a striking woman nonetheless, erect and elegant, though anyone that thin, Mallory guessed, would certainly be considered ugly by local standards. Well, ugliness hadn't slowed up Victoria any, and it didn't seem to bother this one, either. She wasn't too het up over their presence on her island. In a minute she'd make a decision, and not get too het up over it whichever way it went. She would be, Mallory felt, a formidable ally. Or a formidable enemy. "You would find my name difficult to pronounce," she said absently. "You may continue to call me Your Majesty. I call myself Celeste. I very much enjoyed my time in Paris, and my people forgive me the occasional French affectation. They remind me, my name and my desk and my hat, of a happy time. I took my degree in civil engineering at the École des Beaux-Arts. There were only two women in the school, and no colored persons other than myself, but my family has been quite generous with the École over the years and I was permitted to stay. At that time I had the idea of improving my people's conditions when I returned. When I was older and had begun to attain wisdom, I saw that no improvement was necessary. Now and then we permit ourselves extravagances, like the bridge you crossed to come here, or a set of cisterns

I had built for rainwater. But in the main, we live the life that suits us, on the land that suits us, as we have done for nearly six hundred years. What I mean to say is that we were quite happy here before the fates sent Anton Rauth to pollute our . . . source of inspiration, you could say. Our Notre Dame. Our Westminster Abbey. When Monsieur Rauth arrived I dispatched emissaries to reason with him. They were—not well treated. In return he has sent spies, but somehow"—her eyes grew bright and sad—"these persons always meet with the most regrettable accidents . . . "

"We don't come from He' Konau, Queen," Mallory said. "We go there. With your permission, we go there to, ah—" He gave up. "Laurie," he said in English, "tell her we've come to purify the place."

"Ah, '*purify,*'" Queen Celeste said dreamily. "I am acquainted with the word."

She mused for a moment.

"Our history, what you might call our theology," she continued, "exists mostly in the form of songs. We have one, a very old song called 'The Awaited.' According to the song, one day when our people are beset by enemies, when the Dragon's Throne has been claimed by the impious, a man and a woman will walk out of the sea, the woman silver like the moon, the man golden like the sun, and they will be great warriors, and cleanse the Throne with fire. Of course, in this case, it seems to be the man who is the silver one, and the woman gold. A rather dull gold. But I suppose even a song must be permitted the occasional mistake. Are you a great warrior, Monsieur Mallory?"

"No, Queen."

"No?"

"I was a soldier, Queen, some years. And I must fight, in my work. But I am not a great warrior." He nodded toward Laura. "She is."

"Is this so, Mademoiselle Morse?"

"I am skilled at fighting, Your Majesty," Laura said. "I could not call myself great."

"Indeed. But you would both be great warriors, if you were the Awaited. Ah, the phrase amuses you? You didn't know I was such a superstitious old woman? Yes. I was trained in the sciences, Monsieur Mallory and Mademoiselle Morse. But I have two eyes, not one. And I look out of both. And now, we will make a little experiment, in the scientific manner. A tournament with my own soldiers, whom the Awaited would most certainly be able to defeat. Let us see if you are who I hope you are."

"And if we are not these persons, Queen?" Mallory asked.

"If you are not," she said, "I suppose we will all have our reasons to be very disappointed . . . "

6   *1:57 A.M.*

irectly behind the Queen's desk was a smallish clapboard house that perhaps served as palace. The shutters were closed, and Mallory couldn't tell what was inside. But one thing it did seem to have was a diesel generator. Mallory heard it rattle and then cough to droning life, and then unshielded electric lights, one at each corner of the curved metal roof, glowed a dull mustard, and then a hot yellow, and finally a glaring white that peopled the empty rectangle of sand with shadows. The islanders had gathered outside, he saw, in an unbroken wall. They were no longer solemn, but merry. Mallory had stripped off his wet suit and was standing in the center of the arena in his bathing trunks, and his outlandish color and physique, he could tell, were the subject of a certain amount of hilarity. The islanders had put their knives away and brought out their children. These were naked, the youngest ones shaven-headed, the older ones with shaved temples, leaning into their parents' sides and, after the fashion of excited children everywhere, shifting from foot to foot, resting their bare insteps in turn against their own calves. The Queen sat at her desk with the look of polite interest he'd come to recognize as her habitual expression. One of her enormous guards stood directly behind her. K'talo squatted at the right side of her desk, regarding Mallory as blankly as ever. At the other side of the desk squatted a young woman with enormous shining eyes who might be Celeste's granddaughter. Among a people that valued chubbiness, she was obviously a beauty; her sashes and penang were hard-pressed to contain her charms. She regarded Mallory with obvious delight. Mallory wished he had time to do the same.

At the side of the arena, where she stood between two hulking soldiers, Laura looked from Mallory to the young woman and back again, then discreetly consulted her watch.

The glowing dial read 8:41 P.M.

Before Mallory stood the larger of the Queen's two bodyguards, an absolutely enormous young man. Taller than Nemerov, he looked to weigh about twice Mallory's 160 pounds; the vast belly of a *sumotori* sloped out from his broad, hairless chest. The belly looked unwieldy, but Mallory knew it might well not prove to be. He thought of Berlin, and a fat Samoan MP named Tiegs who had once beaten him in the 100-meter dash. Mallory guessed the young man was not as clumsy as he looked. Queen Celeste, Mallory thought, did not hire unskilled labor. And the advantages of size, strength, and youth were entirely on his side.

"Monsieur Mallory," the Queen called. "You are the challenged party. As such, the choice of weapons is yours. We can offer you the *atto,* the long staff, or your own knife. Or, of course, bare hands and feet."

The axe and staff were out of the question; Mallory had never touched the former and was only vaguely acquainted with the latter. With a knife he was expert, particularly with the wedge-bladed alloy knife that now lay in its ankle sheath at the side of the arena.

But the only way to win a knife fight is to kill your opponent. And a death, Mallory thought, wasn't the best way to begin a working relationship.

"With permission, Queen," he said, "I use my hands."

"Indeed?" she said. "Your bare hands against my Dor Hani?"

"Against who you choose, Queen."

"Indeed. Indeed. Are you prepared to begin?"

"Yes, Queen."

She leaned back and set her fingertips on the polished surface of her desk.

"Begin," she said.

Mallory did not move. He continued to stare musingly at his opponent. He was putting into practice what he once used to tell his cadets in the Army. *Start by looking in their eyes,* he'd say. *Before you grab 'em anywhere else, grab 'em by the soul.* What he saw in Dor Hani's eyes was the naïve pride of a young man who'd never met anyone bigger or stronger than himself, a man who'd never known anyone who didn't fear him. He'd be expecting Mallory to rush him in desperation. And for that reason, Mallory was prepared to stand motionless all night.

The dark face atop the immense body was almost impassive, but soon Mallory noticed the beginnings of uncertainty. The warrior was puzzled—not by Mallory's intentions, which would be clear to any experienced fighter, but by Mallory's calm. The seconds dragged by, and then a full minute. Mallory let a bit of amusement creep into his expression and momentarily let his eyes flick around the crowd. He seemed to be wondering, *Is this the best Pali Konau can do?*

And while he was scanning the crowd, Dor Hani charged.

The Konoese rolled forward like a towering brown wave, not gliding after the fashion of a trained martial artist, but stumping along on wide-spread legs, his center of gravity shifting with every step. It was not how Mallory had been trained to move, but he recognized that it had its advantages. It was dynamic, rather than static, and presented a more complex target with, as far as Mallory could see, no loss of balance. Mallory made no move to meet it, standing as motionless as before while the huge warrior rushed upon him. And then Dor Hani gathered his bulk swiftly into the air and, rising on one columnar leg, unleashed a cyclone kick at Mallory's heart.

But Mallory's heart, as many women could testify, was an elusive thing. The blow that should have smashed his ribs and broken his spine met emptiness. Mallory had dipped smoothly backward and let Dor Hani's foot swing past, faintly hissing as it cut the warm air. For an instant, the big warrior was helpless before his own momentum. He fought to stop himself, twisting sharply back toward Mallory. And now Mallory was there to meet him, rising from his back-bend and sweeping the edge of his foot across the huge Konoese's face.

Performed without restraint, it was a killing blow. Performed with force, it was enough to render even a Dor Hani instantly inert. But Mallory was in no hurry to finish this fight. He needed not just to win, but to win unequivocally; to demonstrate that he had won not by means of a trick or a lucky blow, but by virtue of overwhelming skill. He broke the small, round nose and snapped the sleek head back on its neck, and then he was standing behind Dor Hani in the stance called the Horse, waiting.

He did not wait long. The maddened Dor Hani spun and came after him, guarding his wounded face with a massive left arm and searching for an opening with his right hand. Mallory understood that his own arms were too short to be useful now. Grappling with a man of Dor Hani's strength and skill was out of the question, and to draw near enough to try a fist or elbow strike was to risk being swept up in a lethal embrace. He would have to rely on his long legs. He slammed a left foot into Dor Hani's vast hard stomach and danced away again; he smashed his right instep into the side of the big man's neck. That, he judged, was plenty; he must not seem to be taunting a beaten man. Maddened and despairing, the Konoese charged again, and Mallory whirled and sent the ball of his left foot into the warrior's temple.

The big Konoese hit the sand before Mallory's left foot had returned to earth; Mallory felt the ground quiver beneath him.

Dor Hani stirred once, as if dreaming, and then lay still.

Mallory stepped around the mountainous body, faced the Queen, and knelt.

The crowd was silent again. Mallory saw shock in every Konoese face but three: K'talo's blank gaze had not altered, the young beauty's glee was even more pronounced, and the Queen looked thoughtful.

"Your fighting skills," she said slowly, "are superior to your French."

"Fortunately, Queen."

"Indeed. Indeed. Thank you for your trouble, Monsieur Mallory. Please be seated."

Mallory looked around for the soldiers meant to take charge of him. None came forward. None met his gaze. Half a dozen people who seemed to be Dor Hani's family had clustered around the huge body and were poking it gently and whispering. Mallory heard the young man groan. As he walked across the arena and took a seat beside Laura, cross-legged on the sand, they managed to wrestle the fallen warrior up off the ground. Staggering beneath their burden, they carried him off into the crowd.

The Queen turned to Laura and beckoned her forward. Like Mallory, Laura had stripped down to her swimsuit. He'd never seen her looking skinnier. She walked sedately to the center of the arena and stood where Mallory had stood. The Queen's second guard, nearly as immense as Dor Hani, came out to meet her. He stood relaxed, his massive arms at his sides, but made no pretense of certainty. He was watching Laura closely. Whatever advantage of surprise Mallory had had, Laura would be denied.

"Now, child," the Queen said. "It is your turn to choose. *Atto,* staff, knife, or hands?"

"The *atto,* Your Majesty."

"A weapon you can never have used before. This seems danger-ously close to insolence, child."

"A thousand apologies, Your Majesty. No insolence was intended."

"Do my warriors seem so negligible?"

"I am confident," Laura said, "that Heaven recognizes the right-eousness of our cause. But it shall be as Your Majesty chooses."

"Puh," the Queen said.

She spoke rapidly and an attendant stepped from behind her desk bearing two throwing axes. He walked gravely up to Laura and presented them both; she chose the one nearest her right hand and stood hefting it. The other he gave to the huge young guard before retreating into the silent crowd. Laura swung the axe a few times, bounced it in her palm, and then nodded at the Queen.

The Queen looked neither politely interested nor thoughtful now. She looked tensely alert. Her palms lay flat against her desk as if she were ready to rise.

"Begin," she said again.

It was over.

Mallory didn't quite see what had happened. He doubted anyone had. Laura had almost seemed to flicker out of sight, bending sharply forward—or backward?—at the waist as she did so. And abruptly she was standing beside her opponent, quite still, watching him fall to earth. She held her *atto* reversed; she'd used the handle as a club. Her opponent's axe lay in the sand. After a moment, Laura bent and lay her own axe beside it. Mallory had thought the crowd silent before, but the silence now was so deep that even the waves beyond the ridge seemed to have ceased. Laura rose again and stood facing the Queen.

"Is there any other test," she said in her drab voice, "to which Your Majesty would put me?"

The Queen's eyes did not leave Laura's. "Yes. I believe there is. K'talo?"

"Yes, *grand-mère?*"

"Kill her."

He hesitated the barest instant before saying: "How, *grand-mère?*"

"However it seems best to you, child," the Queen said.

And K'talo was on his feet. In the same motion, his *atto* was in his hand, and then not: it was whistling through the air at Laura's breast. She flickered again—

—and was holding it high over her head. Motionless, expressionless, she held the throwing axe aloft until everyone, even those at the edge of the crowd, had seen it.

Then she knelt and lay it in the sand beside the other two.

There was a soft crash. The Queen's chair had fallen over backward; she was on her feet. Both her thin arms were thrust high into the air. *"Name t'hau!"* she cried in a voice that made the metal roof ring. *"The Awaited have come!"*

Jack Mallory never knew what hit him. There was an arm locked around his throat, a small warm arm, and he was being kissed, kissed by, he saw, a small naked boy, and then by the boy's mother, and then by one of the soldiers who had escorted him and Laura from the beach, the one who'd carried their flippers. He seemed to be surrounded by a foaming surf of brown limbs as wave after wave of Konoese flung themselves upon him. A particularly curvy young woman was hugging his thigh with both arms. His hip was firmly wedged in her cleavage. He was about to fall over, but then his other foot left the ground and he was being hoisted up above the crowd. Everyone was singing. He assumed it was the song of the Awaited. The noise under the metal roof was nearly intolerable. Someone Mallory couldn't see was beating time on his rear end. Looking around, he saw that Laura too had been borne into the air, by a crowd of boys and singing women—the men, he noticed, kept their distance. They were being carried out into the night, the Queen leading the way, striding along like a woman of thirty and clapping in time.

Mallory caught Laura's eye. "So that's what you meant on the beach," he mouthed over the din. "When you said you could take him."

She seemed to nod, though she was being bounced around so much it was hard to tell.

"You figured if he threw the axe, you could catch it. But you wanted to find out for sure. And now you know."

"And now I know," Laura said. "Do you think they'll feed us soon? I'm starving."

It was quite a party.

They were carried across the village and set down, none too carefully, in an irregular open area within a circle of huts. In the middle of the clearing was a long, stone-lined trench that looked to Laura like the kind of thing Texans dug for a barbecue. She'd ask Jack later. Just then he was almost hidden from view by a swarm of Konoese who were alternately petting him, wrestling with him, and making him drink a raw, warm liquor that was a bit, Laura thought, like sweet *sake*. They were making her drink it, too. The men hugged Mallory, felt his muscles, and tried to thrust him off balance. The women kissed and frankly rubbed themselves against him. Each of them held out a cup for him to drink from, then drank themselves. A few of the girls got the idea of feeding him liquor from their own mouths. Mallory didn't seem to mind. The children clambered all over him, squeezing his long, thin nose, tugging at the outlandish curls of hair on his chest and arms, pinching his white skin, and poking at his lean, scarred belly. Everyone was laughing merrily. Mallory might be a legendary, long-awaited hero, but he was clearly also the funniest-looking thing they'd ever seen.

Her own circle of admirers was more sedate, and she didn't think she amused them. More likely she made them nervous. In any case, they were being good sports about it. The hugs she received were quick and cautious. The women around her—the men still hadn't gotten up the gumption to approach—bobbed their heads quickly before presenting their cups to drink from. A few tried to chat in bits of French and English; one or two tried to teach her some sort of drinking game that involved her patting numerical sequences out on her knees. Laura was getting quite drunk, and didn't think she made a very apt pupil. The Konoese were a seafaring people, she thought vaguely, and perhaps those who lived or died by their navigational skills tended to be good with numbers. It was very strange to see Jack tickling the small girls and swatting the small boys and gently disengaging those who were trying, in the spirit of scientific inquiry, to get his trunks off. She remembered now that he was the second-oldest of seven. Perhaps it wasn't so surprising that he seemed to get on well with kids. She found herself getting a bit depressed. This might be a very nice party, but she didn't care for parties. She wasn't fond of being touched by strangers, either, or of seeing quite so many pretty young women rubbing up against Jack. Dor Hani had awoken and was sitting, with his nose poulticed and his eyes swollen and one immense arm draped around his conqueror, pouring liquor alternately down Jack's throat and his own. He was singing cheerily in a sweet, high voice. Everyone seemed to be having a lovely time except her.

The heat had been steadily increasing from the coals in the central trench. It was full night now, and stars and the red coals provided the only light. This seemed to be sufficient for the Konoese. They began pulling covered clay pots from the trench with hooked sticks and prying them open. The savory scents of spiced fish and stewed fruit filled the air. Everyone got a broad, shallow bowl brimming with food, everyone except Mallory and Laura, who as honored guests were apparently expected to eat from the plates of their hosts. There was a constant line of people before each of them, holding their bowls out beguilingly. It was delicious, if a bit fruity for Laura's taste. She wished she had a fork. There seemed to be a technique for eating neatly with one's hands, and she and Mallory were the only ones who didn't have it. Everyone was sitting cross-legged on the ground, even the Queen, who had changed into a penang and sashes and, like the rest of the adults, was being steadily assaulted by the smaller children as she ate.

How late was it, anyway? The women had given up on her as a conversationalist and were chatting amongst themselves. A little band was playing: two wooden flutes, a series of scored bamboo tubes that were alternately knocked and rasped together, a rattle made of cowries, and a waterproof aluminum guitar. She'd heard they made such things, for sailors. The older children and younger adults were dancing, and a few mock fights had broken out. They were, Laura saw, reenacting the events of the evening, sucking their bellies and cheeks in to look thin, giving a passable imitation of Jack's appraising squint, and of a fish-eyed gaze that was probably meant to be hers. They took turns playing Dor Hani and being knocked down; they rose in pairs from imaginary water, wearing imaginary scuba masks, and looked surprised; they flung imaginary *atta* and caught them, and flourished them proudly aloft. The movements became more and more stylized. By the end of the evening, Laura guessed, they would have become a dance, to be danced at future feasts in commemoration of this night. Laura sipped from yet another proffered cup and was abruptly quite content, as well as quite drunk enough to pass out. There were already a number of men and women quietly snoring in the shadows. One nearby woman was particularly fat, and Laura briefly considered using her as a pillow. She noticed a young man standing before her, gazing expectantly into her eyes. How long had he been there? He held a copper bowl filled with water. He was going around pouring a little water over each person's hands, to clean them. Laura extended her hands and shivered at the touch of the cool water. Perhaps the feast was over. The Queen was standing. Mallory was getting, a bit unsteadily, to his feet. Laura did the same and stood there trying not to sway. She felt a light touch on her shoulder and looked down as a teenage girl pressed something into her dripping palm, head-bobbed, and scurried away.

It was her own knife. They'd fetched it from the ankle sheath on her wet suit, back in the arena. It lay glinting in her hand.

She saw they'd given Jack his knife as well.

The Queen was holding one palm negligently in the air. The crowd was silent again.

When the Queen spoke, she spoke no more than half a dozen sentences of Konoese. She spoke firmly but with no special emphasis, pivoting slowly back and forth as her eyes roamed the crowd. When she had done, there was a brief pause, and then she turned to Mallory and Laura. "I told them," she said in French, "that there is no need for a speech. We know what hour has arrived. The Awaited hour. We know what we must do. We must fight. And you have come to join our fight."

"Yes, Queen," Mallory said.

"Do you fear death?"

"Not at the moment, Queen."

"Perhaps tomorrow?"

"Probably tomorrow."

"Then it is well we speak tonight. *K'talo,*" she called.

"Yes, *grand-mère?*" came the dull voice from the darkness.

"Pledge."

K'talo emerged from the shadows. He'd sat beside his sister through the entire feast, eating quietly, drinking little, and taking no part in the singing and dancing. He seemed calm and glum as before. He stood before Mallory, pulled the short knife from his belt, and offered it butt-first. Mallory accepted it with a shallow bow. Something more seemed to be expected of him, so he offered his own knife. K'talo took it, then lifted his chin and indicated his own throat with a stubby finger. After a moment, Mallory reached out and touched it with the flat of K'talo's blade. K'talo gently took Mallory's wrist and turned it so that the glittering edge rested against his brown throat, just over the carotid artery. They stood motionless like that for a moment. Then Mallory lowered K'talo's knife and stood still as K'talo reached out and set the hollow alloy blade against Mallory's throat. K'talo returned Mallory's knife, accepted his own, touched the flat of it to his forehead, and turned to Laura. The ceremony was repeated. She noted with approval the complete steadiness of K'talo's hand. Her knife felt cool, even in the warm air.

"Now you are my children," the Queen said. "And what I have is yours. And who harms you, harms me."

Mallory began to kneel again. "Oh, stop flinging yourself about," the Queen said. "We don't do that here. Get up and help us finish the wine."

There was general laughter, to which Mallory responded with an amiably upthrust middle finger—they understood that, all right, and laughed harder—and then the music began again and he strolled over to Laura, idly swinging his knife. He held out a hand and she gave him her knife as well. He caught a passing boy by the elbow and in English said, "Here. The Awaited Ones say go put these damn things away." The boy touched both knives to his forehead and trotted off. Mallory regarded Laura. "You don't look drunk. But you must be."

"I am," she said.

"Seems like we're pledged."

"We have initiated contact," she said, "and are developing a working relationship."

"I like this initiating contact. I like it better now than I'll probably like it in the morning. But this isn't really your kind of throwdown, is it, Laurie? How you doing? Think you'll—"

He broke off. K'talo's sister had tapped his shoulder with a dainty brown finger.

The tiny beauty was the only woman under the age of fifty who hadn't been nuzzling Mallory all evening. Her heart-shaped face was not gleeful now, but imperious. The firelight gleamed on her plump shoulders and firm, round chin. She looked levelly at Laura, then up at Mallory. She held out her hand and in a small, clear voice said, *"Allez se promener avec moi."*

"I believe the princess wants to take a walk with you," Laura said.

"I guess," Mallory said. "Well. I guess I'll talk to you a little later, then."

"See you," she said.

Mallory took the young princess's hand, and she led him off into the night.

Laura watched the girl's round haunches switching serenely from side to side until they vanished into the darkness. Jack's silvery hair caught the firelight a bit longer. They seemed to be heading toward the beach. She'd seen couples wandering in that direction all night. How old was the princess, anyway? Laura touched the corners of her eyes to see if she could feel lines there. If the girl was eighteen, and she was twenty-eight, and eighteen as a percentage of twenty-eight was . . . She noticed that her neighbor was standing silently beside her, offering yet another cup of liquor.

"You really are too, too kind," she said, and drank.

Mallory waded out into the warm ocean waist-deep, dunked his head, and scrubbed his fingers through his hair and over his face. He stood again and brushed his hands down his wet ribs and arms. He'd gotten that damn luau-food all over him. He stood with hands on hips and eyes closed, breathing evenly and waiting for the sea to stop spinning. Behind him, the princess waited, the water swirling around her thighs. Conversation had been flagging a bit. In halting French, they had established that her name was Nilai, that she could not pronounce his first name and preferred to call him Mallory, that she was a princess, that she lived in her grandmother's house, that she was beautiful, that he lived in New York in America, that he lived in a tall building, that he knew how to swim, that he did not know Cliff

Richard, and that he did not like Cliff Richard. Now she politely asked, "It is because you have drunk that you go into the sea?"

"I have drunk, certainly," he said, "and that is why I bathe my head. Why do you laugh?"

"That you are in the water, to try so hard to be not intoxicated."

"I believe any man would be intoxicated who drinks this night all that I drink."

"Yes, but you try to be not intoxicated, and that is humorous. If you have drunk so much why do you not sleep? Half the men are sleeping now. It is because you have drunk that you go into the sea with your clothes?"

"These clothes are, ah, they are for going in the sea with. This is a *bathing suit.*"

"For what reason does one wear it?"

"For no reason, I suppose. To be not unclothed. It is a, a law."

"The salt will discommode you when it dries."

"I guess I'll wash it then," he said wearily, in English. "Why, Nilai, what do you wear when you go swimming?"

"I go in the sea like this," she said. "Like anyone."

Mallory turned and saw her standing on the shore, pulling off the sash that covered her right breast. It bounced free, and she dropped the sash on her penang, which he now saw was already lying in the sand. Only then did Mallory notice the inky triangle of shadow beneath her smooth belly, and the unbroken line of her gleaming hips. She dropped her other sash on the beach, gave her bosom a complacent little pat, and waded out to meet him.

"Like this," she said.

"Your method possesses many advantages," Mallory said.

Nilai set her palms on Mallory's chest and looked up at him, her eyes amused. "I begin to be weary a little of French. And you?"

"Hon," Mallory said in English, setting his hands on her chubby waist, "if I never hear another goddamned stinking word of French again, it's all right with me."

"Perhaps we should speak in our own languages?" she said in Konoese.

"Whatever you say, hon. Just look at you. All of you. Your boy-friends aren't ever cold at night, are they?"

"Yes, it's better in our own languages. So you are the Awaited. I must say I'm surprised. A couple of ignorant savages with no manners. Who spill food on themselves like babies. Who kneel in the dirt like clowns. And such scrawny, ugly devils. Ugly as old sticks."

"Whatever you say, hon. Go on talking. I like it." He squeezed her breast gently. "Lordy. Back home we got an old song, too. It's called 'Built for Comfort.' "

"But you have been sent to lead us. And soon, perhaps tomorrow, *grand-mère* will send you against Rauth."

"I wonder if you folks kiss on the mouth here, or whether that's just some Western deal you don't care for. I mean, I'm willing to learn, but just how do you people get this kind of thing started?"

"It is a holy undertaking, but desperately dangerous. And I cannot say that I myself am hopeful. I would like you to have one night of true happiness before you die. So that at least before you perish, you will have known—"

"*Damn* but you Konoese make a cute noise talking," Mallory said, and kissed her.

Laura had to admit the hut was comfortable. It was furnished with two fragrant, springy beds of bound dried reeds. They were all right, once you got over the feeling of lying on a giant broom. The dirt floor was pounded hard as linoleum. The broad woven leaves that made up the walls and ceiling gave off a faint, surprising odor, like very old leather. Beside each bed lay a small basin of water, and, on a flat-tish wooden bowl, a pyramid of something that looked like bread-fruit. Everything was very tidy. They seemed to be a tidy people, at least when they were sober. Laura liked having a sheet over her, even in warm weather, but she was used to bedding down in all kinds of conditions, and she lay on the reed mat and was soon asleep.

The noise seemed to wake her almost at once. She was instantly alert, with her knife in her hand. She'd set it down close to her head, as she usually did in such situations. Someone, she knew, was moving around outside. Nearby, but not too nearby. The noise was coming from the beach. Perhaps fifty yards away. A young person's voice.

A young woman . . .

Laura relaxed and set her knife back down on the floor by her head. She'd been woken by the sound, rising and falling and rising again, of a young woman's pleasure. And now and then, a soft monosyllable in a Texan drawl.

The glowing dial of her watch read 1:57 A.M.

Five hours and sixteen minutes since he first saw her, Laura thought. *He's slowing up.*

She turned over and went back to sleep.

7 *Squid Ink and Blood*

Mallory woke a bit before seven in the morning. He drank from the water in the basin by his head and decided he was too hungover to go back to sleep. It didn't surprise him that the mat on the other side of the hut was empty. Laurie never did sleep much when there was a job on. His skin and hair were stiff with dried sea-salt. So were his trunks, as Nilai had predicted. He was too dehydrated to piss. His gut was all right, though. Whatever that fruit liquor stuff was, it was kinder to you than bourbon. He used the last of the water to wash his face, stretched, and went outside.

They'd left the sled, he saw, next to the guest hut, or wherever it was he and Laurie had spent the night. Before it, neatly folded, were his and Laurie's wet suits. Atop the wet suits were their diving belts and knives, back in their ankle sheaths. He strapped the knife on, took the keys from his diving belt, and opened the sled. Inside, Laurie's toilet kit was open; she'd taken out her sunblock. It was a good idea, and Mallory did the same. Everything else seemed undisturbed. He assumed Celeste or K'talo had given their equipment a good going-over, but they'd put things back the way they'd found them. He took out his Browning and the silencer, checked the clip, and closed the sled again. Fitting the silencer to the small gun's muzzle, he walked down to the water's edge.

The village was silent, and no one seemed to be around except a clutch of women about a quarter-mile down the shore. A few villagers were still peacefully lying where they'd fallen between the huts. He didn't intend to disturb them. He looked across the lagoon at the western arm of the atoll. The area seemed uninhabited, as the briefing packet had said. He picked a stand of trees about a hundred yards off and stared into them until he was satisfied no one was walking around between or behind. They bore clusters of that breadfruit-looking stuff he'd seen by his mat back in the hut, the small clusters about the size of someone's head; the big clusters maybe twice that. He raised the Browning two-handed, sighted on a big cluster, and fired.

Nothing. Just the silenced report—like the soft grunt of a man struck in the belly—and, a hundred yards off, a stirring of leaves. The first shot he took with a silencer was usually high. He always overcorrected for the silencer's weight. The sleepers behind him had not stirred. The women down the shore hadn't seemed to notice. He raised the gun again, took in a breath, and squeezed off another round. The distant bunch of fruit jerked and swung wildly. He fired again and it dropped from the tree. All right then. He picked a small cluster of fruit and shot it free. He picked another and missed. He steadied himself, picked another target, and knocked it down. He reloaded, knocked down three more and was aware that Laurie was approaching. He lowered his gun and turned as she walked up. "Morning, Jack," she said. "That must be a hundred yards. Your head can't be that bad."

"Morning. Been worse. How's yours? Or did you bring it all up last night?"

Laura's martial arts training had included a daunting array of bodily disciplines. Her muscle control was exceptional, she was effectively double-jointed, she was able to slow her heartbeat and suppress her breathing, and she could effortlessly and noiselessly bring up anything she regretted, upon reflection, having eaten or drunk.

She nodded. "Oh, I got rid of it, of course. I wasn't going to sleep with all that rotgut in me, not when we'd just started a job. But it's funny the way it worked out. I thought I'd picked myself a nice private spot, but as soon as I'd started, a couple of the women walked in on me. So I started making faces, you know, and noises, as if I was doing it because I couldn't help it. I figured, they already think we're peculiar enough. And it turned out to be a very popular thing for me to do. At the feast they'd thought I was standoffish and sort of snobby, but once they found me puking in the bushes, they decided I was one of the girls, and they laughed and stroked my back and cooed at me, and this morning we're all great buddies. We've been cleaning up around the barbecue thing and having a good gossip."

"That's good."

"They were very anxious to tell me what an honor it was that the princess had picked my man to spend the night with. They'd heard outsiders were funny about that sort of thing, but they wanted to assure me that it really put me in the Konoese social register. So I explained that I was very grateful, but that you were really *quite* old, and not good for much anymore, and I was just afraid you might have been a disappointment to Her Highness."

"Hope I wasn't," Mallory said. "Wish I could remember. Lordy, was I stinking. 'Course, I don't think she was stone-cold sober herself."

"What's this, target practice?"

"Yeah. Been a while since I did any shooting, but it doesn't look like I've forgotten how yet."

"Think you'll be done soon?"

"I'm done now."

"Good. Put the gun away. The Queen's waiting."

The white clapboard house behind the arena had dark green shutters and a roof covered with clay-colored asbestos tiles. Inside it was divided into two middle-sized rooms. The one in which they sat was a sort of throne room, or at any rate a living room dominated by a large brocaded armchair. At the far end of the room was a drafting table bearing half-finished plans for what seemed to be a row of broad flat greenhouses. Mallory guessed it was a solar still for desalinating seawater. He'd seen one once at a hashish plantation on St. Kitts. A row of dining chairs stood along one wall, a three-seater sofa faced the throne, and a low coffee table stood in between. The other room seemed to be off-limits, but judging from the noises and smells, part of it was a kitchen. The room was flooded with sunlight, but the electric lamps had been lit, perhaps to make the two citified Americans feel at home. They had just finished a breakfast of tern's-egg omelets—a bit fishy, but good—a basket of the chewy local bread with guava jam, and delicious black coffee in dainty, gold-rimmed cups. The coffee, the Queen explained, was grown on the far side of the atoll. The original beans had been a gift from "a Colombian friend" who seemed to be that country's minister of finance. Laura and Mallory sat side by side on the sofa, the Queen sat on the big chair, and K'talo sat cross-legged on the rug beside them. He'd had a cup of coffee, but had declined food. He wasn't adding much to the merriment. "Thank you, Your Majesty," Laura said, setting down her fork with some regret. "That was delicious."

"Yes, Queen," Mallory said. "You have a very pretty house. Palace," he amended.

"Thank you. It is a palace, of sorts. For official business. My house is out in the village, just a thatched hut like the others you saw. I never grew fond of sleeping in a bed under a plaster roof. And now, if you don't mind, perhaps we may spare a moment for business?"

The stocky Konoese rose silently, opened the side door to the hidden room, and stepped inside. In a moment he was back, followed by a small boy who stacked the breakfast dishes on a tin tray, wiped the table with a clean rag, and returned to the kitchen. K'talo now held a roll of yellow cloth. He swept a palm over the table to make sure it was clean and dry, then lay the cloth down on one end and carefully unrolled it.

It was a map of He' Konau, drawn on the yellow cotton in some dark, purplish substance. Mallory examined it, then reached into the plastic case he'd left beside his chair and pulled out the relief map Analysis had prepared from U-2 photo output, a diazo print scribed with fine, brownish relief lines. He lay it beside the Konoese map.

Aside from color, there wasn't much difference between them.

"That is a very fine map, Queen," Mallory said.

"Thank you, monsieur," she said. "It took quite a bit of reconnaissance. Quite a number of exploratory journeys. Not all of them peaceful, I'm afraid."

"That is a very fine map. Is it drawn in squid ink?"

"You could say," the Queen said sadly, "that it is drawn in the blood of our young men. But yes, the actual substance is squid ink. I see our maps are largely in agreement. The landing place for helicopters here. The subterranean dock here. Observation posts here, here, here, and all through here. Indicated by crosses. What appear to be ventilators for a very considerable underground facility along the shore. Indicated by diamonds. And here a long window—over thirty meters—that Rauth cut into the slope for, we suspect, the sake of the view."

"That is our own thought also."

"Your map was prepared from aerial photos? Yes. And you have in addition prepared a plan of assault?"

Mallory considered the extent of his French and gave up. He glanced at Laura. She said, "A submarine approach, Your Majesty, just here. At low tide, the spot would seem to be half-hidden from this observation post, and fully hidden from all the others. The post is one possible point of entry. These ventilators are another. We were to install miniature acoustic surveillance devices in places where they would not immediately be detected, and then return. The devices broadcast to a recording unit which we had hoped to install here."

"And you would carry out this assault yourselves, just the two of you?"

"Not an assault, Majesty. A penetration. We hoped to depart as quietly as we came, leaving the devices in place. Based on the information they provide, our employer, who commands considerable resources, was to devise a plan for further action."

"You would make this 'penetration' when?"

"The first practicable evening, at, ah, sunset. At one time," Laura said dryly, "we believed this to be a good moment to approach."

"You actually meant to approach with the sun in the sky," the Queen said, shaking her head. "Well, it is understandable. *N'kaluu* are blind. You eat poorly and you live by electric light and if a thing is not shown you in the full of noon, you cannot see it."

"What are *n'kaluu?*" Mallory said.

"You were *n'kaluu.* Outsiders. Now you are my children. And you would travel to He' Konau how? Swimming underwater the entire four miles? That is quite a swim, even for us."

"We were to be towed by vehicle you saw, the undersea sled," Laura said. "It travels at six knots, and the engines are designed to be quite silent."

K'talo sighed. "We hear them," he said. "Yesterday we hear the engines the first time you make, switch them on. We hear your—" He made a gesture of submerging. "Your boat you come on, for many miles, even before we see the bubbles. You put your ear in the water and you hear. Rauth will stand and wait for you when you come, as we waited. And this is your planning?"

"Speak nicely to your brother and sister," the Queen said. She rose, saying to Laura and Mallory, "No, please don't get up. You are always leaping up and flinging yourselves down. You must all have very strong legs in America. K'talo will help you to refine your plan, and give you such assistance as you require. But I must mention one further matter before I go." She paused with a hand on the knob of the kitchen door. "You were shooting off a pistol this morning, Monsieur Mallory?"

"I hope I did not disturb you, Queen."

"It was a very quiet pistol. You planned to bring it to He' Konau?"

"Yes, Queen."

"I am afraid this is impossible. He' Konau is *tapu*. I cannot permit you to bring a firearm, an unclean weapon, to such a place. You may bring your knives, or any weapon in our armory. But gunpowder and lead are impermissible."

"Queen, if we must—"

"Monsieur Mallory. The Throne has already suffered unspeakable desecration. I cannot expect you to understand, but neither can I be party to further defilement. Not even to ensure your success, or your safety. I would not permit it in order to save my own life. While we ate, I had your pistols and ammunition removed to a safe place, as well as your limpet mines. They will be returned to you in good order when you leave us. I am afraid the point is not— what is that wonderful American word? *Negotiable.* I do apologize. Good morning, monsieur and mademoiselle. I hope to see you at dinner."

The Queen slipped through the door and closed it quietly behind her.

There was a brief silence. Laura and Mallory glanced at each other. K'talo regarded them both without enthusiasm.

Then he rolled up the map and stood with a grunt.

In flawless British English he said, "Let's go up to the ridge and have a squint at our target."

They walked in silence into the brilliant sunshine, which seemed to wrap around them like a hot silk scarf. "Over there," K'talo said, jerking his chin. "Up on the ridge. We can get a decent view of the shore without being seen. And I don't want to tell you your jobs, but—"

"We'll keep out of sight," Mallory said. "I'm guessing Rauth surveils your island, and he doesn't need to see a couple of white faces here."

"Might get him thinking," K'talo agreed. "Couldn't help noticing that knife of yours last night. Makes ours look a bit sick. Mind if I have a look?"

"Sure." Bending, Mallory slipped it from the sheath and handed it over.

"This couldn't be Army issue," K'talo said, examining it. "Looks expensive."

"It's one piece of titanium for the handle and blade both. Hollow-ground," Mallory said. "Cutting edge's a surgical steel fillet. Handle's dipped in a little neoprene to make it sticky, then sanded down to keep it from getting too sticky. Grooves there to let your hand breathe. Fella I know in Brooklyn makes 'em. He does custom work for Special Forces guys."

"Light," said K'talo, hefting it. He tossed it away sidearm. The gesture seemed careless, but the knife whirled uphill along a smooth arc and landed with a soft *pok* in one of the trees at the crest of the ridge. "Not too light," he decided. "It's awfully nice."

"I get back to New York, I'll have him send you one."

"Thanks," K'talo said. "Sorry about the guns."

"We'll manage," Mallory said.

"We're not going to shoot our way in," Laura said, "and I doubt we'd be able to shoot our way out. If it gets to where we need guns, we're probably dead anyhow."

"I tried to talk to Granny, but she won't be told. She likes you, you know. She hates bloody Americans, but she really does like you two."

"What's she got against Americans?"

"Bad food, bad clothes, bad politics, and she hates the language. That's why she left us three to get on with it. Because she knows I couldn't do my work in French, and she didn't want to have to listen to a lot of English. She speaks it, all right, but she pretends she can't. Vanity. Her accent's rotten, you see."

"How come you didn't speak English yesterday evening? She wasn't there."

"Didn't know if you were worth speaking to."

"And now you think we are?"

"Now it doesn't matter what I think."

"Sounds like you got a little bit of a London accent."

K'talo's stolid face softened. "Three years at the LSE," he said wistfully. "Granny and I fought a bit when it was time for me to go to Paris. I wanted to go to New York, Washington—hell, even Moscow. Someplace where people *do* things. We compromised on London. And that's a good town. That's an awfully good town. I didn't care for the other students much. The posh ones ignored me because I was a wog, or made up to me because I was a prince, even if I was just a little flyspeck one. The middle-class ones kept asking me, very politely, about our *culture*. And all of 'em kept trying to find out whether I was a darky or Chinese or a mix or what. I told them I was a full-blooded Konoese and that I could trace my ancestry back a lot further than any of them could, and they'd say, Yes, but what are you *really?* No, I didn't care for my fellow students. But at night I'd go to Soho, and down there I wasn't Prince Whatsit. There I was just another spade in a sharp suit. They called me Keith," he said reminiscently. "They never quite got the hang of *K'talo*. They called me

Keith, and we had ourselves some times." He shrugged. "Then Granny got bad, and I had to come home till she was on her feet again. Never did get my degree. Don't miss it. Don't even miss London much anymore, except for sometimes. Here we are. Under that branch is a good spot. Mind your head."

Up on the crest of the ridge, one of the trees had been knocked sideways by some long-ago accident and continued growing that way, writhing along the ground like a snake. It was the tree into which K'talo had thrown Mallory's knife. The meaty, glossy leaves sprouted thickly from its branches, making concealment easy. The earth behind the undulating trunk was packed hard and polished smooth. A well-used observation post. K'talo unrolled the map on the ground, hunkered down beside it, and motioned for Mallory and Laura to join him. Then he nudged back the leaves as if parting lace curtains. Mallory felt his gut tighten, not unpleasurably, as he looked across the glittering water and got his first good look at He' Konau.

The island was dark, naked stone that seemed to drink up all the light. It rose from the sea in a single mighty sweep, its flanks scored and creased like a rhino's hide. The rim of the volcano's cone was jagged and lopsided, and it was easy to see where a vast section had fallen inward. It still didn't look like any chair Mallory ever saw. The steel dome within the crater was invisible from where they were. The shore was dotted with covered ventilators like huge steel mushrooms, perhaps a dozen of them. Two-thirds of the way up the slope, the single slotlike window gleamed like a hundred-foot scar. It would command a good view of both the sunset and Pali Konau. "No one's ever lived there, of course," K'talo said. "Too sacred. You have to fast and purify yourself before you can even set foot on it for the solstice ceremonies. But there used to be trees, turtles, some lizards. All gone. When Rauth moved in, he grubbed up all the trees and fired all the brush. Killed everything that'd been there. Sound tactics, mind. Without trees for cover, the island's a lot harder to approach. Even the bloody birds won't go there now. And of course, we haven't celebrated the solstice for a couple of years, not properly. You know there's only three ways in, right?"

"Four," Laura said. "Dock, helipad, ventilators, and observation posts."

"Forget the ventilators. They're armored."

"We've brought tools."

"And electrified. We tried one in the spring. 'Fraid there wasn't much left of the fellow with the hacksaw."

"We got rubber wet suits," Mallory said, thinking aloud. "And they come with gloves."

"I don't like it, Jack," Laura said.

"Well, it's not real likable," he said. "We'd been thinking mostly of the ventilators, K'talo, or the observation posts. The helipad's sort of up out of reach. Take too long to climb both ways, and with no cover. And we figured the dock's probably the most heavily guarded place in the complex."

"That's right," K'talo said. "You got gadgets we haven't, and you can outfight us. But I don't think you can outsneak us, and we've lost some good people trying the dock. I don't advise it. Or the ventilators."

"Thing is, use the observation posts and you've likely got to take out a guard. And we wanted to be in and out without anybody knowing."

"We've made some drawings of the ventilators. Maybe you can figure something. But Granny's an engineer, and she couldn't. I think you'll find you've got to do a guard."

"Well, we hoped we wouldn't, but we thought we might."

"Suit yourselves. And remember, it'll take luck just to get that far. The water round He' Konau is swept by radar all night. We've got no way of knowing if Rauth uses sonar, too, but we reckon he does. And he plays one little trick it cost us a bit to discover. He's got the island miked. The whole bloody island, and the sea around it—roving shotguns and parabolics, Granny says. Rauth's four and a quarter nautical miles away, but if you were to shout right now? He'd hear you. Not much doubt he heard last night's do, but he probably just thought what you did. There's those Konoese, being simple and childlike again."

"Aw, it wasn't so different from parties back home. Except where I come from, we generally have the fights at the end of the night instead of the beginning. Listen, K'talo. Rauth's got one of the biggest private arsenals in the world. How come he hasn't cleaned out Pali Konau like he did He' Konau? How come you guys're still here?"

"Because of Granny," K'talo said. "You wouldn't think it, but she broke some hearts in Paris, back in the twenties, and she was at school with some pretty prominent blokes. Edmund Torberg, of the newspaper Torbergs. Lord Henry Gossard. Horacio Alba, the Colombian minister fellow. They might not've won her away from Grandpa, but none of 'em have forgotten her. And if Rauth ever tried to do to us what he did to the sea turtles, Granny's old suitors would raise holy hell on four continents. Rauth couldn't stand the racket, not with the sorts of things he's up to. So it's a standoff."

"Rauth could sweep this island in ninety minutes. How would anyone ever know?"

"Shortwave. Granny sends for the newest model every few years. And Lord Henry's a radio buff. Life peers have a lot of time on their hands."

"You know," Laura said, "if we're caught, Rauth might guess you helped us. He might lose his temper and forget about Lord Henry."

"We'll take our chances."

"The Throne means that much to you?" Mallory said.

"The Throne's a lump of rock with a hole in the top," K'talo said.

"Really," Laura said.

"My grandmother's the one who believes all that hugger-mugger about the Dragon and the Awaited. She truly does think you two have been sent to us. The rest of us—most of us, anyway—just go along. Most of us, you drop us in Kansas and we'd be Baptists in a week. Drop us in Delhi and we'd be Hindu. Me, I don't believe much of anything."

"Now, what if she heard you talking like that?" Mallory said.

"She knows what I think," K'talo said. "You'd better get it through your head that Granny knows just about everything. She thinks it's a dirty shame I'm not pious, and she thinks I'll do my job anyway, and she thinks you two are straight. And that's the only reason you're not dead now."

"Well then, I guess it's a good thing she thinks we're straight."

"Listen, Mallory. Granny's bad patches have been getting worse. And she won't go off-island to a proper hospital. She might look fit, but she hasn't much time. My mum drowned when I was a kid. My dad's a commoner. My sister's a little goose, as you've no doubt found out for yourself. We've all talked it through, and when Granny's gone, I'm king. There's twenty-seven islands in the Konau Archipelago. They'll be my job soon. Everything I've ever cared about, everyone I've ever loved, is right here. And Rauth's standing in our light. We can't hold our heads up while he's around. That's what matters, not some tune out of the old hymnal. Granny told me I'm to serve you, so I will. She told me to be your brother, so I am. If you two are who you say you are, I'm ready to die for you. If you're two of Rauth's people playing some bloody game, I'll kill you. I won't be quick about it. I'll turn you into something the buzzards wouldn't touch. Are you paying attention, Mallory? If you let Granny down, you're mine."

Mallory eased back from the lookout, climbed to his feet, pulled his knife from the tree's waxy trunk, and wiped it on the leg of his swimsuit. Tucking it back in its sheath, he said, "I get back to New

York in one piece, I'll send you a knife. Meanwhile, do us a favor, all right? Keith? Learn some goddamned manners."

K'talo rolled up the map and neatened the edges of the roll. He brushed a few crumbs of dirt from it and rose.

"We'll get along," he told Mallory. "Let's go back to the house and make a plan."

8   *Zentrale*

Mallory lay with his head beside Laura's feet and gazed up at the stars. They glided past his face with a series of smooth forward lunges. Swift and almost completely silent, the longboat was approaching the drop point off He' Konau. The oars, though unmuffled, made no more noise than a spoon being dipped into soup. The only sound was the soft distant hubbub of the surf, growing closer every minute. He lay on his side, already wearing a single scuba tank. It wasn't too comfortable, but there was no room in the narrow boat for two people to suit up. And besides, neither Mallory, Laura, nor the oarsmen wanted to risk rising even to their knees in the boat and being picked up by Rauth's radar. As it was, the oarsmen rowed prone—it was apparently something any Konoese soldier could do with ease—so that the low-slung boats and their occupants remained lower than the tallest waves, clinging to the surface of the sea like water striders. It was four minutes to eleven. The previous night had been the night of the new moon, but they'd guessed that Rauth's men might be more vigilant on perfectly black nights and had waited an extra twenty-four hours.

He heard K'talo whisper, "Almost at your stop. Ready?"

"Sure," Mallory said.

"I'll hold here until 0400. After that, it gets too light. If I don't see your signal by then, I'll be back here tomorrow at 2230. We'll have at least three people watching the island twenty-four hours from now on. You signal, any time, from anywhere on this side of the cone, and we'll get it. Try not to blind us with that little laser gadget when you do."

"I'll try." He reached over the side and rinsed his mask in the water, then slipped the strap over his head.

"Miss Morse?"

"Ready," came the cool, quiet voice from the darkness.

"We're about two hundred yards from shore. Any closer and I think we'll be in range of their mikes, so you swim from here. We've got your heads pointed straight at the cove. Bear right like we said and follow the reef in. Clear?"

"Yes," Laura said.

K'talo was silent a moment. Then he whispered, "I don't always talk nicely to my sister. I guess I don't always talk nicely to my brother, either. If you were wrong 'uns, you'd have got ugly by now. Here." Mallory felt a small, dense weight on his chest. He picked it up and felt the familiar checkered grip. His Browning. "Only three rounds left in the clip, but I couldn't get at the ammo. Good luck, Jack."

Mallory zipped the gun into the waterproof bag at his hip.

"Luck to you, Keith," he murmured. "See you soon, I hope. And thanks."

He slipped his mouthpiece in and adjusted the regulator, then reached up and lightly took hold of Laurie's ankle. She flexed it twice: her regulator and mask were in place. He tapped her ankle with a forefinger once, twice, three times. On the third tap he rolled to starboard as she rolled to port and they were, almost without a splash, in the water.

Their weight belts were fully loaded, and they let themselves sink limply to the bottom, trying to create no commotion that might show on Rauth's sonar. If he had a sonar. For the thousandth time Mallory considered how much of a spy's day was spent evading imaginary dangers, while often failing to prepare for real ones. The water was barely two fathoms, and in perhaps twenty seconds Mallory felt the cool sand against his left palm, and then his right knee, and then he was lying on his stomach on the bottom. A slim, hard hand found his shoulder. Good. They were still side by side. The blackness at the bottom was almost complete. It was unpleasantly like being buried alive. Mallory was somewhat claustrophobic—it was one of the reasons he hated submarines—and for a moment he found himself transfixed by pure animal panic, the sense of being trapped under a great weight. It was a moment he'd expected and knew how to deal with. He slipped his hand inside his wet suit and touched his own chest, feeling the beat of his heart. He took a deep, slow breath and pictured the afternoon sun slanting through a shop window at 15th and Armory in Corpus Christi. Through the dusty glass he could see a hex wrench kit, the enameled turquoise lid open, and a row of silvery junction boxes, and behind them, a sheet of pale-yellow pegboard. The hardware store had closed when he was twelve, and he didn't know why the thought of it always steadied him. He took a second breath and a third, and then he was ready to move. Laurie's hand was still on his shoulder. She and Gray were the only ones who knew the trouble he had with enclosed spaces. It was probably the only thing about him Laurie had never made fun of. He found and gently pressed the back of her arm: *I'm all right. Let's go.* Gloved hands outstretched, they began to feel their way along the sandy bottom toward the hook-shaped reef that would lead them to the beach.

Covering the six hundred feet to shore took them fourteen minutes. Twice they paused as a searchlight swept overhead and the water around them became a blinding, milky blur that stabbed at their dark-adapted eyes and left wriggling red and blue trails across their vision. The odds of anyone seeing them through the surface dazzle were slight, but the reflexive urge to hunker down was strong. And besides, there was plenty of time for this phase of the operation, and no point in taking chances to gain a minute or two. Each time the searchlight passed, the lava outcropping toward which they swam appeared as a spreading undersea shadow, and soon they slipped inside it and could swim more vigorously. When the water was no more than four feet deep, they turned off their regulators, pulled off their masks and fins, and shrugged out of their scuba tanks. They left them side by side on the sea-bottom near a beaklike corner of the outcropping, which would hopefully serve as an arrow to point the way to their equipment upon their return. Provided, of course, they ever returned. They stood cautiously and checked the sight lines. It was better than they'd hoped; they were completely shielded from view. They took their first breaths of the air of He' Konau.

According to K'talo, the outcropping was shaped a bit like a shattered and inverted bowl. Just now it was too dark to tell. The outcropping was about four feet high. The strip of gritty beach behind it was perhaps twice that in width. Laura and Mallory hunkered down in the rock's shadow, waited for the searchlight to sweep by, and mentally plotted the boundary between the area lit by its beam and the safe region that remained in darkness. K'talo had said that the searchlight swept the shoreline every twenty-six seconds. They timed it and found his information correct. Crouching in the shadows at the edge of the safe region, they could see a sort of balcony that had been dug from the volcanic slope about thirty feet above them; Jack thought of the gun emplacements at Navarone. Within the balcony, a black-uniformed sentry stood motionless, gazing out into the moonlight.

It was 2318; they'd made good time. The sentry would be relieved at 2330. They would then have forty minutes to kill him, enter Rauth's compound, find and tap three phone lines, leave two transceivers in place, find their way back out, and return to K'talo's boat before the next sentry arrived at 0010. If they couldn't get their business done in those forty minutes, or if the sentry was somehow missed before he was due to be relieved, they'd have to find somewhere in the compound to hole up and then trust luck to lead them out again. If there was no reasonably likely way to approach and neutralize the sentry, they'd try to skirt him and climb to the helipad above; the searchlights swept the shoreline but left the volcano's slopes dark. Each of them carried lightweight climbing tools and a hundred yards of yarn-thin, wire-strong, and startlingly expensive rope braided from Teflon monofilament and silk. The climb, provided it could be made in silence, would take nearly an hour each way; the helipad was accessed by a single door, which might or might not be guarded, and which they might or might not be able to force silently. And that was their fallback.

These things always looked a lot easier when it was Gregory Peck doing them.

Mallory lay on his belly in the sand in the darkness by the base of the outcropping and gazed. The sentry stood about thirty feet above them, in a balcony dug into maybe a sixty-five degree slope. So he was, let's say, no more than a dozen yards away as the bullet flies, silhouetted by the dim golden light of the access tunnel behind him. At that range he was a fat target for any reasonably good shot, and Mallory was a very good shot, but it would have been suicide to fire even a silenced gun while in range of Rauth's microphones. The man looked to be in his mid-thirties, stocky and fair, with wide-set, impassive eyes and brush-cut hair just beginning to thin. He carried what looked like a Kalashnikov RPK with a night sight and a seventy-five-round clip. It was a bulky and, Mallory knew, heavy piece of ordnance, but the man carried it with the ease of long usage. A standard mercenary type. Mallory knew his kind. Hell, Mallory *was* his kind. He crept backward into the lee of the outcropping and let Laura wriggle forward and have a look.

After less than a minute, she was hunkered in the sand beside him again, hugging her knees, staring off at the black horizon. She'd taken a mental snapshot of the observation post, the beach beneath it, and the rocky slope around and above it, and was now pondering this—distances, sight lines, hand- and footholds—like a chess master studying a board. It was something she did better than anyone Mallory knew, and he hoped she could see a way up that he hadn't, but he doubted it. In any case, he left her to get to it. Crawling over to the water's edge, he began working his way along it on hands and knees, peering at the rocks and pebbles cast up by the surf. When he returned, Laura hadn't moved. He nudged her shoulder and held out three smooth pebbles, one the size of a walnut, one the size of a smallish hen's egg, and one almost as big as a tangerine. She raised her eyebrows, hefted the hen's-egg one, then nodded. They both looked at their watches.

It was 2326.

At 2328:16 they watched from the shadow of the rock as the stocky man exchanged a few words with a tall, neatly moustached Oriental, slipped a short, circular key into what looked like a time-clock on the wall, gave it a full turn, and then ambled off down the access tunnel. The Oriental in turn used his own key on the clock, then came to the edge of the balcony, rested a palm on the stone balustrade, and peered around into the night, his right hand lightly cradling the RPK's folding stock. Then he stepped back, took hold of his weapon in a modified Present Arms, and seemed to settle in for his forty-minute vigil, looking alert as a fox and as comfortable as a hen on its roost.

2331:03. The searchlight swept past, momentarily bleaching the dark volcanic pumice a gauzy gray.

2331:07. Dark again. Mallory tapped his boot twice against Laura's.

She rose and silently strolled forward onto the stony slope. She was black-clad against the black stone, and it took the sentry a moment or two to notice that something was out there. As he turned and peered into the darkness, Laura drew her arm smoothly back. And now the sentry was toppling silently over the parapet—the pebble fell with him, clicking once against the rock face—and now, with a single soft clashing of belt buckle against rifle barrel, the man lay still in the sand at the foot of the slope.

Laura was crouching in the shadows beside Mallory again. He felt the warmth of her flank by his cheek.

They listened hard for a long sixty seconds.

2332:06. They emerged from their shelter together, took the sentry by shoulders and legs—a huskily built man, Chinese or perhaps Korean, round-faced and wearing a faint, sweet cologne—and carried him behind the bowl-shaped rock. Laura felt the hinge of his jaw for a pulse, then unsheathed her knife and, frowning briefly, dispatched him with a short upward thrust under the ear. There was very little blood. Mallory was unclipping a heavy ring of keys from the man's belt and fastening it to his own. Rapidly turning out the man's pockets, he found a single clean handkerchief and a small, thick, plastic card punched with an irregular pattern of square holes, which Mallory tucked into the utility pouch at his side. Nothing else. A disciplined man. A disciplined organization. Laura was unstrapping the big gun. Their eyes met briefly: *No.* Tempting, but too clumsy to move fast with and too big to conceal. She rose and waded off into the surf, and Mallory saw with admiration that she meant to hide the gun in the water: if someone happened across the body, they'd think the intruder was armed with the RPK. A nice little bit of PsyOps, and one he wouldn't have thought of. It was the first thing they told you when you got to the Barrens, and it was still the truest: a good partner was everything. For now, they'd leave the body in the lee of the bowl-rock. If they got back to it by 2355, they'd tow the body out to the longboat and bring it back to Pali Konau for

disposal. Without a corpse, Rauth wouldn't know whether to suspect a penetration or a defection. Getting rid of the body would be a
nice touch, if they had time.

Getting home alive would be another nice touch. If they had
time.

A few minutes later they were clinging to the cliff face on either
side of the observation post and peering round the corners. A short
access tunnel leading back to a steel door with a single slotlike
window. Damn. No knob, no obvious lock. On the wall was the key-
operated time-clock. Mallory could see the stubby tubular key on
his belt that would fit it. Maybe they could use it to gimmick the
steel door somehow. Well, they'd worry about that in a minute. Mallory wedged his fingers into a crevice and his heel into a vertical
runnel and began clambering higher. A dozen feet above the post's
balustrade, he found a narrow ledge and nestled a compact, weath-
erproof wireless transceiver into it. It would pick up the signals
from the internal bugs, amplify them, and send them along to the
main unit on the atoll. If somehow he and Laura failed to install the
internal bugs, it was capable of scanning the compound for outgo-
ing radio signals—or even internal wireless communications, like
walkie-talkie traffic—and passing them along as well. Better
than nothing, though the real prize was landline traffic. Mallory
unfolded the tiny, parasol-like antenna, aimed it back the way
they'd come, and turned a metal set screw on the unit's side. The
ready light blinked twice yellow, twice green, and went out again.
The unit was activated.

He climbed back down and slung a long leg over the parapet.
Laura followed, and they stood facing the steel door. No exposed
hinges, not on this side, and nowhere to insert a key or a lockpick. The
window was set at eye-height; Mallory cautiously peered through and
saw that the access tunnel opened onto a cross-tunnel. No one
around. The glass looked like ordinary safety-glass, but the window
itself wasn't much bigger than a mail slot. Maybe Laurie's arm would

fit through, but nothing else. He took the laser pen from his side-pouch and began examining the doorjamb for vulnerable spots, feeling doubtful. They'd already spent too much time to back out and try climbing to the helipad. This might be where they had to abort and head back home. They wouldn't enjoy that, and Gray wouldn't enjoy hearing about it. Mallory sensed deft fingers slipping into the pouch at his side and looked down to see Laurie withdrawing the punched plastic card they'd taken from the sentry. She held the card up and indicated a slot on the side of the time-clock with her chin. Mallory smiled. When she inserted the card, the door emitted a deep, soft clunk and rumbled heavily to one side. They stepped over the threshold and the door slid back into place behind them.

They were in.

Back in New York, Analysis had sat down with Engineering and, extrapolating from the location of the island's dock and the position and number of its observation posts and ventilators, created a series of probable layouts for Rauth's factory and HQ. These had been plotted on color-coded acetate overlays and given nicknames: Starfish, Squared Circle, Double Doughnut, Waffle Iron. Laura studied the curving hallway, then mouthed *"Double Doughnut"* and made a wry face. Double Doughnut had been one of the simplest and most efficient of the layouts. But in Double Doughnut, the communications system was located in three or four nodes well in toward the island's core.

Mallory shrugged, and they started walking.

The cross-corridor, like the access tunnel, had been machined out of the living rock. The floor had been polished to a dull gleam, and the precisely curved stone walls had been painted battleship gray. It was twelve feet wide and brilliantly lit. There was no place to hide, and so they didn't try. Instead, they walked casually, swinging their tool bags, like two wet-suited technicians coming back from some job of underwater maintenance. It was unlikely that the two hundred–odd members of Rauth's team all knew each other by sight, and cut off from the world as they were, it was unlikely that they wore ID badges. The guard hadn't had one, at any rate. Up ahead the corridor intersected one of the radial tunnels leading in toward the core, just as the Double Doughnut plan had indicated. That was nice. Maybe they'd be lucky, and find a communications node without seeing anybody. Otherwise—

No. They rounded the corner and saw at least a dozen black-clad figures scattered along the big tunnel. The nearest was walking straight toward them, rolling a metal cart stacked with sandwiches, each neatly cut on the diagonal and wrapped in waxed paper. By now, Mallory knew, Laurie would be doing one of those damn swami things. She'd have disengaged her bodily emotions from her mind and be cool as a popsicle. Mallory didn't know her tricks. All he could do was lean hard on his nerve. The man rolling the cart looked curiously at them. Mallory nodded slightly and, as he passed, reached out and plucked one of the sandwiches from the top row.

The man with the cart skidded to a halt. " 'Ere now. Don't mess me about," he said. "You know those're counted."

Smiling coolly, Mallory replaced the sandwich. "You must not knock a fellow for trying," he said in a light German accent. "One gets so hungry here."

"Thought you was new," the man said. "And I know *you* are. I'd remember *you*," he told Laura.

"I have no wish that you should remember me," Laura said, matching Mallory's accent. "Piss off, please."

The black-suited Cockney grinned broadly at the two of them. "So that's how it stands. Well," he told Mallory, "like y'say, can't knock a fellow for tryin'."

Both men laughed and moved along.

After a few steps, Laura murmured, "You must also piss off, please, if you intend often in that way to be frightening me."

"Worked, didn't it?" Mallory said. "None of these other folks are giving us a second look now. Here's the turnoff."

Mallory had the habit of keeping running mental tallies of the things he saw on a job. It had been, in the past, an occasionally useful trick. More often it was a distraction. Now he reflected that, not counting the sentries, they'd seen fifteen men and two women on their way in, and that every last one of them had been armed. Walther P-38s, it looked like, the old Bundeswehr service pistol. Mallory had heard they'd started making them again, except these days they were calling it the Pistole 1. A good gun for tight work, and one of the best all-around guns Mallory knew. And these had been fitted with outsized clips that looked to hold about twelve rounds. Mallory wondered if that would throw off the balance, but if Rauth had done the job, probably not.

Two hundred and four bullets, Mallory thought, without particularly wanting to.

The corridor grew wider and broader as they approached the island's core, the stone ceiling gracefully arched and reinforced at regular intervals with gleaming steel bands. Directly ahead of them the corridor opened out into a large, circular room ringed by blinking computer mainframes. Rauth's computer center, most likely, just as the Double Doughnut plan had predicted. The phone nodes would be clustered around it in a ring. If they took a right at the next intersection—

Yes. The second door on their left was marked KOMMUNIKATIONS-SYSTEM 3.

"Bingo," Mallory said in a normal tone of voice. "Now let's see if I can find the damn key. Nope. Nope. Here we go. What time's it, anyway?"

"Eleven forty-one," Laura said.

"Yeah?" he said, opening the door. "This deal might work out."

They let the door click shut behind them and looked around. They were standing in what could have been the phone switching room in any large office. Cinder-block walls, gray metal cabinets labeled with black plastic plaques, snaking bunches of BX and colored wires fastened to the walls with galvanized U-clips. Above them, a cable tray pierced the walls to their right and left. It was arc-shaped, and seemed to follow the curve of the compound's inner ring. One of the cabinets was marked TELEFONKABEL. Mallory nodded at Laura and she flipped off the lights again. No point in arousing curiosity by leaving a line of light under the closed door, if someone passed by who happened to know whether the phones were being worked on or not. Mallory flicked on his flashlight and opened TELEFONKABEL. Inside were neatly labeled bunches of wires: BESPRECHUNGSZIMMER, MITTELGANG, ZENTRALEINHEIT, PLANUNG, ARSENAL, ANLAGE, and HUBSCHRAUBERLANDPLATZ. One simply marked ABD. And the big one: ZENTRALE. The command center. It was a damn shame Celeste had taken their limpet mines. This would be a good place to leave one with a radio fuse, to be lit off in case something went wrong and they needed to create some confusion while they ran for it. Well, he'd have his hands full just planting the bugs in time. The cable tray, Mallory decided, was better than the cabinet. When Rauth discovered the sentry had gone missing, or found his body, he'd order a search for intruders or sabotage. But they couldn't search every inch of a place this size—it would take weeks—and they'd be less likely to climb up and check the cable trays than they would be to pop open the wall cabinet and glance inside. He gestured upward with the flash. Laura understood at once and dropped to one knee. He shoved at the cable cabinet—solid—then stuck the flash in his teeth, planted a foot on Laura's knee, and boosted himself up on top of the cabinet. If the wires up here weren't labeled, he'd drop back down and do the cabinet; there was no time to trace the right wires up. But if they were labeled . . .

They were. Thank God for Teutonic thoroughness. Or Czech thoroughness, or whatever the hell it was.

Unzipping his side pouch, he lay out his tools. First, the Browning, in easy reach. A set of earphones. Then three short lengths of insulated wire—red, blue, and green—with toothed clips at each end and a miniature signal splitter in the middle. The three splitters were attached to small coils of color-coded phone line, each terminating in a tiny single-prong plug. Finally, a lozenge-shaped package about five inches long with three circular outlets on one end, surprisingly heavy for its weight. The internal transceiver. It would take the signal input from the three bugs and relay it to the external unit on the rocky ledge outside, broadcasting an ultra-long signal wave—what they called the sandhogs' frequency—capable of penetrating a thousand feet of rock. Mallory flicked the transceiver on, so that it would begin transmitting as soon as he'd hooked up the first bug. His jaw was getting tired from holding the flash in his teeth, but he didn't want to stop and set the light up in its little stand. He uncoiled the three plugs on the bugs and inserted them into the transceiver, feeling the click and then rocking them once from side to side to make sure they were firmly seated. He set the earphones on his head and plugged them into the main unit as well. He picked out the wire marked PLANUNG— Planning—and gingerly worked it free of the bundle. Taking up the first of the bugs, he closed each of the jawlike clips around the wire at two points perhaps three inches apart. He settled himself more comfortably, took a breath, and got ready to press the clips shut. This would sever the wire and immediately divert its signal through the splitter and into the transceiver. Both clips had to be closed at precisely the same time, or there would be, at best, a brief audible interruption in the traffic, and at worst, a howl of feedback that would send a technician running to the phone room. Mallory took in a breath, as if getting ready to fire at a distant target, and smoothly pressed both his thumbs and forefingers shut. His ears filled with a flat, Midwestern-sounding voice: *"—at the Prime Site. But if that goes well, they'll be wanting more devices pretty damn quick. And that means inventory."*

"My dear Curtis," replied a voice with a heavy Italian accent, *"you are as always—"*

That was enough.

2343:12. Two more lines to bug.

He switched to the blue channel and the earphones went silent again. Working ZENTRALE free from the bunch, he positioned the clips and gently pressed down again. More silence. That might mean he'd made a bad connection, but it was more likely that he'd tapped into a line not currently in use. Was it worth taking the time to test? No, the phone was ringing now. Mallory couldn't hear anything besides the ringing phone, but he was suddenly aware of movement—that Laurie had moved.

He was turning on his knees, the Browning already in his hand, when the room lights blazed on.

Crouching just under the ceiling as he was, Mallory couldn't move quickly, and by the time he'd leapt from the top of the steel cabinet, the black-clad technician was already collapsing to the concrete floor, his neck at an unnatural angle and his Walther slipping from his fingers. No backup, Mallory thought as he landed in a poised crouch, eyes and gun sweeping the room together. Not a guard sent to neutralize an intruder. Just a tech boy who'd picked the wrong moment to twiddle some dials. Laurie already had hold of the dead man's collar. If they could drag him all the way into the room before somebody—

No. Through the door Mallory saw another of Rauth's team out in the hall, whirling in surprise. A thin, scholarly-looking man in steel-rimmed spectacles. A tense hand flashing toward his hip holster.

Mallory shot him through the throat.

Well, Mallory thought, *the curtain's going up.*

"Mainframe," he barked at Laura, tossing her his Browning. "Left and left."

He saw he didn't have to explain. They were hopelessly outgunned. But if they made it to the computer center, Rauth's men wouldn't dare use their guns; the risk of bringing down the mainframe with a stray shot would be too great. They probably didn't have a chance, but if they did, the computer room was it.

Mallory scooped the Walther from the dead technician's hand and then was out in the hall, snatching up the scholarly man's gun. That was twelve bullets, anyway. Laura was sprinting around the corner. He heard the Browning cough once, and then again, and then he rounded the corner just in time to see her hurl the empty gun with deadly accuracy into the face of an oncoming guard.

After that, it got a little confusing. They were in the main tunnel heading to the big computer room, and Mallory was letting off two shots at a computer technician who was still trying to fumble his gun from its holster. Missed; the man ducked down behind a countertop. And then they were in the vast circular central chamber, which was roofed over by a lens-shaped concrete dome. In the center of the dome, where the pupil might have been, was a circular opening onto an even vaster space above. Another angle to cover. There were already too damn many. He whirled, the Walthers in his hands, found two guards charging in from directly behind. Laura was rolling one man's gun-arm between her palms—it seemed to go boneless at her touch—and then turning to the other just as Mallory knocked him over with a lung shot. And then they were alone again. A klaxon was blaring. Above their heads, a mechanical voice repeated, "Intruders, Processor Room. *Eindringlinge, Zentraleinheit.*" He heard boots clattering on the stone floor of one of the radial tunnels. There were five tunnels branching out from the computer room. Impossible to cover them all. There wasn't time to be scared, but he could tell it was no damn good. Another guard appeared, and Mallory took him down and hoped he'd get a chance to tell Laurie goodbye. Glancing over his shoulder, he saw her jerk erect and snatch a silvery something from her shoulder. As he turned to her, a second tranquilizing dart thudded into the muscle of his own biceps. He dropped a gun and reached for it, missed, reached again. Laurie was on the floor now. The huge room was darkening. There was a roaring like cold applause as everything began to rush at him, to rush at him and, sickeningly, straight through him, and as he toppled forward, Mallory forced himself to look up, way up at the circular aperture in the dome, where he glimpsed a gleam of alloy and a face with a blank, ratlike gaze.

Renko.

9 *Angel of the Abyss*

You can't imagine how pleased I am to meet you at last, Mr. Mallory," said Anton Rauth. "And you, Miss Morse, who are quite as lovely as I'd heard. Though that rubber leotard doesn't really do you justice. I understand that there are those who appreciate that sort of thing, and even prefer it, but rubber has always struck me as somehow . . . sweaty. Utilitarian. It pains me to see a lovely woman gotten up like a tire-repair kit. Now, if it were up to me. I'd choose something quite simple for you. Quite classic. Balenciaga, say, or early Dior. A knee-length dropped-waist frock in raw ecru silk. No jewelry, not even pearls. Though I'll admit you're also one of the few with the figure to carry off young Mr. Saint Laurent's more recent innovations. What do you say, Mr. Mallory? I'm told you are, in spite of, or perhaps because of, your rather proletarian background, something of a student of fashion. Do you agree? Some Yves Saint Laurent for Miss Morse?"

The arms, Mallory decided, were absolutely goddamned impossible.

He was sitting in an ordinary steel-framed hospital wheelchair, still wearing his wet suit. He'd been immobilized by the simple expedient of binding his wrists and ankles to the chair arms and footrests with a few yards of heavy, cloth-backed electrician's tape. It was reminiscent of the way he'd been trussed up by Nemerov. Too damn reminiscent. He'd already had to stop twice and think about the hardware store, and now, after half an hour of silently flexing and twisting his forearms, he had to admit he wasn't going anywhere soon. Across the table, Laurie was bound to her own wheelchair. As always, she looked politely uninterested. All Mallory could do was hope he looked the same. He was still groggy, and his left wrist and right biceps were both a little sore. After the tranquilizer dart had put him out, he guessed they'd kept him down with a Nembutal drip. That must have been about eighteen hours ago. Through the thirty-meter glass wall behind Anton Rauth, the sun was now setting over Pali Konau, spangling the waves with molten copper. Like any good host, Rauth had seated his guests so that they had the benefit of the view.

Less than an hour before, Mallory had woken up to find himself and Laura sitting in their wheelchairs at a formal dining table set for four. The table was draped with old lace. The plates were bone china rimmed with tiny blue-and-gold fleurs-de-lis. The silver was substantial, with yellowed ivory handles, and the blades of the knives and the bowls of the spoons gave off a hazy glow bespeaking centuries of careful use. The wineglasses looked fragile as soap bubbles. At the precise center of the table stood a tiny urn-shaped vase in a sort of dull pearly glass, decorated with a relief of plump dancing girls and containing a single waxy orange orchid. Everything on the table would have looked at home in a museum, and nearly everything would have made a serviceable weapon if he'd had a hand free, but he didn't have one and wasn't likely to. The table sat in the center of an expanse of blackish stone floor. As in the other rooms and halls he'd seen, the floor had been machined from the rock of the volcano and polished to a dull gleam. The room was easily as deep as it was long; maybe about five thousand square feet. Aside from the table and a silver chandelier above the table, it was empty of furniture. The chandelier was an old gas-fired one, and hung by a forty-foot steel chain from the shadowed ceiling. The distant walls were ribbed concrete. Mallory could see two doors: a broad double door through which they'd probably entered, and a narrower single door that might lead to the kitchen. Between them stood a row of black-clad servants, waiting to be called. They wore sidearms, like everyone else, and the one in the center held a Sten MK II, which had been rigged up with a flash suppressor and a big snail magazine. 550 rounds per minute, as Mallory recalled. Forget the doors. And the glass wall, Mallory assumed, was bulletproof. Behind Mallory's chair stood a big goop named Erno, who was cutting Mallory's Dover sole into bite-sized pieces and feeding it to him, along with the occasional sip of wine. Behind Laura's chair stood Renko, who was rendering her the same service. Every now and then Renko would gently rub a forkful of food around and around Laura's motionless lips before slipping it into her mouth.

To Mallory's left sat a pale, sweaty-looking, middle-aged man, tall but hunched, who had yet to meet anyone's eyes. This was Herman Treat, the crystallographer Gray had mentioned back in New York—*Lordy*, Mallory thought, *just two and a half months ago.* Each time Renko tucked a piece of food into Laura's mouth, Treat stared help-lessly. In between, he gazed into the bosom of her wet suit, which someone—Renko?—had unzipped nearly to her waist. There was nothing to be seen there but the front of Laura's modest, blue swim-suit, but Treat still couldn't seem to help himself.

To Mallory's right, with his back to the long window, sat Anton Rauth.

Rauth was an unusually good-looking man. Trimly muscular and a bit under medium height, he had a pointed chin, a heart-shaped face, and large, wide-set, green eyes. His thick auburn hair was wavy and grew low on a broad forehead; he brushed it straight back, and only a few tendrils, artfully or not, managed to tumble free. He was quietly dressed in a soft, dark linen suit, an eggshell linen shirt, and a midnight-blue tie. He was forty-four years old and looked ten years younger. He'd entered the room with an athlete's elastic step. Mallory guessed he would be formidable in an unarmed fight. He had a light baritone voice and an actor's knack for modulation. His words were elaborately ironic, but his delivery was quiet and grave. His English was accentless, as the native speaker's never is. He held his right hand in his lap, out of sight, but that was probably just good manners, eating with one hand and leaving the other in your lap. It was impossible to imagine Rauth with his elbows on the table. Or doing anything as vulgar as caressing his goblet as he spoke, but his pleasure in his surroundings was plain. Laurie had been right as usual: Rauth was someone who liked his effects. In spite of his beauty and affectations, Mallory saw no trace of effeminacy. Mallory's impression was of acute intelligence, remorseless discipline, and enormous tension, perfectly controlled. Maybe Rauth was tense about the job he had on, and maybe he was just tense. Some men were. It was the discipline that worried Mallory, even more than the intelligence. Rauth looked like a man who figured all the angles in advance, gave instructions for dealing with each of them, and killed anyone on his staff who dropped a stitch. Mallory's professional instincts told him that they weren't likely to think of a dodge Rauth hadn't anticipated. Their only chance, he guessed, was to try and poke a hole in that discipline. To get Rauth to lose his temper and hope that made him sloppier. Of course, it was pretty terrifying to think what a man like Rauth might do if he slipped the leash, but it probably wasn't any worse than what he already had planned.

Mallory had one last try at freeing his feet under the tablecloth. Nope. It was impossible, unless your legs bent backwards like a cricket's.

"What do you say, Mr. Mallory?" Rauth said pleasantly. "Perhaps you don't care for Yves Saint Laurent?"

"Sorry, Andy," Mallory said. "I wasn't listening. I figured you'd tap a spoon on a glass or something when you were ready to get to the point."

"Yes, you seemed a bit preoccupied. Any luck with your bonds? Think you'll be able to wriggle free? Employing some little-known yogic technique taught you in the wilds of New Jersey?"

"I'll let you know."

"A bit more sole for Mr. Mallory," Rauth said. "And perhaps another forkful of carrots. Don't neglect him, Erno. He needs his strength."

Erno was pretty good at feeding people. Mallory wondered if he'd ever worked as a nurse.

"Fish all right?" Rauth asked. "The wine? I'm fussy about food myself. Pleasure in all its forms interests me. I have a little theory about such matters. I believe that each pleasure one receives in life has a cost, and that the sharpness and fullness of one's pleasure increases with the price one has paid for it. I'll provide an example. It is a great pleasure to see you, Mr. Mallory, and it will be an even greater pleasure to kill you. And that is in part due to the fact that it has cost me quite a bit to secure your company. First of all, of course, there are the costs I paid simply to learn of your existence. The irreparable disruption of a very profitable financial venture in Caracas. The confiscation of a shipment of assorted weaponry meant for a guerrilla group in Rhodesia. And so on. These costs were not exorbitant; in fact, they served to intrigue me. You seemed a capable fellow. I even considered engaging your services myself. But then there was an incident in Copenhagen where you chose to . . . obtrude upon a young woman for whom I myself had conceived a fondness."

"Aw, hell," Mallory said. "You mean Hanny? The Danish consul's girl?"

"Yes, Mr. Mallory. That is whom I meant."

"Andy, that was three damn years ago. You mean to tell me you're still pouting 'cause you didn't get to lay little Hanny? She was pretty good, but Lord, son, you need to get out more. Figure out a way to meet girls without kidnapping 'em."

"An intriguing idea," Rauth said. "Then there are the costs of your adventure in Istanbul, which amounted to some millions of dollars, plus the loss of several months' work on my current project and of a valued senior employee. And finally, the costs of your and Miss Morse's frolic last night. Three of my men killed outright, and three more requiring lengthy hospital stays. Of course, we are unfortunately not in a position to provide lengthy hospital stays, and so were obliged to . . . " Rauth made a small, final gesture. "Employ other expedients. I'll admit I was also a bit concerned about the damage your stray bullets might have done to my computing facilities, but it appears you don't miss very often, Mr. Mallory."

"Can't claim much credit, Andy. It was your fish and your barrel."

"So let's say a half dozen of my men dead, on top of the loss in time, money, and personnel in Istanbul, Caracas, and Rhodesia, as well as the more personal—"

There was a soft popping noise as Laura spat a piece of potato with astonishing force and accuracy at the bud vase in the center of the table. It sent the vase skidding past Mallory's elbow to shatter on the stone floor.

"Well, Andy," Laura said, "I just increased your pleasure by the cost of that little knick-knack. Now tell your boyfriend to stop wiping my dinner around my face. Unless that's your idea of a good time?"

There was a brief pause.

"In fact, it isn't," Rauth said. "Renko, must I speak to you?"

"I'm sorry, Mr. Rauth," Renko said tonelessly.

"You're a talented young man, Renko. But unlike that bit of Lalique, you are not irreplaceable."

"I'm very sorry, Mr. Rauth," the young man said, flushing an unlovely shade of mauve.

"I hope so. You've been quite silent, Miss Morse. We're not boring you?"

"A bit," she said.

Good girl. She was trying to get Rauth angry, too.

" 'Fraid you're not Laurie's type," Mallory told Rauth.

"I wasn't aware, Mr. Mallory, that I was a type at all."

"Sure. Pretty common one. Cripple with a complex."

"I wonder if it's quite proper to call me a cripple," Rauth said. "Quite correct, I mean. Now if this," he said, lifting his right hand, "if this were one of my feet, say, then 'cripple' might be moderately apt. But does 'cripple' really apply to a man with a lamed arm? For what it's worth, I *have* been called a gimp," he said. "Would it relieve your feelings to call me that?"

"Not much."

"A freak?"

Mallory shrugged.

"No further names you'd like to call me?"

"I dunno. How about 'nut case'? What's it like, anyway, being nuts?"

"It's very difficult," Rauth said simply. "It makes everything much more difficult. Especially when there's so much to do. But one manages. I tell myself that, after all, I'm no madder than Hitler was, and he was able to accomplish a great deal."

"For God's *sake*, Anton," Treat burst out. He almost looked Rauth in the face. Then he lowered his head and quickly stuffed down another forkful.

"It upsets Dr. Treat to hear me speak of Hitler," Rauth said, sounding amused for the first time. "He mistakes the nature and extent of my regard for the man. I admire Hitler's audacity, Herman, and his grasp of the theory and practice of propaganda. And, to a certain extent, his taste. He made use of dreadful kitschmeisters like Speer and Breker, of course, but he also hired geniuses like Riefenstahl and Hohlwein. And did you know that the swastika banners at Nuremburg were his own design? Very heartening to a fellow-dabbler like myself. Hitler was really the only modern dictator with a serious aesthetic program. But unfortunately, the man simply wasn't very bright. Why spend valuable time putting people in ovens? Is it useful? Is it *interesting?* And for heaven's sake, why try to conquer the world? He had continental Europe pretty well sewn up by '41, along with some very handy bits of Africa. England would have cut its losses in time. America was quite ready to talk turkey. What in God's name did he want *Russia* for? Even the Soviets haven't been able to find a use for it."

"Now, that's a relief," Mallory said. "You're not gonna take over the world."

"Dear me, no. What would I do with it? No, what I want, Mr. Mallory, is money. Really unseemly and inordinate sums of money. I like beautiful things. I like, within my limitations, to live beautifully. I was born wealthy, quite wealthy enough to buy lovely houses in any of the world's loveliest cities, but my ambitions do extend a bit beyond drapes that match the sofa. What I really want is to take, not the world, but a modest bit of it—say, a middle-sized country—and remake it according to my own aesthetic notions. You could say that He' Konau represents a sort of preliminary study for such a project. Well, securing a parcel like that, doing it over to suit oneself, and amassing the power to enjoy it without interference, all this, Mr. Mallory, requires really exceptional amounts of *cash*, even greater than those I was someday due to inherit. I looked into my heart, I looked into Papa's bank books. And I realized some adjustments would have to be made. And so I've done something rather unusual for a man of my class and background. I've gone into trade. I've become, you might say, a shopkeeper."

"There much more of this, Andy? You're kind of spoiling my dinner."

"Yes, you don't seem very hungry anymore. Nor you, Miss Morse."

"The sole's a bit dry," she said.

"Untrue. You're both trying to pick a fight with me. I wonder why. Well, I'll tell you what we'll do while they're clearing away. Why don't I show you what you both came dog-paddling over here to see? Why don't I take you on a tour of my shop and present my latest line of merchandise? It might interest you, Mr. Mallory. In fact, it was created, in part, with you in mind."

For a healthy young man, Mallory had spent an unusual amount of time in wheelchairs, and it always struck him that a wheelchair-bound man's view of the world was a bit different from anyone else's. Now, as Renko drew Laura's chair smoothly back from the table, Mallory saw something no one else in the room could see. He saw, in the dim light from the gas chandelier, that, impossible as it seemed, Laurie had managed to work her narrow feet out of her foam boots. The boots were still taped firmly to her wheelchair's footrests, and she was pressing her bare ankles against the backs of the boots to conceal them. Rauth, Renko, or any of the guards would have had to bend down and peer to discover it. But both of Laura Morse's legs were now free.

The Double Doughnut plan had predicted an elevator bank in the island's northwest quadrant, and so there was: an ovoid well some four hundred feet deep, stretching into the dim distance above and below them and banded with light at each level of the complex. In the center, two transparent cylinders glided along glistening alloy cables. They entered one of them over a cantilevered aerial bridge. When the glass door rolled shut, they were enveloped in an uncanny silence. "Fabrication Two," Rauth said into the empty air, and the elevator began smoothly to descend.

"This is the Administrative level," Rauth said, in the manner of a tour guide, as they sank past a vast expanse of cubicles interspersed with teletypes and illuminated maps etched into large upright panes of glass. "And here's the Dormitory level. Those banks of lamps are meant to simulate sunlight. My engineers tell me this enhances efficiency, though I've yet to see it. Dock facilities. We're now at sea-level. We'll return here shortly. Inventory on this level and the one below." They were sinking past endless rows of crated weapons, tanks and half-tracks on steel pallets, even ICBMs in their cradles. The next two levels were empty: acres of dusty concrete floor punctuated by thick support columns and sparsely lit by the occasional arc light.

"Seems like you still got some bald patches," Mallory said.

"Room to grow, Mr. Mallory. Room to grow. Now, on this level I do my light fabrication, assembly, and finishing; I've branched out, as you might have gathered, and begun to design and manufacture a few weapons systems of my own. One wearies of writing out packing slips and making change. Here's Heavy Fabrication One, where I take care of welding and stamping. And finally, here we are on the bottommost level, Fabrication Two, one hundred and seventy feet below the ocean floor."

It looked, quite literally, like Hell. At the eastern end of the floor, some hundred and fifty yards distant, stood a row of three blast furnaces, their square mouths unbearably bright. Before them an immense iron ladle was decanting molten metal into a trough, bathing the scene in a sullen orange glow. The monstrous hulk of a drop forge loomed to their right, its jaws inexorably closing. The workers who tended the machines were stripped to the waist and shining with sweat, wearing ear protectors and goggles as if on a shooting range. The omnipresent Walthers swung at their sides. On the opposite side of the floor were thirty-foot industrial lathes, ranks of massive drill presses, and, at intervals, ceiling-mounted robot arms woven around with branching track hoists. "I'll keep the doors shut, if that's all right with you," Rauth said. "It's unpleasantly warm out there, and quite dangerously loud. I can smelt my own aluminum here, forge components up to five long tons in weight, and cast steel components up to twelve long tons. For larger items, I'm still obliged to contract out."

"Seems like I've met up with a couple of your fellas over the years," Mallory said, looking around the floor. "They're nobody I'd invite to a tea dance."

"The worst people in the world," Rauth agreed. "The absolute scum of the criminal classes of five continents. I've taken a fair bit of trouble to find and recruit them. For the work I have on hand, as you'll shortly see, ordinary factory staff wouldn't do. I really can't afford second thoughts or tender consciences. In point of fact, I really can't afford to employ men with any conscience whatsoever. Except for unusual talents like Dr. Treat. For Herman, I've made an exception."

"Thanks," Treat muttered at the floor.

"I find it much easier to teach killers the technical skills they need than to teach technicians how to kill. Let's go back up to the dock, shall we? And I'll show you what all the fuss has been about."

When the glass door slid open on the Dock level, Mallory could smell the sea. They rolled across another cantilevered walkway and into a curving concrete tunnel. The volcanic stone floor here was ground smooth but unpolished, and the noise of waves was soft but certain. The dim tunnel grew brighter as they traveled, the ribs on the concrete walls casting sharper and sharper shadows, until at once it debouched into an enormous space as brightly lit as Yankee Stadium during a night game. Before them, visible through the twisted mouth of a marine cavern, was the dark sea. Leading in from the sea was a huge boat slip; Mallory thought it would easily accommodate a small oil tanker. Set into the cargo slip was a giant turntable, the sort you might see in a railroad switching yard. And on the turntable was a massive segmented device formed of black iron, gray steel, and glittering alloy, like an eighty-foot-long iron centipede tipped with a cluster of heavy, vicious-looking drill bits. At the top, sides, and bottom of each pentagonal segment was a short, cleated caterpillar tread to drive it through the earth. *The gizmo,* Mallory thought. *Just like the one in Istanbul. But this one's all gassed up and ready to go.*

"May I present Project Abbadon?" Rauth said. "Named for the Archangel of Armageddon and Lord of the Abyss, who at the final tribulation is to command the locust army that will lay waste the earth. Do you read the Bible, Mr. Mallory? *And the shapes of the locusts were like unto horses prepared unto battle, and on their heads were crowns like gold, and they had breastplates of iron, and the sound of their wings was as the sound of chariots of many horses running to battle, and they had tails like unto scorpions. And they had a king over them which is the angel of the bottomless pit, whose name in the Hebrew tongue is Abbadon. The lion is come up from its thicket, and the destroyer is on his way; he is gone forth from his place to make your land desolate, and your cities will be laid waste.* Some very good writing in Revelation, I always thought. Though a bit overwrought in spots. Well, there you have it: the Abbadon. It may not look much like an angel, but I assure you it is quite capable of sounding the last trump. I'll let my technical adviser Dr. Treat explain. Dr. Treat?"

"Well," the scientist said, "the idea behind the device—not that I can take credit . . ." He frowned at the floor " 'Credit,' " he muttered to himself. "Anyway. About two years ago I was working on ways to create standing waves in superheated igneous rock. You know what a standing wave is?"

"Nope," Mallory said.

"It's a wave that reinforces itself," Laura said. "The interval is such that each oscillation makes the next one stronger."

"That's right," Treat said. "It's what brought down the Tacoma Narrows Bridge. A steady wind across the cables, at just the right speed . . . " He chewed his lip for a moment. "And Anton, Mr. Rauth heard about my research. He called to ask me whether P waves, the primary waves in a seismic release, didn't behave much the same as sound waves, and of course they do. And we, ah, the principle of the thing is that you pick a fault trace and a likely hypocenter. And you, you've got a good survey of the mechanical properties of the surrounding rock and soil, which is, that survey's mostly been done, governmentally, and so you can plot a point of insertion, for where you want to start your standing wave. It has to be the right frequency, of course, but you don't need to start with much power. Not in geologic terms. And you can predict for reflection and refraction, and sort of, ah, control the amplitude and the—" He flung his hands out. "Area. The meizoseismal area."

"Treat," Mallory said, "what in the hell are you talking about?"

"Well," Treat said, going briefly red. "In lay language, the thing tunnels underground and starts an earthquake."

For a few moments, there was no sound but the waves lapping against the dock.

"Think of it," Rauth said invitingly. "An earthquake, in virtually any spot one chooses—provided, of course, that there is a workable fault trace in the vicinity, as there usually is—and of almost any degree of intensity. You are familiar, I'm sure, with the Richter scale. Each unit represents a tenfold increase in magnitude over the next. History's largest earthquakes, including Lisbon in 1755 and Yokohama in 1923, have never exceeded 9 on the Richter scale. A scale value of 15 is generally regarded as signifying planetary destruction. Dr. Treat and I are fairly confident that we can engender quakes and earthquake swarms—picturesque phrase, that—of perhaps Richter 9.8. This would represent an energy release far greater than the world's massed atomic arsenals. Imagine the ability to direct such force with surgical precision. To create, at will, what we in the reinsurance business call Acts of God. Imagine the beauty of a weapon that can devastate entire nations without—here's the neatest bit—*without the nation's ever knowing it's been attacked.* No danger of reprisals. No messy and hard-to-predict political reper- cussions. War, Miss Morse and Mr. Mallory, has been described as the exercise of diplomacy by other means. The Abbadon will make both obsolete."

Rauth stepped up to a console at the edge of the great turntable and flicked on a bank of floodlights that bathed the device in a ghastly white glow. "Pretty, isn't it?" he said. He tapped a foot pedal at the console's base, and, with a deep shudder that made the Abbadon rock slightly on its treads, the turntable began to revolve. "The platform still doesn't start up quite smoothly," Rauth com- plained. "Can't we do something about that?"

"Eventually," Treat said.

"Just so. As you can see, the theory behind our little toy is com- plicated, but the execution is quite straightforward. The device is unpiloted, of course: it destroys itself during use, so you wouldn't get many volunteers. We control it from the surface, using this con- sole. One sets the angle of descent here. Turns it right and left like so. Controls speed here. This timer activates the main oscillating unit, which engenders the standing wave. The whole business is about as complex to use as a washing machine." Rauth halted the turntable with a second tap on the pedal, and frowned briefly as the device jolted again on its treads. He touched a button, and a hatch slowly opened in the nose. Inside was a single padded seat, criss- crossed with leather straps. "We were actually able to provide the device with windows: solid slabs of quartz eighteen inches thick. Until the windows are abraded to opacity around the middle of the second day, the device's occupant will be able to watch the strata grind by. The seat is upholstered in hand-stitched calfskin. I think it looks rather comfy, don't you?"

"I thought you said this dingus didn't need a pilot," Mallory said.

"It doesn't. That seat is for a single passenger. That seat, Mr. Mal- lory, is for you."

"Well," Mallory said, after a pause. "Then I guess I'm glad you made the thing comfy."

"Originally," Rauth continued, "I'd meant you to ride the Abbadon on its voyage under Istanbul, which, for various reasons that are neither here nor there, I had selected as my test site. That project, as you well know, suffered . . . reverses. And I was forced to postpone, and to revise my plans somewhat. The device had been designed for one passenger; I hadn't the heart to eliminate the passenger compartment when I rebuilt it. And now I find, to my delight, that you will be part of the Abbadon's maiden voyage after all."

"Think you can fool INSTA twice?" Mallory said.

Rauth smiled. "Oh, Istanbul is no longer my target. Not now."

"I never much cared for Twenty Questions. You going to get to the point?"

"I am," Rauth said. "How long since you've been home, Mr. Mallory? I don't mean home to New York City. I mean to your home town, your birthplace. How long since you've been to Corpus Christi? Thirteen years or so, isn't it? You never liked the place much, I'm told—and I must admit it doesn't sound very charming—or had much to say to your brothers and sisters. You were the only one who left. And since your mother died, you haven't been much inclined to go back, have you? I wonder what you'll say when I tell you that I'm not impressed with Corpus Christi either. I wonder what you'll say when I tell you that in a little over two weeks, Corpus Christi—along with New Orleans, Tampa, and most of the cities and towns along the Gulf of Mexico—will largely cease to exist. Not that I propose an earthquake in downtown Corpus Christi. It would hardly be worth the trouble. No, the hypocenter will be six degrees of latitude to the south, beneath the sea, at a cusp of the Caribbean's Grand Traverse Fault. What will erase Corpus Christi from the earth's face, along with your remaining family, is the two-hundred-foot tsunami which will follow. The quake and its aftershocks will take with it the bulk of America's domestic oil-producing capacity, as well as creating, I'm told, a really unprecedented oil slick from Tampa to Mérida. A quite substantial body blow to the United States of America, and one that will be entirely proof against retaliation. The KGB's Political Section is paying me three hundred and fifty million dollars to bring it off. I'd say that's money well spent, wouldn't you? And if this first outing is as successful as we expect, we have follow-up missions on the drawing board for New York, Chicago, Washington, and, of course, Los Angeles. We have hopes of knocking a great portion of California into the sea. By the time the Soviets begin their land invasion, there may well be no U.S. government to surrender. In fact, your countrymen will quite likely be pleading with the occupying forces to restore order. And, as a sort of bonus, I will at the same time have brought a quite decisive end to the House of Mallory."

There was a wisecrack in there somewhere, Mallory thought dully. But just now he couldn't think what it was.

"The new Abbadon is complete. We're nearly done with our final round of pre-launch tests. In thirty-six hours, the device will depart on a converted oil tanker to the Gulf. And you, Mr. Mallory, will go with it, to the Gulf of Mexico, and beneath. The Abbadon is equipped with sufficient oxygen and refrigeration to keep a man alive and conscious for the two-day trip down to the base of the Grand Traverse, some three miles deep. The view out the ports may, I fear, become a bit monotonous, but I can promise you some excitement at the trip's end. You, and you alone, will be privileged to hear the beginning—though only, alas, the very beginning—of the Abbadon's song. And as the bones of your skull begin to disintegrate, you will have the satisfaction of knowing that, at that moment of dazzling beauty, Miss Morse and I will be celebrating our, shall we say . . . our honeymoon."

There was another brief silence. Mallory's mouth was dry.

Laura said, "And that's the big plan?"

"Yes, Miss Morse. That's the big plan."

She shrugged. Her voice was the usual cool monotone when she said, "Pretty good, Andy, if you can bring it off. But I thought you were aiming for a bit of aesthetic quality. If you don't mind my saying so, all this is pretty predictable stuff."

"Is it?"

"Oh yeah. The sort of thing a sick kid might dream up when the big boys have been teasing him. Comic-book fantasies of making everyone pay. Not much of interest, unless you're a child psychologist. The only thing that surprises me is you, Treat—what you're doing here. The man of science. How much is Andy paying you for this . . . stuff? I'm guessing he bought you out of petty cash."

Treat flinched, his face shinier than ever. He turned away with a despairing grunt, then strode back to Laura again, his big jaw working earnestly. "Look," he said. "Look. The Grand Traverse is due for a quake anyway, sometime in the next hundred years. It's coming, no matter what we do. All right? It can't be stopped. And whenever it comes, it'll be bad. And there's nothing to be done about that. So why not get it over with now? Especially if we can learn something in the process?"

Laura nodded thoughtfully, her eyes never leaving Treat's.

"I see what you mean," she said.

Then, as it had in the Pera Palas Hotel, her right leg flashed heavenward, carrying her slight body into the air, so that the wheelchair, bound to her wrists, was dragged briefly aloft, and the edge of her bare foot sank with a crunch into Treat's adam's apple. He flopped over backward as her wheelchair landed crookedly on one wheel and capsized, and the two of them sprawled beside each other on the floor. A guard jammed the muzzle of his Sten against Laura's temple and looked anxiously at Rauth. Erno and Renko rushed forward to help. But Rauth in a faraway voice said:

"No. Don't bother. His windpipe's crushed."

Treat knew what had been done to him. His feet kicked spastically behind him as he gripped his throat, trying to squeeze his pharynx open again. He was making a faint, inhuman squeaking noise, like someone making balloon sculptures. He stared unbelievingly into Laura's face.

"Look at it this way, Herman," she told him sweetly. "You were due to die anyway, sometime in the next hundred years. So why not get it over with now? Especially if we can learn something in the process."

It took the pale scientist four more minutes to die. No one spoke until his body had gone quite limp.

Then into the silence Rauth said, "And just what have we learned, Miss Morse?"

She said, "We learned, Andy, that you better keep me trussed up good and tight, or we'll have a damn short honeymoon. And I wouldn't think that'd be much fun, even for a little freak like you."

For a moment Mallory thought: *She's done it. She's goddamned done it. There he goes.* Rauth's pale-green eyes shone with dreadful brightness in a taut, white face. He, too, seemed to be strangling.

Then, bit by bit, they watched him wrestle his rage under control. Slowly, he seemed by force of will to withdraw the brightness from his eyes, the tension from his face, to send the blood back into his cheeks. And then his good left hand relaxed. And last of all, his right hand lost its tautness.

Rauth's voice was courteous and almost disinterested when he finally spoke.

"You're right, Miss Morse," he said. "Our honeymoon wouldn't be much fun after all. I'll just have to think of something else."

10   *The Well of Truth*

Laura Morse's martial arts training had included a variety of methods for slowing her heartbeat, depressing her respiration, relaxing her muscles, and clearing her mind. She knew Jack thought these enabled her to dispel fear.

She wished it were true.

She was in a windowless room, perhaps ten by fifteen feet, illumined by indirect lighting that flowed evenly from the seam where the walls met the ceiling. The ceiling was ivory in color; the walls were a deep beige. The floor was the ubiquitous polished black rock. The bed on which she lay was comfortable, placed in the precise center of the room, and covered with taupe sheets that seemed to be raw silk. She might have been lying on a massage table in an elegant and impossibly expensive spa. Even the fact that her ankles and wrists had been wrapped in heavy felt and then tightly bound together with leather straps might have been part of some recherché beauty treatment. The straps binding her ankles were fastened to the foot of the bed; those at her wrists were fastened to the head. The door was directly behind her, so that she wouldn't be able to see who came in when it next opened. That bothered her unreasonably. She knew it was meant to. She'd spent the last half an hour trying to slip her bonds and was now exhausted and glistening with sweat; sweat had puddled inside her wet suit and was beginning to cool. Her mind was beginning to slither into panic. She called it to order. *They can kill you quick,* she thought, *or slowly. They can cause you pain until you lose the ability to feel it. They can pry your jaws open and feed you horrible things. They can deny you sleep. They can drug you. They can grind you down until there's nothing left, no person you or anyone would recognize as Laura Morse, make you forget your name, make you forget there ever was a you. But that's all they can do. There's a finite number of bad things anyone can do to anyone, and they've all been done to somebody sometime. Some you can survive. Some you can't. If you don't survive, all it means is you're dead, which is how everyone ends up anyway. You've trained for this, trained for years; you're as well prepared to meet this as anyone in the world.* She was awash in terror, sick with it, but felt almost sure she could bear what was coming, if only she knew what they were doing to Jack. If she knew Jack was going to be all right, if she had that one good thing to hang onto, she felt she could see this business through, and survive or die the way she'd been trained to do.

Behind her, the door quietly opened.

She willed herself not to crane her head.

The footsteps on the stone floor were almost silent. It was a disciplined gait, a martial artist's gait. Male. Long-legged. Probably young.

She knew who it was before she looked up into the ratlike pale-brown eyes.

"He sent me for you," Renko said.

She did not reply.

"He told me to get you ready," he added.

Raising his right arm, he drew back the sleeve of his loose black jumpsuit and extended it before her eyes, turning it slowly so that she could see the long surgical scars crossing his forearm, bisecting his elbow.

"Two operations," Renko said. "From what your boyfriend did. He's good. You taught him, maybe? You taught him good. I can move the arm now. I can even fight a little, though not so good like I used to fight. The doctor told me, that's not going to be like it used to again. Not anymore." The young Serb dropped his arm.

When he raised it again, he held the trench knife.

They'd zipped up her wet suit again. Renko reached out and set the knife against the sponge rubber covering her collarbone. Slowly, lightly, he brushed the edge of the blade down over her left breast. He lingered over the point of her breast, gave it a little slap with the flat of the blade. Then, delicately, between thumb and blade, he pinched up the fabric of her wet suit and the nylon swimsuit beneath.

With an abrupt jerk, he gouged out a rough circle of cloth. She felt the cool air of the room moving around her nipple.

"For what he's going to do," Renko explained, "you don't have clothes on."

He dropped the scrap of cloth on the floor and repeated the procedure on her right breast. Then lowered his arm and began to stroke the knife over her mons veneris. She forced herself to keep her eyes open and fixed on his face. She forced her body to remain limp and relaxed. Renko pinched up the cloth covering the base of her belly, and she felt his knife gliding in a broad semicircle to the left, and then another to the right. "What he's going to do, you know, it's not what you think," he said.

He'd separated a leaf-shaped flap of rubber and nylon eight inches across. He lifted it now, nipped off its base, and dropped it on the floor, and she felt the cool air, and then the flat of his knife, moving lightly over the tops of her thighs.

"It's worse," Renko said.

He studied her, knife poised. "He doesn't like your clothes. But I think you look quite pretty now."

He inserted the tip of the knife under her collar and with a single economical stroke, laid her wetsuit and swimsuit open from neck to groin, and then with four more strokes laid open her wet suit along her legs and arms. "Like skinning a mink," he remarked. Setting the knife aside, he slipped a broad hand beneath the small of her back, lifted her hips easily from the bed, and with a brisk tug whipped the remnants of her clothes from beneath her like a magician flicking the tablecloth from a fully set table. He dropped the shapeless mass of rubber and nylon on the floor with a slapping noise and lowered her buttocks to the bed. Aside from the felt swathing her hands and feet, she was naked now. She could feel her wet flesh goose-pimpling. Her eyes had not left his face. Her breathing remained steady and slow. Controlling her face, controlling her breathing; she was grateful to have something to do. He slipped a hand between her thighs and wiggled it to see how much room there was.

"A pity your legs are tied close like this," he said. "Or I could do things you might like."

He slid his hand up her thighs and took hold of her, and for a moment his hard fingers were busy. The muscles of her jaw flickered once before she could will them slack again.

"Ah," he said, noticing. "Hello there."

He trailed his damp thumb lightly along her belly, delicately circled her navel with it, then along her gleaming breastbone. He touched it to her lips.

"But I still have your mouth," he said.

"And I still have my teeth," she replied levelly.

"And I still have my knife."

"It won't help you much once I've used my teeth. Besides, Rauth would kill you. Badly. He wants me in one piece, without a mark on me. That's what the felt's for, isn't it?"

"Yes, you are correct," Renko admitted. "It's a great pity. So now, this way, I can't do nice things. I can only do things you won't like. Things that nobody could like." He began stroking her forehead, as if soothing a feverish child. "Now, if I had my own way, I would take you somewhere and do all those things to you for a long time. For a long . . . long . . . long time. Until you forget there was ever a time when somebody wasn't doing those things to you. Until you forget nobody could like those things. Until you begin to like them. Until, when I get tired, you say, Why do you stop? But the way it is, I have only a few short hours until he wants you. And so you will dislike what I do the entire time. You will dislike it all very much."

He set a foot on the edge of the bed and with a single, agile movement was standing astride her, his feet bracketing her hips, looking down into Laura's face. *Don't think,* she told herself. *Still your mind. Do your job. Do your job.*

"And then I must give you to Rauth," Renko said. "And when he begins, you will wish I was still doing all those things to you. You will wish you were back here with me."

He bent toward her.

There was a rap on the door. "Tesic?" said a muffled male voice. "Garland here. What's taking you?"

Renko stared past Laura at the door.

"You've had more than enough time to get the girl ready, Tesic," said the voice. It had a faint Western twang. "And Rauth told me you weren't to be left alone with her for longer than absolutely necessary. He knows you, fella, and so do I. I'll expect you out here in fifteen seconds. Don't disappoint me."

One day, Laura knew, she'd forget the look on Renko's face.

At least, she hoped so.

Nothing, Mallory thought savagely. *Not a goddamn thing.* No windows, no electrical outlets, no exposed ventilator grilles. Nothing that could be broken or unscrewed or pulled loose and used as a weapon. Walls some kind of heavy padding over concrete. Ceiling a single slab of polished concrete. Lights and ventilators recessed out of reach. Bed fastened to the floor the way they did it in the maximum security prisons, with heavy rivets, not bolts. There weren't any springs underneath; just flexible strips of steel. Welded on. His hands were shackled, but in front of him, not behind, and his fingers were free; he could tear the sheets into strips if he wanted to. And then what, weave a lanyard? He didn't even have a pipe to hang himself from. He paced around the room; it was maybe ten by fifteen and didn't have a goddamn thing in it he could use. He wondered if he could kill himself by jumping off the bed head-first onto the stone floor. Maybe. And what the hell good would that do? He wasn't thinking right. He wasn't as clear as he wanted to be. It was hard to be clear when he didn't know where Laurie was, what they were doing to her. He'd wanted to tweak Rauth off, shake the little man's control, and goddamn her, she'd gotten in ahead of him, and now what the hell had she let herself in for? Goddamn her, if she was just the hell out of this place, if he only had to worry about himself, then maybe he could think.

Behind him, the door quietly opened.

Mallory spun and was met with the steady muzzles of two Stens. The man standing between the two armed guards was middle-aged and nondescript, with steady, unimpressed eyes. Mallory heard a faint Western twang as he said, "Doctor'll see you now. And in case you were thinking of doing something silly, like making us kill you? My men have orders not to. They'll kneecap you and carry you in on a stretcher. Stretcher's right outside. Will you walk, or ride?"

"I wouldn't mind stretching my legs a bit," Mallory said.

The Westerner led the way, keeping just far enough in front of Mallory to be out of range of a flying kick. He didn't bother looking back. One of the big guards had snapped a padded nylon collar around Mallory's neck and clipped it to eight feet of heavy chain, and was now walking Mallory like a dog on a leash. The other guard kept pace with the Sten aimed at the ceiling just above Mallory's head, ready to bring the gun into play in an instant. The stretcher bearers padded along behind. They walked down a short length of curving corridor and through automatic double doors of armored glass.

When the doors rolled open, Mallory smelled cold stone and, again, the sea. He was being led out onto a circular gallery surrounding a vast concrete well. The walls stretched up endlessly; they were the weathered naked rock of the volcano's crater. He looked up and saw the jagged mouth of the crater directly above him. The articulated steel dome that sealed off the crater, the one built like a camera shutter, had irised open, and he could see the bright tropic stars.

In the center of the star-filled crater's mouth, perhaps seventy feet over Mallory's head, hung a shadowy package, much longer than it was wide, suspended from the crater's rim by three long cables.

The vast conical chamber was shrouded in dimness except for a single tiny light from the opposite side of the circular balcony. As they rounded the great concrete curve, and the light grew nearer, Mallory saw that the light sat on a small writing desk, and that behind the desk sat a man, and that the man was Anton Rauth. Behind him stood Erno. Mallory fought down a brief spasm of disappointment; he realized he'd hoped to see Laura there. Almost anything would be better than this not knowing where she was. They led Mallory to within ten feet of the desk and halted with a jerk on the chain around his neck.

The desk was another of Rauth's damn antiques, a fancy little thing on those feet that were supposed to look like a lion's paws. There was a snarling lion's face carved into each corner. On the table was a covered silver dish, a small radio-control unit with a stubby antenna, and a stack of papers, which Rauth was signing, quickly and fluently, with his left hand. This little creep had trained himself to write lefty. It was as disheartening a display of iron disci-

pline as anything else Mallory had seen, and he glumly watched
Rauth writing for a full fifteen seconds before he recognized the
pen he was using.

It was the Waterman Superba that Gray had given him in Cannes.

"Sorry. Won't be a moment," Rauth said pleasantly. He examined
a final paper, made a quick correction to it, signed it, and capped the
pen. Looking up, he said, "I'd like to thank you for this most thoughtful gift, Mr. Mallory. Each time I use this handsome pen in years to
come, I shall think fondly of you both."

"Don't mention it," Mallory said.

"Do you like this place? I find it quite restful, as well as useful. I
call it the Well of Truth. Like the author of Revelation, I enjoy the
occasional note of high drama. Perhaps you've already guessed the
function of that largish hole before us?"

"Sure," Mallory said. "It's where you put folks you don't like. I
guess shooting us would lack that little note of high drama."

"Indeed it would. And drama is a key element in any successful
scheme of deterrence."

"Uh huh. You going to keep telling me how much you like drama,
or were you thinking of maybe getting down to business?"

"Oh, we shall be quite businesslike this evening, Mr. Mallory. But
first, a little snack to refresh you? Free his hands, Erno. I think he's a
bit tired of having you feed him."

Mallory sensed rather than heard one of the guards approaching
behind him, then felt the cool tip of a gun barrel against his neck.
Erno slung his Sten around his shoulder and unfastened Mallory's
handcuffs. He then took up his position behind Rauth again, submachine gun at the ready.

Rauth uncovered the silver dish at his elbow. Within were an egg-
slicer and a shallow celadon bowl containing a single peeled hard-
boiled egg. He opened the slicer and set the egg inside. He
gestured. "Would you do the honors, Mr. Mallory?"

Mallory felt the two guns tracking him; one aimed at his head, one at his back. The chain behind him tautened slightly. If he stepped forward, Rauth would be within range of at least three killing blows Mallory could think of, and Mallory would need no more than three-eighths of a second to execute any of them. But the guards with the guns weren't likely to let him have even that much time. And as long as they had Laurie somewhere . . . He moved carefully toward the desk, feeling the drag of the collar at his neck. Slowly, he reached out a forefinger and pressed down the handle of the egg-slicer. The feeling of sharp wires sinking through the meat of the egg was, for some reason, very nasty.

Mallory stepped back, and Rauth emptied the egg slicer into the celadon dish. "Please," he said, offering it to Mallory.

Mallory picked up a slice and hesitated.

Rauth took a slice of his own and ate it in two neat nibbles. "Don't you like eggs, Mr. Mallory? This one's *very* fresh. I wouldn't feed a guest a stale egg."

Mallory slipped the bit of dead white flesh into his mouth and swallowed. It required an effort. He could feel it in his throat, rubbery, inching downward.

"There, now," Rauth said. "Refreshed?"

"Not much," Mallory said.

"Get the idea yet?"

"No."

"Tut. Have a look in the Well."

Mallory felt the chain behind him slacken a bit. Still moving with care, he stepped over to the concrete balustrade and looked down into the blackness. He heard a click from Rauth's desk—the radio control—and a bank of lights rimming the great well flicked on.

The mouth of the Well was perhaps sixty feet across, and strung edge to edge like a harp with gleaming parallel strands of wire.

"By the way," Rauth said behind him. "I'm afraid I neglected an introduction. Mr. Mallory, your escort this evening is Mr. Harold Garland, my Director of Security."

"Pleased to meet you," said the Westerner.

"Likewise," Mallory said, examining the wire. It was very thin, very taut, and glittered dully, like a fine metal rasp. The Well beneath was quite black. From far below, he could hear water lapping at its concrete walls.

"Mr. Garland's function is a particularly vital one in our little firm. He is the man responsible for, among other things, preventing hostile agents from entering my compound."

There was a moment of utter silence.

"Mr. R—" Garland began. Mallory turned just in time to see one of the stretcher bearers swing the skeleton butt of his Sten into the nape of Garland's neck. The man staggered, his eyes stunned, and in a moment the bearers had bundled him backward onto the stretcher. And then, with a deft heave, swung him up and out into the Well.

Garland let out a howl as he found himself in midair. It ended abruptly in a brief wet noise as he struck the wires and seemed to vanish in a burst of red and off-white pulp.

And then he was gone, with only a coppery tint along a stretch of wire to mark his passing. In perhaps five seconds they heard a splash, as if a bucket of offal had been emptied into a distant tub of water.

Mallory turned around and looked at Rauth again.

"Mr. Garland was a disappointment," Rauth said.

"And you don't deal too well with disappointment," Mallory said.

"Perhaps not. Get the idea yet?"

"Yeah." The taste of sliced hard-boiled egg was thick in his mouth.

"Good. You are now going to tell me all about Gray and the Consultancy. I understand my ex-employee Piotr Nemerov made a clumsy attempt to pump you on the subject in Istanbul. I, on the other hand, have more confidence in your abilities as a storyteller. I shall give you free rein to tell me anything you consider of interest, in your own words, just as it occurs to you. I'll sort it all out later."

Mallory gave himself a little shake. "Hell," he said, almost to himself. "I was worried this'd be tricky. I was really worried. And here you've gone and made it all simple for me. I don't discuss my business with little craps like you," Mallory said, white-faced. "Just go on and throw me in there, if that's the best you can think of."

"I wouldn't dream of it," Rauth said, and picked up the radio control again.

The second bank of lights sent their glare directly overhead. They struck the long package suspended high overhead and made it glow like heated silver.

It was a naked woman, dangling seventy feet above their heads like mistletoe at Christmas. Her arms were bound behind her back, her legs strapped together at ankle and knee. Her wheat-blonde hair hung loose, partly hiding her face, and even at that distance, Mallory could see she was almost too thin. He felt the tightly controlled stillness of his mind begin to dissolve into a silent roar of panic. *Goddamn her,* he thought numbly. *Goddamn her anyhow.*

"I wouldn't dream of sending you after Mr. Garland," Rauth repeated. "Not and interrupt our nice little chat before it's really begun. But Miss Morse, who presumably lacks your special knowledge? Who is after all not a proper employee of the Consultancy? Miss Morse is another matter." He uncapped the pen again. "Let's start with Gray. Don't worry about going too fast. I've taught myself shorthand."

"No," Laura shouted from above them, her voice echoing off the rock. *"Don't tell him anything. Do your job, Jack. Do your job. Forget me and see what you can do about the job."*

Mallory looked back at Rauth again. He shook his head slowly.

"Goddamn it, Jack, forget me and play for time. You're the one he needs. You're the one he needs alive, Jack. Let me go, Jack."

Mallory cleared his throat. "Well," he said raggedly.

"Just let me go. He'll kill me anyway. I'm already dead, Jack. I'm already dead."

"Well," Mallory said again. "Damn, shorty. Damn if you don't know how to put an awkward pause in a conversation."

"Indeed," Rauth said. "Well, shall we begin? You don't really want to watch your sweetheart being julienned, do you, Mr. Mallory? Feeling for her as you do, I imagine it would be highly unpleasant for you."

"No," Mallory said slowly, staring hard into Rauth's eyes. "No, I don't think you can imagine." He cleared his throat and went on, deliberately. "From what I've seen of you, I don't think you can imagine what a healthy man feels for a woman. I'm guessing old Hanny was lucky in more ways than one. I'm guessing that flipper of yours isn't the only thing you got that doesn't work right."

In the end, it was as simple as that.

Rauth dropped the pen and came out of his chair with a strangled noise and stood quivering, his eyes horribly bright.

"I don't—" he said. "I don't . . . "

He swallowed and squeezed his eyes shut.

The little man's control was gone now, all right. Mallory waited.

At last Rauth opened his eyes.

"I don't think," he said hoarsely, "that I want to talk to you anymore."

He picked up the radio control and pressed the third button. The straps binding Laura Morse clicked open.

She let out a single brief cry and began to fall.

For a moment, everyone's eyes were drawn helplessly upwards. All except Mallory's. His were fixed on the uncapped pen on Rauth's desk. He seemed to see every curlicue chased into its silver nib, to see every crease on the knuckles of his own right hand, as he lunged forward and swept the pen from the desktop. The collar around his neck dragged him back then, but he'd already brought his other hand forward and given the pen's barrel a twist. And then another.

And then an unbearable line of crimson light flashed across his vision.

The line became a flame-bright sheet as Mallory whipped the laser around and burned a trench into Erno's face and chest before the big man could bring his Sten into play. Rauth dodged sideways as Mallory spun and cut the chain binding him. He saw the guards staggering back in shock. From the corner of his eye he saw Laura plunging toward the wires. Still spinning, still playing out the precise choreography he'd been refining in his head since he'd first stood before Rauth's desk, Mallory brought the beam slashing downward across the mouth of the Well, then thumbed the laser off and dove for the floor as, with a noise like a gigantic piano destroyed by machine-gun fire, the wires parted, the severed ends sizzling backward through the air. Rauth leapt backward, a red stripe appearing along his face. Another strand of wire sliced a guard's head and gun arm diagonally from his body. Then Mallory was on his feet again and vaulting over the concrete balustrade as Laura reached the mouth of the Well. The darkness swallowed them up together.

Five seconds to the bottom, perhaps. No time to tell Laurie everything. He wanted to tell her that there had to be an underwater pump at the bottom of the Well to flush away the mangled scraps of its victims. Otherwise there'd be an awful stink, and Mallory had smelled nothing but salt water and cold stone. He wanted to tell her to go deep when they hit and let the pump suck them out to the open sea. He wanted to tell her he knew her legs were dead from being bound so long, and that she needed to grab his collar and let him tow her. He wanted to warn her to get herself turned around and hit the water right, like a diver, or, falling from this height, she'd snap her neck, but saw she was already plunging head-first like a golden spear, her hands ready to part the surface. He wanted to tell her to puff out hard just before they hit and take a deep breath, but when the hell was *just before,* anyway? How long had they been falling, as the black walls blurred past them, seeming to slow time to a crawl? He'd lost track of—*Three? Two?* "Grab a hold!" he shouted, hoping she'd understand, then huffed his lungs empty and dragged in a chestful of air. Had he been too—

An instant of icy obliteration.

Then they were deep in the dense black water. He groped out, felt Laurie's ribs, hugged her closer and felt hard fingers scrabbling at the back of his collar just as the pump's suction found them and drew them smoothly in. He had a moment of panic as it sucked them still further downward, a blind urge to escape, thrash his way back to the surface, try something, anything else, and then the rim of a big pipe slammed his ribs and nearly startled the air out of him. And then they were in the pipe, gliding forward at a speed impossible to judge. How many feet to the outfall? Fifty yards? A hundred? More? Should he be kicking harder to get them to the outlet sooner, or going limp to conserve breath and letting the pump carry them out? He found himself thinking what he hadn't let himself think before, that if Rauth had installed a grate across the pipe—He could imagine the steel bars. He could almost see them. If so, would they be able to swim back to the Well? Against the current? No, if they met a grate they couldn't squeeze through, it was lights out. To drown in a cement pipe buried under a mountain; it was a perfect claustrophobe's nightmare. The pain in Mallory's lungs was growing, joining the pain in his ears and, in his head, the squealing, chattering onrush of fear. They'd stopped moving forward. They were still. Stuck. He was buried, buried deep—He had to breathe now. Now, *now*, even if it was water.

The pipe was gone from around them. They were in the sea. He opened his eyes and saw nothingness. Laura had released his collar. He could feel his lungs letting go; he couldn't stop it now. He groped out again, found a small, flat buttock, and roughly shoved it surfaceward. And now he felt his throat opening . . .

Laura was frightened for Jack, coldly terrified. She'd throttled her need for oxygen down to its bottom limit and was good for at least eight or nine minutes more, but how long could an untrained thirty-four-year-old like Jack hold his breath? Two minutes, even? Ninety *seconds?* It was past ninety seconds already. She knew they were in the open sea now; was Jack really going to drown, now, so close to freedom? He'd gone still—had he drowned already? If she could get him to the surface, could she resuscitate him? When her own legs were too numb to tread water? She let go of his collar and groped out for an arm to drag him up with, and then felt a rough hand clamp painfully on her behind as he thrust her upward. And himself downward. The *idiot.*

And then, without meaning to, she'd broken the surface.

And a moment later Jack, hacking and retching, had floundered up beside her.

He tried to say something. It came out mostly water. He reached out and slipped an arm beneath her, gagged again, hauled in his first good breath. "All right?" he said hoarsely, and coughed again, spraying droplets across her breasts.

"Yes," she said. "I'm all right."

"Good," he said, coughing. "Good."

The tropic night spread out around them, dreamily soft, weirdly peaceful. The stars above them were thick as mist. The moon silvered the slopes of He' Konau. Jack was cradling her now, treading water with one arm beneath her shoulders and the other beneath her numbed legs, bearing her up. She was waiting for the sirens. She heard nothing, just Jack drawing in breath after breath, calming himself, squeezing out the last bits of his fear, readying himself for action. She wriggled her toes and felt sharp pains shoot up her legs. She began slowly flexing and stretching her deadened calves.

"Well," Jack said at last, "you do have curves, Laurie. Where've you been keeping them?"

"Go to hell, Jack," she said.

"You all right? They didn't hurt you, did they? I was a little bit jumpy about what they might be doing."

"I'm all right."

"Guess I gave you sort of a scare."

"Sort of. Jack, those little bits of the security man—"

"Yeah, I know."

"They'll be out here with us. Drawing sharks."

"I know."

"Have you seen anything?"

"I might've seen a fin," he admitted. "We'll start swimming in a minute, soon as you got your legs under control."

"I can almost use them now," she said.

And then they heard it. A distant snarling noise like a chainsaw revving up. And then another. And then a third.

"What the hell's that?" Mallory said.

"Surface sleds," Laura said grimly. "We used them on the Canal job last year. You were in Frankfurt."

"Well, what in the hell are surface sleds?"

"They're not good news," she said.

11 *The Dragon Rises*

They were listening hard. The harsh note of the sleds' engines rose, fell, as if they were calling to each other, and then steadied. Two of the engines began growing softer. One grew louder.

"They're splitting up," Mallory said. "Heading in different directions."

"There must be more than one outfall," Laura said. "Maybe there's three. They don't know which one we came out of."

She slipped from his arms, and without a word they began slowly sculling away from each other. It was better not to present a single target. At fifteen yards apart, Mallory stopped and scanned the horizon. Where was the dock, in front of them or behind? He glanced at his wrist, remembered Rauth had taken their compasses. Judging from the sounds, in front of them, somewhere behind that spit of land. He reached around and found the fastenings of his nylon collar, with its stub of chain. He undid them and let it sink beneath the waves. His eyes were adjusting to the moonlight, and he saw a steely triangular glint, cresting the waves and then rolling calmly under. "Nice and slow, Laurie," he said.

"I saw it, too," she said.

Mallory listened again. "Only one of those sled deals is coming this way," he decided. "We'll need a little more luck like that. How many do they carry?"

"Just one rider. Two at most. It's like a motorcycle on water, and almost as fast. You sit astride and steer it with handlebars. Wedge-shaped pontoon hull, split keel. Speed up and you get a hydrofoil effect. The ones we used would do seventy-five knots."

"Jesus. And you've driven one of these things?"

"I'm not an expert, but yes."

"All right. When he gets here, I'm going to draw him my way. Lay low and be ready to grab the sled if you get an opening."

"Right. Here he comes."

There was a long bright glint on the water beyond the spit, as from a glaring light parallel to the surface, and then almost at once a tiny sleek vehicle shot into sight, a single headlight glittering in its nose. It moved with nightmarish speed. Mallory had never seen anything move that fast on the water, not even a cigarette boat. It swung in a tightly controlled arc, banking like a fighter jet, and in a moment the searchlight was shining straight at him, half-blinding him, bleaching the ocean white. Hunched behind it was the rider, straddling the short, sleekly humped hull like one of those old sea-god guys riding a dolphin, gripping an oddly bulky handgun instead of a trident. Goggles and a helmet. But at least no windscreen. Mallory glanced toward Laura and saw empty ocean, then a nose and forehead just breaking the surface for a quick breath, and then nothing again. Good. Mallory was riding as high in the water as he could without kicking up a froth that might stir a shark, while unsnapping the jacket of his wet suit from the leggings and easing himself out of it, when he heard the first heavy crack of pistol-fire, and simultaneously a hiss as the bullet cut the water beside him.

Well, he'd gotten the man's attention. He hoped he wouldn't regret that. There was that shark fin off at two o'clock, or maybe another one. They were probably wondering what all the commotion was about. Another shot, and Mallory still had one arm stuck in his sleeve. *Hell.* He sank deep into the water, eyes open, and watched from beneath as the sled's phosphorescent wake shot toward him and past. An underwater shock wave shoved him back and down.

When he rose again, he was gripping his wet suit jacket in his right hand, holding it by the cuffs.

One more fast pass like that, he prayed. *Don't smarten up on me now.*

The driver was a hundred yards past them before he could slow himself. He cut around in the tightest possible circle, and Mallory saw the sled's rear hunker down in the water as the man cranked the throttle. Mallory began to swim toward Laurie, taking long, slow strokes, trying to keep himself in view while not presenting too perfect a target, trying not to thrash, keeping the sled on his right side. He saw the gun muzzle lift again, and sank into the water just as the driver let off another shot. From sixty damn yards off. Thank God for fools. Shooting one-handed with a pistol, at night, from a moving, bouncing platform, struck Mallory as a bad deal, but the guy could always get lucky. Or be a better shot than Mallory. When Mallory next surfaced, the sled was barely fifty feet away, heading straight at him. He sank once more and watched the glowing white wake above him draw nearer. A whitish ray of bubbles appeared beside him as the driver fired into the water, then another, beneath him, and still the white wake was drawing nearer. *Like a damn bullfighter,* Mallory thought. *Dear Jesus, this is dumb.*

Now.

Mallory lunged from the water as the sled whipped past him, swinging his waterlogged rubber jacket up and around like a flail across the driver's goggled face. The impact nearly wrenched his arm from the socket.

And then the gun was spinning through the moonlit air, the sled was past him, and the driver was tumbling backward into the water. With Mallory.

Mallory had fought all his life and, though he never took victory for granted, had grown used to it. In the Army he'd been considered an unusually effective instructor in hand-to-hand. He was a fair amateur wrestler and, without the benefit of any formal training, a capable boxer. But he'd never fought a man while treading water and trying not to attract sharks, and he quickly saw that he didn't know how. Neither did the driver. And so in a moment they were locked in a plain old playground shoving match. Mallory slugged the man in the jaw. Without his feet under him or his weight behind it, it wasn't much punch. The man's answering blow took him in the neck and told Mallory what he'd rather not have known: the man was strong. Mallory tried to push him under, but the driver had a life jacket under his nylon jumpsuit. He was riding higher in the water than Mallory, and in fisticuffs as in artillery, high ground conveys a critical advantage. He was coming around from that slap in the face too fast; his helmet had saved him from the worst of the blow. But his mouth and nose were bleeding. *More blood in the water.* Mallory thought. *All we needed. Get on the sled, Laurie.* The driver rolled forward over Mallory and they both went down. Mallory struck at the thick arms, took hold of the clutching fingers to break them, but couldn't get a grip through the man's heavy gloves. Again he felt a shock wave break against him, this time from below. A shark had just passed beneath them. Sometimes they made a few passes before they got up the nerve to dig in. Mallory hadn't had a proper breath before going under, and his lungs were beginning to spasm. He grabbed at the driver's life jacket, angling for a grip, and suddenly remembered Laurie's hand gliding along his chest in the Pera Palas hotel. He stroked his hand up the man's chest, along his throat, and up under his helmet, until his fingers rested just under the man's right ear. Where the hell was it? There? There?

There. Mallory jammed two fingers with all his strength into the driver's Peony Crescent.

He felt him relax into death.

Mallory shoved up hard, thrusting the body desperately aside, broke the surface, and took a sobbing gulp of air, clutching the floating corpse for support. Then was jolted as something yanked it away from him. The body jerked twice in the water. Then it was drawn smoothly down out of sight.

He was aware of a grinding roar close behind him, and turned to see Laura Morse astride the surface sled. She was steering with her left hand and cradling the driver's pistol in her right.

"You both kept rolling around," she said. "I couldn't get a shot in."

Her dripping hair twined around her throat and shoulders, and her breasts glittered in the reflected glare of the headlamp. She gripped the sled's hull between long, bare thighs. *I'm alive,* Mallory thought dazedly. *And lookit that.*

"Jack," she said patiently. "That wasn't the only shark in the South Pacific."

She tucked the gun under her knee and held out a hand. They gripped each other's wrists as trapeze artists do, and Laura leaned back hard as Mallory swung himself aboard the sled and settled in behind her. "Here," he said, handing her his jacket. "You might want this."

"I do," she said. "You might want this." She passed back the gun. "The big aluminum casing's hollow, and makes it float. I think it's recoilless."

"Twelve-shot clip," Mallory reported as Laura zipped herself into his jacket. "Seven left. Guess the shark's got the spare ammo. All right. I'm going to be shoving up pretty close behind you, so it's not too obvious there's two people on this thing. Sorry to get fresh."

"We're going hunting?"

"That's right."

"Hang on," Laura said, and twisted the throttle.

Not that much different from water-skiing, Mallory thought. Then, as they accelerated, he thought, Well, a little quicker. More like a speedboat. By the time Laura had wound out the big engine beneath their rumps, Mallory had admit this was like nothing he'd ever done, except maybe riding an old shovel-head Harley flat-out once on a disused Montana highway. And this sea wasn't near as smooth as that concrete had been. Mallory let his spine go lax, as Laura was doing, so the sled's jouncing wouldn't knock a disk loose, and clamped his jaws to keep from biting off the tip of his tongue. They rounded the spit from behind which the first sled had come and sighted the second sled in not much more than a minute. Its driver glanced back over his shoulder into the glare of their headlight, then kept riding, unconcerned.

"Conned him. Laurie, I need your shoulder for a gun-rest," Mallory roared, his lips close to Laura's ear. *"Gonna hurt some."*

She understood and screamed back, *"My ear won't do me much good if we let them catch us."*

He rested his right forearm on her right shoulder, brought his left arm around Laura's collarbone, and gripped his own wrist, hugging her body back hard against his. *"Try to kill the bounce a little,"* he bellowed.

She eased the sled starboard so it was more parallel to the waves. Their path began to diverge from their quarry's, but they were riding smoother. Mallory would have maybe ten seconds to get his shot in before they'd diverged completely.

He let himself go a little dreamy, as he did on the target range, as if the target were a sunset he'd come out to admire. For three or four seconds, he pondered the creases crossing driver's nylon-clad back. Then he squeezed off a stacked burst of two, one a fraction of a degree above the other.

The second took the driver between the shoulder blades, and he spiraled off his sled into the sea.

"*Nice*," Laura roared. "*But we might not be able to surprise the last one.*"

"*You got that right. Here he comes.*"

The last sled was closing in fast from about ten o'clock, catching them broadside. Mallory didn't have to tell Laura to narrow their profile by cutting to starboard and meeting the attack head-on. They weren't more than halfway through the turn when three shots raked the water before them. A fourth sliced the waves behind as Laura accelerated again, and then the sleds were barreling straight at each other, headlight to headlight. *Middle of the goddamn South Pacific*, Mallory thought, *and we're playing chicken. Might as well never left Texas.* He mashed his gun arm down on Laura's shoulder and squeezed off a shot between the driver's hunched shoulders. Both sleds were bouncing hard now, and Mallory couldn't see where the shot went, couldn't even tell if he needed to correct up or down, right or left. A shot puffed past his wet, bare arm and he squeezed off two more. The target was getting fatter, anyway. Another dozen seconds and they'd be rubbing noses, and Mallory had just two rounds left. And the sled driver was probably flush. Another shot dug into the waves before them.

"*Fuel tank, Jack*," Laura screamed. "*Amidships.*"

Goddamn it, maybe one day he'd grow some brains. Mallory quit aiming for the hunched little driver and threw down on the big, fat hull. He squeezed out his second-to-last shot.

Twenty yards ahead of them, the sled blossomed into an orange-white fireball. The driver spun limply in the night sky above them. One flaming leg traced a separate arc out toward the black horizon. There was no time to stop; Laura wrenched the sled hard to port and sailed into a rain of hot debris, and the edge of the fireball licked their faces as they skimmed through. And then they were coasting to a halt in the dark waters beyond.

Mallory said, "Get us away from the firelight, hon, and then let's hunker down a minute and think."

Laura eased the rumbling sled into the blackness to the east, brought it around to face the island, and cut the engine and lights. For a moment they listened to the ticking of the cooling hull and the rustling of the flames. The wrecked sled had sunk; only a slick of burning gasoline remained, and a blazing corpse bobbing almost invisibly in its bright center.

Beyond was the volcano and the floodlit mouth of the dock, from which, in eerie silence, one boat after another was putting out to sea. They were big Zodiacs, motorized inflatable rafts, each carrying upward of half a dozen armed men. Laura and Mallory could barely hear the clatter of their outboards.

"Nice driving," Mallory told Laura.

"I think that's the last one," Laura said. "Five Zodiacs. An average of seven men in each, armed with the RPKs. One man in each raft with a handheld searchlight and one with a shoulder-mounted bazooka. And we've got a not-terribly-accurate pistol and, I believe, one bullet."

"One left," Mallory confirmed.

"We're about three times faster than they are," Laura said musingly, "and we've still got most of a full tank. Even now, we might make a wide arc and beat them back to Pali Konau. But we couldn't hide from them once we got there. They'd burn the place out like a hornet's nest, and that would be it for all of us. The Konoese, too."

They watched in silence.

"They're fanning out to the west," she said. "Blanketing the water between here and the atoll. Setting up a cordon on each side. They don't know for sure that we came from there, but they know that's the only place we've got to run."

"No," Mallory said.

She turned her head inquiringly.

"We got one other place to go," he said. "One place they won't be looking for us."

Laura was silent. Then her shoulders shook, and she let out one of her rare, unlovely snorts of laughter.

She kicked over the engine and pointed the sled back toward He' Konau.

The mouth of the landing slip was ablaze with light. They made a wide arc and hugged the shore, their lights off, slowly easing up to the edge of the darkness. "Can you beach this thing so we can push off in a hurry?" Mallory whispered. "I think here's where we start climbing. Looks like they left just one guard minding the store, but I still don't want to stroll in through the front door."

"I do," Laura said, and Mallory heard her unzipping her jacket. "Would you take this, please?" Steering one-handed, she extended her other arm as if waiting for him to remove her wrap in the foyer of Le Bernardin.

After a moment, Mallory slipped the rubber jacket from her shoulders.

"Thanks," she said, and they puttered out into the circle of flood-lit ocean. The guard spun at the noise, bringing the big gun up in a single smooth motion so that his gaze and gunsights found them at the same moment. Then he froze. Laura smiled and waved. The guard had been on He' Konau for sixteen months, and for a moment all he could do was goggle.

Mallory punched a neat hole in the center of his chest.

The guard pivoted on his heel, as if about to run off and tell his friends, and pitched forward out of sight. They heard his gun clatter on the concrete. Then silence.

"You never smile at me like that," Mallory said as Laura brought the sled around the corner of the dock. A long steel staircase led down to the water's edge, where there was a little landing platform for small boats.

"I don't, do I?" she said. "Give me my blouse back, please." Gripping a sleeve between her teeth, she sprang ashore and began tying up the sled. Mallory leapt around her and, gun foremost, sprinted up the stairs. At the top he whirled in a crouch, pistol barrel sweeping the docking facilities.

"The gun's empty, Jack," Laura said as she reached the top of the stairs, zipping up Mallory's jacket. There before them stood the Abbadon on its turntable, the hatch open, the floodlights glittering balefully on its digging screws and cleated treads.

"Well, if there'd been anyone here, they wouldn't've known that," Mallory said, tossing the pistol into the water and scooping up the dead guard's machine gun. "Here. Take this and cover me while I set the gizmo."

Ignoring the gun, Laura bent and unbuckled the guard's belt. She dragged off his trousers and stepped into them, then quickly rolled up the cuffs. "In a minute," she muttered, glaring at the floor and yanking the belt tight. "This is important, too. Are you doing what I think you're doing?"

"Gonna try," Mallory said.

She took the gun and he trotted off to the control console that stood beside the Abbadon's great turntable. Summoning his memory of Rauth's demonstration—there was the big dial that governed speed, there the joystick that turned the device right and left—he began punching in coordinates. Meanwhile Laura pivoted slowly, the machine gun against her hip, as she moved through the cave looking for hiding places and vantage points. "Digging angle, eighty degrees," Mallory said as he worked. "Depth, ah, say a hundred fifty yards. 'Bout a hundred feet under the main factory floor."

"Not too deep," Laura said. "We don't want an actual earthquake."

"Oscillator activated in, what do you think, two minutes? We oughta be clear by then. You know, those pants are nice and roomy, but I miss the old ensemble. It had this nice little habit of riding up."

"I know," she said, working her way back toward the Abbadon. "But I'm afraid the show's over."

"Yes," said a Serb-accented voice. "She's quite right. The show is over."

Laura and Mallory became quite still.

"Very good," Renko told them. "I am very covered up right now, little Laurie, just a little bit of me to hit, and I have in my sights the base of your boyfriend's spine. That's not such a nice place to be hit. He isn't such a good boyfriend anymore if I do that. So you will be intelligent now and let the gun fall down on the ground. Very nice and slowly—yes. And now you will get down on your knees, slowly, yes, like that. Because I don't like how quick you move when you're standing up. And because I enjoy you on your knees. Isn't she nice on her knees, Jack? Don't you like her that way? That's a very nice obedient girl you have."

Renko was behind the nose of the Abbadon, resting his pistol on the edge of the open cockpit, everything but his gun hand and a bit of face covered up by twelve hundred tons of steel. Now he rose and stepped into view, his gun steady. "And now, Jack, I have my gun on your little girl. On the little place where the babies come out, so now you'll be sweet and obedient also, like her. You know, when I met your girl, Jack, I didn't know how nice she could be. We didn't get along when we met. She told me I was ugly. And it's true, I'm not handsome like you, and she hurt my feelings. But then this afternoon while you were having your nap, Laurie and I got to know each other better. I got to know her very well. And I found out how nice and obedient she could be. She didn't tell you how nice she was to me? She didn't tell you how well we got to know each other?"

"No," Mallory said after a moment. His voice was soft but clear. There was very little Texas in it now. "I guess she didn't think it was worth mentioning. You must not've made much of an impression."

"Jack," she said. "He didn't do anything. Jack, it's not true."

Mallory's long body was as still as a sword in its scabbard. He wasn't listening.

"*Jack,*" she said.

"Oh, I think maybe I made an impression," Renko said. "I think I gave Laurie some very big memories she won't forget. Just like you gave me some big memories when we met in Istanbul. Except now I'm going to make everybody forget everything. But I have this problem now, that I can't decide which one of you dies first. Maybe I should begin with you, Jack. Because I'll miss the little place where the babies come out, and maybe I can't bear to say good-bye to it yet. But then I think it would be better if I could see you watch your woman die. So maybe after all it should be ladies first."

"No," Mallory said again, and turned to him. "No, it isn't going to be ladies first. Or gentlemen, either." He began walking deliberately toward the young Serb.

"And here you come? You think I'm not going to shoot you?" Renko said, amused. "You think you just walk over and I give you my gun?"

Laura saw what Jack meant to do and clamped her jaws to keep from screaming. It was impossible. Even for someone as fast as she was, it was impossible.

"Yes, Renko," Mallory said, drawing steadily nearer. "Matter of fact, that's what I do think."

Renko shook his head pityingly, and his forefinger tightened on the trigger. And Mallory's foot landed on the pedal by the edge of the turntable.

It started up with the familiar lurch that jostled the Abbadon on its tracks, and sent Renko stumbling to the side. In what almost seemed like silence Laura watched a pale-red furrow trace itself along Jack's ribs as he plunged spinning, almost cartwheeling forward, and swept the pistol from Renko's hand. On the return journey, his hand grasped the Serb's wrist, and then with the same economical swipe of the left palm he'd used in Istanbul, Mallory jammed the arm backward until it snapped at the elbow.

Renko fell mewling against the Abbadon, and Mallory took him by the jaw and rapped his skull against the device's iron flank.

The young Serb slid to the floor.

"Okay, Jack," Laura said.

But Mallory had Renko under the arms and was dragging him to his feet. His eyes were lit from behind. *He doesn't look much saner than Rauth now,* Laura thought. Renko was in the air now, balanced on Mallory's shoulder, and then Mallory had bundled him into the Abbadon's cockpit and was buckling the straps with a series of harsh clacks. "Jack, no," she said. There was no breath behind her words. "Let's just go, Jack. *Jack,*" she screamed. *"No."*

Mallory turned to the console and slapped the power button.

The Abbadon came to life with a swelling, thunderous rumble Laura could feel in the concrete floor beneath her knees. The cockpit hatch, heavy as a safe door, began to close. From where she knelt she could not see Renko's face, could not see Renko at all, but the noise seemed to rouse him, and from within the cockpit came a shriek as he realized where he was and what was happening. She saw his good hand fly up and strain madly at the hatch as the hydraulic pistons drew it shut. Then the hatch closed with an echoing thud and his screams were cut off as if someone had flipped a switch. A dim white fist began to beat against the inside of the thick quartz port. The massed drill bits in the nose began to turn, slowly and then more rapidly, and then, with a riotous grinding noise, the Abbadon began rolling forward, emitting a deafening roar and raising its fearsome head as it went, like a cottonmouth preparing to strike. *"Jack,"* Laura screamed again. When the front third of the segmented vehicle had hunched itself into the air, the fanged head plunged forward and dug into the floor, emitting a chattering screech, spraying bits of concrete and stone in all directions. She could still see the pale fist beating at the cockpit window, leaving a faint red smear each time. Then the cockpit disappeared into the growing crater, and then the rest of the Abbadon slithered after it with shocking speed and ease: the cottonmouth slipping into a pond. And then it was gone.

Jack turned to her. The light of fury was fading from his eyes. He was coming back to her again.

Poor Laurie was still kneeling as Mallory walked up, her arms limp at her sides, staring at him, horrorstruck. Goddamn it, he shouldn't have done it like that, with her watching. Well, it couldn't be helped now. When she spoke, Mallory couldn't hear her over the buried roar. He had to read the words from her lips.

"That was worse," she whispered. "That was worse than what he did."

He said. "It was meant to be."

His voice had been harsh, and he cleared his throat. Laurie didn't respond. He touched her shoulder.

"C'mon, hon," he said. "Come on. Let's go home."

He might not have set the controls quite right, because by the time they cast off from the landing platform, a ghastly note was already rising from the steel steps, from the concrete dock, from everywhere, and the first chunks of stone were beginning to drop from the ceiling. A boulder the size of a summer cottage began to ease free as they sped clear of the cave's mouth, and then they heard the first of the explosions as they swung around the point and caught sight of Pali Konau.

Mallory was brandishing the dead guard's machine gun as a deterrent, though he knew that if he fired thing the recoil would likely knock him overboard. But the rifle proved not to be needed. The swarming Zodiacs were in chaos as the Abbadon set off explosion after explosion in the island's vast subterranean arms depot. Flinging their guns in the water, the guards were making for the open sea, or heading pell-mell toward Pali Konau. One dutiful or confused crew was even racing back to He' Konau. Laura and Mallory shot between them unhindered and almost unnoticed, and Mallory shrugged, consigned the gun to the waves, and used both arms to hang on. *It can't be this easy,* he thought. *It can't.* He twisted around in his seat to glance back toward He' Konau.

It isn't, he thought grimly.

A peculiar shimmer in the moonlit water along the volcanic island's shore. As if the ocean were coming loose from the beach somehow, and rippling like curtains in a breeze.

And then rising.

There it is. Goddamnit, I should've seen that coming.

He glanced ahead at Pali Konau, at the gap in the shoreline that led to the atoll's sheltered inner lagoon, then back at the volcano again, trying to gauge distances.

"*Stay still,*" Laura roared over her shoulder. "*You'll throw off my balance.*"

"*Being followed,*" he shouted in her ear.

"*How many?*"

"*We're being followed by the whole damn ocean,*" he said.

The shimmering waves were rising behind them to form a wall of black water. It was as if the black horizon were drawing nearer, driving a band of glittering silver before it. By now Laura and Jack were almost halfway between the He' Konau and Pali Konau, with two miles of open water before them and two behind them. But the onrushing wave was beginning to close the gap. As Mallory watched, it lifted the furthest Zodiacs, then kept rising until it began to hide the flame-pierced island. At its topmost edge, a bit of curling froth began to form.

"*Tsunami,*" Mallory bellowed. "*Head for the gap. Try to make the lagoon.*"

"*We'll hit the bridge,*" she bellowed back.

"*It'll be gone by the time we get there,*" he promised.

At these speeds, Mallory knew, the water would be hard as wood, and just falling off could be fatal. Beneath them, the moonlight on the blurring waves was like a shower of sparks thrown from a grinding wheel. And then the waves began to darken as the rising wall of water behind them blotted out the moon. Mallory looked back carefully, turning just his head, and saw a Zodiac sliding helplessly up the slope of the massive wave and then go spinning like a flipped nickel as it reached the top, scattering men in all directions. They were doing about eighty, he guessed, but the wave was doing about ninety. The mouth of the lagoon was opening up before them now, but slowly, slowly. Another Zodiac buckled halfway up the shining mountain of water, and at once was sucked inside.

"Running flat-out," Laura shouted, reading his thoughts.

He felt a sickening levitating feeling as they, too, began to slide up the tsunami's slope. They weren't going to make it in time.

"Get your feet under you," she bawled. *"Ready to jump with me on three."*

"Right." They had a better chance if they could get away from the sled. Slim instead of none. They were well up the slope now, approaching the atoll from a greater and greater height. The water was drawing back from the beach; he saw the bridge ahead of them looping across gleaming mud—but they were already riding far above the bridge's level, looking down on it—he saw mossy banks of coral laid bare to the moon for the first time in centuries, and then disappearing again into the onrushing shadow. They kept sliding hideously up and backward.

"One," Laura shouted.

Halfway up the slope of the wave and beginning to turn over on their noses.

"Two."

The sled's nose starting to dig in.

And *"Three"*—and they were spinning free. Just behind them, the vast wave smashed into the face of the atoll with an echoing roar. But now they were through the gap in the ridge, inside the sheltering circle, flying forward through the dark sky at eighty miles an hour and accelerating downward at thirty-two feet per second per second. The sled was tumbling away from them, to the left; Laura and Mallory were spiraling off to the right. And Mallory was reaching out, wrapping Laura in his arms, hanging on as she struggled to get free, twisting their bodies through a barrel roll, so that when at last they struck the lagoon like a pebble skimmed across a pond, he was beneath her, and took the full impact on the flat of his back.

He was aware of the taste of seawater, and then of the quite similar taste of blood. Someone was making a horrible squealing noise. That was him, trying to get a breath in. He listened for a while. Someone else was holding him up by the arms.

"*Please* wake up, Jack," said the familiar voice. "You're getting heavy."

He staggered to his feet and looked wildly around at Laura. There was blood on her collar. But it was all right, he saw. It was fine. It was his blood. He got a little air into his lungs and nodded, and almost fell again. The lagoon was heaving and slopping and the water in which they stood was now knee-high, now chest-high; Laura had to take his arm again. He was breathing now, and it hurt. A few ribs had let go. The salt stung the wound in his side. Good. Keep it clean. The suspension bridge, he saw, was gone now. Just a smashed stump of telephone pole left, vanishing and reappearing in the waves. The village huts were festooned with sea-wrack and leaned crazily in all directions. But the seaward face of the ridge had taken the brunt of the tsunami, and the palace and metal-roofed arena seemed drenched but sound. Konoese were pouring from these two shelters and trotting purposefully among their disheveled homes. Mallory glanced around: seventy feet behind them, the crushed surface sled burned brightly in a stand of shattered trees. "Are you all right, Jack?" Laura said.

He nodded again, more gingerly. It still hurt his head.

She took his shoulders and turned him toward He' Konau.

"Look," she said.

A helicopter was just lifting off from the top of the volcano. Beneath it, the long window Rauth had cut into the slopes of He' Konau had become a single line of unbearable white light. As they watched, the line of light brimmed over and began to spill down the volcano's lower slopes. The crump of exploding munitions had given way to a series of blasts so deep that they were felt more than heard. A pale yellow spume broke from the crater, carrying with it the massive steel dome, which revolved lazily in the air, shedding vast steel segments like a dead flower shedding petals in a gust of wind, and then a second gout of lava shot still higher and caught the rising helicopter amidships. It bloomed into a orange ball. Bright streams ran down the ridged black cone of He' Konau; bright rivers wandered to the sea and were lost in massive banks of steam. Bright cracks appeared as the hollowed-out mountain filled with magma and began to dissolve, to fall in upon itself and rise again as thick floods of light. Mallory staggered, and Laura set a steadying hand against his back. He draped an arm around her shoulders. Side by side they stood and watched as the Dragon rose to reclaim his Throne.

12 *Never Change*

S o that's the end of Anton Rauth," Mallory said.

He and Gray were in their familiar places in the tiny conference room on Madison Avenue. As often happened when
Mallory came back from a difficult job, the place seemed strange
and new. He traced the scars on the old conference table with a finger. They gleamed like meteor trails on the moon. He tried once
again to figure out how they'd shoehorned a table that big into a
room that small. He marveled again at the grubbiness of the walls
and carpet, the stingy dimness of the lights. And watching Gray
packing up the debriefing materials, he wondered how a man in a
sweater-vest like that could be so finicky about the arrangement of
papers in a folder. "Well, I guess it comes to us all," Mallory said
philosophically, and waited.

"You've seen his body, have you?" Gray asked, not looking up
from his papers.

Mallory smiled faintly.

"I wish you wouldn't try to annoy me, Jack," Gray said. "It wastes time."

"And that annoys you?" Mallory said.

Gray got the file arranged to his satisfaction, closed it, and set it aside. "Anton Rauth," he said, "is an exceptionally able individual with a high regard for his own survival. You may rest assured that he had a detailed standing plan, complete with fallbacks and cut-throughs, for his own evacuation in the event of a successful assault on He' Konau. I suppose he might have been seen off by a glob of magma or whatnot. One can't plan for everything. But I fancy, and of course hope, that we'll be hearing from him again."

"You hope we will?"

"Rauth and his initiatives have been, one way or another, a sub-stantial source of revenues for this firm."

"Well, hell, then," Mallory said. "I'm sorry I put such a good source of revenue in danger. Next time I'll be more careful. How come you're not frying my tail about exceeding instructions?"

"Your instructions were to return alive with data. If you hadn't taken Rauth's *apparat* out of play, he'd have killed you before you'd had a chance to report."

"He'd likely have killed a bunch of Konoese, too. As it is, I guess we were pretty tough on them. You yanked us out of there so quick we didn't get a chance to say good-bye, but it seems like we wrecked the place pretty good."

"The island will require a bit of tidying."

"Any word on casualties?"

"Konoese casualties? There were none."

"That can't be right. They got hit with a seventy-foot tsunami. I didn't expect that part."

"They did," Gray said, "Bear in mind, Jack, the tribe have been living around volcanoes for the last six hundred years. By the time He' Konau blew, they were all safely on the leeward side of the atoll's ridge where, you'll notice, most of them live to begin with.

Had to rebuild the beachside huts, but they do that twice a year any-way, to freshen the leaves. No, rest assured, Jack, the Konoese are doing quite nicely, and very well pleased indeed with the state of affairs. They've done a remarkable job of rounding up the survivors of Rauth's team, you know. By the time Interpol arrived, the tribe had, ah, persuaded the great majority of these fellows to identify themselves, sorted them by nationality, and gotten them patched up and ready to be shipped home for trial on a rather interminable list of old charges. And it seems every man jack of them was eager to go. They weren't happy to see Interpol, of course, but they were simply terrified of Queen Celeste. Remarkable woman," Gray said mus-ingly. "Remarkable mind. We chatted a bit. I'd quite like to have her on staff, but I don't suppose one offers queens jobs. She wants to know how soon you two can come back and be feasted. And Prince K'talo asked me to tell you that kid brothers are always annoying, and that he hopes you aren't too annoyed with him."

Mallory laughed. "Tell him I'm sending him a knife, a fifth of George Dickel, and a book on etiquette."

"Just as you say. Well. I think that's about everything. I see Laura's still in the outer office."

There was a row of miniature TV monitors at Gray's elbow. He hadn't seemed to be watching them.

"Yep," Mallory said. "I'm taking her out tonight. Celebrate get-ting home with a whole skin. Wasn't always sure we would this time."

"I thought she was looking rather dressy. Well, you've both cer-tainly earned a nice night out on the town, and I hope you'll enjoy it very much. Just one last thing. As you say, this was a rather trouble-some assignment, and Laura had a fairly bad time of it."

"I know," Mallory said. "She tell you what happened with the Tesic kid?"

"Yes."

"She keeps telling me he didn't get a chance to do anything."

"Perhaps you should believe her."

"Yeah, perhaps," Mallory said unhappily. "Anyway. I thought it might be good to take her out someplace nice. Try to show her a good time. Take her mind off things."

"Yes, and that's what I wanted to talk to you about. Your intentions are laudable, Jack, but where women are concerned, I'm afraid you're not entirely to be trusted. In this regard you are, in fact, childish and often careless. Miss Morse is a valuable asset to this firm. You are not to be careless with Miss Morse."

Mallory was silent. Then he said, "I don't know that Laurie much notices whether I'm careless or not."

"I disagree. Laura's as tough as they come when it's a matter of being shot at and tortured and so forth. But every operative has his or her weakness, and Laura's weakness is you."

"I wish you knew how funny that was."

"I fear I don't."

"Look, Gray, this isn't your area of expertise, all right?"

"Nor yours," Gray said. "For a man with your opportunities to learn, Jack, you know remarkably little about women."

"I believe Laurie can take care of herself," Mallory said evenly.

"Not in this particular instance, no. Treat her carefully, Jack. And as I like to say: that isn't a suggestion."

Mallory was silent again.

"That's all, Jack. Do please charge your dinners and so forth to the firm. And have a pleasant evening."

"So all I could think of to say," Mallory said, "was, 'Well, sir. Could you at least give me back my hat?' "

Laura laughed even harder. She laughed, Mallory thought, like someone who hadn't had much practice. She squeezed her eyes shut and bared her teeth, which were surprisingly large, and heeled over to one side, gripping desperately at her wineglass. Laurie wasn't as pretty when she laughed, but she was a whole lot more attractive. Mallory had been watching her carefully all evening, and by now he was pretty sure Gray was wrong. If there was one thing Mallory knew after all these years, it was which women wanted to go home with him. And Laurie didn't. She was having a good time. She was glad to be alive. But that was it. *She just thinks of me as her partner,* Mallory thought, and was surprised to find himself a little sad about it.

"Oh dear," Laura said, fanning herself. "And did he?"

"Nope. 'Course, the hat wasn't in much shape by then, anyhow."

"Your poor hat. That you looked so handsome in."

"I looked like Halloween," Jack said. "Every man in Texas thinks he looks good in a black Stetson, and ninety-five percent of us're wrong. That old boy did me a favor. He cured me of cowboy hats. Been twenty years, and I haven't worn one since."

"Oh dear. Well, it doesn't sound like you had a very good time in Corpus Christi, Jack, but you did come out with some good stories."

"Yeah, that's about what Corpus's good for," he said. "Stories."

"That's too bad. You know, I like Newton. It makes me happy to have come from there. It's a pity you don't like your home town better."

"Aw, I guess it wasn't that bad a place. You know, maybe it wasn't . . . " He gestured around him.

"Yes, Jack," Laura said. "You have taken me to the world-famous Rainbow Room. No need to remind me again."

"All right, Laurie," he said, grinning. "Uncle. I thought you'd like it. If I guessed wrong, just say so."

She patted his arm. "I'm just teasing. It's wonderful, and I'm having a wonderful time. In fact, I'm a little guilty. If anything, *I* should be taking *you* to dinner."

"Don't start that again."

"It's true. I should be buying you dinner for the rest of your life. You could have broken your back."

"Well, I didn't."

"Taking the impact for both of us, at that speed—by rights you ought to have killed yourself. You *did* crack a few ribs, didn't you?"

"I'm all right. I figured I would be. I wish you'd drop it."

"And if you hadn't figured you'd be all right, you'd have done the same anyway."

"Don't be so sure."

"You would have."

"Well, what if I would've? I'd rather keep you in one piece, if I can. I work a lot better when you're backing me up."

"I'm glad you think I'm useful."

"You're not *useful,* goddamn it," Mallory said. "You're my partner. I don't know where I'd get another partner like you."

She didn't answer him.

After a few moments, they both dropped their eyes, and Laura pushed back her wineglass. "That's enough for me," she said, "until dinner comes. Or I'll float entirely away."

"Yep," he said. "Speaking of which, it was probably a mistake for me to go with beer."

"Need to be excused?"

"If you would," he said, rising.

"You've got five minutes," she said.

Mallory stopped. "Sorry?"

"You've got five minutes," Laura repeated.

Her eyes were merry, and her face was still lightly flushed with wine and laughter.

She said, "Little black-haired darling in the shell pink, over at the bar. Third stool from the left. You've looked at her twice since we came in. She's looked at you maybe four times. I agree, she's perfect for you—a little bottom-heavy, to my eye, but quite lovely—and it'd be a shame to let her get away. But you're out with me tonight, Jack. Not her. So. You've got five minutes. That's plenty of time for you to get a phone number and return to your date for the evening."

"You got a hell of a nerve," Mallory said after a pause.

"I suppose I do," Laura said.

"You got a nasty low suspicious mind."

"That, too."

"I don't think she's so bottom-heavy."

"Just a little," she said. "Four and a half minutes."

"Four and a half minutes," Mallory said, and headed for the bar.

For a moment Laura watched the composed, loose-jointed walk she'd have known anywhere in the world. In spite of his best efforts, he was moving a bit stiffly. He'd cracked a couple of ribs all right. She took another sip. The room was crowded and the diners' voices sounded like the hissing of surf. She heard a constant soft clashing of silver and china. An organ was playing some old Artie Shaw tune. A hidden mechanism was projecting colored lights on the domed ceiling. They gleamed on the parquetry disk of the revolving dance floor, on which no one was dancing. A vulgar, overpriced tourist trap, she thought, and just the sort of place Jack hated, too. But it was his idea of what a rich girl might like, and she found herself touched by his attempt to please her, and enjoying it quite as much as he'd meant her to. And the view *was* wonderful: the whole of New York City, laid out before her like pearls on a black velvet tray. There was the Williamsburg Bridge, and the Brooklyn Bridge just behind it, and then the lights of Brooklyn, looking a bit like the Asian Side of Istanbul seen across the Golden Horn. The Empire State Building was lit in yellow and blue. It looked very strange after He' Konau. She was, she realized, happy. It was odd, but she was. She was alive. She was with Jack. They'd done a difficult and important job of work together. It didn't matter tonight that he was chatting up a new little darling. The girl would be gone in a few nights, forgotten in a few weeks. And Laura would still be Jack's partner, the only partner he had, in the one thing that truly mattered to him. Not many people had a true partner in this life. But she was Jack's. And Jack was hers. And tonight, that was all she wanted.

The little darling was laughing now. Maybe he was telling her the story about the hat.

Some things never change, Laura thought, and took a paperback novel from her purse.

Author's Note

First thanks are due to Her Serene Highness N'ke Il'leakatanea and the rest of the Konoese royal family for their gracious hospitality, and for sanctioning the addition of two entirely fictitious islands, Pali Konau and He' Konau, to their archipelago; it goes without saying that the doings of the Konoese royal family in this book are equally fictitious. I also owe a great debt to my friends and former colleagues at INSTA for making me welcome during my time in Turkey, as well as to weapons consultant Charles Ardai, who, on the page as in the field, has long been a stalwart ally.

This book is dedicated with deep respect to the memory of John Foster Dulles.

And to T'llila, my light.

—*F. DeV.*
Kanea Konau
July 1963